Rain slashed against the patio doors, turning the glass into sheets of gray velvet. Then lightning flared again, turning them into blazing platinum rectangles.

In that brief, brilliant flash of light, Garland saw someone crouched outside the door.

Unable to move, unable to breathe, she watched the spot where she'd seen the figure. It had looked shapeless and hulking, its head sunk between its shoulders. *Creature of the night.*

A bolt of lightning crackled overhead, then another and another, strobe-light fast and intense. Like frames in an animated movie, scenes flashed across her vision with each succeeding bolt: crouched figure, standing figure—hooded jacket/baseball cap/wide-shouldered male/something shiny in his hand . . .

And then she screamed.

Prepare Yourself for

PATRICIA WALLACE

LULLABYE (2917, $3.95/$4.95)
Eight-year-old Bronwyn knew she wasn't like other girls. She didn't have a mother. At least, not a real one. Her mother had been in a coma at the hospital for as long as Bronwyn could remember. She couldn't feel any pain, her father said. But when Bronwyn sat with her mother, she knew her mother was angry—angry at the nurses and doctors, and her own helplessness. Soon, she would show them all the true meaning of suffering . . .

MONDAY'S CHILD (2760, $3.95/$4.95)
Jill Baker was such a pretty little girl, with long, honey-blond hair and haunting gray-green eyes. Just one look at her angelic features could dispel all the nasty rumors that had been spreading around town. There were all those terrible accidents that had begun to plague the community, too. But the fact that each accident occurred after little Jill had been angered had to be coincidence . . .

SEE NO EVIL (2429, $3.95/$4.95)
For young Caryn Dearborn, the cornea operation enabled her to see more than light and shadow for the first time. For Todd Reynolds, it was his chance to run and play like other little boys. For these two children, the sudden death of another child had been the miracle they had been waiting for. But with their eyesight came another kind of vision—of evil, horror, destruction. They could see into other people's minds, their worst fears and deepest terrors. And they could see the gruesome deaths that awaited the unwary . . .

THRILL (3142, $4.50/$5.50)
It was an amusement park like no other in the world. A tri-level marvel of modern technology enhanced by the special effects wizardry of holograms, lasers, and advanced robotics. Nothing could go wrong—until it did. As the crowds swarmed through the gates on Opening Day, they were unprepared for the disaster about to strike. Rich and poor, young and old would be taken for the ride of their lives, trapped in a game of epic proportions where only the winners survived . . .

Available wherever paperbacks are sold, or order direct from the Publisher. Send cover price plus 50¢ per copy for mailing and handling to Zebra Books, Dept. 3750, 475 Park Avenue South, New York, N.Y. 10016. Residents of New York and Tennessee must include sales tax. DO NOT SEND CASH. For a free Zebra/Pinnacle catalog please write to the above address.

SHADOW WHISPERS

WENDY HALEY

ZEBRA BOOKS
KENSINGTON PUBLISHING CORP.

This book is dedicated to
Corporal Bob Haynes
of the Norfolk Police Dept.
Thanks, Bob. We will all miss
your support and vision.

ZEBRA BOOKS

are published by

Kensington Publishing Corp.
475 Park Avenue South
New York, NY 10016

First printing: May, 1992

Printed in the United States of America

Prologue

The man reached under his bed and pulled out a shoebox. At first, he didn't open it. His big hands smoothed over the cardboard. To his eyes, the hands weren't those of a man, hair-sprinkled, spare, and strong, but the soft-fleshed hands of a child. A ten-year-old child.

The box the child had possessed was blue, with a red and white stripe and the words LITTLE YANK printed on it. He'd found it in the trash behind someone's house; his own shoes, either hand-me-downs from a kindly neighbor or obtained from the local shelter, never came in a box. He'd always wanted a pair of shoes that smelled new, and that came in their own box.

The man sighed. His shoebox had held the few, precious things that had lightened his stark childhood. There had been the teddy bear, long-since deprived of its stuffing. Its flat, empty arms were crossed over its chest as though it were praying. A dozen marbles surrounded it, glass offerings to a toy deity. The boy would hold the hard little spheres in his cupped hands, watching their swirl-color cat's-eyes wink eerily in the neon light that speared into the room from the motel sign across the street. Treasures.

And whenever the laughter began downstairs in his mother's room, the shrieks and grunts of copulation, the frenzied squeaking of bed springs, he would snatch the teddy bear from its resting place and hold it over his ears. A talisman against the ugly sounds. But soon, once the man left—he was always a different man—his mother would come upstairs. There was no talisman against her.

He came to himself abruptly. Cold sweat beaded his forehead, and his breathing was harsh in the quiet room. Take it easy, he told himself. You're out of her reach forever. Yes. Grown-up. Bigger and stronger than she could ever be. Yes.

Still, he could hear the echoes of her voice running across his mind like tiny, sharp-clawed mouse feet. Scratching, hurting, ugly, leaving a trail of filth and blood . . . Abruptly becoming aware that he had crumpled the shoebox between his hands, he forced himself to relax. Gently, he straightened the wrinkled cardboard. This box was brown and white, man-sized, for man-sized shoes. His shoes. And the treasures inside were different from his childhood ones. But they were just as comforting, just as special and secret.

He reached into the box and pulled out a braid of straight dark hair, tied with a ribbon. Closing his eyes, he ran the end of the braid along his right cheek, across his chin, and up his left cheek to his temple. He reversed direction—left cheek, chin, right cheek, then back again. And again. A shiver went through him.

It was almost time.

Chapter One

Norfolk, Virginia

Garland looked at her watch for the sixth time in as many minutes, then crossed her arms and settled back in the black plastic seat. Airport sights and sounds surrounded her: the powerful, high-pitched whine of a jet taxiing toward the runway, the rumble of conversation from the steady stream of people passing her chair. Someone ran past, a quick flash of white tennis shoes, nearly soundless on the carpeting. The man sitting next to Garland lit a cigarette. She eyed the only unoccupied seat, which was beside a woman who was trying unsuccessfully to pacify a fretful toddler and an even more fretful infant, and opted for the cigarette.

"Come *on,* Milo!" she muttered. With jet lag, a suitcase that weighed a ton and a ride that was forty-five minutes late, this was turning out to be one hell of a long day.

The man with the cigarette stiffened, his whole body coming to attention like a bird dog's on point. Curious, Garland turned to see what had caused his reaction. A strikingly lovely blond woman was striding gracefully through the crowd toward them.

"Well, that explains everything," Garland murmured under her breath. Charla was always, *always* late. With a sigh, she fished her suitcase out from beneath her chair and stood up.

"Garland, darling!" the blonde called, rushing forward with outstretched arms. "Have you been waiting long?"

"Nearly an hour." Garland returned the hug, torn between irritation and true pleasure at seeing her sister again.

"Forgive me?" Charla batted her eyelashes in outrageous humility. "Pleeeeease?"

Garland laughed. She just couldn't stay mad at Charla; no one could. "What happened to Milo?" she asked. "He was supposed to pick me up."

"Oh, I told him I'd meet you. After all, I haven't seen my sister in nearly a week. Come on, let's get out of here. We've got a lot of catching up to do."

As Garland swung her bag over her shoulder, she caught a glimpse of the man who'd been sitting beside her. He was looking from her to Charla and back again, his face registering profound surprise. It wasn't the first time someone had been astonished to discover that small, dark, ordinary-looking Garland and tall, knock-em-dead gorgeous Charla were sisters. With a grin, Garland looked up at the woman who towered a full head over her. Charla was her *little* sister.

"Want to get something to eat before I take you home?" Charla asked, sliding adroitly into a gap in the crowd.

"Thanks, I'm starved." Garland fell into step beside her, lengthening her stride to match Charla's. "But afterward just drop me at the store. Milo will still be there, and I can't wait to show him what I got at that estate auction." With a self-satisfied smile, Garland shifted her carry-on to the other shoulder. "I've got books in here that are going to send him straight to heaven."

Charla reached back and hefted the bag. "It weighs a ton! What did you do with your clothes?"

"I sent them UPS. These are first editions, and I didn't dare take a chance—"

"Don't you think about anything but books? I swear, you're going to work yourself to death! Ever since you opened that bookstore, you've done nothing else."

Garland shrugged. "It's what I like to do." Actually, The Tome was more what she *was* than what she did; since her divorce, the bookstore had been her husband, child, hobby, social life, and career all rolled into one. Was it normal? She didn't know. Normal or not, it was better than being married to Garry.

"Well, I think you're out of your mind," Charla said.

"I probably am," Garland agreed good-naturedly, shifting the heavy bag again.

A group of teenage girls trotted past. They looked hard at Charla as they went by, and one of them said, "Isn't that Charla Ross? Don't you remember, Julie? We saw her on the cover of *Cosmo* a while back!"

Hearing the overloud comment, a group of businessmen swung around to stare. Charla swept past, acknowledging the statement with a brief nod. Garland trailed along in her wake, fascinated by the way her sister took the attention as her due, seeming to absorb it and become even more beautiful because of it.

Then two of the businessmen shifted, and beyond them, near the far wall of the concourse, Garland caught a glimpse of another man. He, too, was staring, and with an intensity that brought his whole torso forward. With a swift little dart of surprise, she realized he was looking, not at Charla, but at her. She bumped into someone, excused herself, then turned to look at the man again. He was gone. Strange, she thought.

"Do you want Mexican or Italian?" Charla asked.

Giving herself a mental shake, Garland replied, "Italian."

"Good. I'll take you over to the Vincenza. I'd kill for a salad and a basket of those wonderful breadsticks."

"Sounds great." Garland let herself be hustled down the elevator and outside, where Charla's silver Mercedes occupied one of the curbside parking places. The red EXPIRED sign showed on the meter, and a parking ticket decorated the car's wiper blade.

"Sorry," Garland said. "I'll pay it."

"Don't be silly." Charla extracted the offending paper and held it in her mouth while she unlocked the car. "I've got a half-dozen others in the glove box. I'll just add it to the pile."

"Charla—"

"Oh, don't worry about it." With a laugh, Charla added, "My dear husband pays a lawyer a lot of money to take care of things like this."

Garland slid into the buttery softness of the leather seat and tucked her bag beneath her feet. As the car pulled away from the curb, she leaned her head against the headrest and pondered Charla's comment. It had been a rich woman's statement, the assurance that anything could be fixed if the right strings were pulled. Although the Ross girls came from a hardworking middle-class family, Charla had made a fortune as a top photographer's model. Ten years ago she had married Frank Hollister, a prominent psychiatrist whose family came from old money. A real "catch." Fame and fortune, Garland thought, glancing at her sister's profile. But happiness? She took a longer look, for the first time noticing the discontented set of Charla's mouth, the fine lines that were beginning to show at the corners of her eyes. No, maybe happiness was the one thing beauty couldn't buy.

"Is something wrong, baby sister?" she asked.

"Actually, things are going wonderfully." Charla turned onto Military Highway and began weaving expertly through the rush-hour traffic. "I've been offered a job as spokesmodel for Angelique Bei Cosmetics, beginning Monday."

"That's great!"

"Not so great; the shoot is going to be in France. I'll have to be gone at least a month." The stoplight ahead turned red. As soon as the car stopped, Charla swiveled to face Garland. "Frank has a very important conference in Los Angeles at the same time. There's no way he can get out of it."

"So you want me to stay with the twins," Garland said, mentally checking her schedule. "How long is Frank going to be away?"

"Two weeks."

"Two weeks! Charla, you know I love those girls, but I'm up to my ears in work right now. I've got three collections to appraise and—"

"I know, I know. But the nanny quit today and I'll never be able to find a replacement in time. You know how awful it is to find someone suitable."

Garland knew; she'd done the interviewing for Charla last time. "Why'd she quit?"

"Oh, something about not having enough days off." Charla pouted. "The least she could have done was to give two weeks' notice. This has really put me in a bind."

Garland grimaced, but not because of the twins. She took them two weekends a month as it was, just because she wanted to; Amber and Annalese were great kids. But it was a shame that Charla and Frank didn't spend a little more time at home so they, too, could find out just how nice their children were. "Look, Charla—"

"Please, don't say no! The girls don't get home from school until after three. You'll have plenty of time to work."

With a sigh, Garland closed her eyes. Plenty of time? Now that was an interesting assessment from someone who knew absolutely nothing about her business. She could hear Milo now: "You're letting her take advantage of you again, Garland! Just say no!"

The light turned green. The car behind them honked, and Charla faced forward hurriedly and stepped on the gas. "Garland, I really need this job."

Startled, Garland opened her eyes. "What—"

"I'm thirty-four. I'm losing it, fast."

"I'm five years older than you, and I don't exactly think of myself as a crone," Garland pointed out.

Charla waved her hand, dismissing that logic. "In my

business, thirty-four is *old*. You heard those girls talking about me in there. That issue of *Cosmopolitan* came out a year ago, and I haven't had a call from a major magazine since." Her voice cracked, and she cleared her throat before going on. "Angelique Bei is starting a new line: cosmetics for the nineties woman—mature, vital, and beautiful. Face it, sis, I can't compete with these fifteen- and sixteen-year-old girls coming up. But this Bei campaign is aimed at women our age. If I play my cards right, this can take me right to the top again."

Again Garland looked at the tiny lines at the corners of her sister's eyes, the slight downturn of her mouth. Strangely, she had never thought about Charla getting older; that beautiful face was somehow separate from the flesh-and-blood woman, as perfectly preserved and ageless as the magazine covers it graced. Her gaze dropped to Charla's hands, which gripped the steering wheel with white-knuckled force.

"All right, Charla. I'll take care of the girls for you," she said, feeling only half a fool for letting herself be talked into doing this yet again.

"Thank you," Charla said, reaching over to squeeze Garland's hand. "I'll bring them to your house Sunday morning, okay? This will be the last time, I promise!"

Garland drove slowly down Botetourt Street, enjoying the rolling jiggle of the car on the brick surface. It gave her a cozy feeling, this small tie with the past. She could almost imagine what it had been like to drive a carriage down this street long ago, unhurried by clocks and schedules or impatient traffic. No blaring stereo, just the rhythmic clop-clop of horseshoes against the bricks.

She turned left onto Bute Street and, seeing that there were no empty spots along the street, pulled into the parking lot across from the bookstore. Welcoming yellow light spilled from the store's big front window, against which the painted Old English letters that spelled *The Tome* stood out starkly.

Excitement stirred in her as she opened the door and heard a murmur of conversation from the rear of the store. The aroma of fresh-brewed coffee mingled agreeably with the leather-musk smell of old books. A lingering trace of Murphy's Oil Soap told her that Milo had cleaned today. The front desk was empty, but when she closed the door behind her, a man appeared at the far end of one of the floor-to-ceiling shelves that ran nearly the length of the store. Although she couldn't see his face, she could tell who he was by his stance and mane of dark blond hair. Her partner, Milo. Handsome, witty Milo—Renaissance man, gambler, care-free collector of women's hearts.

"Hey, Garland! Robbie and Troll are going at it again," he called. "Lock up and hurry, or you'll miss it." He disappeared behind the shelf again.

With a smile, Garland locked the deadbolt, then took her jacket off and hung it on the hook beside the desk. Wild as Milo was, she reflected, he knew books. His taste ran from horror and the occult to mystery and science fiction, while she preferred history and the classics. Milo was flamboyant, Garland quiet, even a little shy. Or as Milo had described it in his own inimical way, peacock and sparrow. Still, they made an excellent team; his flair, coupled with her steady, down-to-earth common sense, had made The Tome a thriving business.

"And I tell you, he didn't mean that at all!" a woman shouted. "He just didn't like the mingling of pagan and Christian elements—"

"Good God, Troll, it took a damn lot of hubris for the man to go around slamming Milton!" Robbie's voice quivered with indignation.

A third voice came into the fray, George's mellifluous British tones rolling through the store like smooth brandy. "Come, children, let's not get angry."

"Yeah. Old Samuel's been dead for more than two

hundred years; no one but you two atavists gives a shit why he hated *Lycidas*," Milo said, pouring oil on the flames.

Troll's voice went up a notch. "I suppose we ought to spend our evening discussing Conan the Barbarian's motivations?"

"Why not? It might broaden your horizons," Milo retorted. "Bring you out into the real world."

Garland rolled her eyes upward as she walked toward the rear of the store. The argument had risen in acrimony and volume, and she felt as though she were broaching a solid wall of sound as she entered the small open space at the far end.

This was the heart of The Tome. The bookshelf-lined walls were pierced by two doors, one the back exit, the other leading to the storeroom that Milo called the Tomb. A braided rug and two electric heaters fought the cold seeping through the plank floor. Five people sat at the battered mahogany table that occupied the center of the room.

Garland joined them, feeling as though she'd come home. These were the regulars. They came here every Friday night to drink coffee, eat doughnuts, and talk. The love of books had brought them together, but their discussions ranged the gamut from politics to gossip. Robbie and Troll had been the first; the others had come into the bookstore as customers, been sucked into one conversation or another, and had left as friends. One Friday night Milo had plugged a pot of coffee in, and that was the beginning of a ritual that had lasted for more than three years.

Milo had managed to turn Troll's attention from Robbie to himself. Troll—Linda Berenson to the rest of the world—was glaring at him, her sharp little chin thrust aggressively forward as she spoke. She'd raked her hands through her short reddish hair, making it stand up in spikes. Despite the feistiness that had earned her her nickname, Troll was cute—dimpled, pug-nosed cute—and hated it. Garland knew Milo had it bad for her, and also knew that he had batted zero.

George Pattie, the retired Shakespearean actor, had given up his peacemaking efforts. With his silver head bent and his hands folded on his belly, he looked asleep. He wasn't, though; he flashed Garland a wink from beneath his grizzled eyebrows. What a love of a man, she thought. If he were thirty years younger, she'd grab him.

To Garland's right was Robbie Schuyler, the lawyer whose love for Milton's poems had started this argument. He leaned back in his chair and watched the combatants with amusement, a sardonic smile creasing his dark, sharp-featured face. His wife had died last year, a heart attack at age forty-five, and Garland knew these Friday nights were his lifeline.

She glanced at the man sitting to her left, who was busily scribbling in a notebook. Colin Kingsley. He'd been coming to the Friday night sessions for about six months now, but she didn't know him well. He was a quiet man, only rarely talking about himself. He didn't talk much at all, actually. Although his face was craggy, almost homely, his eyes were beautiful, an unusual variegated green like cracked bottle glass. The twins adored him.

He glanced up briefly, nodded, then returned his attention to the notebook. Garland's interest sharpened. He'd told them that he'd taken up art, but this was the first time she'd seen him bring anything here. She hitched her chair a few inches closer to his, trying to peer over his arm.

He turned his head to look at her, a smile quirking his lips upward. Then he slid the notebook across the table to her. He'd caught Troll perfectly. Not just her physical features, but the woman herself. Essence of Troll, with her mouth wide open and one finger raised in exposition. *He really is good,* Garland thought. She glanced at Colin from the corner of her eye and gave him a thumbs-up.

With a grin, he retrieved the drawing and bent over it

again. Garland watched his profile. That drawing had given her a new perspective on him. *So quiet, watching us all with an all-too-perceptive artists' eye, filing it away until he strips our secrets away in one of his pictures.* And of course, she couldn't help falling into the trap of curiosity: *I wonder what he'd see in me.*

Then, noticing that George had managed to turn the conversation to a slightly less incendiary subject—theater—she sat forward and began to listen more closely.

Someone knocked at the front door, then rattled the knob urgently. Garland started to rise, but Milo pushed away from the table, saying, "I'll get it."

He came back a moment later, followed by Charla and the twins. The other men rose quickly to their feet, their faces mirroring Garland's surprise; in the five years the bookstore had been open, this was only the second time Charla had come here.

"Please, sit down, gentlemen," Charla said with a smile. "I'm only going to interrupt for a moment or two."

Amber and Annalese swarmed past their mother to envelop Garland in a pair of whirlwind hugs. "We get to spend the weekend with you, Aunt Garland!" Amber said excitedly. They left Garland and made a beeline for George.

"Fait accompli, Charla?" Milo asked.

"Don't be a cat, Milo," Charla murmured, her smile turning brittle.

Milo opened his mouth to retort, but Garland shot him a warning look. With a grimace, he sat down and crossed his arms over his chest.

Satisfied, Garland turned back to Charla. "Did you come to join our evening of conversation?"

"Sorry, but no." Laughter glinted in Charla's eyes. "No offense, dear, but I'll leave it to you intellectual types. My interests don't run to things that have been all but forgotten for hundreds of years."

"Like Shakespeare," Milo murmured. "No one remembers *him,* do they?"

Meow! Garland thought. If she hadn't been so eager to avoid trouble, it might even be funny. She glared at him from beneath half-closed lids, hoping her eyes were expressing her feelings clearly. Apparently they were, for he subsided. She noticed that Charla seemed oblivious to Milo's jibe, but then Charla had a knack for hearing only what she wanted to hear.

"I got a call from Angelique Bei this afternoon," Charla said. "They've moved the shoot up. Emergency shuffle, darling; I'm booked on a flight to Newark in"—she glanced at her watch—"less than an hour. I knew you wouldn't mind taking the girls a little early." Her gaze flicked to her daughters. Amber was ensconced on George's lap and Annalese had wrapped herself like a flesh-and-blood shawl around Colin's burly shoulders. "Right at home here, aren't they?"

"Yes, they are." Garland smiled. Physically, the girls were eight-year-old replicas of Charla, but mentally, they were just like their maternal grandmother: gregarious, stubborn, and intelligent, curious as anything. On the weekends they stayed with Garland, they insisted on coming to these Friday night sessions. Pepsi and politics, doughnuts and Donne . . . An unconventional education perhaps, but what better way for a kid to learn about the arts than from people who loved them, and in George's case, who'd lived them?

"So, this is your Friday night get-together?" Charla asked. "The girls talk about it all the time. They say you have *such* fun."

George laughed. "Actually, we're all eccentric billionaires, come to bask in your sister's beauty, wit, and charm."

Charla smiled at him a little vaguely, then stepped forward to take Garland's hands in hers. "You don't mind, do you?"

Garland opened her mouth to say she did, then closed

it again. Not for the world would she make Amber and Annalese think she didn't want them. "No, I don't mind," she said. She didn't dare look at Milo.

"Thanks, sister mine. Here's the key to the house. The alarm is on, so be careful to turn it off when you get in. You know the code." Charla took a gold key ring out of her purse and handed it to Garland. "Oh, I left a message at Frank's hotel for him to call you. You can tell him the change in plans."

Garland shrugged. In for a penny, in for a pound.

Holding her arms wide, Charla called, "Come, darlings. Give Mommy a goodbye kiss."

They obeyed, clinging to their mother with childish intensity until Charla gently disengaged herself. "I'll be back in a month, sweethearts. Have fun with Aunt Garland, and I'll call you as soon as I can."

With a wave of her hand to include the entire group in her goodbye, Charla swept out. Opium perfume lingered in the air. Garland risked a glance at Milo, to find him glaring at her, his mouth pursed in a maiden-aunt's pout of disapproval. It wasn't that he minded the girls being here, she knew; it was just that he felt Charla took advantage of her too easily and too often.

Well, Milo was an only child. He couldn't understand the responsibility she felt for both her sister and her nieces. Oh sure, Charla had money enough to hire a nanny for the girls, but that was no substitute for family.

Slipping the keys into the pocket of her jeans, she turned back to the table. "Now, where were we?" she asked.

The discussion resumed where it had left off. The next two hours passed quickly, with the conversation skipping from history to current events to movies and back again. When Garland saw the twins' eyelids drooping, she got up reluctantly.

"I'd better get them home," she said. "Good night, all."

"I've got an early morning, myself," Colin said, climbing to his feet. "I'll walk you to your car."

He helped her get the girls into their coats, then held her jacket for her. Silently, he accompanied them out to Garland's five-year-old minivan. She was grateful for his company, for there had been a few robberies in the neighborhood lately. Although he wasn't tall, he was wide-shouldered and powerful, and just a frown on that craggy face would probably be enough to send a mugger running. Amber and Annalese, however, weren't fooled at all by his rough-hewn exterior; each gave him a hug and a powdered-sugar kiss before climbing into the van.

He leaned against the side of the van and regarded Garland solemnly, obviously unaware of the smears of white powder that decorated his cheek. "Good night," he said.

" 'Night, Colin."

She slid into the driver's seat and closed the door. He gave her a mocking salute, then pushed off from the van and walked away.

"Hey, you two," she called to the twins over her shoulder. "Do you want to go home, or stay at my house this weekend?"

"Your house!" the girls said in eerie unison.

Twins, Garland thought. They looked and talked alike, sometimes even finishing one another's sentences. Frank wanted to put them in separate schools to foster their independence, but Garland didn't agree. Never mind that her brother-in-law was a psychiatrist; this was gut feeling.

She pulled the seatbelt across her chest and was startled by the rattle of paper from her breast pocket. "What . . .?" she muttered, retrieving the paper. It was one of Colin's drawings, but it was too dark in the car to see it clearly.

She reached up to flick the overhead light on, and her breath went out in a long sigh when she got a good look at the drawing. Colin had drawn her as St. Joan. She was tied to a stake, her hands folded, her eyes uplifted in prayer as a plume of smoke rose from the wood piled at her feet.

For a moment she was tempted to crumple the paper. Then, suddenly, she began to laugh.

"What's so funny?" Annalese demanded.

"Oh, nothing, honey. Just Colin being silly."

Chapter Two

The phone shrilled, bringing Garland up from her pillow with a gasp. Her gaze automatically went to the clock. Twelve-thirty. The phone rang again, making her jump. Before it could ring yet again, she snatched the receiver up. "Hello?"

Silence. "Frank, is that you?" More silence. With a grimace, she hung up and burrowed back into her pillow. Her heart still pounded with reaction. It had been twenty years since the night a ringing phone had awakened her to the news that her parents had been killed in an auto crash. Twenty years, and she still hadn't shrugged off the remembered terror. Phones in the night—bad news, sad news. It had been late at night when her husband had called from his mistress's house to tell his wife that he wouldn't be home—ever.

The phone rang again, bringing her back to a sitting position with a jolt. Irritation sparked her voice this time when she answered. "Hello!"

"Garland, this is Frank. Charla left a message for me to contact you." His voice was crisp, almost brusque.

"Did you call a minute ago?" she asked.

"No, I didn't. Look, I only have a few minutes between engagements. What did Charla want you to tell me?"

Garland scraped a stray lock of hair back from her forehead with the heel of her hand, then reached to flick the bedside light on. "She had to leave early. Um, something about the shoot being moved up." As always, she found herself rushing, speaking too fast as though doing otherwise might waste her brother-in-law's precious time. "She left the girls with me, so you don't have to worry."

There was a long silence at the other end. Garland could hear him breathing. "Frank?" she prompted.

"When did she leave?"

"Tonight. She was going to stay in New York, then fly out to Paris tomorrow."

"Are you sure?"

The intensity in his voice startled her. Usually, Frank's tones were cool and remote, as colorless as the man himself. "Is something wrong?" she asked.

"No . . . I was just surprised. I wasn't expecting her to leave until . . . Just a moment." His voice became muffled, as though he'd put his hand over the receiver. "Go on down. I'll meet you there in a minute." His voice resumed normal volume. "Sorry, Garland. Things are very hectic here. Do you have a key to the house?"

"Yes. Do you want to talk to the girls? I'll wake them up for you."

"No time, I'm afraid. I'm late now. Tell them I'll try to call sometime, but between my schedule and the time difference, I can't guarantee it. Goodbye."

Click. The dial tone came back, and Garland slowly replaced the receiver. "You're welcome, Frank," she said, shaking her head in mingled bewilderment and annoyance. "And I'll be sure to give the girls your love." Christ, what a strange man! Maybe he saved all his warmth and sympathy for his patients.

With a shrug, she turned the light out and lay back down. If Charla was happy, who was she to criticize? Oh, she knew Charla had been attracted mostly by Frank's money. *She'd* chosen Garry purely for love—hormones, really, but it had felt like love—and had been miserable once the glow had worn off.

Irritated, she pushed the thought away. Garry had caused her enough sleepless nights while she'd been married to him; she wasn't about to let him do it to her now. Closing her eyes, she reached for serenity. To her surprise, she actually found it.

Maybe, she thought as she floated off into a pleasant sleep-fog, she was getting to the point where remembering him wouldn't bother her at all.

Charla arched in mindless passion, digging her nails into her lover's slick, straining back. "Harder," she moaned. "Harder!"

He buried his face against her neck and obeyed, his thrusts pushing her up to the head of the bed. Gasping, she took hold of the headboard and held on, vaguely registering how cool the brass felt against the skin of her hands. She was hot, so hot—she was burning, aching, ready! A shattering climax ripped through her, and she screamed.

He collapsed on her, his body shuddering. Her hands roamed over his back. Up, down, across, and back again, reveling in the smooth hard muscles, the long clean sweep of his spine.

"That was so good," she murmured into his hair.

"Mmmm." He rolled onto his side, propping himself on his elbow to look at her. "I'm glad you managed to spend the weekend with me. You're sure your husband won't find out?"

"I'm sure. I told everyone I had to be in Paris two days early." Playfully, she traced the line of hair that ran down his torso to his belly. "Two whole nights together. I hate to waste a moment of it."

"Sorry, baby," he said, moving her hand up to his chest. "Three times, and there ain't no more. Even for you."

Flopping onto his back, he sighed and closed his

eyes. His breathing deepened. Charla watched him sleep. Jay Cohen—tall, handsome, charming, and incredibly passionate. Some people might call him, at twenty-four, a little young for her. But he was everything she'd ever wanted in a man. Except for money—a welder by day, drama student by night, Jay didn't make enough to keep her in eyeshadow. She'd even had to give him the deposit for this townhouse, or they'd still be trysting in that squalid apartment he'd had in downtown Norfolk.

But money or no money, Jay was ten times better than her husband. She'd been so young, so completely foolish when she'd married Frank. Blinded by his brilliance, manners, and wealth, she hadn't realized that he had passion for nothing but his practice and patients. Even his money hadn't been all he'd advertised it to be; much of his inheritance had gone into his research. Well, things were going to change. As soon as she got back from Paris, she was going to file for divorce. Frank probably wouldn't care—probably wouldn't even notice. A frown creased her forehead, and she rubbed it away with her fingertips. Frowns made wrinkles. Besides, divorce wasn't the worst thing in the world.

Charla ran her fingertip along the hard curve of Jay's cheek. Maybe, if he was very, very good, she'd marry him. There was one small problem with that: he didn't like children. And the twins, those strange little beings she hardly understood herself, were sure to dislike him in return.

She sighed. Garland was able to get by without the Franks and the Jays. Garland was tough. After Garry had walked out on her, she'd rebuilt her life. She'd done it alone, and seemed happy to stay that way. Charla admired that; she always had to have some adoring male around to fill her days and nights.

"But that's not all bad," she murmured, stroking Jay's cheek again.

She turned out the light and lay down, snuggling into her lover's warm side. Everything always worked out, one way or another. And now, with the Bei job ready to send her sagging career to the moon, she was beginning to look forward to creating a new life for herself.

Garland rooted the twins out of bed early. After a quick breakfast, she packed them into the van and headed back to The Tome. To her surprise, Milo was already there.

"What are you doing here so early?" she demanded, hanging her and the twins' jackets on the hooks beside the door.

"Playing catch up," he said. "Hi, sweethearts. There are fresh doughnuts in the back." He watched the twins disappear around the end of the bookshelf, then folded his arms over his chest and regarded Garland from under lowered brows. "Did you talk to Frank?"

She nodded. "Honestly, Milo, the man pays no attention to those kids at all, and it's getting worse all the time. It seems he only notices people with psychoses."

"That should be an indicator of the girls' mental health. If he suddenly starts paying attention to them, look out." He propped one hip on the corner of the desk. "It's *your* mental health I'm worried about. How long are you going to let them do this to you?"

"C'mon, Milo. What else do I have to do?"

"Date. Party. Have fun. Fall in love. Anything but sitting at home alone."

"I've dated. Enough to know it usually isn't worth the time and trouble." There were all different kinds of loneliness, and the solitary kind wasn't the worst.

He grinned at her. "Then just go in for some healthy screwing."

"Like you do?" she asked, remembering Colin's drawing. "And has it solved *your* problems?"

"That's dirty pool," he said, raising his hands in a gesture of defeat. "Okay, okay, I'll stay out of your affairs—or lack thereof. But mark my words, the more you give Charla and Frank, the more they'll take. And when you finally decide to come out of your cocoon and make a life for yourself, there won't be anything left."

"Thank you, O wise one."

His eyes were impudent, like a small boy's. "I bet you don't even remember what sex feels like."

"Oh, I remember, despite my advanced years." Unembarrassed, Garland brushed her hair back from her face. "I'm not dead, you know, just picky. Now, which job do you want—minding the store, or spending the morning in the Tomb cataloging those new books?"

With a sigh, he straightened and went to flip the sign in the window to OPEN. "I'll go bury myself in the back. By the way, I brought my Monopoly game in with me. You and the twins can play between customers."

"Okay." As he turned away, she put her hand on his arm to stop him. "I understand what you're trying to do, Milo. I appreciate it, but I have to handle my own problems in my own way."

He sighed, then reached out and ruffled her hair. "Okay. Now let me retreat to my dark and odorous lair."

A smile curved her lips as she watched him disappear around the corner. He wasn't as hardened as he'd like to think. Sir Milo, hiding a tender heart beneath the veneer of a rutting male on the make. Too bad Troll couldn't see it.

"C'mon, Aunt Garland," Amber called. "We're all set up."

"Okay," she said. "Are you sure you know how to play?"

"Well, we read the instructions," Amber said. Two

pairs of blue eyes regarded her with exaggerated innocence. "But this *is* a grown-up game. Want to spot us a railroad each?"

Instantly suspicious, Garland shook her head. "Uh-uh. If you want to play adult games, you've got to take your knocks."

She pulled up a chair. Although business was brisk and the interruptions in the game correspondingly frequent, she was bankrupt by lunchtime.

"Sharks," she grumbled, handing her last property to Annalese. "Who taught you to play, anyway?"

"Milo," Amber said.

"That explains it." Garland shook her head in disgust. She was truly pitiful if she couldn't beat a couple of eight-year-olds at Monopoly. It was a good thing she hadn't gone into real estate. The very idea made her shudder; that was one of the professions her ex-husband had tried to push her into. There were others, completely unrelated except that Garry saw them as quick money-makers. How he'd laughed when she told him she wanted to open a bookstore!

"Excuse me, miss."

The voice was deeply masculine, and jerked Garland out of her reverie. The man matched the voice; tall and dark and lean, with a not-quite-handsome-but-who-the-hell-cares sort of face that made her want to drop one wing and run in circles. He was somewhere in his forties, if those patches of silver at his temples were any indication.

"Could you direct me to the history section, please?" he asked.

"Sure. It's the first bookcase to your right. Wars are grouped together, the rest are in approximately chronological order."

He smiled. "Very efficient. Perhaps you could tell me if you have Toland's *Hitler.*"

"Sorry, but we sold that a couple of weeks ago."

Wow, she thought, look at the way his eyes crinkle up when he smiles. I thought that just happened in the movies. "If you want, I can try to get a copy for you."

"Well . . . let me look around a bit. Maybe something else will catch my fancy." He sauntered off down the aisle.

Against her better judgment, Garland let herself be talked into another game of Monopoly. Luck was with her for once; by the time the first few rounds were over, she had acquired Broadway, Park Place, and three railroads. "Now," she said, rubbing her hands together in ostentatious glee, "I'm going to build hotels and bleed you two dry."

"C'mon, Aunt Garland. Have a heart!" Annalese cried.

"Heck, no. Did you have any sympathy for my feelings last time? No, you beat me into the ground without a qualm. Well, let me tell you . . ." A muffled noise from the back of the store caught her attention. "Hey, do you hear something?"

The girls moved their heads like twin tracking radar. "It sounds like Milo."

"Uh-oh!" Garland bolted from her chair and headed for the back. Reaching the closed door of the Tomb, she grasped the knob and gave it a yank. The doorknob came off in her hand.

"Milo, are you all right?" she called through the door.

"Let me out, Garland." His voice was plaintive.

"Those hinges have to come off." Cupping her hands around her mouth, she called, "Amber, there's a screwdriver in the middle drawer of the desk. Bring it to me, will you, honey?"

The twins came running. Garland began working on the hinges to the accompaniment of Milo's comments from the other side of the door. He told her where to stand, how to hold the screwdriver, which screws to remove first and how fast to do it. Garland stopped working.

"I don't hear anything getting done," he called.

"You're right," she said, leaning her shoulder against the doorjamb. "And you won't, unless you shut up."

Blessed silence. Shooting the giggling twins a grin, she began on the hinges again. A few customers stopped to watch the proceedings with interest. When Milo finally walked out of the storeroom, it was to applause.

"Thank you, thank you," he murmured, bowing.

With a snort, Garland headed back to the front. She found the attractive customer waiting at the desk, a stack of books cradled in his arms.

"I still want the Toland book," he said, adding with a smile, "But I found a few other things."

"A few," she agreed, matching his smile.

"By the way, I admired the way you dealt with the door." One corner of his mouth went up. "And the commentary from the other side. Are you always so forceful and efficient?"

She laughed. "I'm great with hinges anyway."

"Is this your store?"

"Half. Milo Freeman is my partner. Milo"—she pointed toward the back of the store—"was the commentary."

His smile widened. "Well, you should both be proud of what you've got here. This is the finest selection of used books I've seen anywhere."

"Thank *you.*"

He handed her a business card with his American Express. It said STEVEN DAWSON, ACCOUNT EXECUTIVE, GARRIDION ADVERTISING. She turned it over to write the name of the book he wanted on the back, then slipped it into the Rolodex.

"It may take a few weeks," she said. "But I'll call you as soon as it comes in."

"Thanks." After signing the charge slip, he picked up his books and turned toward the door. Then, so suddenly that Garland gave a start of surprise, he swung back around to look at her. "Look, miss . . . what's your name anyway?"

She stared up at him wide-eyed. "Ross. Garland Ross."

"I'm not going to beat around the bush. I find you attractive and interesting, and I don't want to wait weeks to hear your voice again. How about coming to lunch"—he paused to look at his watch—"no, dinner with me?"

She was tempted. Very tempted. But . . . with a sigh, she said, "I'm sorry, Mr.—"

"Steven."

"Steven. But my nieces are staying with me this weekend and I'm afraid—"

"I was planning on taking the girls to a movie tonight," Milo said from behind her.

Steven grinned at him, then turned his attention back to Garland. "You were saying?"

She hesitated. After all, she didn't know the man at all. Milo moved close enough to poke her in the ribs. She could almost hear him thinking, *Go for it, you idiot!* Feeling reckless, she said, "All right, Steven. But just dinner; I've got to work tomorrow."

"Just dinner," he agreed. "When will you be finished here?"

"Six o'clock. But I ought to go home and change," she said, indicating her sweater, denim skirt, and ancient but comfortable boots.

"You look great as you are. I'll come get you at six." A moment later he was gone.

Garland shook her head, not quite believing what had happened. "Milo, did you hypnotize me or something? I just let that guy pick me up. I don't know a thing about him!"

"Oh, come *on,* Garland! You've got his American Express number, work number, and home telephone number," Milo said, rolling his eyes in exasperation. "Besides, what are you risking here—a measly couple of hours of your time? Take a chance, for Christ's sake!"

She wanted to. Recklessness kicked in again, and she said, "Are you sure you don't mind taking the twins for a couple of hours?"

"Positive. You may have trouble believing this, but I have absolutely nothing going on tonight."

"Thanks, Milo." She patted his cheek. "If any of your women knew how nice you really are . . ."

"God forbid!" He staggered backward in mock horror. "I'm going to fix that doorknob before you have me married off."

"Only to Troll," she called to his retreating back. He paused, did a little stutter-step, then continued on.

By the time six o'clock rolled around, Garland found herself actually looking forward to her date. Milo and the twins had left an hour ago, bound for the five-fifteen show at Janaf Cinema. The girls had already gotten him to promise to buy them a pizza afterward.

Garland checked her makeup one more time. God, she was as nervous as a kid on a first date. Probably because it had been nearly seven months since her last date. *That* evening could best be described as grisly. Then Steven came in, looking unbelievably sexy in jeans and a leather flight jacket, and she suddenly began looking forward to the evening.

"Ready?" he asked, giving her a crooked smile that raised her internal temperature several degrees.

"Just let me lock up, and I will be."

He waited while she switched off the lights and locked the door, then took her by the elbow and steered her toward a blue Impulse parked at the curb. "Are you as nervous as I am?" he asked.

"Yes." Then they both laughed, and Garland didn't

feel self-conscious anymore. "Where are we going?" she asked.

"Have you ever eaten at El Pejero? It's that new Mexican restaurant in Ghent."

"I'd love to try it out," she said. A small lie. After having eaten her way through southern Texas, she doubted she'd care for the sort of upscale Tex-Mex that would appeal to Ghent tastes. But with a man as handsome as this across the table, who cared what the food tasted like?

To her surprise, El Pejero was reminiscent of some of the Mexican restaurants she'd been to in Texas: red-checked tablecloths, black metal chairs with red vinyl cushions, metal sconces on the wall. Each table held a fat glass candleholder like the citronella candles her mother used to set out on the patio every summer. The best touch was the green neon mockingbird in the front window.

"I like it," she said.

Steven chuckled. "Let's hope the food matches the decor."

She never even tasted the food. They talked and laughed and talked some more, and she couldn't remember when she'd had so much fun with a date. Steven ordered sopapillas for dessert, but the little puffs of pastry sat untouched until they were cold. Finally noticing that their waiter was beginning to hover, Garland glanced at her watch.

"Holy cow, it's after nine!" she said. "I really have to go rescue Milo."

Steven gestured for the bill, then stood up and held her jacket for her. "I hate for the evening to end so soon. I'm really enjoying myself."

"So am I. But duty calls. It's going to be nearly eleven o'clock before I get the kids to bed as it is."

He slipped his arm around her waist as they walked back to his car. Instead of opening the door for her, he pressed her against the car and gave her a kiss that seared her to her toes. Wow, she thought, he's stirring juices I didn't even know I *had!*

"I want to see you again," he murmured huskily into the hair at her temple.

"That can be arranged." Two couples walked past and she straightened, a little embarrassed at being caught necking like a teenager.

He helped her into the car, then slid behind the wheel and slid smoothly out into traffic. Smiling, he reached over and took her hand, raising it to his lips in a courtly gesture that made her pulse speed up.

"Oh, hell!" he exploded suddenly. Muttering under his breath, he pulled over to the side of the road.

Coming back to earth with a jolt, Garland glanced over her shoulder to see the blue flash of police lights behind them. "Uh-oh."

Steven rolled the window down as the officer walked up. "Is something the matter, officer?" he asked.

"Sir, did you notice that the traffic signal back there was red?"

"No." Steven sighed. "I'm afraid I didn't."

"May I see your license and registration, please?" the policeman asked.

With a muttered curse, Steven flicked his overhead light on and leaned over to open his glove compartment. His vehicle registration fell out, catching on the edge of the small door for a moment, then fluttering down to Garland's feet. She felt Steven's hand caress her calf as he retrieved it.

Shock held her motionless. Not shock at his touch, shock at what she had seen on the registration. Two names: Steven J. Dawson and Laura M. Dawson. Then anger kicked in. Anger both for herself and the woman who was waiting at home for him. She waited silently while he signed his ticket and waited for the police car to pull out around him, then plucked the registration out of his hands and held it up.

"Would you care to explain this?" she asked.

"Damn." He turned to face her. "Garland, look—"

"You're married!" she hissed. "Why did you take me out when you're married?"

With a sigh, he ran one hand across his jaw. "Because I'm attracted to you, and because I wanted to get to know you better."

"Kids?"

"Three. A boy thirteen, a girl ten, my youngest son six." He grabbed her hands and held them tightly. "I've never done this before, believe me. You hit me like a ton of bricks."

"Bullshit," she said wearily, pulling her hands out of his grasp. When she grabbed for the door handle, intending to leave the car, he stopped her.

"It's a good mile back to The Tome," he said. "Come on, Garland; at least let me see you safely back."

She nodded. Fixing her gaze on the dashboard in front of her, she remained silent during the short drive. *Damn* him, she thought bitterly. Damn him for showing her how great it could be, and damn him for being a lie. In five years of the single life, she'd learned to spot the fakes. Or thought she had. Steven had seemed so nice, so thoughtful. But she'd found out the hard way that any man—*any* man—who'd go out on his wife had a selfish streak a mile wide. She'd been there.

He pulled up behind her van. "Are you sure—"

"Quite." She slid out of the car and began walking rapidly toward the van.

"Garland, I'm sorry," he called.

Her hand was shaking so badly it took three tries before she finally got the key into the lock. Once she was safely in the van, Steven's car pulled around and accelerated around the corner.

"Men!" she muttered, jamming the key into the ignition. "Let their penises do their thinking for them . . .

This is it, really it! No more dating. It's not worth the trouble."

The van started, then suddenly died. When she tried to start it again, all she got was a few coughs. She tried twice more with the same result, then turned it off and waited. *Give it a moment to . . . what?* the cynical part of her mind asked. For the damn thing to heal itself miraculously? Still, she couldn't keep herself from trying one more time. But there were no miracles for her tonight; the van stayed dead.

"Great. The perfect end to a perfect evening." She climbed out of the van and headed across the street toward The Tome. A battered station wagon passed behind her, going slowly as though its occupants were checking her out. Brakelights flashed red as it stopped at the corner. Garland lengthened her stride. Just in case—a woman alone, on a dark, quiet street, had better have caution these days. Moving quickly and efficiently, she unlocked the store's deadbolt, slipped inside, then locked it again.

The store was dark, the only illumination coming from the streetlight outside. Garland left it that way while she dialed Milo's number.

"Hello?" He sounded tired. In the background, she could hear the girls' voices.

"Men are toads," Garland snarled.

"Always, sweetheart," he said. "What happened? Did he make a pass? Did he *not* make a pass?"

She glanced out the window to find that the station wagon was gone. False alarm. "He's married."

"Some people might not care about that."

"Well, *he* didn't, that's for sure." Picking up a nearby pen, she began making angry slash marks on the blotter. "Look, my car won't start. Can you come pick me up?"

"Sure. Are you at the store?"

"All locked up, safe and sound."

"Well, stay there. We'll be there in, oh, twenty minutes." He hung up.

Twenty minutes. Enough time for her to get some work done. She pulled some invoices out of the file cabinet and sat down at the desk. After flicking on the desk light, she settled into the big swivel chair and began to work.

"Bills, bills, bills," she grumbled, sorting the invoices into three stacks. This job always depressed her; buying books was one thing, but spending money for utilities, postage, and office supplies was like draining her lifeblood.

With a gut-clenching stab of alarm, she suddenly became aware of movement outside the big plate glass window in front of her. The desk light, reflecting off the glass, prevented her from seeing anything other than an amorphous shadow lurking there. Its very ambiguity was more frightening than a brandished weapon. Was it one person, or several? He or they were surely looking at her; she could feel their eyes. Staring at her. Trapped in the circle of lamplight like a butterfly pinned to a board, she knew she was visible to . . . whomever. Exposed.

She rose to her feet with pretended casualness, taking the phone with her. Just as she was debating whether or not to call 911, headlights flared outside. The shadow disappeared so fast that she began to doubt she'd even seen it at all. Her terror evaporated. Maybe it had been an optical illusion of some kind, born of the reflection on the light on the glass. She forced herself to approach the window and look outside. The street was empty.

"Well, what did you expect, idiot?" she asked aloud, feeling a trifle foolish now. "Did you think you were going to see the bogeyman standing on the sidewalk?"

Another incandescent stab of headlights speared toward her, and a moment later she made out the shape of Milo's Corolla. She grabbed her purse and unlocked the door.

Annalese, who was sitting in the passenger seat, rolled down the window. "Aunt Garland, you would have *loved—*"

Milo put his hand over her mouth. "You talked all the way over here. Now its my turn." Still keeping his hand over her mouth, he winked at Garland. "Now, what's wrong with the van?"

"I don't know." Garland shrugged. "It started right away, then suddenly died. I tried several more times but got nothing but a cough out of it."

"A cough, huh?" Milo climbed out of his car and held out his hand. "Let me have your key."

"What for? You know less about cars than I do," Garland said.

"Gimme your key, woman."

She tossed the key ring to him. "Lock the doors," she told the twins before hurrying after Milo. "Milo, we don't need to do this right now. I'll have somebody come look at it tomorrow."

Ignoring her completely, he unlocked the van and climbed inside. A moment later the engine purred to life. He peered at her, his eyebrows raised in mocking inquiry.

"It *was* broken," she said in self-defense. He opened his mouth to say something, but she raised her voice to override him. "And if you make one of your comments about PMS hallucinations, I'll kill you."

He grinned. "Okay. Why don't you pack the girls in and move out? I'll follow you to make sure nothing happens on the way."

A few minutes later Garland was heading home, absentmindedly listening to the twins' chatter. All in all, she thought, it had been one hell of a disturbing evening. A good night's sleep was what she needed to sweep the cobwebs from her head. After this, she'd be grateful for her secure, if boring (by Milo's standards, anyway) life.

Chapter Three

"A rehearsal? At eight o'clock on Sunday morning?" Charla demanded, sliding up in bed so she could look at Jay.

He stood with his back to her, combing his wet hair away from his forehead. "The play opens Friday, Charla. We've got a hell of a lot of work to do between now and then. Besides, don't you have to leave for the airport?"

"Not for an hour or so, love. Time enough for a real nice goodbye." She crossed her arms over her chest, squeezing her breasts together; she knew he liked that. "Turn around."

He did, and she could see the awareness of her in his eyes. Awareness, and desire. Now she had him! Her triumph faded quickly, however, for instead of moving toward the bed, he shrugged into the Louis Vuitton sportcoat she'd bought him the other day. She did notice that he was still looking at her breasts.

"Baby, if I had time, I'd kiss those pretty things for you," he said. "But I'm late as it is."

A moment later he was gone. With a sigh, Charla tossed the sheet aside and padded into the bathroom. After taking a hot shower, she wiped the fog from the mirror and leaned close to examine her face. The tiny lines around her eyes were plumped somewhat by the moist heat, but they were definitely there. The time had come to do something; she wasn't about to surrender to the ravages of age without a fight. The mirror began to cloud over again, giving her the fresh, dewy look she'd had years ago. It wasn't fair. Here she was, thirty-four years old, and already she was on the slide to nowhere. The modeling world had a very short memory. If this Angelique Bei thing didn't hit big, five years from now—no, two years from now—no one would remember Charla Ross. She'd be nobody. And she didn't know how to be nobody.

"Hell!" she muttered, flicking the fan on to dissipate the moisture. "I don't want to be a *mature* model. I don't want to be old!"

It took her the better part of an hour to do her hair and makeup, and by the time she went downstairs, there was barely time to make her flight. Ignoring the pot of fresh coffee Jay had left for her, she grabbed her purse and headed out to the garage where the Mercedes was parked. The big car gleamed like old iron in the dimness at the far side of the space.

She flipped the light switch, but nothing happened. "Damn you, Jay," she said aloud. "You could have put a new bulb in before you left." Stepping gingerly—Jay's clunker leaked oil like a sieve—she made it to the Mercedes without fouling her new shoes.

There was a sound behind her, a stealthy footstep that jerked her head up in alarm. She whirled, sucking in her breath for a scream. Before she could let it out again, a hand clamped over her mouth, and a heavy body bore her backward to slam against the car. She beat at her attacker with her heavy makeup kit, but he tore it from her grasp, sending tubes and jars spilling out over the floor. Catching both her wrists in his free hand, he immobilized her with his weight. A jagged knife-edge of panic shot through her. Caught. Pinned. Helpless. She peered up at her captor, but could see nothing but that he was male and had dark hair.

He leaned close; she could feel his hot breath on her cheek. "You're a pretty one," he whispered. "Not my type, but pretty."

She surged against his restraining hand. He leaned more of his weight on her, pressing her cruelly against the fender of the car. She wanted to scream—tried to scream—but the hand gripping her mouth was like a vise. Her breath came in ragged, frightened pants.

He let go, so suddenly that she didn't react for a moment. When she did open her mouth to scream, he jammed a gag into it. After that, it was only a few seconds before he'd tied her hands and feet. Then he blindfolded her. Surely, she thought, he wouldn't blindfold her if he planned to kill her. She clutched that small bit of hope desperately, not daring to think of what might happen if it weren't true. Money. That was all he wanted. Frank would give it to him, and then she'd be safe.

He moved away from her, and a moment later she was aware of light through the layers of cloth over her eyes. She heard him moving about the garage . . . doing what? Ah, picking up her scattered makeup. Why would he do that?

She heard the jingle of keys, then the familiar sound of the Mercedes's trunk being opened. Her captor's footsteps seemed to echo in her head as he came toward her, and her body curled up reflexively. He grabbed her beneath her armpits. Handling her as though she were a sack of flour and not a human being, he dragged her to the rear of the car and dumped her into the trunk. Her makeup kit was tossed in beside her. As the trunk lid closed with a solid *thunk,* she whimpered deep in her throat. She shifted restlessly. The tinkle of broken glass came from the makeup kit and the smell of Opium perfume permeated the small space. She didn't think she'd ever buy that brand again.

The garage door slid open with metallic smoothness. Then the car purred to life and began to move. She could feel it turn right, left, then right again, and a moment later the sudden punch of acceleration. The freeway! He was taking her . . . where? For the first time in many years, she prayed. Really prayed; not the bored routine of words that sufficed at church, but an outpouring of emotion so profound that He had to hear it. *Please, God, stop this. Please! I'm scared, so scared. He might hurt me. I don't take pain well, I never did take pain well, I don't want to be hurt . . .* She began to cry. Tears soaked the blindfold, then over-soaked it, and began to flow along her cheeks in warm rivulets.

The air in the trunk felt as hot and thick as flannel, or maybe it was terror that settled over her in a smothering blanket. She wanted to faint; whatever was going to happen, she didn't want to feel it. But the air just got denser, her bonds more confining, her fear more profound. And under her, around her, the car moved with smooth power. Taking her to her fate. Every turn of the wheels, every bump, every passing second seemed to imprint itself in her flesh. Her brain twisted and turned and folded in and over on itself, trying to find a way out. An accident, a policeman stopping the Mercedes for speeding . . . anything so that she could try to attract someone's attention.

The car decelerated, and a moment later she felt it swing into a long right turn. An exit ramp. She began to whimper deep in her throat again. The drive went on and on, but whether hours or minutes passed, she didn't know. It felt like a lifetime. The outside world seemed strangely remote; all reality now was encompassed by the dark confines of the trunk. As long as it remained closed, nothing *really* bad could happen to her. But her captor had the key, and the time would come when he would enter her world. And then, and then . . . she flinched back from that thought, concentrating instead on the discomfort in her bound hands.

The car slowed to make a left turn. The surface beneath the wheels was badly pitted, and although she braced herself as best she could, her head banged painfully against the carpeted floor of the trunk. Suddenly the sound of the engine changed—they were inside a building. The car door opened and closed, then came the unmistakable sound of a metal garage door closing. Quiet. The only sound was her heartbeat fluttering in her ears. He was coming.

Panting in terror, she squirmed as far back in the trunk as she could. *Please, God, make him go away! I'll be good, I'll never see Jay again, I'll be the best wife and mother you ever saw . . . Nooooo!*

The trunk was open; she could feel the change in the air, feel him looking at her. The car shifted as he leaned his weight on it. He grasped the front of her shirt and used it to pull her forward. She moaned as she was dragged over the lip of the trunk and dumped on a cool, hard surface. Paralyzed by fear, she lay curled on her side.

She flinched when she felt his hands groping through her hair, but he only untied her blindfold. As soon as the cloth was pulled away from her eyes, she turned her head to look at him. Her first thought was *He's so young!* Then she noticed that his eyes were cold and flat, like a shark's. Terror, sharp and sickening, clenched her throat. He was wearing black leather driving gloves.

He reached toward her, and she flinched back from those black-clad fingers. But he didn't hurt her, just began sifting through her hair again. He seemed to be fascinated with her hair. "Pretty," he said. "So pretty."

Hope. Just a shred, but she clutched it frantically.

Good! He seemed interested in her; maybe he'd keep her for a while.

"I bet men like you," he said.

She nodded, praying that he would like her, too. Was he going to rape her now? God, he didn't have to use force; she'd do anything for him, anything!

His fingers delved slowly through her hair. She stared up at him, trying to read some emotion into those strange blue eyes. If only he'd take the gag off, give her a chance to talk to him.

As though reading her thoughts, he untied the gag and tossed it away. "There's no one to hear if you scream," he said.

"Please . . ." The inside of her mouth was dry and sore, her voice raspy, so she cleared her throat and tried again. "Please, could I have some water?"

"Okay." He turned toward a stained concrete sink that stood against the right wall.

Rolling onto her side, she watched him take a glass from a shelf above the sink and fill it with water. Her teeth sank into the inside of her bottom lip as she resisted the urge to scream. The fact that he hadn't hesitated to walk away from her showed that he'd told the truth about no one being able to hear her. If she screamed, she'd only make him angry.

As he came back toward her, she tried to wriggle to a sitting position. He watched her impassively for a moment, then bent to help her.

"Thank you," she murmured. "Please, won't you untie me?"

He shook his head. Then, going down on one knee beside her, he held the glass so she could drink. It was a strangely solicitous gesture, and her hope soared. He was taking care of her. He was human. More, he was a *man*. Reachable.

The water was gone. When he took the glass away

from her lips, she asked, "Why did you take me?"

His shoulders lifted in a shrug.

She tried again. "My husband will pay a great deal of money to have me home safely." Instead of answering, he got to his feet and started playing with her hair again.

A wave of nausea went through her. *Don't be weak, Charla. He's a man. Remember that. A man. One thing you've learned in your life, and that's how to make men do what you want. Find out what he wants and give it to him. Make him happy.* "Do you like my hair?" she asked.

"Yes," he said. "It's pretty. Like moonlight. Pale, not dark." Clumsily, he tried to remake her tumbled chignon, then sighed and spread her hair out over her shoulders.

Such a childlike gesture, she thought. But then he couldn't be more than nineteen or twenty. *Too young for you,* a cynical voice whispered in her head. But she knew better. Here, there were no such rules. This was his world. Here, he owned her.

"Mrs. Hollister."

She jerked in surprise; somehow, she hadn't expected to hear her name. His hands left her hair. And his voice had hardened, the dreamy, childlike quality gone. Her emotions reeled, trying to find balance in a changed world.

"Mrs. Hollister," he said again.

"Yes?" her voice was shrill.

"You have a lover."

Not knowing what he wanted to hear, she remained silent. Then his hands returned to her hair, his fingers sliding along the length of the strands, then delving deep again. She relaxed slightly.

"Tell me about your lover," he said.

"What . . . what do you want to know?"

"He's younger than you, isn't he?"

She swallowed convulsively. "A little."

"Ten years is more than a little," he said, moving around behind her and trying to redo the chignon again. "Does it bother you?"

"No." *If only I could see his face, I'd know what he wants.* Taking a couple of deep breaths to calm herself, she added, "I don't think it matters . . . as long as the people are attracted to one another."

"I'm even younger than your lover, Mrs. Hollister. Are you attracted to me?"

Relief and dread swept through her. He wanted her. He'd let her please him. If only she could look at him, *see* his desire, this would be so much easier! "Yes, I find you attractive," she said, forcing the words through stiff lips.

"I'm not . . . experienced with women," he whispered.

"I'll show you," she said. "I'll be everything you ever dreamed of. I'll—"

"Slut. I *hate* sluts."

At first she didn't comprehend what he'd said. Or its consequences. His fingers tightened in her hair, using that hold to haul her to her knees. Her startled gaze caught the flash of metal, but she didn't realize what it was at first. And then she knew: a knife. A big kitchen knife, sharp-edged and cruel. *No, it can't be. Not here, not like this! I can't do this, I can't bear it!* She screamed then, letting all her accumulated terror out at once.

"Nooooo!" she shrieked, twisting her bound wrists until trickles of wetness ran down her hands. "You can't! Oh, please, you can't!"

And he laughed. *Laughed!* His hand left her hair to grip her jaw with numbing force, stilling her scream and lifting her chin up even higher. Time seemed to pass with unutterable slowness as the glittering blade descended toward her throat. A cold touch. Not pain, just . . . coldness. Was he teasing her, playing at terror games just for fun? Some sick kind of foreplay?

When the knife ascended again it was red, not silver. A pulsing crimson fountain sprayed out in front of her. Her blood. Her life. She wasn't ready. *She wasn't ready!* He let go of her, and she fell forward onto her face with a force that cracked bone.

But for once she wasn't worried about her face; she was watching a swiftly running stream of blood disappear down the drain that was set in the middle of the floor. A moment later, even that didn't matter. Blackness rushed in on her, roaring.

And then silence.

Chapter Four

Garland dropped her suitcase beside the kitchen table, then poured herself a cup of coffee and sat down to wait for the twins to finish packing. The girls always hated to leave this house. So did she. This had been her parents' home, and the essence of the Ross family had been absorbed somehow by the modern suburban dwelling. The child Garland had eaten at this oak table, at this very spot. Near her coffee cup was the neat square of cross-hatched scratches she'd made when she was eight. Oh, Mom had been mad about that! And here, near her left elbow, was the dark burn mark she'd made when she had accidentally set her napkin aflame with a candle from her eleventh birthday cake. Somehow, Mom had never gotten around to having the table refinished. Neither had Garland.

Five years ago, when Garry had moved out for good, she'd had the wall knocked out between the dining room and kitchen, making a big, airy informal dining area. The change was great, but she'd picked out the same wallpaper her mother had chosen years ago: copper teapots and groupings of vegetables on a beige background. Charla had laughed and laughed before offering to send her designer over. "Oh, Garland, *really!*" she'd said. Garland had refused politely but firmly; she liked the teapots and veggies. They felt like home.

The twins finally walked in, carrying matching overnight bags. Garland was struck by how grown-up they were getting; it wouldn't be too long before they'd be as tall as she was.

"Ready?" she asked, getting to her feet.

"I don't know why we can't stay here," Annalese complained.

"Because you have school tomorrow and your bus doesn't come out to Elizabeth Park," Garland said.

"We could play hooky, just this once," Amber pleaded.

Garland shook her head. "Absolutely not. Your parents would kill me, and rightly so. You know how important your education is."

The statement was greeted by a silence that made the air vibrate with its intensity. Garland picked her coffee cup up and took it to the sink. Then, leaning her back against the edge of the counter, she confronted that tense hush. "What's the matter?" she asked.

"Dad's going to send us to separate schools next year. *Boarding* schools." Amber was calm, strangely adult in her pain. "He says we're old enough to start learning to be independent of one another."

Anger made a hard knot in Garland's chest. "I see." She took a deep breath. "What does your mother say about it?"

"Mom says it's for the best," Amber said. "She's going to be busy working all next year."

Holy cow! Garland thought. Shuffled aside like . . . like a couple of inconvenient pets. She knew Charla loved these girls. Frank, too. But somewhere along the way they'd lost sight of what their children were and what they needed.

She saw the way the twins stood shoulder to shoulder, shoring one another up. Together they were strong. Together they could face anything the world threw at them. How could anyone think that tearing them apart would be good? Oh, sure—someday they'd have to separate to find their individual destinies. It was already happening a little; Amber was interested in math and science, while Annalese gravitated toward language arts. But *they* ought to be the ones to do it—at their own pace and in their own time.

"Can't you do something, Aunt Garland?" Annalese asked. Her chin quivered just a little. "Can't you talk to him, make him understand?"

Garland knelt and put her arms around them. "I'll try, honey. I'll do my very best." And she would. But in the ten years she'd known Frank Hollister, no one had ever made him change his mind about anything. If only Charla . . . With a sigh, she stood up. "Come on, let's get you home."

She drove them downtown to Frank and Charla's posh Ghent house. It was a three-story brick structure of a style Garland jokingly called Federal Nouveau. A brass plate beside the door was tastefully inscribed with *Dr. and Mrs. Hollister.*

Since Garland didn't have the remote that opened the security gates across the driveway at the back of the house, she parked the van at the front curb. Whistling under her breath, she unloaded the twins and luggage and headed up the brick steps.

"Remember the alarm," Annalese said.

Garland let her breath out in a long sigh. "Thanks. I'd completely forgotten."

"You always do." Annalese jabbed her twin with her elbow, and both giggled. "Remember the time the alarm went off and the police came?"

"How could I forget?" Shifting her suitcase to her left hand, Garland inserted the key while mentally reviewing the proper sequence for canceling the alarm. "Two squad cars came screaming up the street, lights flashing, tires squealing. I thought they were going to shoot first and ask questions later."

She pushed the door open and hurried inside, knowing that she had less than a minute to get the ID code punched into the control panel. *Talk about stress!* she grumbled to herself. *Can't even walk in a house anymore without having to sacrifice to the resident computer god.*

Once she'd pacified it, however, the computer very kindly turned the living room and hallway lights on. The interior of the house was nothing like the pseudo-traditional exterior; this was Charla's domain, and Charla was *modern.* The decor had been done wholly in black and white, with a few stray touches of color brought in by floral arrangements.

Beautiful and sterile, Garland thought. Surely even dust didn't dare to settle here. As always, the house brought out her rebellious instincts; the first thing she did was toss her green plaid jacket untidily on the hideously expensive black lacquer chest in the foyer. Defiantly—although they'd never have dared to do it if their mother had been here—the twins dumped hats, coats, and shoes on the floor and ran shrieking toward the family room and the Nintendo.

"Want some popcorn or something?" Garland called after them.

"You bet!"

Smiling, Garland stepped over the mess on the floor and went into the kitchen. Blond oak cabinets added buttery warmth to the room, balancing the sleek modern functionalism of the appliances. A marvel of design. Garland preferred her teapots and vegetables; all that shiny chrome and black glass attracted fingerprints like crazy and the floor, a huge stretch of alternating black and white squares, always made her feel a little seasick. She caught sight of the answering machine, its red light blinking urgently.

Pulling a note pad out of a drawer, she rewound the tape and began listening to the messages. Some were the usual: requests for Charla and Frank to attend social functions, friends wanting to talk, a couple of sales calls. Garland wrote them down in sequence. Then came a series of calls from Ted Ballard, Charla's agent.

"Charla, darling," he said, his gravelly bass voice so loud that Garland turned the volume down a bit, "I'm catching a plane to Paris in an hour. See you there." *Click.* "Charla, I'm meeting with the Bei people first thing in the morning. Call me at the Plaza-Athenée Hotel as soon as you get in, it's important." *Click.* "Charla, damn it, where the fucking hell are you? Call me, and call me now!" *Click.* "Charla, don't do this to me. It's two o'clock in the morning—*Monday* morning, goddamn it. In case you've forgotten, the shoot is scheduled to start in six hours. Angelique Bei is ready to have a cow. If you don't have your ass on an airplane right this minute, you'd better get it on the Concorde *tout de suite.*" His voice rose to a bellow. "I don't know what kind of game you're playing, but I'm tired of covering your spoiled prima-donna ass for you. If you screw this up, you're fucking *through,* do you hear me?"

Garland dropped the pen. Charla wasn't there? She had to be there; she'd left Friday!

"Aunt Garland?"

Amber! The pen rolled off the counter and Garland bent to retrieve it, glad to have a chance to compose her face. "What do you need, honey?"

"Can we have Twinkies instead of popcorn?"

"Sure."

Amber hoisted herself onto the counter and opened one of the upper cabinets. The Twinkies were way, way in the back. Evidence that they weren't supposed to be eaten, Garland knew. For once, she didn't feel like enforcing household rules.

"Want one?" Amber asked.

"No, thanks."

Her mouth stuffed with Twinkie, Amber headed back to the family room. Garland pulled the phone book out of the drawer and looked up the number for TWA. Charla always flew TWA to Europe. The reservation agent's manicured voice cooled when Garland asked if a Ms. Ross had been on a Friday night flight to New York.

"I'm afraid we can't give out that information, ma'am," she said. "I can only tell you if she had a reservation. Mrs. Ross, you said?"

"Charla Ross. She was going to take the last Friday night flight from Norfolk to Newark. . . . I'm afraid I don't have the flight number."

There was a moment's pause. "I'm sorry, ma'am, but there was no reservation made by a Mrs. Ross on any flight that day. Let me try Saturday, just in case. No, nothing. Are you sure she was flying TWA?"

"I was." Garland raked her hand through her hair, damning herself for not getting more information out of Charla. "Well, thank you for your help," she said.

After checking to make sure the twins were occupied with their Nintendo, she began calling the rest of the airlines that served Norfolk International. After the last call, she sat numbly for a few moments, the receiver forgotten in her hand. No airline showed a reservation for Charla Ross for either Friday or Saturday. Could Charla have traveled under another name? If so, it was the first time ever; she *liked* being recognized. What the hell was going on?

The phone beeped at her, then a recorded voice said, "If you'd like to make a call, please hang up and dial again. If you need help . . ."

She hung up. "Now what?" she muttered. Call

Frank? Call the police? Frank first. No, Ted Ballard first. Maybe Charla had shown up in Paris after all. It took her a few minutes to get through to the Plaza-Athenée Hotel.

Ballard answered on the first ring, sounding tired and irritated. *"Allo?"*

"Mr. Ballard, this is Garland Ross, Charla's sister."

"Where the hell is she?"

"I don't know," Garland said. "Isn't she supposed to be staying there?"

"Yes."

"Maybe she changed her mind and went to another hotel."

"Uh-uh. The whole crew is staying here by order of Angelique Bei, Inc.," he said.

Garland worried at her bottom lip with her teeth. "I don't know what could have happened, Mr. Ballard. Charla told me she was leaving for Paris Friday night—"

"Friday? What for?"

"The shoot had been moved up." There was silence at the other end, and Garland's throat started to ache. "That wasn't true?"

He snorted. "No, it wasn't true."

She drummed her fingertips on the countertop, trying to make some sense out of her sister's actions. Ballard seemed to find her lack of response amusing.

"Well, Miss Ross," he said, chuckling. "It looks like Charla's diddling both of us, doesn't it? Well, I just hope her little game is worth fucking her career up for."

Forgetting that he couldn't see her, Garland shook her head. "I can't believe she'd do anything to jeopardize this job."

"Ahhh, she's pulled this crap before." he growled. "I've put up with it for more than ten years. The Ross grand entrance scene—she's famous for it. Well, she got away with it when she was on top. Now she's just another middle-aged model. There are fifty other women who'd kill for this job, and who'll do it without any bullshit."

All Garland's protective instincts surfaced. "Now look here, Mr. Ballard—"

"No, *you* look!" he shouted. "I've been up all night grabbing hell from the Bei people, my ulcer is killing me, and I'm extremely pissed off at your sister. If she doesn't show up at six this morning—six, not six-thirty, not six-oh-*five*—not only will she be finished in this business, she's gonna get sued for breach of contract. First by Angelique Bei and then by me. I've *had* it, Miss Ross."

The phone went dead. Numbly, Garland replaced the receiver. Charla had seemed so eager for this job . . . then why hadn't she gone to Paris? Why had she lied about leaving Friday? Obviously, she'd lied to Frank, too—or rather, as a cynical little voice in Garland's mind said—she'd gotten her sister to lie to Frank. Now Garland was torn between being worried about her and covering up for her.

"Charla, you really did it this time." With a sigh, Garland rested her forehead against the cool marble countertop. She couldn't call Frank yet, or the police. Yet. But if Charla didn't show up somewhere soon, there wouldn't be a choice. And if it got Charla in trouble, well, too bad. She was going to have to take full responsibility for this one.

Garland straightened, her gaze going to the clock on the wall above her. Nine o'clock, time to get the girls to bed. At least then she wouldn't have to be so careful not to let her worry show. She shook her head to clear the cobwebs, then went in to the family room to roust the twins upstairs.

It took her nearly an hour to get Amber and Annalese bathed and combed and in bed. Ignoring the whispered giggles from behind their closed door, she went downstairs to Charla's study and began searching through her desk drawers. There was nothing but the usual sort of desk clutter: magazines, bills from Saks and Neiman Marcus, invitations to one party or another, a few letters. Garland opened her sister's appointment book. The pages of an entire month, from the third week of January to the third week in February, had been x'd through with red marker, and "Angelique Bei, Paris" written above each date in Charla's bold, looping script. Each date; thirty notations of Angelique Bei. Charla had *enjoyed* writing that.

Garland's stomach knotted as concern warred with resentment. "Take it easy," she muttered under her breath. "You're worse than an old nursemaid. And you know Charla. She probably spent the weekend shopping in New York or London and will walk into the shoot, looking cool and beautiful while everyone else has been tearing their hair out. No wonder Ted Ballard has an ulcer."

With a sigh of exasperation, Garland scooped the appointment book up and went to sit on the white damask sofa in front of the fireplace. Mirroring the twins' defiance, she put her feet, shoes and all, up on the cushion and began to read. Every page through July was heavily penciled in. Dates, times, places. Hair appointments, nail appointments, appointments for photos, fittings and charity luncheons. Garland shuddered. *And Charla thinks my life is boring?*

The phone rang, and she bounced up to answer it. "Hello?"

There was no reply. But the line was still open, she could tell. Maybe it was a bad connection from Paris. "Hello," she said, louder this time. "Charla, is that you? Hello? Hello!"

Still nothing. With the receiver still pressed to her ear, Garland swung around to look at the clock on the wall behind her. Ten minutes to midnight; nearly six o'clock in Paris. Final countdown for Charla's career.

Garland pressed the disconnect button with her thumb. The aborted call might have been from Ted Ballard; she'd better try calling him back. Realizing that she'd left the notebook with his number in the kitchen, she went back to retrieve it.

The dark kitchen was like a cave, spooky and silent. The appliances were hulking shadows in the dimness, a few faint reflections on glass or chrome looking like the flash of animals' eyes in the light. An involuntary shiver made goose bumps rise up on Garland's skin. She recalled memories of the child she had been, watching the corners of her room at night—wedges of deep shadow, blacker than the rest of the room. If she stared hard at those spots, she could see movement. She'd stare and stare and stare, terrified that the movement was real, and that if she looked away, something awful would come out of the shadow into her room.

"Shit," the adult Garland said, fumbling for the light switch. A moment later a bright fluorescent glare filled the room. Her childhood memory fled, taking its attendant bogeymen with it.

The phone rang as she reached for it, startling her heart into fear mode again. She snatched the receiver up. "Hello?"

Silence.

"Charla, is that you?" she asked. "Operator? Is anyone there?"

No answer. She pressed the disconnect button with her thumb, holding it there while she flipped through the notebook with her other hand. "Where is it?" she muttered as she turned pages. "I know it's right . . . ah, there it is!"

But when she released the button, there was no dial tone. The caller hadn't hung up yet.

For five minutes—Garland counted all three hundred revolutions the second hand made around the clock face—she stood holding the useless phone and cursing under her breath. Then the dial tone came back with startling suddenness.

Frustration made her hand tremble as she dialed the number of Ted Ballard's hotel. He wasn't there, of course, but she left a message for him to call her back.

The man stared at the phone, his fingers twitching with the desire to pick it up again. He repressed that desire; it wasn't time yet. Slow and sure won the race. Pleasure was increased by waiting. Denial made it grow and sharpen. He'd learned that in the past.

His shoebox was on the bed beside him. He opened it and lifted out his newest treasure: a hank of smooth blond hair, tied at one end with a pink ribbon. A pretty thing. Pale and fine, like spun platinum.

Absently, he curled the loose end around his finger. Pretty, but not right. Not satisfying. He laid the hair aside and reached into the box again. Taking out a handful of ribbon-tied hanks of hair, he arranged them in a circle around the blond one. Only the center one was light; the rest were dark, ranging from chestnut to black. He counted them, stroking them with his fingertips. Eleven. There was one he had failed to obtain, the one he'd always missed—twelve. An even dozen.

With a sigh, he rearranged the hair, placing them in a line from lightest to darkest, left to right. He left the third spot from the right empty. The other one would go there. He was a good judge of color.

He looked at the blond one, vivid among the dark. That woman hadn't been right at all. Even her terror had been pallid, a pale shadow of what he'd come to expect. But he'd been told, over and over, that his preference for a particular sort of woman was dangerous, and he'd come to believe it. So now he had to branch out, stop limiting himself.

His mouth twisted. The blonde had been a slut, sure enough. She'd thought he wanted to . . . wanted to . . . With a wordless snarl, he snatched the blond hair and tossed it into the ashtray on the nightstand, then struck a match. The hair shriveled and stank, curling frantically away from the flame as though trying to escape. Strange, he thought, how hard it was to burn hair. He persisted, however, using match after match until there was nothing left but a pasty mass of ash. *There, that's better!*

He put his treasures away. For a moment he sat hugging the shoebox to his chest, his eyes closed. Sometimes it was hard to wait. That woman . . . the other one. The sister. Last night, when she had sensed him standing outside the window of the bookstore, fear had come into her eyes. Dark eyes. Dark eyes and straight dark hair and face pale with fear. The sight had nearly sent him over the edge. He could have taken her. Oh, he'd toyed with the idea; he'd even disabled her car by stuffing a rag up the tailpipe. It wasn't time yet, though, so he'd left her alone.

She was perfect, the best one yet. Even her voice was dark. Dark and rich as honey, as cream, as the pit of hell.

"A poem!" Beating out time against the bedspread with his open hand, he chanted, "Dark and rich as honey, as cream, as the pit of hell. Ahhh, woman of my dreams, I know you well!"

He laughed. Miss Thomason, one of his fourth-grade

teachers, had liked his poems. She had written to him at the home they'd sent him to after his mother died, but his poetry had turned black and ugly and her letters soon stopped.

His laughter dried up, shriveling like Charla Hollister's hair. With a grunt, he swung his feet down to the floor and stood up. It was time to get her to a place where she was sure to be found. This, too, felt wrong. Until now he'd always tried to hide his victims. Some had *never* been found.

But this was necessary, at least for now. A hunter had to adapt as his surroundings changed. He'd heard it so many times that it was like a song in his head. Self-denial. Self-control. Good for the psyche, good for the soul.

Chapter Five

Garland dozed fitfully on the sofa in Charla's office. Her dreams were heavy and frightening, filled with an overpowering sense of dread. Finally unable to sleep at all, she sat in the chair beside the desk and watched the red LED numbers on the clock change. Five o'clock, five-fifteen, five-thirty.

There were times when she reached for the phone, intending to call Frank, but didn't. There were more times when she'd nearly called the police, but didn't. That call had been harder to resist; the only reason she hadn't made it was the fact that Charla had lied to her about leaving. A nagging little internal voice kept saying, *She didn't tell you what she was doing. She didn't trust you.*

"So what?" she retorted. "Charla's all grown up. She doesn't have to tell her big sister everything!"

Doesn't she?

"No." Still, it hurt. Really hurt.

There was only one call she dared make—to Ted Ballard—and she made it so many times she lost count. Each time she failed to reach him. Why the hell hadn't she thought to get the number of the shoot from him?

At 6 A.M. she called Ted Ballard's hotel again. She knew she ought to wait; it was only noon in Paris, and if Charla had shown up, the shoot would be going full speed. But Ted had become her only link to Charla, and she could no more stop herself from calling than she could stop breathing.

The desk clerk recognized her voice. "I am very sorry, Mademoiselle Ross, but Monsieur Ballard has not yet returned. Yes, yes, I will ask him to call you the moment he does. No, your sister has not arrived. No, I have not heard from her. No, I do not know if Monsieur Ballard has heard from her. I am sorry, mademoiselle."

Garland tossed the receiver back into its resting place, feeling scared and angry, frustrated and helpless all at once. If she could find out whether or not Charla actually arrived at the shoot, she'd know what to do. Now, however, it was time to get the twins up. Her muscles protested as she rose to her feet. Feeling a hundred years old, she trudged upstairs to wake the girls.

"Come on, come on, move it!" she called through the bedroom door, pitching her voice in the drill sergeant's bark that was needed to get the twins moving on school days.

There was a groan from inside. Garland opened the door and looked into the frilly pink-and-white-lace room to see both girls roll over, putting their backs to her. "Come on, you two. Time's a-wasting."

They flipped over and glared at her. "We're tired," Amber said.

"Uh-uh, don't even try it," Garland said. "I've seen you in action, remember? Now get things in gear; your bus is due in twenty-five minutes."

"You look awful," Annalese said. "Is something wrong?"

They're too perceptive, Garland thought. I've got to hide this better. They don't need to know anything, not yet. *I* don't know anything. "I'm not tired. I'm just in a very bad mood."

Amber nodded. "PMS."

"Get!" Garland said, more forcefully than she had intended.

They got. For Garland, the next twenty minutes passed in a blur. She was grateful that the mindless mechanics of routine allowed her to fix breakfasts and lunches, check the contents of matching neon green and pink backpacks, and even make the proper verbal responses to the girls' chatter. Once they were out the door, however, she rushed to the phone and called Ted Ballard again.

This time she was put through to his room. The phone rang four times, five. The knot in her stomach tightened with every ring. The world narrowed, seeming to beat in time with her heart. This was it.

There was a click, then she heard Ballard's gravelly *"Allo."*

"Mr. Ballard, this is Garland Ross."

"I was just going to call you," he said. This time his tone was thoughtful, not irritated. "Charla never showed."

Garland sagged in the chair, feeling as though someone had punched her in the stomach. Her breath moved in and out, in and out, feeling almost too big for her throat to contain.

"Are you all right?" Ballard asked.

It took her a moment to find her voice. "What do you think about all this, Mr. Ballard?"

"Well, I have to admit that for all the BS Charla's given me over the years, she's never failed to show up on an assignment. There's a first time for everything, though."

"I know my own sister," Garland said. "There's no way she would have missed this assignment deliberately."

He sighed, the gusty exhalation of a tired, tired man.

"Look, I'm catching a plane to New York as soon as I can throw my clothes in a suitcase. I'll call you as soon as I get back to the office." There was an awkward silence, then he said, "I hope she's all right."

Garland couldn't speak. After a moment she hung up. Tears threatened, tears she didn't have time for. She pressed the heels of her hands against her eyes, hard.

"Okay," she muttered. "You've got to hold things together. First, call Frank. He's got a right to know what's going on."

Her brother-in-law answered on the fifth ring, his voice fuzzy with sleep. "Hollister."

"Frank, this is Garland."

"Garland?" She heard him fumbling around in the background, probably looking for his reading glasses. "What's the matter? Is something wrong?"

"Everything's wrong," she said. "Charla never made it to Paris."

"She's home then. If you let me speak to her—"

"She's not home!" Although Garland tried to control her voice, it went up shrilly. "She's not *anywhere!*"

She could hear him breathing, and knew he was examining all the ramifications of that statement. It was infuriating, the coolly deliberate process of his mind.

"She has to be somewhere," he said at last.

It was a reasonable thing to say, but Garland didn't want to be reasonable. This was *Charla* they were talking about. "She's not in Paris and she's not here. No one has heard from her. I called all the airlines and there was no reservation for her on Friday night, and then—"

"Easy, Garland," he soothed. "Take a deep breath. Calm yourself."

He's right, she thought. She took several deep breaths while he waited patiently, then told him the story as concisely as possible. "I'm worried enough to call the police," she said at the end.

"Yes, I think that would be best," he agreed. "I'll call the hospitals from here and see if she was admitted to any of them over the weekend. Perhaps she had an accident of some kind."

"That would be a big help; you know who to talk to." A tremendous wave of relief washed over Garland; it was great to have someone to share the responsibility. She found herself wishing again that she and Frank had been closer. He'd showed his mettle just now by ignoring Charla's lie and concentrating on the important issue: finding out what had happened.

"I have a few loose ends to tie up here," he said. "I'll catch the earliest flight possible." He cleared his throat, a nervous sound. "I hate to ask you to do this, but will you tell the girls? You never know how things like this get out, but they do, and I'd rather they didn't hear about it from a stranger."

"Of course." Actually, it had never occurred to her *not* to tell them. Not wanting to strain her newfound rapport with Frank, however, she didn't say so.

"I'm sure there's a perfectly rational explanation for what's happened. Charla is probably stranded in an airport somewhere."

"All weekend? Without calling? I don't think so," Garland said. "I'm really frightened."

"Now, Garland, don't panic."

Reasonable words again, she thought, as unsatisfying now as they had been earlier. Oh, Frank was good at it, very good; after all, he made his living soothing the distraught. But Garland didn't want to be soothed. She wanted Charla back. But she also hated losing control; in that respect, she was very much like Frank. So she said, "I'm not going to panic. I can't do anyone any good if I panic."

"I know I can count on you," Frank said. "Now, let

me go. The sooner I get started, the sooner I can get home."

He hung up. As soon as the dial tone returned, Garland dialed the number of the Norfolk Police. She was proud that her hand shook only a little.

A surprisingly short time later, she found herself sitting on the sofa in Charla's office, looking a bit dazedly at the police detective who had come to take the report. No Peter Falk sloppiness here, she noted, but a gray business suit, white shirt, and conservative tie. Garb to reassure, matching the politely sympathetic expression on his rather broad Slavic face. It should have worked. "If you're ever in trouble, Garland, go to a policeman," her parents had always told her. But answering the detective's questions had only sharpened her fear for Charla. A missing person's report. Seemingly bland questions, seemingly bland answers, but actually a stinging, sharp-edged reality that cut deeper with every passing moment. *This* missing person was her sister.

"Miss Ross?"

Her gaze focused, and her mind struggled to catch up. "Oh! I'm sorry, ah . . ." After a frenzied moment of scrabbling through her memory, she remembered his name. "Detective Pulkowski. I was just thinking about . . . never mind. What did you say?"

"What kind of car does your sister drive?" he asked.

"A silver-gray 1990 Mercedes 520SL, license plate 'CRoss.' "

"Was she planning to take it to the airport?"

"I assumed so." Garland clasped her hands and put them in her lap. "It isn't in the garage. I checked."

He smiled. "That was going to be my next question." After writing something in his notebook, he asked, "Would it be possible that she decided to drive to New York?"

"Possible, but unlikely," Garland replied. "It's what . . . eight hours by car? If she'd missed her flight for some reason, she'd have taken the first plane to New York in the morning. Besides, she hates long car trips." A knot of dread tightened her chest, and she cleared her throat before continuing. "I called the airlines, of course. They wouldn't give me much information, but they *did* tell me that she hadn't made reservations for either Friday or Saturday."

He looked up from the notebook, surprise sharpening his brown eyes. "No? But your sister told you she was taking a Friday night flight, didn't she?"

"Yes, she did." There it is, she thought. That lie. That damned lie. She examined the detective's face for some clue as to what he was thinking, but his expression was neutral. Carefully neutral. "Look, Detective Pulkowski, I know how that sounds. I mean, lots of things went through my head when I found out she'd lied. That's why I waited until she failed to show up in Paris before calling you. I didn't even call her husband until this morning, ah—"

"In case she'd gone off with another man?" he asked.

Garland was surprised to find that his blunt question made her feel easier; it was out in the open now. She spread her hands wide. "I think it would be strange for her *not* to tell me if she were having an affair. You, see, I'm older than she is . . . I pretty much raised her after our parents died, and we're closer than most sisters. She'd . . . well, she'd tell me about the affair, expecting me to cover for her."

"Would you cover for her?"

"Yes. Oh, I'd give her the standard lecture about right and wrong and point out the risks, but my loyalty would be with her. Always has been, and always will be. She knows that."

The angle of the detective's jaw showed that he had

some doubt about the last statement. And although she hated to admit it, Garland knew he had some basis for it. Charla *had* lied. She *had* concealed something from her older sister.

"Has she ever gone away like this before?" he asked.

"No." With a sigh, Garland pushed her hair back and met his gaze directly. She had a pretty good idea of what was going on in his mind, and she didn't like it. "I know what you're thinking," she said.

He looked up from his notebook, his brows going up in obvious surprise. "You do?"

"Yes. You think Charla dumped her kids on me and took off on . . . on some kind of lark."

"You'd be surprised how many people do that sort of thing, Miss Ross."

Garland considered that, remembering Charla's lie, then shook her head. "*If* my sister took off on some wild escapade, you can be sure that it would have ended Monday morning. The Angelique Bei job was very important to her. Besides, she's never, *never* no-showed on an assignment before. If you want, you can call her agent, Ted Ballard, and ask him. He's represented her for ten years."

Pulkowski jotted something in his notebook. "She's a model, you said."

"A *top* model. And she didn't get to the top by not showing up for assignments."

The notebook sagged in the detective's hand as he glanced around at the photographs that covered almost every square foot of wall space in the room. Garland watched his gaze move from one photo to another: Charla in a sequined evening gown, Charla in a swimsuit, Charla in Rome, in Egypt, in New York and Paris. Charla on the covers of *Elle, Cosmopolitan, Glamour.* Garland wondered if he noticed there were no pictures of the rest of the family in the room. Probably; he didn't seem to miss much.

After drumming her fingers on her knees thoughtfully for a moment, Garland said, "Charla is thirty-four, which is considered old for a model. Just the other day she told me that her career hasn't been doing so well. She said the Angelique Bei campaign would put her right on top again." Taking a deep breath, Garland willed him to believe her. "She *needed* this job. I can't think of anything that would keep her from getting to Paris on time. Anything she had control over, that is."

"I see." He glanced at the big photograph over the desk, the one that showed Charla standing on a black sand beach, a diaphanous emerald dress wind-molded to her long, graceful body. It was Garland's favorite.

She pulled her gaze away from it with an effort, fixing it instead on the man's face. "Maybe she never intended to make a reservation Friday night. Maybe she just planned to buy a ticket and get on that flight. She always flies first class; there are almost always seats available there."

"Well, let's see what we can find out. I'll make some calls—the airlines first—and get back to you."

"Thank you." Garland let out her breath in a sigh of mingled relief and fear. Relief because he seemed to be taking her seriously, fear because it meant that she was right to be afraid for her sister's safety.

"You'll be able to supply me with a recent photo of your sister, I suppose?" he asked, smiling faintly.

Unfolding herself from the sofa, she went to the file cabinet and pulled out the folder where Charla kept her publicity photos. Some were recent, some several years old, judging from the hairstyles. "Here, take your pick." She handed the folder to him, feeling a vague stirring of indignation as she watched him sift through the pictures. After all, this was Charla's property. Her image, her past and her future.

He chose one of the smaller color photographs, then picked up one of the black and white shots Charla kept for newspaper releases. "I'll take these two."

"Will this get into the newspaper?" Garland asked. The idea grated on her nerves like sandpaper—thousands of faceless strangers peering into what ought to be her family's private hell.

"Can't help it. These reports are made available to the media—or anyone, for that matter—on a daily basis," he said. "I'm sorry, but that's the way it is. Besides, it doesn't hurt to alert the public in these cases. Do you remember reading about that elderly woman who wandered away from her home a few weeks ago? Well, that story got us a lot of help from the community."

"It didn't help *her,*" Garland pointed out. "She was dead when they found her."

There, she thought. The word had been said. Dead. Dead, dead, dead. It hung in the air between them, harsh and ugly and final.

Pulkowski neither admitted or denied its existence. "You've had no calls to indicate your sister has been kidnapped?"

"No. I almost wish I had." *At least then I'd know she was alive.* "It's like she vanished into thin air."

Her voice quivered on the last word. She was on the edge of control, and knew it.

So did Pulkowski, for he said, "Look, Miss Ross, I know this is very difficult for you. Until your sister shows up, it's going to continue to be difficult. But those two little girls are going to need you to be strong."

She nodded, unable to speak. Yes, the twins would need her, just as Charla had needed her when their parents had died. And that need had made her strong. But what if Charla never showed up? Oh God, what if something awful had happened to her? Was anyone strong enough for that?

"I think I've got everything I need for now." Closing the notebook, he slipped a rubber band around it with an emphatic snap. "Here's my card. Would you please ask your brother-in-law to get in touch with me as soon as possible? Call me if you think of anything else. It doesn't matter how trivial; sometimes a seemingly unimportant fact is the one that breaks a case wide open for us. And of course, call me immediately if you hear from your sister."

Interview over, Garland thought, moving forward. He rose to his feet, slipping the notebook into the inside pocket of his suitcoat. As she walked him to the door, she heard herself say, "Thank you for coming so quickly, Detective Pulkowski." Automatic politeness, drilled into her from childhood, taking over when she wanted to grab the man's lapels and insist that he find her sister right now. She wanted him to tell her that everything was going to be all right. But he couldn't, and until or unless Charla was back home safely, things weren't going to be all right.

He waited at the door while Garland went to the foyer closet to get his coat. "Please don't get upset, Miss Ross. More often than not in these cases, people turn up on their own."

"Thank you, Detective Pulkowski," Garland said again. But she wasn't reassured.

Just as his car pulled away, the phone began to ring. The nearest one was in the kitchen. Garland ran for it, her sneakers squealing on the ceramic tiles underfoot. Rubber-squeaky sounds of alarm, of hope that she'd hear Charla's voice.

Snatching the receiver up, she said breathlessly, "Hello?"

There was no answer, only silence echoing her ragged breathing. Somehow, mocking her. She slammed the receiver down.

"Must be the same jerk who called last night," she muttered, turning away. "Got nothing better to do than play games at a time like this—"

The phone rang again. She counted to five before answering. "Hello? Hello!" Nothing. Nothing but that pregnant, *listening* silence. That damned prankster! At another time she wouldn't have given something like this a second thought, but now it triggered all the frustration that had been festering inside her.

"Damn you!" she screamed. "You'd better stop this. Do you hear me? If you call again, I'll have your number traced. I'll have you put in jail! I'll—"

There was a click, then the dial tone returned. She stood with the receiver pressed to her ear, her chest heaving as though she'd run a race.

"There." She hung up, hoping she'd taught the caller a lesson. "Go pull your tricks on someone who has time for them."

The phone didn't ring again. As the afternoon wore on, the silence in the house grew oppressive. Garland would almost have welcomed a call from the prankster. Almost. She began pacing, making the rounds of living room, kitchen, and family room like a caged animal. She avoided Charla's office; alone, with the big empty house around her, those photographs were too much to take.

The knots in her stomach tightened as it got closer to three-thirty. Amber and Annalese would be home soon. How was she going to tell them their mother was missing? What words could she use to soften the news?

At three-twenty, the doorbell rang. That would be the twins. Cupping the reassuring warmth of her teacup in her hand, she went to let them in. When the door swung open, however, she saw not the girls, but George Pattie and Colin Kingsley. Garland's mug crashed to the floor, scattering shards of porcelain and hot, sugary tea across the tiles.

Colin took her by the elbows and steered her to one side, leaving George to close the door. "Where's the kitchen?" he asked.

Garland pointed. Colin disappeared through the doorway, emerging a few moments later with a roll of paper towels.

"What are you doing here?" she asked.

"Milo called us. He has to mind the store until five, but George and I came over as soon as we could," Colin said as he began cleaning the mess on the floor. "Did you think we'd let you face this all alone?"

"Why . . . I mean, I never expected—"

"Us to come?" After tossing the last piece of porcelain onto a towel, Colin straightened. "We're your friends, Garland. Don't you think we'd want to help?"

She looked from one to the other, George towering, cranelike, over short, burly Colin. If anyone needed a friend right now, she did. "I've got to tell the girls; this is going to hit the newspapers, and I don't want them hearing about it from some stranger." She felt her bottom lip quiver. *Ridiculous— like a little kid!*

The two men moved forward. "Come, my dear," George said, his deep, mellow voice flowing over her nerves like honey. "I'll fix you another cup of tea. The girls will be here soon. You must be ready to deal with them."

"I'll check the TV and see if anything's hit the news yet," Colin said, bending to pick up the pile of sodden paper towels. "Don't answer the phone; I'll run interference for you."

"Thanks." Garland rested her forehead against George's arm for a moment. "Until you two showed up, I didn't know how alone I was. I just hope I don't break down and make a fool of myself."

" 'One's friends are that part of the human race with which one can be human,' " George quoted. "Truly, dear, I'm old enough to have seen every kind of fool there is, and you're definitely *not* one of those."

There was a double tattoo of knocks on the front door. The twins. So eager, so ready to have fun with their aunt. She'd promised to order a pizza tonight; she wondered if they'd still want it. "Well," Garland murmured, "here goes. I hope I do this right."

"You'll do fine," Colin said. "Now, do you want us to stay with you while you tell them?"

"Yes, but I think it would be better if I talked to them alone." Squaring her shoulders, she went to let the twins in.

The man sat in his car and watched the two little girls go into the house. Two men had preceded them, an old one and one that looked to be in his forties. The woman certainly had a lot of company. Like a funeral. Gathering her friends around for comfort.

He wanted to call her again. He would, once the others were gone. But next time he'd do it from a pay phone. His fingers tightened on the steering wheel. She'd shouted at him. She'd *threatened* him. Her voice, going from smooth to shrill, her anger beating at him. Like the other. Love/hate/kiss/kill. So much like the other that he'd lost it for a minute. When he'd come back to awareness again, he found himself curled up on the bed, tears and snot smeared over his face. His treasures wet with it. Still sobbing, he'd cleaned them with tissues and put them away.

Taking a deep breath, then another, he forced himself to relax. Later. He'd deal with her later. But there was a need within him, an itch, a burning, and it would have to be satisfied. It would be dark soon. The prostitutes came out with the waning light. He'd cruise out to Ocean View and pick one up. Creatures of the night. Easy pickings, easy prey. No one watched over them, no one cared. Except him.

"Come to my lair, said the spider, and I'll treat you fair." He smiled, running his palms around the circle of the steering wheel. The plastic ridges tickled his palms nearly as much as his poetry tickled his fancy.

Light hair, he reminded himself, running his tongue over his lips. Red, blond, it didn't matter as long as it was light hair. There was little savor to that thought—like popcorn without salt.

His gaze focused on a shadow that crossed one of the bay windows in the front of the big house. It was a small shadow. Perhaps one of the little girls, perhaps the woman. He'd seen her with the children—laughing, hugging, having fun. Well, she wasn't laughing now. He tried to imagine the scene in the room. Tried to imagine himself there, but couldn't.

Reaching up, he ran his thumb along the line of his jaw. His attention was on the house, but he was vaguely aware of his thumbnail scraping over his whiskers. *Scritch, scritch.* Small and dark, small and dark. Small. And. Dark.

He pushed the refrain aside. Not now. He'd learned his lesson well—set no pattern, give them nothing to connect him with what had happened in that other place. He'd almost gotten himself caught there.

Putting his car into gear, he eased down the street.

Chapter Six

Garland stood looking out the kitchen window, seeing, yet not seeing, the alley that ran behind the house. The room behind her was dark, illumined only by the faint light sifting along the hall from the family room. This time she didn't notice the shadows lurking in the corners; the bugaboos were all in her mind.

The phone rang, but she felt oddly detached from it, as though the sound came from miles away. It had rung many times this afternoon. Colin and George, and later Milo, had fielded them for her, leaving her to tend to the distraught twins.

Something blocked the faint light coming in the doorway, and she glanced over her shoulder to see Colin's blocky form silhouetted in the opening. "Detective Pulkowski," he said. "I thought you might want to take this one."

She took three quick steps to the phone and snatched it up. "Yes?" Her whole body felt like one big heartbeat.

"Miss Ross, I called the airlines. As they told you, your sister had no reservations for either Friday or Saturday. But she did have one for Sunday." He paused, and Garland's pulse kicked into high gear. Then he added, "She didn't take that flight, or any other since."

"I see." It came out a whisper, and she cleared her throat and tried again. "What . . . what are you going to do now?"

"Well, I'll just have to keep working. Probably show her picture to reservation agents to see if anyone remembers her. She may have traveled under another name. I'll call you as soon as I have more information."

"All right. Thank you." She stood motionless for a while after he hung up, then Colin took the receiver out of her hand. "Charla had a reservation on Sunday," Garland said. "She didn't keep it. Didn't make another."

Colin's hand closed on her arm briefly, but that warm human contact was comforting. She was glad that he didn't try to give her empty assurances.

"Are they asleep?" he asked.

"Yeah. For now." She turned back to the window and leaned her forehead against the cool glass. There was a pounding ache behind her eyes, part long-withheld tears, part tension. "They're scared to . . ." Death, she'd been about to say. The word stuck in her throat, too big and hard-edged to be spoken out loud. "They're scared. So am I."

A car moved into the alley. The twin incandescent beams of its headlights fingered slowly through the darkness as though searching for something. Could it be Frank, perhaps? Garland tracked the lights, feeling her eyes grate in their sockets as though they'd been lined with sandpaper. The car moved on. Not Frank, not yet. Garland wanted him here. Their relationship had always been more polite than warm, but their conversation today had changed that. Charla's disappearance linked them by ties more binding than mere likes or dislikes. His wife, her sister; shared pain, shared responsibility. Family.

"How are you doing?" Colin asked.

To Garland's surprise, his voice came from immediately behind her. She hadn't heard him move. "I'm fine," she said, closing her eyes. *Fine, fine, fine. My sister seems to have disappeared off the face of the earth, but I'm* fine, *damn it!*

His hands came down on her shoulders. Unable to bear the silent sympathy of his touch, she tried to pull away. But he held on, his grip tightening enough to spear through her internal pain.

"You can let go now," he said. "The girls can't see."

Silently, she shook her head. There was no letting go, not for her. He heaved a sigh, then dropped his hands and stepped back. After a moment, she scrubbed the back of her hand over her forehead and turned to face him. She could see little of his features in the dimness. Hopefully, he couldn't see hers either.

"Who called earlier?" she asked.

"Robbie and Troll, wanting to know if there was anything they could do for you. And Ted Ballard called—"

"Did he hear from Charla?" Garland's question was eager, automatic, but the set of Colin's shoulders drained the hope out of her.

"No," he said. "I'm sorry, Garland."

The loss of that flash of hope, however brief, left a bitter taste in her mouth. "So am I."

There was a clank outside. Garland looked out to see the gates that separated the driveway from the alley swing open. Beyond them was Frank's BMW, limned in a ghostly backlit exhaust-fog.

"Thank God," Garland murmured.

The sound of the garage door sliding upward was loud in the quiet room. Colin went to turn on the overhead light, making Garland blink in the sudden fluorescent brightness.

Frank came into the kitchen, setting his briefcase on the counter in a motion that spoke of long practice. Another man might have looked tired after flying across the country, but Frank looked only a bit grayer than usual. Gray eyes, prematurely silver hair, gray suit—even the overcoat hung over his arm in precise folds was gray.

Garland hurried toward him, her hands outstretched. "I'm so glad you're back!" she said.

Instead of embracing her, he grasped her hands. His arms were stiff and straight, holding her away from his body. Garland felt as though an invisible barrier had dropped between them. Don't touch. Don't get too close. Then he smiled, and she began to think she'd been mistaken.

"I called the police from the plane," he said. "Detective Pulkowski filled me in on everything."

"Oh. So you know about Charla not making her flight on Sunday morning."

"Yes, I do."

Feeling his grip on her hands loosen, Garland stepped back. Did he believe something had really happened to Charla, or did he believe she'd run away with another man? Was he jealous, concerned, maybe even frightened? If so, none of it showed. "What do you think about all this, Frank?" she asked. *What do you feel?*

"I don't know. I just don't know." He ran his hand over his jaw, suddenly looking completely exhausted. "Charla told you nothing of her plans?"

Garland shook her head. There was an awkward silence, with the two of them staring at the floor. Middle ground, she thought, feeling hideously uncomfortable. It seemed that Frank didn't want to address the implications of Charla's lie any more than she did. Then her shoulders straightened; they *had* to face it, either privately or together, and she preferred to do it together.

"I'm sorry, Frank," she said softly. "I really don't know what she was doing."

His iron-gray gaze flicked over her, indecipherable

and calm, then moved to a point behind her. "I see you have company."

"Oh, geez, I forgot my manners," Garland said, then quickly introduced the two men.

"You've got other things on your mind," Colin said, stepping forward to shake hands. "Hello, Dr. Hollister. Sorry we had to meet under such circumstances."

"So am I." Frank's gaze moved to Garland, and for the first time she saw a crack in that calm, professional manner of his. She saw anger. It was obvious he didn't like finding a stranger here. It must have been obvious to Colin, too, for he excused himself and left the room.

"Is there a problem with my friends being here?" she asked.

"Wrong? Of course not." Frank's face closed immediately. It was like a shutter had slammed down, hiding everything behind a polite, urbane mask.

"That's not the impression I got. Or Colin either."

"Don't be silly, Garland. The man obviously felt a little awkward listening in to a private family conversation, that's all. I certainly would, if I were him." Frank put his hand on her shoulder. "And I think you would, too."

She sighed. Warmth, remoteness, anger, warmth again—his abrupt shifts were getting confusing. But then he was tired, she was tired, and their whole world had been turned upside down. Neither was reacting normally. So she chose to respond to the warmth and disregard the rest. "I'm really scared. I can't imagine Charla just running off without telling anyone."

"Neither can I. But hopefully we'll know more tomorrow." He patted her shoulder again, then brushed past her and headed for the door.

"Frank?"

He paused, glancing at her over his shoulder. "Yes?"

"The girls are sleeping right now, but I know they'll

want to see you right away."

"I'll let them rest a bit," he said. "Thank you for taking such good care of them for me. Now I think it's time *you* went home and got some sleep."

"But what if the girls need me? I mean, they're very upset about this, and I was planning to stay—"

"I'm sure I'll be able to deal with them adequately. The best thing we can all do is try to keep our lives as normal as possible until we have more information. And don't worry; if I hear anything from either Charla or Detective Pulkowski, I'll contact you immediately."

"But—"

"You can call the girls in the morning." He cut in so smoothly that an observer might have missed the firmness of the interruption. Garland, however, did not. "Now," he said, "I really must wish you—and your friend—good night."

He left the room, leaving Garland to stare openmouthed at the empty doorway. She was stunned by what he'd done. She'd been dismissed. Neatly, firmly dismissed. As she realized the full scope of what had happened, anger began a slow burn in the pit of her stomach. Frank had just defined the borders of this crisis, and had placed her outside them. *His* wife, *his* children, *his* home.

Well, it wasn't going to work. If he thought she was going to let him walk over her like this, he was wrong, wrong, wrong. He'd always pegged her as Charla's quiet, plain sister. The peacemaker, the smoother-over of difficulties with his wife and children, the always-available babysitter who never disagreed with the great doctor's pronouncements. She hadn't, but that was because she hadn't given a damn about his opinion.

This time, however, he'd hit her where it hurt. Charla was *her* sister, those two little girls upstairs *her* nieces. Like it or not, Frank was going to have to make room for her in his chill little world.

"Tonight you get the benefit of the doubt, Frank," she muttered under her breath. "But as Scarlett says, tomorrow's another day."

Although exhaustion gritted her eyes and fogged her brain, Garland couldn't sleep. She tried counting sheep. She tried reading *Ulysses,* always an excellent anesthetic. Except for tonight. The air in the house was stifling, the walls seeming to hover claustrophobically close.

By the time 4 A.M. rolled around, she couldn't stand the confinement another moment. Pulling on two layers of sweats, she went outside for a walk. The neighborhood was dark and very quiet. A soft glow of moonlight silvered the white stucco walls of the apartments across the street, giving the squat one-story boxes a clean purity they lacked in the sterner light of day.

Thrusting her hands into her jacket pockets, she strode into, then out of, the circle of yellow light cast by a streetlight. A door opened and closed in one of the apartments across the street. Garland glanced over her shoulder to see a man striding down the sidewalk, his walk and the set of his shoulders stiff with rage. *Whoops,* she thought, *Gene and Sharon are on the outs again.* At least they were going about it quietly tonight; last time, Sharon had tossed most of the breakables out of the house along with her husband.

With a sigh and a shake of her head, Garland turned around and resumed walking. Gene and Sharon's volatile relationship provided most of the gossip in this staid middle-class neighborhood. If her neighbors knew half of what went on over there, Garland reflected, the furor would *never* end.

The sidewalk stretched ahead of her, a ribbon-beacon

in the quiet, tree-lined street. She heard Gene's car start, then the squeal of tires as he turned the corner. As soon as he reached the main drag, he took off like a rocket. The noise faded quickly, however, and the neighborhood returned to its usual serenity.

It took a couple of blocks before Garland really hit her stride. Head up, arms swinging, she walked as fast as she could, hoping somehow to outrun her worry. It didn't work. She'd gotten to the point that she *wished* Charla had gone off on some wild, last-chance-before-middle-age-strikes fling. A lover, two lovers, anything. Somehow, she didn't think it had happened—at least, not at the cost of the Angelique Bei job.

Up the street, Mr. Farley's beagles burst into startled baying. *Aaa-wooo, aaa-wooo!* The alarm was picked up by the retriever two doors down. And on down the block, each dog taking up the call. Each successive voice, Garland noted, was closer, as though whatever was bothering them was moving toward her. House by house, step by step.

She peered into the darkness, for the first time disliking the neighborhood's burgeoning growth of azaleas. The street was empty—seemed empty. But the agitated voices of the dogs filled the night, crying caution.

A few feet farther on, a mass of low-hanging pine branches cast a pocket of dense shadow over the sidewalk. She slid into it, pressing close to the trunk. Her breath puffed out in a steam cloud, hovering eerily in the cold, still air beneath the trees. She felt the roughness of the bark beneath her palms and the chill trickle of sweat beneath her clothes.

God, it had been stupid to come out here at night! Stupid to think that in this day and age even this neighborhood was safe. She strained her eyes and ears, seeking any sign of movement. There was nothing but the darkness and the dogs and her own fear. *Intruder, beware, intruder!* the dog voices cried. Could it be a cat or racoon, come to relieve the boredom by teasing the dogs into nervous prostration? Probably. Still, she couldn't force herself to step out of the security of her hiding place as long as the dogs were barking. Her skin prickled, feeling the alarm as an almost tactile thing.

A floodlight burst into sudden life at the house on her right—the Olsons'—a brilliant cone of light piercing the darkness. Garland almost passed out with relief when she heard Jack Olson's sleep-blurred voice call out, "What's going on out here?"

"It's only me, Jack," she called, stepping out from under the trees so he could see her. "Garland Ross."

"Garland? What the hell are you doing out at this hour?"

"I couldn't sleep and thought a walk might help me relax," she said. "Then the dogs started up."

He grunted. "Damn dogs."

"They weren't barking at me."

"No?" He leaned farther out. "Then who?"

"I don't know. But *they* were sure in a stew over something. Maybe a cat or something?"

"Damn dogs," he said again. "Come on, I'll drive you home."

"Thanks." Goose bumps crawled up her spine as she walked forward into the circle of light in his front yard; she couldn't shake the feeling that something or someone was watching every step she took.

"Come inside while I get my keys." He held the door open for her.

Garland stepped into the foyer. Her rescuer yawned and scratched his head, making his thin brown hair fluff up in an aureole around his ears. His pajamas, she noted, were red. Not just a *little* red, but flaming, fire-engine red. Outside, the dogs began to settle down.

"Just let me tell Ann where I'm going," he said.

He disappeared into the back of the house, emerging a couple of minutes later wearing a coat over his pajamas and jogging shoes without socks.

"I really appreciate this," she said.

"S'okay. I had to get up for work anyway." He opened the door again and shooed her toward his car.

They pulled up in front of her house just as the paper "boy"—Marty Sutton was nearing seventy—tossed the morning newspaper onto the sidewalk. His eyebrows soared when he saw Garland get out of Jack's car. *I wonder what he'd think of Jack's pajamas,* she mused, waving at the departing car.

"Morning, Mr. Sutton," she said, scooping the paper up as she went by.

"Morning, Garland." He cleared his throat. "Uh, I'm sorry about your sister."

Everything stopped moving—her feet, her hands, her brain. "What . . . ?"

"The paper," he explained.

She whipped it open, snapping the rubber band securing it. The headline read, WHERE IS CHARLA ROSS? Bold, black letters. Uncompromisingly, brutally stark. Below it was a smaller headline: *Norfolk model disappears, police giving no clues.* And Charla's picture, that beautiful face smiling at the camera with such poise, such confidence . . .

"Hey! That isn't one of the photos I gave Pulkowski!" she muttered. She saw Ted Ballard's name in the first sentence of the article below. "Wait 'til I get my hands on you, you greedy, grasping, publicity-grubbing son of . . ." Seeing that the old man was still watching her, she snapped her mouth shut on the rest of the sentence. "Thanks, Mr. Sutton."

Turning her attention back to the paper, she walked up the steps and across the porch, her feet knowing the way without her mind's direction. Her hands, too, must have known their job, unlocking the door, opening it, closing it behind her again, for she found herself standing in the foyer.

The newspaper people had obviously gotten to Frank last night; there were several quotes from the doctor, all sounding very distraught. With a sigh, she gave herself a mental kick for being unfair. Frank surely *was* distraught. And Ballard had done her the favor of keeping her name out of it. So, the man had *some* scruples. It was only a matter of time, however, before the reporters tracked her down.

Her head began to pound, probably from not having eaten since lunch yesterday. "Better get something in your stomach while you can," she said, folding the paper back up and tossing it on the seat of the nearest chair. There was nothing else in it she wanted to see.

She made scrambled eggs, bacon, and toast, then sat down at the table to eat. With her stomach full, and surrounded by the familiar sights and sounds of her own kitchen, she felt some of the tension drain out of her.

She jerked when the phone rang, but managed to resist the urge to jump up and answer it immediately. The answering machine clicked on at the fourth ring. The caller identified himself as a reporter from the *New York Times* and urgently requested a return call. Garland sighed. Charla was well known in New York; the *Times* was probably the first paper Ted Ballard had called.

Several more calls came in during the next half hour, all from reporters from various newspapers and television stations. It seemed that everyone on the East Coast wanted an in-depth interview with Charla Ross's sister. Then another call came, a man who didn't identify himself.

"I think your sister is a damned slut," he said, bringing Garland to her feet with a lurch that sent her chair skittering across the linoleum. His voice went on, cruel and ugly. "I hope she's dead. I hope she's rotting in a ditch somewhere."

He was still talking when Garland rushed out of the room. Staggering, bumping into walls and furniture, she made it to the bathroom just in time to spew her breakfast into the toilet.

Chapter Seven

Harold Simms pulled into the parking garage only to find another car parked in his reserved place near the entrance. Instant outrage rose in him as he realized that it was the same gray Mercedes that had been there yesterday. He tried to read the license plate as he went by, but someone was riding his tail hard and he didn't dare slow down.

"Goddamn it," he snarled. "This time I'm going to have you towed."

Not wanting to squeeze his brand-new car into one of the tight spaces allowed the hoi polloi of Admiral Banking Tower, he drove all the way to the nearly empty fourth level. There, he straddled two parking places.

He took the stairs down to the first level, then marched to his stolen parking spot. The Mercedes's nose was almost touching the sign that said RESERVED FOR H. SIMMS, SR. VP.

"Can't read, huh?" he muttered under his breath.

There was something spattered over the license plate, nearly obscuring it. He bent close, rubbing at the brown stuff with his finger. It wasn't mud. Strange. *Too* strange.

The trunk wasn't closed properly. He tucked his briefcase under one arm and opened the trunk lid with the other. At first he thought there was a mannequin inside, for the pale, waxlike skin didn't seem even remotely human. Then he saw the open, milky-filmed eyes and the slashed throat. Dried blood crusted the wound and the front of the dead woman's clothing, even the rope that bound her ankles and wrists.

"Holy shit!" he said, backing away hastily. "Holy shit!"

Dropping his briefcase, he ran for the nearest phone.

Garland spent the morning waiting for the phone to ring, and dreading what she might hear when it did. But other than a few more calls from press people, there was nothing. No news of Charla.

"How can a person just disappear off the face of the earth like this?" she demanded of the empty house. "Why can't someone find out where she went?" *And what happened.* But she didn't say that aloud.

By noon, she couldn't stand it another moment. Pulling on jeans and a flannel shirt, she put some mascara and blush on and went to the bookstore. Milo took one look at her, then locked the door and steered her toward the back of the store.

"We're supposed to be open!" she protested.

"There aren't any customers right now," he said, adding, "You look like hell."

"I feel like hell."

He sat her down at the table and handed her a cup of coffee. She took a sip of the sweet, hot stuff, then another. Registering that it was eye-popping strong, she drained the cup and sat back to wait for the caffeine to hit her system. When it did, the jolt made her shudder.

"Thanks," she said, holding the cup out for a refill. "Did you see the newspaper this morning?"

"Yup. Are you holding up?"

"I'm not gibbering yet, but I'm close." With a sigh,

she told him about the disgusting phone call. "What kind of person would *do* that?"

He poured coffee into her cup, then added sugar and cream before handing it back to her. "There are plenty of sickos out there. Something like this brings 'em out of the woodwork."

"Like cockroaches."

"Yeah," he agreed, sitting down across from her and leaning his elbows on the table. "Some reporter already called here looking for you."

She grimaced. "Damn. I don't want to talk to anybody."

"Do you think Frank would let you take the girls out of town for a while?"

"After last night, I don't know what to think about Frank." Letting her breath out in a hiss of exasperation, she added, "I called the house this morning, to be informed by the maid service that Frank had taken the girls to school."

"Bastard."

Garland tilted her head to one side and considered that comment. As much as she'd like to agree, she couldn't. "Maybe he's doing the right thing. That school has pretty good security, and ought to be able to insulate the twins from the worst of the publicity."

"Maybe. But I–damn, somebody's at the door," he said, shoving his chair back and rising to his feet. "If it's the press, duck into the Tomb."

"Just don't let them in!"

"If I do that, they'll know you're here for sure. I'll let them snoop around for a while, then sweet-talk them into looking elsewhere." He shook his head, stopping Garland's protest before it got started. "Listen to Uncle Milo, darlin'. This is the way to go, or they'll camp on our doorstep for the duration."

The knocking grew louder and more imperative. After

raising one finger in an admonishing gesture, Milo headed toward the front of the store.

Garland heard the door open, then Milo's voice saying, "Feel free to come in, but I'm not expecting Miss Ross to be in at all today."

Evidently the press had arrived. Quietly, she slid out of her chair and ran to the storeroom, remembering to bring her coffee cup with her. Pressing her ear to the closed door, she eavesdropped on the conversation outside. Well, it wasn't exactly a conversation; Milo was the only one talking, and with a speed and flexibility a door-to-door salesman would envy. Finally, however, he stopped for breath, giving the visitor a chance to speak at last.

"You're a friend of the family, aren't you?" the stranger asked.

"Absolutely," Milo said. "Have been for years."

"Ah. Then you could tell me something about them."

"My friend, I can tell you everything and anything."

The man chuckled. "Do that, and I'll make it worth your while."

"Come on, sit down and have a cup of coffee." Milo's voice was fairly throbbing with the promise of juicy confidences. Having heard that tone before—and seen the results—Garland began to relax. Milo didn't disappoint her. With much digression and stupefying detail, he told her life story almost from birth, and *still* managed to leave out anything that might be remotely interesting to the public.

With a nod of satisfaction, she shrugged out of her coat and began logging new acquisitions into the computer. This had always been one of her favorite jobs—actually handling the books, assessing their condition, all the while wondering what story each could tell if it could speak. Now the task was familiar and comforting, the windowless room safe and secure, like a womb.

She buried herself in the work, hoping to use it to hold her fear and worry at bay. It wasn't completely effective, but it was better than sitting at home waiting for the phone to ring.

There was a knock at the door, then Milo called, "All clear!"

Garland was astonished to find that more than an hour had passed. After stretching to remove the kinks made by sitting in one place for so long, she unlocked the door.

"When did he leave?" she asked.

"A couple of minutes ago."

"He lasted this long?" she asked in surprise. "Boy, he was persistent."

"Writes for one of the tabloids. I have to admit he's got good reflexes; it took him less than thirty seconds to hit the door when I had to answer the phone." Milo smiled, that impudent small boy's grin that had melted the hearts of more women than Garland had ever been able to keep track of.

Reaching up, she patted him on the cheek. "Well, good riddance."

"We ain't rid of him. He hasn't given up. He just doesn't want to listen to *me* any longer. Last time I checked, he was sitting in his car outside. Looks like he's settled in for the duration." He grimaced. "And you can bet he's not going to be the only one sniffing around."

A knot twisted Garland's stomach. "They're probably at my house."

"That would be my guess. Where's your coat?"

She jerked her head toward the storeroom. He went inside, reappearing a moment later carrying her coat. Before she could react, he began putting the coat on her, taking her arms and poking them into the sleeves as though she were a child.

Coming out of her bemusement abruptly, she slapped his hands away. "What the hell do you think you're doing?"

"I'm getting you out of here; of all the people you *don't* want interviewing you, that guy out there is tops. Now, Colin's going to be here any minute . . ." There was a soft honk from the alley behind the store. "Correction: Colin is here to spirit you away."

"Huh?"

"A truly erudite comment, darlin'." Holding up his hands in patently false terror, he exclaimed, "Don't hurt me, don't hurt me! I'll explain! See, the phone call that released my victim was from Colin. When he asked if there was anything he could do, I told him to come rescue you. Lunch at Waterside, he said."

"But my phone! What if—"

"If Charla comes back, let *her* take the heat from the press. If she doesn't . . . no, look at me," he said, putting his hands on her shoulders to keep her from turning away. "If she doesn't come back, a couple of hours aren't going to make any difference."

His statement was blunt and bald and utterly true, and she flinched away from it. "But—"

"Do what I tell you." With one hand firmly planted at the small of her back, he pushed her toward the back exit. "If I hear anything, I'll come find you. Meanwhile you can spare yourself some grief by getting lost."

She sighed. All she wanted was to be left alone. But Milo was determined to do this, and she just didn't have the energy to fight him. Correctly interpreting silence as acquiescence, he hustled her out the door and into the alley beyond.

A white van, K & K Plumbing painted on its side, was waiting. Leaving the engine running, Colin jumped out and came around to open the door for her.

"Hi, Garland." He glanced over his shoulder at Milo. "I'll call you later to see if the coast is clear."

Colin backed the van out of the alley and headed down Boush Street toward Waterside. He was uncommonly quiet, even for him, and his manner didn't invite conversation. Garland clasped her hands in her lap, uncomfortable in the silence.

"I appreciate you coming to get me," she said.

"No problem."

Silence again. Garland decided to leave it like that, but curiosity was too strong for her. Swiveling in her seat, she looked in the back of the van, taking note of the neatly racked tools, the hoses, and other, less easily identifiable plumber's helpers. She glanced at Colin's neat sweater, blue jeans, and tennis shoes. "Is this your van?"

"Yes."

She cocked her head to one side and studied his profile. It was strange that she'd known this man for so long and hadn't had any idea what he did for a living. There were a lot of questions she'd like to ask just now, but his unresponsiveness kept them locked in her throat. She turned around and settled back in her seat.

"My work boots and overalls are in the back," he said after a few minutes. "Now you know my deep, dark secret."

Ah, now I see! Outrage kicked in, and she said, "You think we're snobs!"

"Oh, come on, Garland." He raked his hand through his hair. "Why do you think I never voice an opinion in the group? Hell, I never even finished high school—got my GED ten years ago. Everything I've learned about literature I learned right there at The Tome."

Their gazes locked for a moment, then he turned his attention back to his driving. After a moment Garland said, "You *do* think we're snobs."

"Well," he glanced at her from the corner of his eye, "*I* sure don't give a damn whether Samuel Johnson liked *Paradise Lost* or not."

Startled, Garland drew her breath in sharply. Then she smiled. "Actually, I don't either."

He chuckled, then fell silent again. This time, however, the silence was a comfortable one. It lasted until he parked in the garage across from Waterside and came around to open her door.

"What about your art?" she asked. "You're very good, you know."

"I've been taking night classes." He shrugged. "I'd like to make a living with it someday, but I've got to face reality. With a family to support—"

"You're married?"

"Was. My daughter Kathy's thirteen, a great kid. But by the time I finish paying off her braces, she'll be ready to go to college. And now she's talking medical school."

There was no hint of resentment in his voice, only pride. Garland knew he didn't mind making the sacrifice. When he offered his arm in an old-fashioned, courtly gesture, she tucked her hand in the crook of his elbow and let him lead her toward the glass-walled walkway that crossed high over Waterside Drive. They stopped to watch the traffic moving below.

"I always feel weird doing this," he said. "It's strange, like standing in a window to the world, being able to see and hear, but not touch. And those people down there don't even know we exist."

"Maybe this is the way ghosts feel," Garland said without thinking. The words seemed to hang frozen in the air, crystalline shards of her own fear. Her hands tightened on the metal rail.

"Let's go eat," Colin said. "I'm starved."

Slowly, Garland's grip loosened. "All right."

He offered his arm again. She took it, grateful that he wasn't pushing her to talk about Charla.

Waterside loomed ahead, its bright blue walls enveloping the end of the walkway. A moment later they went through the double glass doors and entered the vast, airy space beyond. Although she'd been here many times before, Garland never failed to enjoy the initial visual effect the huge shopping/eating/entertainment center always had on her. The far wall was a many-faceted expanse of glass that looked out over the Elizabeth River. The water was robin's egg blue, sunlight reflecting in thousands of golden pinpoints on the waves.

"Eat or shop?" Colin asked.

Garland moved to the railing. Leaning her elbows on it, she gazed down at the restaurant booths that lined the entire first floor.

After a moment Colin joined her, adopting her position at the rail. His hands were square and strong, his forearms twice as big around as hers. He was solid and real, and his presence ought to have been comforting. It might have been, had she wanted to be here in the first place.

"You don't have to entertain me," she said.

"I'm not entertaining you, I'm rescuing you."

She tried to smile, but her face felt stiff, as though plaster had dried upon her skin. "Milo is the knight in shining armor, remember?"

"And I'm the plumber."

"So, you're the plumber." Shifting her weight to her left elbow, she turned and looked at him. Really looked at him for the first time today. For all the muscle he packed in his five-eight frame, he looked oddly hesitant. It was obvious that he wanted to help, but wasn't sure if she'd accept it.

Garland didn't have the heart to reject him. "Let's

eat, Mr. Plumber. All I've had all day is some of Milo's coffee."

"I'm yours to command." His hand closed on her wrist. Gently, he tugged her toward the escalators.

Lunch was an international mishmash. Colin chose dishes seemingly at random from Italian, Japanese, Greek, and Filipino restaurants, finishing the meal off with New York cheesecake. Garland ate a little of everything and felt better for it. Afterward, they strolled toward the river end of the building.

"Coffee?" Colin asked as they passed a gourmet coffee shop.

She shook her head. "With all the spices inside me right now, a dose of caffeine might start spontaneous combustion."

"How about some ice cream, then?"

"No, thanks." *He's going to talk about the weather next,* she thought. *Anything but Charla.*

"It's such a beautiful day," he said. "Makes me wish summer were here."

Suddenly, completely tired of avoiding the subject of Charla, Garland pulled Colin to a stop and turned him to face her. "Tell me the truth, Colin. Do you think Charla's dead?"

"My opinion doesn't matter." His eyes were brilliant green, mesmerizing in their intensity. "*You* think she is."

"Of course I don't . . ." The automatic protest froze in her throat. Ever since Charla had turned up missing, Garland had held that fear in her heart, insulating it, but so terrified of it that she hadn't dared bring it out into the open. Now, just when she wanted to deny it most, she couldn't. She looked away from Colin, not wanting to read affirmation in his eyes.

He put his arm around her waist and led her to one of the benches that were scattered throughout the area.

Once they were seated, he draped his arm across her shoulders.

"I feel so helpless. I'm going crazy waiting!" Although her voice was low, nearly a whisper, her fist pounded the bench beside her. "I've always taken care of her. Even before Mom and Dad were killed, I always watched out for her. Whenever things went wrong, she came to me. I always do my best to fix . . ." Too close to losing control, Garland took a couple of deep breaths before going on. "I think that detective believed Charla had run off with a lover. But she'd *never* do something like that without telling me."

"There are plenty of things people don't tell their mothers, at least until afterward. I imagine extramarital affairs are pretty high on the list."

"I'm her sister, not her mother!"

"I know that." Heaving a sigh, he crossed his arms over his chest. "But I'm not sure whether you and Charla know it."

Garland stood up, out of the circle of his arm. "You're out of your mind."

"I don't . . ." He looked past her. "There's Milo."

She glanced over her shoulder, then slowly turned around. Milo was standing about ten feet away, his hands jammed into his jacket pockets. His face told her everything.

"No," she said.

He came to stand in front of her, reaching down to take her limp hands in his. "I'm sorry, Garland. They found her this morning. Frank has already identified her."

Garland took a deep breath, feeling as though she'd swallowed acid. "Tell me the rest."

"Let's go back to the store," Milo said. "I'll tell you everything over a cup of coffee."

"Now," she hissed.

"All right!" His face was drawn and grim, and he looked as though he'd aged ten years in just a few minutes. "She was murdered."

Murdered. Garland heard a moan, and realized it had come from her. Colin's arms came around her from behind, pressing her against his chest. Milo kept his grip on her hands. Locked together by grief, the three of them stood silently amid the passing crowd of people.

"Take it easy," Milo murmured. "We're with you, honey."

She blinked, hardly registering his words at all. Everything was in preternaturally sharp focus: dust drifting like tiny snowflakes upon a beam of sunlight, the sweet-sharp aroma of some nearby chrysanthemums, the black, grinding pain in her chest.

"I've got to get to the girls," she said in a voice that didn't sound remotely like hers.

"Uh-uh." Milo shook his head. "Two homicide detectives are at the house now, as well as the swarm of reporters who've set up camp outside. I don't know if you're up to dealing with that."

She looked at him, and he quickly let go of her hands. "I've got to get to the girls," she said again. "Go call Frank. Tell him to open the back gates for us."

Chapter Eight

"That was a simply wonderful service!" Estelle Hollister sighed. "The flowers were lovely, really lovely."

The statement fairly echoed in the leather-scented silence of the funeral home's limousine. Garland, who had been staring out the window, turned to look at the other woman. Frank's aunt was sitting in the opposite seat, her tall, thin body encased in layers of blue georgette. Beside her was her older sister, Julia. Estelle had gotten the Hollister looks, Julia the brains. Garland noted that Julia was staring at Estelle intently, probably trying to send a mental message to shut up. It wasn't going to work; after ten years of dealing with the various members of the Hollister clan, Garland knew that nothing short of a sledgehammer could stop Estelle once she got going.

"Such a wonderful ceremony," Estelle said again. "I'm sure Charla would have been pleased."

Garland crossed her arms over her chest. Charla would have hated it. She would have scorned the entire ponderous process, from the solemn eulogy to the sleek, brass-fitted coffin and the oversized car needed to carry it. "Models don't die," she'd said jokingly. "They just go to smaller and smaller magazines and finally disappear."

Estelle burbled on. "I thought Ted Ballard gave a simply marvelous eulogy. What do you think, Garland?"

I think Ted Ballard's a publicity-grubbing prick. Aloud, however, she said, "It was very nice." Another of those automatic politenesses drilled into her since childhood. "Very nice" had been her mother's standby; no matter what she'd thought privately, in public everything had been "very nice."

Judging by the look on Julia's face, she was seriously thinking of strangling her sister. Garland glanced longingly at the limo just ahead, wishing she'd insisted on riding with Frank and the twins. But she'd let herself get talked into sharing a car with the aunts, and now she had to pay the price.

With a sigh, she turned to look out the back window. Colin's blue Oldsmobile, bearing the group from The Tome, maintained a steady ten yards to the rear. Beyond them stretched a long line of cars, their headlights bleached pale lemon yellow by the bright sunlight. Charla's entourage. It wasn't the one she would have chosen.

"Poor Frank," Estelle said. "He looks terribly upset by it all."

Garland turned around, wondering if and what she should reply to that statement. Before she could decide, however, Julia reached over and patted her hand. Garland accepted the apology in the same silence in which it had been given. Maybe the silence would even last until they got to the cemetery.

A moment later, however, Estelle spoke up again. "Well, the girls are certainly taking this all in stride," she said.

"They are?" Garland had spent the past two nights with the distraught twins, letting them cry it out, holding them whenever the nightmares got too bad. "What makes you say that, Estelle?"

"Good heavens, Garland! They didn't shed a single tear at the funeral home. Besides, kids don't really understand death. They just think their mother is asleep or something." Before Garland could respond to that astounding observation, Estelle continued, "And Charla looked so lovely, don't you think? They really did a marvelous job on her. You'd never know that—"

"Oh, shut up, Estelle," Julia snapped.

Garland found herself clutching the armrest with white-knuckled force. Slowly she relaxed, concentrating on her hand to keep from screaming at Estelle. She couldn't let this bother her; she'd heard worse than this at her parents' funeral.

One thing Estelle had said, however, was the absolute truth: Frank seemed to be taking it very hard. Garland had expected him to maintain the lines of distance he'd drawn Monday night. She'd expected to have to fight even to see the twins. But the confirmation of Charla's death had changed everything. Emotionally, Frank had turned off, tuned out, and headed south for the winter. A walking husk of a man, neither accepting or giving comfort. To Garland had fallen the tasks of arranging the funeral, choosing Charla's burial dress, comforting Charla's children. She welcomed them, wondering all the while when she'd be thrust out of the inner circle again.

"Here we are," Estelle burbled. "Such a lovely day. Aren't you glad it's not raining, Garland?"

Garland made an ambiguous noise, hoping to keep from being drawn into conversation again. The car slowed to make the right turn onto the drive leading to Colonial Gardens Memorial Cemetery, then passed through the massive stone and wrought-iron gates that guarded the entrance. Up ahead, Garland could see the long silver hearse moving along the curving drive.

When they finally arrived at the gravesite, they found the spot crawling with people. As the limo carrying Frank and the twins drew to a stop, a forest of cameras and microphones focused on it. Frank, Amber, and Annalese emerged, and a shouting, shoving group of reporters dashed to surround it.

An adrenaline rush went through Garland. Before her limo had quite stopped, she flung the door open and jumped out.

"Garland, wait!" Julia cried.

Garland ignored her. She couldn't see the girls now; there were too many people around them. But she could tell where they were by the angle of the cameras. Shoving, jabbing with her elbows, even kicking a few shins, she pushed through the crowd surrounding Frank and the twins. The girls were huddled against the fender of the car, sobbing. Garland held out her arms. The twins ran to her, hiding their faces against her body.

"We've got to get them out of here," she shouted at Frank over the din.

He didn't raise his voice, so she only caught part of his reply, something about "attending the burial would help them accept their mother's death."

Garland pointed at the host of staring camera eyes. So many flashes went off that they looked like strobe lights. After a moment, Frank nodded. Keeping the girls tucked close to her sides, Garland turned back toward her limo. The newsmen, however, closed in, blocking her path. A quick glance over her shoulder told her that Frank had either moved or been drawn away from her.

"Let us through!" Garland shouted.

A man reached out and grasped Amber's arm, obviously trying to get the child to look up for a picture. Garland shoved him away. Another grabbed her sleeve. With a hiss, she jerked her arm out of his grasp, only to have a dozen microphones thrust at her.

"How do you feel about your sister's murder, Miss

Ross?" one reporter shouted.

Another voice, a woman's. "The police are calling it a robbery. What do you think about that?"

"Did your sister have any enemies?"

"Was she raped?"

Garland shook her head, more to reject the situation than as a reply to the question. As though held by a single hand, the microphones darted forward. A forest of eager snake heads, ready to strike.

"Your sister took out a million-dollar insurance policy on herself a couple of years ago. Can you tell us—"

"Who's going to take your sister's position with Angelique Bei?"

"Have the police told you whether or not they have a suspect?"

"Did your sister—"

Garland watched the mouths open and close, but the voices merged into one meaningless babble of sound. And faces everywhere, bobbing like balloons in and out of her field of view. Only the fact that she had the girls with her kept her from losing control.

Suddenly the crowd parted, and she saw her friends coming through. The five were in a wedge, Colin's burly form taking the point. There was a bit of jostling, a bit more verbal exchange, but her friends finally surrounded her and the girls and began to move back toward the cars. Unabashed, the reporters followed, shouting questions as they went.

Colin bulled his way to his car, pulling the rest of them with him. Opening the driver's door, he fended off the cameras while Garland and the twins ducked inside and climbed over into the back seat. Pulling the girls into her arms, Garland shielded them from the faces that peered at them through the windows.

Troll took the passenger seat. "Ghouls," she snarled.

"Come *on,* Colin! Milo and the others can meet us later!"

Colin slid behind the wheel and started the car. Easing forward, he carefully used the vehicle to clear a way through the throng. The moment he was through he gunned it, leaving the gravesite behind in a spray of dirt and torn grass.

"I'd have run the lot of them over," Troll said.

"Tempting," Colin murmured. "But that would only make them happier. More grist for their publicity mill."

Although his tone was soft, Garland could tell by the set of his jaw that he was very angry. The car's wheels squealed in protest as he took the turn onto the street much too fast, then squealed again as he made another turn.

Through it all, the twins clung to Garland. They'd stopped crying, but there was a bruised look in their eyes that made her want to smash something. Damn it, it was bad enough for them to lose their mother in such a sudden, brutal way, but to be subjected to that . . . that circus!

Troll hooked her arm over the back of the seat, her gaze going from Amber to Annalese, then settling on Garland. "Where do you guys want to hide out?"

"I'm taking them to my house," Colin said. "That should be safe—at least for a while. And—"

"Garland, you're hurt!" Troll said sharply.

"Hurt? No, I don't think so—"

"Drop that rose!"

Surprised, Garland looked down to see that she was clutching a single red rose in her left hand. Dried blood crusted her fingers. She opened her hand and examined the line of punctures that matched the pattern of thorns on the rose's stem. "Someone must have given it to me at the cemetery," she said in bewilderment. "I don't . . . all I remember is all the faces, and the shouting."

"They're supposed to trim the thorns off those things," Troll said as she climbed over the back of the seat and all but fell in Garland's lap. After inspecting Garland's wounds, she drew in her breath with a hiss. "Some of those are pretty deep. Maybe we should get a doctor to look at them."

"They don't hurt," Garland said. Not entirely true, but the small pain in her hand didn't begin to compete with what she was feeling inside. She let the rose fall to the floor. "I'll put something on them later."

Annalese started to cry again, and Garland pulled her close. Instead of returning to the front seat, Troll wriggled into what little space was left and put her arm around Amber. The four of them huddled thigh to thigh, trying to let simple human closeness hold the loss at bay for a little while.

It seemed to work for the twins; Annalese settled down after a few minutes, propping her head against Garland's breast as though comforted by her aunt's heartbeat. Amber fell asleep.

For Garland, however, there was no ease. It wasn't only grief that made a burning knot of pain in her chest. There was also anger—sheer, unadulterated rage at the person or persons who had killed her sister and shattered her family like this.

So she stared out the window seeing, not the scenery outside, but Charla as she'd last seen her: in the coffin, framed in shining folds of white satin. That still, waxen face had been as beautiful in death as it had been in life, perhaps more so, for death had erased the faintly dissatisfied look that had begun to show. Because of that, and because she was wearing a high-necked dress to hide the terrible wound in her neck, she looked shockingly young.

Tears stung Garland's eyes but refused to fall. For as

long as she lived, the memory of Charla's dead face would haunt her. She might recite all the rationalizations in the world, but the "if only" specter refused to be banished. *If only I'd called the police sooner . . . If only Charla had confided in me, I might have been able to stop her from going to her death last weekend* . . . If only, if only, if only. Like hot needles, stabbing her brain, burning her heart. *I tried, Mom and Dad. I tried so hard to take care of her!*

There was no answer. No comfort, no lessening of guilt. She closed her left hand into a fist, welcoming the physical sting of her wounds.

After turning on the TV, he settled in the recliner and opened a can of soda. No beer for him; he didn't approve of alcohol.

The news came on. Quickly, he set the soda aside and picked up the remote control to switch the VCR to Record. The first story was about Charla Ross's funeral. Big time for the news people, and *he* had done it.

As the footage from the cemetery ran, the anchorwoman read, "There is still no break in the Charla Ross murder case. Although the police are following up every lead, they have no suspect as of yet. It's been confirmed that Lisle Argenti has taken Miss Ross's place with the Angelique Bei cosmetics firm."

The man ignored the voice as he watched the doctor and the two young girls emerge from the limousine and be surrounded by reporters. Leaning forward, he waited impatiently while the camera focused in on the children's faces. Where was the woman . . . ah, there she was! He could see her now, pushing her way through the crowd to reach the girls. The camera zoomed in on the action, panning across a number of faces as it did. For a moment, a brief, precious moment, he saw his own.

He squirmed on recliner's slick pseudo-leather seat. He'd actually stood beside her. Close enough to touch. The knife had been in his pocket then—cool and deadly. He'd looked at her neck, so smooth and pale and vulnerable beneath her dark hair, and had almost done it right then. Could have gotten away with it easy; the noisy, jostling crowd would have been better cover than the darkest night. But she'd been so fiercely protective of the children, like a mother hawk defending her young against a flock of ravens, that admiration for her had held him frozen.

Long ago, his mother had been like that. He remembered how she'd screamed at Mr. Johnston for swatting him when he rode his tricycle through the old man's flowerbed. He remembered how she'd taken a broom to some boys who had teased him, how she'd stood up to the social worker who had come to the house, concerned that he wasn't being sent to school regularly. Afterward, she'd packed up their belongings and moved to another part of the city. She'd done it for him, she'd said. To keep him with her.

There had been beatings, sure, but only on those nights she was really plastered. Weekends, mostly. He grew to hate weekends. He still hated weekends. TGIF—he'd like to get his hands on the jerk who had come up with *that*.

Suddenly realizing that the news had moved on to something else, he hit the Stop button. The phone rang while he was rewinding the tape. He let it ring until he was finished, automatically counting the rings—seven, eight, nine. On the tenth, he picked it up.

"Hello?"

"I saw you at the cemetery today," the caller said. "Why did you go?"

Shifting the phone to his other ear, he hit Play and began watching the tape again. "I've never been to a funeral before."

"Well, this one was the wrong place to start. It was very ill advised."

He picked up his soda and took a sip. The woman came on screen again, pulling the girls against her and turning to face the crowd of reporters. And there *he* was, looking down on her with the faintest of smiles on his face. The rose had been a nice touch. Subtle, yet satisfying. He wondered if she'd liked it.

A rush of remembered pleasure made him wriggle. He'd seen her blood, red against the skin of her hands, red as the rose he'd given her. Even in the midst of the crowd he'd been able to smell the sweetly metallic tang of it.

"David!" the caller shouted in his ear. "Are you listening to me at all?"

"Sure." He hit Rewind and watched everyone move backward at a furious pace.

"Going there was very dangerous," the caller continued.

A dark tendril of annoyance coiled through him, sullying the glow of his satisfaction. "What's your problem anyway? I did everything you wanted me to do."

"Of course you did." The voice became soothing. "I only have your best interests at heart, you know. There were cameras everywhere. Someone might recognize you."

The tape stopped rewinding. He held his finger poised over the Play button, but didn't push it. Not yet. He didn't want to be distracted when he watched it. "No one knows me."

"*I* know you," the caller said. "I'm your friend. Your only friend. Always remember that, David."

"Sure, I remember."

There were several moments of silence while he waited for the caller either to speak or to hang up. Finally the other man said, "I sense that something is bothering you tonight, David. Do you want to talk about it?"

"No." His hand tightened possessively on the remote control. This was his. Only his. As precious and private as his other treasures.

"Ah, something personal, I see," the caller said. "Well, friends can talk about personal things, you know."

"No." *Mine, mine, mine.*

"Very well, David. But remember that I'm here for you if you want to discuss it. Do you need some more money?"

He straightened. Ah, he'd forgotten all about that! Quickly, he tallied what was in his wallet. "Yeah. I need money."

"Why don't you come over tonight, then? We can talk."

"Not tonight. Tomorrow."

"All right, David. Tomorrow. Nine o'clock?"

"Yeah." Without saying goodbye—he never said goodbye—he hung up the phone. *At last.* Smiling, he hit Play. He watched the woman push through the crowd. He watched himself standing behind her, within a hand's-breadth of touching her. Rewind. Play. Watch the woman rush to the children, pull them into her arms. Watch his own face, blissful with the knowledge of what he could do if he wanted. Yes, he wanted. Soon. But not yet. He wanted . . . he wanted . . .

He played the tape again. Watched her. Watched himself. Saw his desire, saw his need. He picked up the phone again and dialed her number. The machine answered. It had her voice. "You have reached 555-7237. We can't come to the phone right now, but if you leave a message at the beep, we'll get back to you as soon as possible." *Beeeeeep!*

He hung up. Absently, he wiped his clammy hands on his jeans. Long, slow strokes, from his hips to his knees. Over and over, until his palms were stinging from the friction. It was only a machine, he knew, but it still had her voice—dark, sweet, vile. He reached for the phone again, then withdrew his hand and closed it into a fist.

The hunger rose up inside him. Raw and hurting, yet infinitely promising. Pleasure/pain, pain/pleasure. He went into the bedroom and got his treasure box and opened it, taking the hanks of brown hair out one by one and arranging them according to shade. Shades of darkness, chestnut to midnight, deep to deepest. After a few minutes of contemplation, he put them away and stood up.

He was going out. After all, it was Friday night. Time to head out to Ocean View again; there was a woman waiting for him on some street corner. He had no idea who she'd be or what she'd look like, but he'd know her when he saw her.

TGIF.

He cruised down Shore Drive, his gloved hands sure and steady on the wheel. It was a little warmer tonight; the whores were out in force. None tempted him. Still, he slowed down to check them out. Several stepped forward to peer into the car's windows as he went by. He stopped, making sure it was in a place where there was a good bit of shadow inside the car.

Rolling down his window, he called, "Hi, girls."

They sauntered closer, opening their coats to show off their wares. His heartbeat went up a notch. *Pick and choose/Pick and choose/It's your lucky night/You can't lose!* They all wanted him. Any one of them was his, for the taking. Point. Choose. He felt powerful, like a king, like a god. It would be especially good tonight.

"Hiya, honey," a big redhead called. "You just off the ship?"

He nodded, smiling. He'd taken to wearing his hair in a Navy cut. Perfect camouflage in a Navy town. With his unremarkable features, that would be the one thing people would remember most. Blend with the herd, pretend to be one of them even as he culled the ones he wanted. Most hunters never achieved that.

The redhead reached the car. Leaning her elbows on the sill of the open window, she said, "Are you lonely, my man?"

Her low-cut blouse fell open, giving him a clear view of most of her big breasts. Ugly. Big, white pillows. Then, behind her, he caught sight of the one he wanted. Not short, not tall, small, high breasts beneath her tight T-shirt. He liked the way her blunt-cut brown hair moved against her neck.

"Not you," he told the redhead. "I don't like big tits."

He pointed to the one he wanted. As the redhead flounced off, the chosen one approached the window.

"Want to go for a ride?" he asked.

"Fifty bucks," she said.

He leaned across the car to unlock the passenger door. She slid into the seat. When he'd put the car into gear and moved away from the watching whores, he asked, "How much for you to come out to my place for a few hours?"

"That long?" She opened her purse, took a stick of gum out, and popped it into her mouth. "What did you have in mind?"

He thought of the pantyhose he had ready for her. Something new. For her, for him. "Just the regular stuff," he said. "I just don't like doing it in cars. At least you won't have to stand out here in the cold."

"Okay. A hundred bucks. Two hours of unlimited joy, sport."

He smiled. Once was all it took.

"Let me see the cash," she said, taking a grip on the door handle beside her. "I see the money, or I'm gone."

Keeping his right hand on the wheel, he reached into his pocket and pulled out a wad of bills. Mostly ones and fives, he knew, but there were enough twenties to make her let go of the door handle. It was all he had, but tomorrow he was going to get more.

She complained the whole way, saying she didn't know he lived way the hell out in East Jesus, she couldn't understand why *anyone* would want to live out here with the cows and chipmunks, she ought to charge him extra for time lost for travel, et cetera, et cetera. He pacified her by tossing the cash into her lap.

Instead of parking in the garage behind his house, he stopped the car just outside the front door. The whore talked all the way into the house, but he'd stopped hearing her; his only reality now was the deed. The sensation. The lift and the power that would soon be his. He could almost taste it.

His throat was dry. "I need a drink," he said. "Do you want something?"

"Got any champagne?"

He shook his head. "Pepsi, Sprite, or pineapple juice."

"Cripes." She plopped down on the sofa. "Pepsi."

He went into the kitchen and took his gloves off to get himself a drink of water. The power was coursing through him like the tide, vast, irresistible. Whistling softly, he took the pantyhose out of the drawer and stretched it between his fists. It felt strange. His hand crept into his pocket to feel the knife he always kept there. His knife, the one he always used. Until now.

Self-denial/Self-control/Good for the psyche/Good for the soul. He could almost hear his friend: "Use the pantyhose, David. A hunter cannot afford to fall into a pattern." He stuffed the pantyhose into his pocket and went to get a Pepsi from the refrigerator. Then he put his gloves back on, the smooth leather sliding over his skin like silk, cool and sensual. Still whistling, he walked back to the living room.

The whore was sprawled naked on his sofa. He skidded to a stop, feeling his mouth drop open with surprise.

"What's the matter, sailor?" she asked. "Haven't you ever seen a woman naked before?"

She opened her legs wide. A cloud of black wiry hair crowned their juncture, framing the pink-and-brown folds of her sex.

He couldn't move. Couldn't think. Couldn't tear his gaze away.

"Cat got your tongue?" Laughing, she reached down to spread herself open. "Hey, honey, do you like what you see?"

Do you like what you see? Another voice, another room. His mother coming toward him, weaving drunkenly. Her face a slack-mouthed mask, her hair, mussed by the lover who had left a few moments before, standing up like Medusa's snaky coils. Her robe was open. His nine-year-old eyes couldn't seem to stop looking at her. Breasts/nipples/belly. And below, curly black hair. *He* didn't have hair down there.

"Do you like what you see?" his mother said again. Her lips pulled back in a snarl. "Come on if you're so goddamn curious, you little bastard. Come and get a closer look."

"No! Please, Mommy, no!" Horror. Disgust. His bed against the back of his legs, trapping him. Nowhere to go, nowhere to hide. A spreading rush of hot liquid down the front of his pants, a puddle of it beneath his feet.

"Look what you did, you little fucker! Come here!" She grabbed his arm and twisted it, forcing him to his knees. Then she wound her other hand in the hair at the back of his head and thrust his face into her groin.

The hair was coarse, not at all like the hair on her head. A thousand little points sticking into his skin. It was wet, horribly wet, painting slimy little snail trails across his face. And the smell: heat and musk, sweat and sex, woman and man mingled, overshadowing even the reek of her cheap perfume.

He screamed. Fought to raise his head, to breathe air untainted by *that.*

"You like that?" she shrieked, grinding his face into the prickly curls. "You like that?"

Her voice was a screech, turned animal-like by beer and gin and cigarettes. It dug into his brain like a rusty file. And all around him, the smell and feel of hate. His. Hers. His.

"How about it, you little bastard? You think I don't see you watching me? Always watching me, always staring, those big, dumb eyes always staring . . ."

A loud roaring filled his ears, drowning out her voice. He welcomed it, embraced it, holding it against him for comfort.

It took him a minute to figure out that the roaring came from him. *His* voice. The picture shifted. Not that room, long ago, not that woman, but here and now.

And then he saw the blood.

Chapter Nine

Garland lay still, listening as the twins' breathing slowed and deepened. Propping herself on one elbow, she studied their sleep-softened faces. They looked so small, so completely vulnerable like this. Thank God Colin had offered them the use of his home; for now at least, they were safe from the rest of the world.

Annalese made a soft sound. She was sucking her thumb, a habit discarded long ago. Or at least, her parents had thought so. Frank would have a cow if he knew; he was the one who'd insisted on breaking the habit when Annalese had turned four.

"Eight isn't so old, is it, baby?" she whispered under her breath.

Amber rolled over, burrowing closer to her sister. Twin-bonded, even in sleep. Garland's heart contracted with love for them. They were all she had now, all that remained of Charla.

Sighing, Garland lay down again and closed her eyes, willing herself to sleep. But despite the fatigue that made every muscle in her body ache, her mind refused to shut down. It was torment to lie in a comfortable bed and not be able to fall asleep. Slowly, so as not to wake the girls, she extricated herself from the tangle of bedclothes. Wrapping herself in Colin's much-too-large bathrobe, she padded down the hall to the living room, navigating by the nightlight in the bathroom.

She curled up on Colin's sofa, feeling the nubbly texture of the fabric against her legs. If she remembered correctly, it was some sort of brown-and-beige tweedy thing, as comfortingly well used as her own. Paper crackled as she leaned back.

Reaching behind her, she switched the lamp on. She'd sat on the afternoon newspaper, she realized. Charla's funeral had hit the front page. There was a picture of Frank, looking like he'd stepped out of a Brooks Brothers catalog, and one of her, looking like Medea—wild-eyed, her mouth open, one palm out to the camera and her other arm clutching the girls. After one glance, she refused to look. The article itself wasn't bad, although there was one startling item: Robbie Schuyler had identified himself as her lawyer.

"Can't sleep?" Colin asked from the hallway behind her.

She jerked, startled. "Nope."

"Me either. Want company?"

"Yes," she said, surprised to find it was true.

He sat down beside her, propping his feet on the coffee table in front of him. Garland waited in vain for him to say something. Only a quiet man, she thought, would interpret silence as keeping someone company. But then, maybe it was. Milo's bright, witty chatter would have sent her screaming out of the room. Feeling comforted, she settled back and finished reading the article.

"Did you read this?" she asked, tapping the paper with her knuckles.

He nodded.

"This isn't Robbie's sort of thing at all; he's a high-priced, high-profile criminal lawyer."

"He said to tell you to lie low for a couple of days and leave the press to him. Take his advice, Garland; he's very good at this."

Her eyes stung. How strange it was that it had taken something like this to make her realize she had such good friends. "Thanks for letting us stay here. I don't think the girls could have stood another go-round with the press."

"I know you'd rather be home."

She drew her legs up in front of her, pulling the thick terry warmth of the robe over her knees. "Actually, it's easier here. There's too much of Charla in my house, and in hers. Memories, everywhere I turn. Too many memories."

He didn't respond. His head was bowed, and for a moment she thought he'd fallen asleep. Then he shifted, crossing his legs at the ankles. His silence freed the specter Garland had been holding at bay for far too long. Rage. Outrage. All of a sudden she found herself breathing hard. In, out, in, out. Air feeding the blaze of her anger.

"Have the police told you anything?" Colin asked.

A calm, logical question, spoken just when she needed calmness and logic the most. She forced herself to concentrate on answering it coherently, using it to regain her wavering self-control. "Not much. Now that the case is officially a . . . a homicide, two new detectives have taken over. Ah, Grange and Baedecker. All they've had time to do is take statements from Frank, me, and the girls. But one of those reporters said that the police think Charla was killed during a robbery."

Colin cocked his head to one side. "Don't you agree?"

"Does it matter? Whatever the reason, Charla is still dead, and that's what I've got to deal with." Her hands pleated the fabric of the robe. "All I can think about is that killer walking around loose, thinking he's gotten away with it."

She didn't want to cry; she wanted to hold her anger inside, to fill herself up with it so she couldn't feel the pain. But the tears came anyway, great, gasping sobs that hurt. She pressed the heels of her hands against her eyes, but the hot, salty flood seeped out from under to run down her cheeks.

Colin said something she didn't understand, then pulled her onto his lap and held her. Slowly, he rocked her in the warm, wordless embrace of human sympathy. She needed it. Needed it and hated her own vulnerability at the same time. Hated him for not being her mother or father or sister or husband, hated herself for not being able to simply accept the comfort he was trying to give. Her sobs grew deeper and more painful, feeling as though they were being ripped from her guts.

"Cry it out, get rid of it," he murmured against her hair. "I understand."

"Understand? How can you understand?" she raged through her tears. "That was my *sister!* He cut her throat, Colin. Ear to ear like . . . like a steer sent to slaughter." The words fell, hard and flat and ugly. She couldn't stop them, no matter how much pain they caused her. "And for what? A few hundred dollars, some jewelry? She'd been tied up, helpless—it wasn't like she could have fought back."

He let her cry. He let her pound her fists against his chest and shoulders, absorbing her grief, her anger and frustration, with quiet patience. When Garland finally passed through the worst of it, she pressed her forehead against his tear-dampened T-shirt in embarrassment. As though none of it had happened, he took up the conversation where it had left off.

"There can be no possible justification for your sister's murder," he said. "But things like that happen all the time, and for a lot less than what Charla had."

"And I've got to live with it."

"You've got to live with it. And with the fact that he—or they—might never be caught."

"That stinks, Colin."

"Yeah." He lifted her off his lap and deposited her on the seat beside him, then shifted so that his back was against the armrest. "You know, when I first started coming to The Tome, I thought you and Milo were lovers."

She stared at him for a moment, startled by the sudden shift of subject. "Me and Milo? Why?"

He shrugged. "It was the obvious conclusion, at least until I got to know you better."

"Milo and I both have taken a lot of heat over this," she said with some asperity. "Why is it so strange for a man and woman to be 'just' friends?"

"It isn't. Most people assume that a woman will choose another woman as her best friend, that's all."

"I did," she said, her voice flat. "Charla."

Was she? Was she really? Garland could almost hear the thought, although Colin wisely hadn't said it aloud. "I know what you're thinking," she said.

"No, you don't."

There was a scratch at the front door. When Colin didn't react immediately, there was a loud meow, then the thump of a heavy body hitting the door.

"Milord awaits," he said, sighing as he got to his feet.

He opened the door a crack, and the biggest cat Garland had ever seen squeezed through. A rakehell tom, she thought, noting his ragged ears and scarred, orange-tabby body. She welcomed the distraction—any distraction. There would be a whole lifetime to think about Charla, and to miss her.

"I didn't know you had a cat," she said.

"I don't. He came with the house. Sometimes he honors me with his presence, sometimes I don't see him for several days. He's probably come to check you out." Colin switched on the table lamp beside the door, then returned to his seat.

"What's his name?" Garland held her hand out, inviting the cat to sniff. He stalked forward, but stopped several feet from her outstretched fingers.

"Don't try to pick him up," Colin said. "He doesn't like to be touched."

Garland withdrew her hand. "What's his name?"

"Well, I don't exactly know. The guy next door said it was Numbnuts."

"Numbnuts? Numbnuts?" Outraged, Garland turned to stare at Colin. "You've got to be kidding! Who would do that to a cat?"

"Who would do that to *himself?"* With a grin, he added, "Can you imagine some guy running through the neighborhood calling, "Here, Numbnuts! Here, Numbnuts!"

She laughed. Or rather, half laughed, half sobbed; there was still plenty of crying lurking just beneath the surface. "You poor cat," she murmured, deciding that "dear" or "kitty" were most unsuitable for such as he.

"I call him Milord," Colin said. "He takes it as his due, along with fourteen cans of tuna a week."

Sitting down, the cat stretched out his hind leg and began cleaning it. Fascinated, Garland watched his pink tongue work its way over and around, even catching between the toes. Once finished, he drilled her with a yellow basilisk stare, then jumped into her lap and curled up. She smoothed his fur, then scratched behind his battered ears. He began to purr.

"I don't believe it," Colin said. "All he's ever let me do is feed him."

Garland kept scratching. The purr got stronger, the vibrations making their way through the thick terrycloth covering her legs. Rather like being under instead of upon one of those vibrating beds you find in motels, she thought.

The cat yawned. Garland echoed the yawn reflexively.

"Chuck him off if you're ready for bed," Colin said.

"I'm not ready." She pointed to the television. "I wouldn't mind watching TV for a while, though. Something not too taxing."

"I've got a ton of movies." Sliding off the sofa, he went to paw through the stack of movies on the TV stand. "I know there's something . . . nope, nope, that's not . . . Ah! How about *Star Wars?*"

"Perfect. I haven't seen it in years." She shifted her legs beneath the cat's limp bulk.

Colin started the movie and returned to the sofa, turning out the light as he did. He sat beside her, close enough this time that his shoulder was touching hers. Garland settled against his warm, undemanding solidity as the movie began. A wonderful fable, *Star Wars*—a land far, far away, where the Force was with you and the good guys won.

She yawned, lulled by her purring lap massager and the flickering movie light across the room. God, that cat was better than a sleeping pill, she thought. She really ought to get up and go to bed, but she was just too tired to move.

"Are you comfortable?" Colin asked.

"Yup." Lazily, she stroked the cat's back, then yawned again. "Y'know, Colin, it's one hell of a screwed-up world we live in."

"Yup." His shoulder came more firmly against hers.

The movie played on, but Garland soon found herself watching the insides of her eyelids more often than not. Finally she gave up trying to stay awake, and slipped peacefully into oblivion.

She woke up sometime later—Luke Skywalker was just leading his valiant team of fighters against the Death Star—to find the cat gone and her head lying in Colin's lap. He had an erection. For a moment she lay there, paralyzed with shock, then bolted to a sitting position.

To her surprise, Colin laughed. "At least you didn't scream 'What is that?' and run out of the room."

"I know what it is," she retorted. Despite his matter-of-fact acceptance of the situation, she was horribly embarrassed. "Colin, look . . ."

"Just ignore it," he said. "I am."

"Why?"

"Why am I aroused, or why am I ignoring it?"

"Both." She spoke without thinking, and was surprised to discover that she really did want to know the answer to both.

Colin sighed. "I'm in love with you, Garland. Always have been. But this is the wrong time and place for it."

"I . . . had no idea."

"I suppose you didn't. You never really looked at me, did you?" he asked. "I was right in front of you every Friday night, but you never really *saw* me. Just good old Colin, the quiet one. Everyone else in the group knew."

This ought to be absurd. But it wasn't. Colin was in love with her—a man and an emotion to be taken seriously. Searching inside for a reaction, however, she found only the vast black hole of her grief. In time, maybe there might be more, for herself and for Colin. Not now. Although she knew he deserved much more than she could give him, she found herself unwilling to turn him down flat. "I'm just not ready to deal with this right now," she said.

"I thought *I* was the one who said this was neither the time nor the place for it. Look Garland, I'm not asking you for an answer—I'm not asking you for anything."

"Thank you." She let her breath out in a sigh of relief, then pushed herself off the sofa. "I'm going to crawl back in with the girls. Good night, Colin."

"Good night."

As she went past, his big, square hand engulfed her wrist, stopping her in her tracks. It was the first time she'd been truly aware of his touch. As a man. A possible lover. There was great strength behind the gentleness of his grip, iron sheathed in velvet. She sensed it would always stay sheathed, for this man had found other ways of dealing with the world.

"We *will* have to resolve it someday," he said.

"I know." Impulse caught her. Spurred by the knowledge that he wouldn't make her pay the price for it, she leaned down and kissed him. His lips were firm and warm, his mouth burning hot, and she found herself responding in a way she wouldn't have believed possible a few seconds ago. He tasted good, and he felt good. *Surprise, surprise!* she thought.

After a moment she pulled away. Slowly though, her breath mingling with his, her mouth disengaging reluctantly. He let her go, as she knew he would. She put her hand on his chest, feeling his heart beat a rapid tattoo against her palm. *I did that!*

"What was that for?" he asked, his voice showing no trace of emotion. "An experiment? A promise?"

"Maybe a little of both. But I've got some things to work out before I know. Give me some time."

"Some." He heaved a sigh. "But I'm not sure that kiss was a good idea."

She turned to go.

"Garland?" He waited until she turned to face him again. "Amber and Annalese are going to be all right. They're are a lot stronger than you might think; they've got a lot of their aunt's courage in them."

Garland suddenly felt a hundred years old. Tired, bone-and-blood-and-heart-weary. "I'm glad someone's got some. *I* seem to be fresh out."

"Sure," he agreed, his voice turning sarcastic. "Just like today at the cemetery. You really fell apart there, didn't you? Sobbed into your handkerchief and left the twins to the mercy of the press."

It was such a deliberately Milo-ish statement that she almost laughed. Almost. "Good night, Colin," she said, and left the room.

* * *

The shrill ring of his phone pulled Kurt Baedecker out of a deep sleep. "Christ Almighty," he muttered, groping blindly across the top of the nightstand in an attempt to shut the thing up before it woke Ginny. Then he remembered Ginny was gone. For good. *Finis.* Kaput, thanks to his career.

He lay back down and glared at the phone, which blissfully kept ringing. He knew who it was. If he answered it, ten to one he'd end up working today. Finally, he couldn't stand it any longer. Snatching up the phone, he growled. "Damn it, Jeff, it's my day off!"

"It *was* your day off," his partner said. "We've got another body," his partner said. "White female, mid-twenties—"

"Old or new?"

"Brand, spanking new. This one's Chesapeake's, but they said we were welcome to take a look. Stabbed to death and some other funny stuff."

Intrigued, Baedecker sat up and swung his feet over the side of the bed. "What kind of funny stuff?"

"Uh-uh. You're going to have to come see for yourself. If *I* have to work on my day off, by God, so do you."

"Where was she found?"

"In the woods beside I-64—just before the Deep Creek exit. Some fella pulled off the road to take a pee and got the shit scared out of him for his trouble."

"I'll be there in a half hour," Kurt said, and hung up.

It was closer to forty-five minutes when he walked into the Virginia State Examiner's office. The place always seemed cold, even when it wasn't. Jeff was sitting in the waiting room, his face buried in the sports section of the newspaper.

"What's the score, buddy?" Kurt asked.

"Damn Celtics got beat." Tossing the paper aside, Jeff rose to his feet.

Baedecker looked up, and up, and up. An ex-college football, basketball, and baseball player, Jeff Grange was six-feet-seven of solid muscle covered with skin the color of strong Columbian coffee. As always, the sight of all that well-trained sinew made Kurt overly aware of his own middle-aged paunch and thinning hair. But Jeff was as smart as they came, a real stand-up guy, and there was no one Baedecker would rather work with.

"Where's your corpse?" he asked.

Jeff led the way to a small viewing room, where a sheet-shrouded form lay on a gurney. Baedecker peeled the covering back to the dead woman's waist, noting the lividity on her left side, the bruises on her jaw and cheekbone. There were three deep stab wounds in her chest.

"Note the cuts on her palms," Jeff said. "She tried to defend herself from the knife."

Kurt grunted. "Yeah. What's the funny stuff you were talking about?"

With a jerk of his hand, Jeff whipped the sheet down to the end of the gurney. Kurt swallowed hard; the woman's pubic area had so many stab wounds that it looked like a piece of hamburger. What he could see of her genitals looked even worse. He was glad he hadn't had time to have breakfast.

"What the hell?" he burst out.

"What the hell is right," Jeff agreed. "She was nude when found, by the by."

"Rape?"

"Who could tell? Maybe the autopsy will show some sign of it, but if they can find anything resembling a vagina in that mess, I'm a white man."

Kurt pulled the sheet up over the body, glad to cover the mauled and pitiful remains of what had once been a human being. "I've seen enough," he said, leading the way out into the hall.

"Want to get something to eat?"

"Christ, man! After that?"

"It's all in the mind." Jeff took a small, leather-covered notebook out of his pocket and began thumbing through it. "Her prints are on file; prostitution, three arrests in the past seven months. Name of Bambi Henks."

Kurt snorted. "Bambi?"

"Hey, it doesn't matter now, does it?"

"Shit."

"She worked the Ocean View area. One of Bibb's girls."

Kurt grunted. "Who's got the case?"

"Harry Lobello and Rog Thompson. They're on their way to roust Bibb out of bed." Jeff handed Kurt a photograph. "Here's our Bambi in happier times."

Baedecker studied Bambi Henk's picture, taken at the time of her last arrest. She hadn't been bad-looking. Long dark hair, blue eyes, olive complexion. Average height, average build. Average in everything but the manner of her dying. What accident of fate had put her in a killer's hands last night?

"What do you think, Jeff?"

"I think it's ugly, real ugly. Doesn't seem to have much to do with the Ross case, though." Jeff opened the outer door and gestured Kurt through. Both men stood blinking in the bright sunlight. Too bright, after what they'd seen inside.

"I don't like it," Kurt said. He tapped the side of his nose. "This smells bad, partner. Even if it doesn't have anything to do with Charla Ross's murder, I don't like it. I'd really like to get the person who did it behind bars."

Chapter Ten

"Are you sure you don't want to stay?" Colin asked. "It's only been three days since the funeral."

"Frank wants the girls home. He's into setting boundaries again, and I'm back on the outside." Garland folded a kid-sized pair of blue jeans and stuffed them ungently into the suitcase Colin had lent her. A sweater followed, then another. She and the twins had had such fun looking for bargains at K-Mart.

"He's going through a rough time," Colin said.

"I know." With a sigh, she sat down on the edge of the bed. "I'm just tired of getting jerked around. One day I'm the princess, the next the outcast. And this is the guy who advocated unwavering consistency when his kids were born!"

"Maybe he'll settle down once the hoorah is over." Colin's burly shoulders lifted in a shrug. "At least Charla's name wasn't on the front page this morning; that was reserved for that rape—excuse me, alleged rape—among the rich and famous."

"I just wish—"

"Aunt Garland!" There was a rush of running footsteps, then Amber and Annalese burst into the room. Their voices tumbled over each other excitedly. "Colin's got the neatest cat, he let us pet him and everything. He caught a mouse last night, it's just the grossest thing, brown and kinda ripped-up and its tongue hanging out. . . . Annalese thought we should bury it, but the cat wouldn't let us touch it. And—"

Garland held up her hands, trying to stem the flood, but it swept on relentlessly.

". . . And there's a creek behind those trees over there, and we saw a boy catch a crab. Do you think we could try to catch a crab? And the guy across the street is an actual *clown,* can you believe it? He came over and showed us some magic tricks, and Colin's cat bit him on the leg! What's his name anyway?"

"The clown's?" Colin asked.

"No, the cat's," Amber said.

"Don't you dare!" Garland hissed.

"I call him Milord," Colin said, absolutely deadpan.

Annalese peered into the suitcase. "Hey, that's our stuff! What are you doing?"

"Your father called while you were outside," Garland said. "He wants you to come home." She raised her hand, cutting off a chorused "Awwwwww." "He's all alone, and he needs you."

"You can come back anytime," Colin said. "I'll take you crabbing. You'll like my daughter Kathy. She's thirteen, but she still likes to do fun stuff like that."

The twins turned two pairs of beseeching blue eyes to Garland, who nodded. "Of course. Now go get cleaned up; you've got mud up to your eyebrows, and your father's going to be here soon to pick you up."

They disappeared as fast as they'd appeared, and a moment later Garland heard water running in the bathroom. *They're beginning to heal.* Oh, they'd never stop missing their mother, perhaps even more when they were grown. It had been that way with her; every day she regretted the loss of the friendship she and her own mother had begun to explore. Not mother-daughter friendship, but the bonds two women shared when they also shared a home, a family, and a past.

"It's getting close to lunchtime," Colin said, holding out his hand to her. "How 'bout I make us all some sandwiches?"

Garland scrubbed the back of her fist across her forehead, trying to banish the memory cobwebs. The present had to be dealt with now. "Sounds great, Colin," she said, putting her hand in his.

The kitchen was as comfortably well lived in as the rest of the house. The oak cabinets needed refinishing, and the stove looked as though it had come out of the Stone Age, but it was a nice room. It was also painfully clean.

"You don't cook much, do you?" she asked.

His voice was muffled somewhat; he was in the process of rummaging through the refrigerator. "There doesn't seem to be much incentive to cook for one person. When Kathy's here, we usually end up eating pizza or hamburgers; her mother makes her eat *good* stuff at home."

"Occupational hazard of a weekend father?"

"Yeah." Tucking several jars and packages into his arms, he emerged from the depths of the refrigerator. "How come you never had any kids?"

"We couldn't. *Garry* couldn't." She turned away. Both from Colin and from the wounds that were still too raw and too deep for anyone else to see. Conscious of his gaze on her, she began opening and closing cabinets. "Where do you keep your glasses?"

"Third door to your right. Silverware is in the drawer next to the dishwasher, placemats and things in the one beneath that."

To her relief, he didn't ask any more questions about her marriage. Gathering up the utensils and placemats, she went into the eating area and began to set the table. Sunlight slanted through the big bay window on the back wall, gilding the Formica tabletop and warming the back of her hands.

No sooner had Colin put the last slice of bread on the last sandwich, however, than the doorbell rang.

"Works every time," he said. "Will you get it? I've got mayonnaise all over my hands."

Garland looked through the peephole. Frank stood on the tiny porch outside, his body distorted by the bull's-eye lens. He reached up to smooth his hair. His hands shook slightly. Garland had never seen him show nerves before, and sympathy replaced the irritation she'd felt earlier.

Opening the door, she said, "Hello, Frank. Come on in."

"Thank you." He stepped inside and glanced around Colin's modest living room. "And thank Mr. Kingsley for me. It was very kind of him to let the girls stay here."

"Why don't you come into the kitchen and tell him yourself?" she asked. "And have something to eat while you're at it; we've just made a ton of sandwiches."

Not the slightest shred of interest lit Frank's cool gray eyes. "Thank you, but I'm afraid I don't have time."

The bough of friendship had been refused, Garland thought. Coolly and politely, with ne'er a hard word. She let her breath out in a sound that was a cross between a sigh and a hiss. It was always like this with him. Try as she might to establish some kind of rapport with him, he always slid out from under. If it weren't for Amber and Annalese, she'd write him off as a loss. But she was uncomfortably aware of how few rights she had as far as the twins were concerned. With Charla gone, seeing Amber and Annalese depended on Frank's goodwill. So she'd try again and again, and as many times as was necessary.

"How was your weekend?" she asked.

"Very stressful. You and the girls were better off here, believe me."

"Are the reporters leaving you alone?"

"Relatively. Fortunately, their attention span is fairly short. I did agree to give an exclusive interview to one of the local people, however. I suggest you do the same. That should satisfy the public's curiosity once and for all."

Garland recoiled inwardly. "I'll talk to Robbie about it."

"Robbie? Oh yes, your lawyer friend. I must admit, he did an admirable job of handling the press." Frank smoothed his hair again. "When you receive his bill, send it along to me. It's the least I can do."

"Robbie isn't going to charge me."

His eyebrows went up. "A great imposition, even on the best of friendships."

"I offered to pay him, Frank," Garland said, hoping her voice didn't show her mounting irritation. "He wouldn't take it. And he won't take it from you. So I suggest we say thank you politely and sincerely, and go on to other things."

Frank waved his hand, dismissing that. "I'll talk to him about it tomorrow. Where are the girls? I promised Estelle we'd be at her house for lunch."

And Garland wasn't invited. *Boy, he's drawing those lines with thick, dark ink.* Temper kicked in. She opened her mouth to let him have it, but the cat chose that moment to scratch at the door—loudly enough, she noted, to make Frank jump.

She opened the door. The cat sauntered in, tail held high, then sat on her foot and fixed Frank with a malevolent yellow stare. Garland turned back to her brother-in-law, but the urge to argue had passed. Oh, she planned to discuss this with him sooner or later, but not in anger.

"You know I don't like cats," Frank said, returning the cat's stare with equal fervor.

"His name," Garland said, "is Numbnuts."

Much to her disappointment, Amber and Annalese came in then and saved Frank from replying. While everyone greeted and got greeted, Garland surreptitiously removed her foot from under the cat's behind.

"Come on, girls, you can tell me the story on the way to Aunt Estelle's," Frank said. "Go say goodbye to Mr. Kingsley and get your coats."

As always, they obeyed their father without argument. There was no sign of the bold, talkative little girls who had come running into the house a short time ago. Just good little Hollisters, Garland thought. Make 'em mind their manners and tongues and feelings, and maybe they'll turn out as colorless as the rest of the clan. *Over my dead body!*

The twins returned a moment later. Colin was with them, but he stopped in the doorway, distancing himself. Amber and Annalese flung their arms around Garland.

"Are you coming over tonight, Aunt Garland?" Annalese asked in a voice that shook with suppressed tears.

"Not tonight, sweetheart." Garland met Frank's gaze levelly. "But soon. Very soon."

"I love you," Amber said.

Garland held them close, laying her cheek atop each blond head for a moment. "And I love you both very much. Be good for your father now."

Glancing up at Frank, she saw that the emotional little scene was making him uncomfortable. He smoothed his hair, over and over, until Garland was sure he was going to slide it right out of his scalp. Odd. Why, in all the years she'd known him, hadn't she noticed that habit before?

Gently disengaging the twins' arms from around her waist, she said, "Come on, now. Your father needs you now."

Frank held out his hands to the girls. Annalese took the right, Amber the left. Garland watched them walk down the sidewalk toward Frank's car. Annalese glanced at the house over her shoulder, and there was such longing on her face that Garland's heart clenched.

"He shouldn't be doing this!" she said through clenched teeth. In sudden decision, she whirled away from the window. "We're going to have this out right now!"

"No!" Colin grabbed her by the arm.

"He doesn't know what they need. He's never taken the

time to know *them* at all!"

Without letting her go, Colin said, "Maybe now he'll make the effort. Garland, you can't let it tear you up like this. They're not yours."

"I know they're not mine!" She wrenched away from him. "Frank has already made that abundantly clear, thank you!"

"Garland—"

"Why do you have to *see* so damn much! Why can't you let me keep anything to myself!"

He raked his hand through his hair. "I can't help it."

"Take me home, Colin."

"All right." He turned away, then whipped back around. "No, it isn't all right. Look, somebody's got to say this."

"What?"

"You love too damn much. You make yourself responsible for everything. You did it for Charla, and now you're doing it for the twins."

The words felt like a physical attack, each syllable hitting straight and hard. Garland stepped backward until the sofa hit the back of her knees, making her sit down abruptly.

Colin followed her. "You're trying to make the whole world right for them. But you can't give them their mother back. And Charla . . ." He flung his arms wide, a gesture full of frustration. "Damn it, Charla was thirty-four years old and you *never made her grow up!*"

Outrage flooded through her. "Jesus Christ, Colin! You make me out to be some kind of *Mommy Dearest!*"

"That's not what I meant at all, and you know it." Sitting down beside her, he took her hands. "Charla was the kind of person who wouldn't be responsible as long as she had someone else to do it for her. And you were always there, weren't you? Always ready to make things right, no matter what the personal cost. When are you going to live for yourself and not for other people?"

Garland tried to pull free, but he tightened his grip

and continued, "I'm not saying you're wrong to want to help the twins. But you've got to find some balance here. Let other people take a share of the pain."

"They're just kids. And their father—"

"Is their father. Right, wrong, or indifferent, they've got to live with it. And the worst thing you can do for them right now is to make them ride an emotional boomerang between you and Frank."

"What makes you the expert?" she asked, her voice bitter.

"During our divorce, my ex and I put Kathy through hell before we figured out what we were doing to her. We agreed on a truce, because we loved her more than we hated each other."

This time he let her go when she tried to pull away. Garland sat with her face averted, wishing she could refute what he'd said. But she couldn't. The truth lodged in her chest like a lump of smoldering coal; it hurt, it stung, it raised demons of conscience she'd rather not deal with just now. The best she was going to be able to do with it was to cool the fire enough to make it bearable. And that was going to take time.

"You've had your say," she said, feeling a hundred years old. "Will you take me home now?"

He sighed. "All right."

She didn't speak during the ride home, and neither did Colin. The atmosphere in the car was uncomfortable, thick with the things that had been said and charged with those that hadn't. Yet. Garland knew he *would* say them, and she didn't want to hear them. Not now. Not yet.

The car pulled up in front of her house. Before Colin had a chance to switch off the ignition, Garland released her seatbelt and opened the door.

"You don't have to leap out," he said. "I wasn't going to push my way into your house."

"Why not?" she snapped. "You've pushed your way into everything else."

To her surprise, she saw no responding anger in his green eyes, only sadness. It tugged at her, letting her own anger out like air from a punctured balloon. She turned away from it. She had to; he pressed too hard, wanted things she wasn't ready to give right now. Maybe she'd never be ready.

"Goodbye, Colin," she said, getting out of the car. "Thanks for letting us stay with you."

"Take care of yourself." He leaned across the seat to pull the door closed.

She watched the car move down the street, then make the turn that would take it out of the neighborhood. There was nothing inside her right now—no regret, no desire to call him back, nothing. If she banged her fist on her chest, she'd probably rattle like the Tin Man.

Heaving a sigh, she went inside. There were several messages on the answering machine: one from Milo, telling her everything was under control at The Tome, two from reporters, and one from Detective Baedecker of Homicide. She started to call Baedecker, then stabbed her forefinger down on the disconnect button and dialed the phone company's number instead.

"Should have done this last week," she muttered under her breath.

It took her only a few minutes to arrange to have her number changed to an unlisted one. Until that went through, she'd let her answering machine screen her calls. Then, her heart beating faster with dread and anticipation, she called Baedecker.

He sounded tired. "Hello, Miss Ross. Thanks for getting back to me so soon. I'm sorry you had such a rough time at the funeral."

"My sister was frequently in the news when alive," Garland said. "I guess I should have expected her death to be as public."

"More," Baedecker said.

"Is it always like this?"

"I'm afraid so. It's hard on the family, puts tremendous pressure on people who already have the death of a loved one to deal with."

"Tell me about it," she agreed. She felt as tired as he sounded. Out of energy, out of patience, out of everything. "Did you want to ask me something, Detective Baedecker?"

"I wanted to tell you that your sister's purse and luggage were found this morning in a dumpster behind Janaf Shopping Center."

"Oh." There was a smudge on the light switch. Garland rubbed at it with her thumb, concentrating on the small task in an effort to keep her emotions under control. "Have you gone through them yet?"

"Yeah. From what you described earlier as to the probable contents, the only things that seem to be missing are her cash and jewelry. Possibly traveler's checks, but you weren't sure whether or not she had any."

The light switch was clean. Garland closed her hand into a fist and dropped it to her side. "So. Cash and jewelry. You think it was a robbery, then?"

"So far, all the evidence points to that."

"Are you getting close to finding my sister's killer?" She no longer flinched from the word. Killer. Charla's killer.

"Not yet." He made a faint, exasperated sound. "Miss Ross, investigating a case like this is a huge, complicated job. Most murders are committed by someone the victim knows, for some logical—at least to the killer—reason. As far as your sister's case goes, it looks like it was a matter of her being at the wrong place at the wrong time. We've got no witnesses. We don't even know *where* she was killed."

"So what do you do?"

"We talk to every man who has been recently released from prison after serving a sentence for a violent crime. We go through everything your sister had fiber by fiber. We hope a witness turns up . . ."

"I get the picture," she said. Her mind conjured up the

picture of a man, faceless and nameless, walking around with Charla's blood on his hands. Smiling. "Detective . . ." Her hand tightened on the phone. "Are you going to return my sister's things?"

"The car will be returned to your brother-in-law in a week or so. But the rest, probably not anytime soon; we never know what may turn out to be significant at a later time. Why? Is there something you want?"

"No. It's just that, well, it feels as though Charla's life is spread out for everyone to see. Strangers going through her things, poking through the remains of her life. It bothers me."

There was a moment of silence. She could hear him breathing. Finally he said, "Death puts us all in the public domain, Miss Ross."

"You ought to be a poet, Detective Baedecker." She hoped she didn't sound as sour as she felt.

She must have, for he shifted back to his official tone. "If you want to discuss anything, Miss Ross, anything at all, call me. Remember, the most important thing for all of us is to find whoever killed your sister and put him away. Right?"

"Right."

He hung up. Absently, Garland tapped the phone against the palm of her other hand. Funny, that last statement of his. It was almost as if he thought she hadn't told him everything she knew.

That damned lie. Charla's lie. Evidently Baedecker didn't quite believe that Charla would fail to confide in her loyal big sister, no matter how dreadful the secret. Neither had Garland, until today. But now she did—thanks to Colin, damn him. If only he hadn't been right!

Crack!

The sudden sharp noise came from the front of the house. Dropping the phone, she ran into the living room. The curtains were pulled back from the big, many-paned picture window, letting a flood of sunlight into the room.

"What the . . ." Then she noticed the cracked pane in

the upper-left-hand section of the window. There was no hole, no circular impact pattern like a BB would have made. Thirty years of living in a neighborhood full of kids had given her plenty of experience with BB holes.

"A pebble thrown by a truck?" she muttered, rising on tiptoe to trace the line of the crack with her fingernail.

She went out to the front porch to investigate further. There she found the broken-necked body of a cardinal, its feathers a vivid splash of red against the dark slate of the porch. Even as she watched, the bright beads of its eyes glazed over.

"Poor thing. Flew right into the window, didn't you?" She picked the bird up and gently smoothed the scarlet feathers. Its head dangled bonelessly against her wrist. "Let's get you taken care of."

It didn't take long to dig a hole in the back flowerbed. She laid the small broken body inside, then pushed the dirt and pine straw over it.

She knelt there for a moment, looking down at the rude little grave. And then her grief came out in a flood, unbearable and uncontrollable.

Digging her fingers into the cold dirt, she cried. She cursed Fate, she cursed God, she cursed Charla, and she cursed herself. When there were no more tears left, she climbed to her feet and went into the house. She had things to do.

Charla's killer was walking around loose. Somehow, there had to be a way to change that.

Chapter Eleven

David dragged the sofa out to the back yard. Picking a spot where the tree branches didn't overhang, he doused the sofa with gasoline, then struck a match and tossed it onto the soaked cushion. Flames exploded into being with a *whoosh* that sent him a couple of steps backward. Hot, hungry flames ate at the brown-stained fabric. Cleansing it. Fire, the great purifier, the great destroyer. The curse and the savior.

Turning his back on it, he went into the house. Now that the sofa was gone, the room was empty but for a paint can, brushes, and rollers. The worst of the blood had either been washed or sanded off the walls. Ceiling, too. The carpet, however, was a different matter; great splatters of rusty brown surrounded the spot where the sofa had been. From there, a two-foot-wide trail led into the hallway. Drag marks.

He hated mess. He'd already cleaned the linoleum in the hall, first with a mop, then with a brush. Finally, it was returned to its former pine-scented shininess.

"S-s-s-scrubbing bubbles/Always ease my troubles," he warbled as he took the lid off the paint can and began to stir. White, white, white. Walls, ceiling, trim.

He glanced into the kitchen, where a roll of carpet lay. He'd bought it this morning at one of those outlet places. A nice, restrained gray. Much more serviceable than the beige that had been there before.

The paint was ready. Pure, stark white. Like snow, like

porcelain. He dipped into it with his forefinger, then rubbed the pad of his thumb over his paint-covered skin.

The phone rang, making him jump. "Oh, shut up," he said, picking up a paintbrush. Again, the phone rang. He held the brush poised over the smooth surface of the paint, wanting to put it in but distracted by the annoying, imperative sound.

Realizing that it wasn't going to go away, he put the brush down and strode into the kitchen. Snatching the phone up, he snarled, "What?"

"Hello, David."

"Oh. You again." Sullenly. "I was painting."

"Did you read the paper this morning?"

"No." With one finger, he pushed the curtain aside far enough for him to see the fire outside. The couch was burning well.

"The police found a woman's body in the woods off a remote section of highway. She'd been murdered—stabbed several times. Does that scenario sound familiar, David?"

He shrugged.

The caller persisted, sounding more upset than David had ever heard before. "Why are you painting?" he asked. "Did you do it there in the house? In *my* house?"

Shrugging again, he asked, "Did it hit the front page?"

"Dead prostitutes don't usually get the front page," the caller snapped.

"Just dead society women."

There was a stretch of silence, then, "You're falling into those old patterns again, David. You promised me you'd be careful about that."

Annoyance, sharp and grating, swept through him. His house was torn up, everything was out of place, and he hated mess. The paint was open, probably getting scummy already. "You got what you wanted, didn't you? Why do you keep *bugging* me?"

"Now, David, don't get upset. But you must understand that if you persist in . . . hunting in predictable ways, you're going to be caught."

And then he'd never get to hunt again. He'd never get to

talk to her *again*. "I know all that," he said peevishly. "I've changed."

"How? This one was dark, just like all the rest."

"Not all," he said. "There were *two* blondes."

The caller hesitated for a moment, then said, "The police didn't find the other one."

"Is that my fault?"

"No, David." The other man's voice was soothing, flowing smooth as oil over his nerves. "You've done wonderfully."

"I worked hard to change my technique." It was true; he hadn't taken his usual "trophy" from the last one. It had hurt—all that lovely dark hair, and he hadn't taken even a little for his treasure box. That was the second one that had gotten away from him. *Third time's a charm!*

"David," the voice prompted.

"Hmmh?"

"Perhaps the police need a little help."

"Help?" Frowning, he cocked his head to one side.

"They just don't know where to look for this other blonde, do they?"

A smile replaced his frown as he realized what the other man wanted. It fit in well with *his* plans. "Okay. I can take care of that."

"That's very good, David. Will you call me later to tell me how it went?"

"Sure." He hung up, then leaned forward to look out the window again. Smoke rose in a fat column in the windless air. It would be worse when he burned the carpeting. Good thing he lived way out in the country where nobody cared about things like that.

He'd see that the police got the blonde. Actually, he'd see that they got more than one. But not all at once; there was a time and place for everything. And *he* was the one who decided where and when. The only one.

Maybe the police would like a redhead. He'd never had a redhead. They weren't his type, but then, neither were blondes.

"She walks in beauty like the night/Dark and sweet, my

heart's delight," he murmured, letting the curtain fall back into place.

Coming to Virginia had been the best thing he'd ever done for himself. He'd learned so much in such a short time. Useful things. Clever things. He could hardly wait to put some of those new ideas into practice.

He laughed. Almost of its own volition, his hand reached for the phone. To call *her.* To hear her voice, to imagine . . . No! Later. After all, she was his. His. He'd marked her, as the lumberjack marked the trees he was going to cut.

The time would come. He didn't know when, but he'd recognize it when it did. And then he'd collect his property. No, not property, that was the wrong word. Treasure. He'd better get the house fixed up; he wanted everything to be perfect.

Humming the theme song from *Rocky,* he went into the living room and began stirring the paint again.

Garland pulled up to the curb in front of The Tome and parked in the rectangle of light that spilled from the window. Friday night. A significant day, Friday. Two weeks ago today, Charla had walked out that door. A week ago, she'd been buried.

Milo's head bobbed into sight in the window, then disappeared. A moment later the door opened. He stood silhouetted against the light, beckoning her in with an impatient wave. Garland turned off the ignition and got out of the van.

"You're holding things up," he called. "Move it."

"You didn't have to wait for me," she said. "You never did before."

He gave her a withering look. "You've got the coffee."

"Oh." Amusement washed through her, sparkling like a woodland stream. "Well, puncture *my* ego," she said, glad to fall into the old bantering mode.

"Always eager to serve."

"So I hear."

"Gimme the coffee." He ushered her through the door, then closed it and locked the deadbolt.

Voices came from the back, Troll's and Robbie's. Troll was beginning to get excited; although she wasn't yelling yet, there was an edge to her voice that showed it wouldn't be long. Garland sighed; between the familiar voices engaged in the familiar argument, and the comforting leather-and-Murphy's Oil Soap smell of the books, it was like coming home after a trip through hell.

"Milton again?" she asked.

"What else?" Under his breath, Milo added, "Fuddy-duddies." Then, "I thought you were going to bring the girls."

"Frank," Garland said through her teeth, "decided they needed a quiet weekend at home."

"Oh. Maybe—"

"He isn't home. They're with the new nanny. Xenia."

"Xenia?" he echoed. "No shit?"

"You should have heard her, Milo." Garland's voice went up in a nasal twang. "I'm sorry, Miss Ross, but Dr. Hollister left orders that Amber and Annalese spend a quiet evening at home. No, you may not speak to him. He's at his office, not to be disturbed. Perhaps next time you might have better luck if you gave us a few days' notice."

"No shit?" he said again. Then he took her hand, contrition written across his expressive face. "I'm sorry, sweetheart. Sometimes I get carried away. Want to talk about it?"

"No, talking about it just makes me madder." She raked her hand through her hair. "Is everyone here?"

"Yeah. And Colin, too."

Bull's-eye, Garland thought. She might as well have asked the question outright. No privacy at all. "Did he tell you we had an argument?"

"No, he told me he was a plumber."

She shouldn't ask. She knew she shouldn't. But temptation was stronger than resolve. "And?"

"And what?" Milo's eyebrows went up. "I tried to get

him to come to the apartment and fix the leak in my sink, of course."

Garland gave him a shove. "Get out of my sight."

"Okay, okay." He trotted toward the back, giving her his bad-little-boy grin over his shoulder.

She stayed in the front long enough to hang up her coat and check the day's receipts. Then, after a hasty and unaccustomed check in the mirror, she headed toward the voices.

The table was littered with soda cans and wire-handled take-out boxes from Chang's. Garland registered Troll and Robbie's waves of greeting, Milo's presence at the coffeepot and George's smile, but her attention was on Colin. His green eyes were warm and just a bit wary. In a way, she didn't want to forgive him for seeing something in her she hadn't wanted to admit even to herself. But she had. Maybe it had been deliberate, that offering of himself as a target for her anger. But that didn't excuse her for taking him up on it.

As she went past him to her chair, she laid her hand on his shoulder. He leaned back briefly and covered her hand with his. Apology accepted. Silently and without frills, just like the man himself.

"Where are the girls?" Troll asked.

"Wrong question," Milo said from his post at the coffeepot.

"Whoops," Robbie murmured.

Garland flopped down in her chair and planted her elbows on the table. "Does everyone know my business?"

"Yes," Troll said, putting her hands on her hips.

"Now, Garland," George reached over and patted Garland's hand, "we *have* rather been keeping up on things, you know."

With a sigh, she capitulated. "All right, all right. If my friends can't pry into my private life, then who can?"

"Damn straight," Milo said. "Who wants coffee?"

Robbie raised his forefinger. "By the way, Garland, your brother-in-law sent me a check this week. For services rendered, his letter said."

"Sorry, Robbie. I told him not to."

"There are plenty of people who are wary of lawyers bearing gifts," Robbie said.

George chuckled. " 'A grateful mind/By owing owes not, but still pays, at once/Indebted and discharged.' "

"Not Milton!" Milo wailed.

Colin, who had begun sketching, looked up at Garland and winked. With a smile, she took the pencil out of his hand and wrote *Paradise Lost* in the corner of the paper. He nodded.

"Hey, is that the phone?" Troll asked.

Milo nodded. "I'll get it."

He disappeared around the corner of the bookshelf. A few moments later he reappeared, frowning. "Garland, it's for you. Some guy. He won't tell me anything, just says he's got to talk to you. About Charla."

"Who is he?"

"He won't say." Milo spread his hands wide. "I've taken calls from every Joe Blow Nutcase in the city this week, and he doesn't sound like one of them. He just sounds . . . urgent."

"I'll talk to him," Garland said, pushing her chair back hurriedly.

The trip to the front of the store seemed to take forever. When she caught sight of the desk she saw the phone waiting for her, the twin circles of speaker and mouthpiece seeming to track her like the sights of a gun.

She picked it up, put it to her ear. "Hello?"

"Is this Garland Ross?" A man's tenor, clear and well modulated. When she affirmed that fact, he said, "I know where she was that weekend. That *last* weekend."

Feeling her heartbeat jolt into a gallop, she asked, "Where?"

"She was with me. At my place."

"What are you trying to say?" she asked.

"We were lovers. For over a year."

Garland gripped the phone as though it was the only thing holding her up. "Who are you?"

"Uh-uh, lady. I'm not getting involved in this. In fact,

I'm leaving town tomorrow. But I couldn't leave without telling you what was going on."

"But—"

"I'm giving it to you straight: we were lovers. And if you doubt it, I've got proof. Remember that locket you gave her for her seventh birthday? Remember how you painted it with clear nail-polish to keep it from turning her neck green, and ended up gluing it to her skin?"

"Yes," she whispered. "I remember."

"Do you believe me now?"

She closed her eyes. "Yes." This man knew Charla. Had known her.

"Charla hated that jerk she was married to. Really despised him. She was planning to file for divorce when she got back from the Paris job."

"Are you saying *Frank* had something to do with her death?" Garland demanded, her eyes popping open in shock.

"Isn't it always the husband?"

"Frank was in California that weekend. I called him at the hotel myself."

"Hell." He made an odd sound, half snort, half chuckle. "I really wanted to blame him."

Garland understood; she wanted to be able to blame *someone*. She wanted to be able to point at her sister's murderer and say 'He did it.' "Look, Mr.—" He didn't volunteer his name, so she continued without it. "You have to go to the police with this."

"No, I don't. Look, lady, I liked Charla a lot. Maybe I even loved her—I don't know. We had some real good times. But I'm not getting mixed up in a murder case."

"But—"

"And don't give me that crap about doing the right thing. I was good to Charla. Now she's dead, and I've got to look out for myself."

"Don't you want her killer caught?" Garland asked softly.

He made that strange noise again, part snort and part

chuckle. "Yeah, I want him caught. But what I know won't help that."

"You can't be sure of that," she said, desperate to convince him before he slipped away from her. "Something small, something you might think insignificant, might be the key to finding him. You *can't* walk away. Promise me you'll talk to the police!"

"I had a little trouble with the law a couple of years ago," he said. "Do you really think the police are going to believe *me?* Hell, they'll probably throw my butt in jail; after all, I was probably the last one to see Charla alive."

"I'll get you a lawyer—"

"There aren't any lawyers that good."

"Please!"

The phone went dead.

"Oh, don't go!" she muttered under her breath as she stabbed at the disconnect button with her forefinger. "Oh, please!"

It was no use. He was gone. She knew he wasn't going to call the police. Well, *she* didn't have such qualms. He said he'd had trouble with the police before, and that meant mug shots and fingerprints. He could be found.

But first, she had to have a talk with Frank. Maybe he already knew about his wife's affair. He certainly wouldn't be the first husband—or wife, for that matter—who had endured an intolerable situation in the hope of salvaging his marriage. Garland certainly knew what *that* was like. And if he didn't know, she wanted to be the one to tell him. Not strangers, not police detectives, and certainly not the newspapers.

"No, Milo, I'm not going to discuss it with you first," she murmured under her breath. He'd probably insist on going with her, or worse, put her decision up to a committee vote. Garland began to understand how Charla must have felt about *her* sometimes.

She did leave a note saying where she was going, however. After propping the paper against the telephone, she put her coat on and slipped out of the store.

Chapter Twelve

Garland parked in front of the tidy brick building that housed Frank's practice. Big old oak trees hovered close, their winter-nude lower branches eerily illumined by the floodlights. The perfect setting for the Gingerbread Cottage, waiting with sinister patience for greedy little girls and boys to come take a taste.

But the building itself was much too prosaically red-brick and square for any such night-borne fancies. Staid, that was the word for it, Garland thought. The door precisely in the center. Two windows precisely positioned on either side of it. Out front, in the precise center of the small strip of grass that separated the office from the parking lot, was a tastefully painted sign said *Granby Psychiatric Associates, Director: Franklin R. Hollister, M.D.*

Frank was still working, she knew; his car was parked in the spot nearest the entrance.

She sat in the van for a few moments, trying to get her thoughts in order. As much as she wanted to learn if Frank knew about Charla's infidelity, she hated to just walk in and ask, "Did you know Charla was having an affair?" There had to be a gentler way.

Resting her forehead on the steering wheel, she muttered, "Charla, Charla, Charla—you really left things in a mess, honey."

Then she straightened, gathered up her purse and keys, and strode to the front door. To her surprise, she found it unlocked. It was nearly ten o'clock—odd that Frank was seeing patients at this hour. The waiting room was dark, lit only by a single lamp in the far corner. There was no one at the reception desk, so she went through the door at the back.

Beyond that was a short hallway, pierced by three doors. The first one she tried was the bathroom. The second, a storage closet. The third must be Frank's office, then. After knocking and getting no answer, she opened the door and peered in. It was a pleasant room, undoubtedly arranged to put people at ease. A sofa and two chairs were arranged cozily around a cherry coffee table. A few paintings, nonthreatening in their pastel simplicity, hung upon the walls. Frank, however, was nowhere to be seen.

"Frank?" she called softly. "Frank?"

There was no answer. Strange that he would go out, even for a short time, and leave the place unlocked. As she turned to go, she noticed another door half-hidden behind a lovely Japanese screen. Frank's private office perhaps? She moved forward, her footsteps silent upon the thick, fawn-colored carpet.

"Here goes," she said under her breath. Her stomach churned with apprehension.

The door was closed but not latched, and swung ajar easily under the pressure of her hand. A large traditional desk occupied the center of the room. A brown leather executive chair was turned away from the door, but Garland could see the top of Frank's neat gray head above the back of the chair. He was facing the portrait of Charla that hung on the wall behind the desk. His right hand, just visible from this angle, was holding a glass.

Garland's gaze moved over the ice bucket and half-empty bottle of Scotch upon the desk, then lifted to the portrait. It was a large painting, nearly life-size. Charla was wearing a strapless red evening gown and long white gloves. A white fur cape was draped over her left shoulder, and a magnificent diamond-and-ruby necklace adorned her slim throat. Her hair was pulled back in a severe chignon that made her look cool and austere—ice against the flame red of her dress.

Trembling, Garland raised her hand to her own throat. That picture had graced the cover of *Cosmopolitan* twelve years ago. Charla's first big break. Seeing it brought back memories in a flood that held her speechless for a moment. And Frank . . . did he look at it and mourn the loss of the woman he loved? Or did he look at it and see a faithless wife?

It was time to find out. Taking a deep breath, she opened the door wider. Before she could speak, however, Frank rose from the chair with an abrupt movement that surprised her. He stepped closer to the painting and tilted his head back to look at it.

Then he hurled his glass into Charla's face.

Garland stood transfixed for a moment, staring at the liquid dripping down the canvas. Her gaze shifted to Frank. His shoulders were hunched forward—she could see the strain on his expensive suit jacket—and he looked like a man in pain.

No, not pain. Hate. She didn't know why she was so certain of it, but she was. The force of his hate was an almost palpable thing to her, a sickening blow in the guts. She had to talk to him. She had to look into his face when she asked him if he knew Charla was having an affair. But not now. She couldn't bear the thought of seeing that hate on his face.

So she backed away, then turned and stumbled back to the waiting room. A few minutes' respite was what she needed; maybe it would blunt the power of what she had seen. A few minutes, and then she'd go back in and ask him what she wanted to know.

Standing in the doorway of the dimly lit room, she could almost see phantoms lurking in the dark places behind the furniture. The ghosts of Frank and Charla's marriage: lies, secrets and betrayal, lost years and shattered dreams. Garland knew them all. She'd felt them all. There had been times during her divorce when she'd wished something terrible would happen to Garry. But not death. Never death. Had Frank been the same? Had he wished for his wife's death, then been horrified when his wish had come true? Or was there only the hatred?

"Hell," she muttered, feeling along the wall for the light switch. She didn't want to sit in the dark with those demons, either Frank's or her own.

The fluorescent overhead lights flared to comforting life. Garland sat in a chair facing the front door and picked up a magazine from the table beside her. *National Geographic.* The first article was about snow leopards, and quite interesting.

Cold air swirled around her ankles. Surprised, she looked up to see a man standing just inside the door. She hadn't heard a thing. Before her surprise could turn to alarm, however, he slid into a chair and picked up a magazine. Her breath went out in relief; obviously, he was one of Frank's patients. She returned her attention to the *Geographic.*

She couldn't seem to concentrate, however, for some sixth sense kept nagging at her to look up. Finally, she did. The newcomer was staring at her. He didn't speak, so she forced herself to return to the magazine. Still overly aware of his gaze on her, she found herself reading the same sentence over and over.

After a while, she glanced up to find him still staring at her. He was young, somewhere around twenty. Regular features, the sort of face you see every day. But his eyes, a washed-out-looking blue, were incredibly intense, made even more so by the fact that he had virtually no eyelashes.

Without looking away from her, he turned a page of his magazine. He was still wearing his gloves, she noticed. Odd. The thought occurred to her that Frank was a psychiatrist, and that some of his patients might not be screwed in all that well. *This* one, perhaps. Maybe she should try to talk to him.

"Are you waiting for Dr. Hollister?" she asked.

His eyes didn't waver. "Yes. Are you?"

"I was, but if you have an appointment, I should come back another time."

"I don't have an appointment," he said. "I just need to talk to him."

Garland crossed her legs nervously, then uncrossed them. *Need* to talk to him, he'd said. Why would he *need* to talk to his psychiatrist at ten o'clock at night?

"Do you always wear your hair like that?" he asked.

She reached up automatically to touch her blunt-cut shoulder-length hair. "Y-yes, I do." *Oh, boy!*

"It's pretty."

"Thanks." Slowly, she got up from her chair. "I think I'll go see if Dr. Hollister is available."

He opened his magazine, but didn't look away from her. Just before Garland reached the hall door, however, Frank opened it and peered into the waiting room. His startled gaze went to Garland, then moved past her to the young man. Surprise turned to consternation, and then Frank's face became impassive. Garland watched with interest; it was as though an invisible hand had passed over the doctor's face, erasing emotion as it moved.

Frank's gaze was still focused on the young man. "What are you doing here?" the doctor asked.

"Talking to this nice lady," the young man said. He rose from his seat, turning briefly to return the magazine from the stack from which he'd gotten it. "Do you have a couple of minutes to spare, Dr. Hollister?"

"Yes." Frank ran his hands over his hair again. There it was, Garland thought. That telltale nervous movement she was coming to know well. "Yes, of course. Come on back."

As he turned away, the doctor glanced over his shoulder at Garland. "I'm sorry, Garland. Perhaps another time . . ."

"We need to talk, Frank. Tonight." she said. He wasn't going to slip away from her. Not this time. Not after what she'd seen in the other room.

"Very well." Turning away again, he ushered the young man through the rear door.

Before sitting down again, Garland went and locked the front door. She wasn't about to share this waiting room with any more of Frank's patients. The last one had given her the willies.

Frank returned a few minutes later without the young man. "I let him out the back door," he explained.

"That didn't take long," Garland said.

"He only wanted a bit of reassurance." Settling in the chair beside Garland's, he said, "Now what can I do for you?"

"I want to talk to you. How about coming with me to the All Nightspot for a cup of coffee?"

He shook his head. "Come into the office. I'll make us some."

Garland would have preferred the neutral ground of a restaurant. But then, she reflected as she followed him back to his inner sanctum, maybe there was no neutral ground. Not with what they had to discuss.

Charla's portrait had been wiped dry. And Frank looked as cool as a cucumber, not even glancing at the picture as he entered the room.

"Let's get some coffee going," he said. He swung open the doors of a built-in cabinet to reveal a neat little kitchenette. Taking a streamlined chrome coffeemaker down from a shelf, he did things to its innards and then plugged it in.

"Come, my dear, sit down while we wait for it to brew." Extending his arm, he shepherded Garland to one of the leather armchairs in front of his desk.

He sat in the executive chair, putting the polished width of the desk and several inches in height between them. It also put Garland at a psychological disadvantage, which she was sure was deliberate.

She decided to dive right in. "I came here to talk to you about Charla."

"Charla? I don't know what—"

"A man called me tonight." Taking a deep breath, Garland let the next sentence spill out fast and hard. "He said he and Charla had been having an affair."

Frank's face might have been made of stone for all the emotion it showed. "I don't believe it."

Yes, you do. "He was very convincing."

"I don't believe it." His knuckles had turned white, she

noticed. "Who was he? What did he tell you?"

Suddenly she felt very sorry for him. "Frank, if you know something that might help the police find Charla's killer, you have to tell them."

"The police have already asked a great many questions about my marriage," he snapped. "After that, they moved on to the amount of her insurance policy and who was the beneficiary."

"It's their job to ask those questions, Frank. And you're avoiding the issue: did you or did you not know that Charla was having an affair?"

"My wife was *not* having an affair."

Garland shook her head. "This guy knew something only a very good friend of Charla's—or mine—would know. Something from our childhood. *I* believed him."

"I do not."

Garland folded her arms over her chest. "I've got to go to the police with this. I'm sorry."

"Of course you must do what you think is right. I will, of course, have to disagree if the police ask me about it." His mouth was stretched so tight that Garland almost thought she saw the outlines of his teeth behind them.

"Of course." If he were another person, Garland would have reached out and taken his hands in hers. She knew his pain. And for Frank, this terribly inward-turning and private person, to have his wife's infidelities tossed into the public arena would be intolerable.

This was the first time since Charla's murder that Garland felt she'd actually connected with him. There might never be another, so she brought up a subject she hadn't intended to discuss.

"Frank, about Amber and Annalese—"

"The girls?" He stared at her in surprise. "What about the girls?"

"I feel as though you're shutting me away from them, Frank."

"Why do you feel that way?" he asked. His voice was coolly remote; they might as well have been discussing a matter completely unrelated to him.

Garland was not about to let him get away so easily. "Your nanny refused to let me see them tonight, and all but told me to make an appointment next time."

"Xenia was only following instructions. As a psychiatrist and a father, I thought it best that they spend a few quiet evenings at home after all the excitement they've had lately. I must admit that Xenia is very correct and formal. If her manner offended you, I'm sorry."

Garland shook her head again. "I don't think we're on the same track here."

"Charla took great advantage of you where the children were concerned," he said. "I don't intend to do the same. Xenia is an excellent nanny, and comes with numerous recommendations."

She closed her eyes, opened them again. *The man is a psychiatrist, for God's sake! How can he be so damn blind about his own children?* "They don't need a nanny, Frank. They need me. And most of all, they need you."

"And I've been there for them. I've explained every stage of grief. They know what they're feeling and why, and what to expect as time goes on."

Garland rose to her feet. Putting her hands flat on the desk, she leaned forward, right into his "personal space." Although he didn't move, she saw the withdrawal in his eyes. "Go home, Frank. Talk to Amber and Annalese. Don't analyze them. *Talk* to them. Ask them about school. Ask them about clothes or their friends or, or anything! Be their friend."

He shook his head. "A parent's role is not to be a friend. Children need guidance and discipline."

"Oh, Frank." Garland sighed. He was right, and yet so very wrong. *His* daughters needed his love and friendship along with the discipline, they needed to comfort him and be comforted. "You've missed so much," she said, sinking back into her chair.

Frank stared at her, obviously not getting it at all. Then he clasped his hands on the desktop again. "I'll speak to Xenia tomorrow. We'll set up some sort of schedule for you to visit with the girls."

"How kind of you." Garland's temper was going, and fast. She controlled it; seeing the girls—even on Frank's schedule—was more important than the personal satisfaction she'd get from telling him exactly what she thought of him.

He stood up. "It's very late. Come, I'll walk you to your car."

"Oh, that won't be necessary," Garland said, rising to her feet. "I'm parked right out front."

"I'm leaving anyway." Retrieving a briefcase from the floor beside his chair, he came around the desk.

As she followed him out the door, Garland paused to look over her shoulder at Charla's portrait. "She was very beautiful, wasn't she?"

"Yes." Frank smoothed his hair with his free hand. "Very, very beautiful." *He* didn't look at the portrait.

He turned off lights as they went through the office, leaving only the corner light on in the waiting room. Escorting Garland to her van, he waited until she locked the door.

Garland rolled her window down. "Think about what I said, Frank. About the girls."

"I will . . . Ah!" With a hiss of surprise, he said, "I forgot to unplug the coffeepot. Go on home, Garland. I'll be fine." He strode back toward the building.

Garland waited to see if he was going to come out, or if he'd just used that excuse to get rid of her. It was cold in the van, so she started the engine and pushed the button marked HEAT. A glance in the rearview mirror told her that she could give Medusa a run for her money. She dug through her purse for her brush.

She brushed her hair slowly, thinking about the conversation she and Frank had had. Talking to Frank always left her unsatisfied. Something deeper than speech—some connection that didn't get made no matter how clear the words had been. Had it been like that for Charla? If so, Garland could understood a little of her sister's motivation to stray.

Five minutes went by, and still no Frank. Garland's

brush moved slower and slower, more as something to do to pass the time than to actually groom her hair. Ten more minutes went by, and she realized Frank wasn't coming out anytime soon.

"Face it, darlin'," she said in her best Milo-ish manner, "you've been given the bum's rush. And you didn't even get that cup of coffee he promised you."

Putting the van into gear, she backed out of the parking lot and headed for home.

The man watched the van pull out. He'd parked here, waiting for her to come out. Perfect camouflage; these old houses had been divided into apartments, and there were dozens of other cars parked along the street. The tree branches hung out over the street, holding the darkness pooled beneath them.

She drew up beside him for a moment, so close that he could have spoken to her had their windows been open. But she didn't look. No one ever did. No one ever really *saw* the hunter until it was too late. *She* wouldn't either. But there was one thing that would be different with her: she would know him, at the end. She would understand the hunt. He'd make sure she understood.

He ran his thumbnail over his chin as the van moved away. Soon the only thing visible was the swiftly disappearing glow of the taillights.

He stared at the twin red points through narrowed eyes. She really was perfect. The best one yet. In one way he wanted to take her now, this minute; in another, he wanted to draw it out as long as possible. To savor the anticipation.

She fascinated him. He'd never felt so close, so completely in tune with anyone before. The sight of her brushing her hair just a few yards away had nearly pulled him out of his car to her. The brush—a white one—had moved through her smooth dark hair slowly, oh, so slowly, while the sweat broke out on his face.

He closed his eyes. But he didn't stop seeing the brush.

But this was a blue brush, wielded by a different hand. A child's hand, chubby and unformed, a bit grubby around the fingernails.

His hand. Brushing and brushing. His mother's hair, brushing and brushing.

"Oh, that feels good, Davey," she crooned, dipping her head forward so the weight of her shoulder-length hair swung forward against her cheeks.

He was on the sofa, his skinny kid-legs tucked beneath him.

His mother was sitting on the floor in front of him. The TV was on—*Dallas*, her favorite. The dingy little apartment was hot despite the fan that stirred the stale air. A trickle of sweat inched down his spine.

He kept brushing. Slowly, to make it last. One hundred strokes every night. He loved doing this, loved the closeness and the way her eyes closed in pleasure. Loved how the brush moved through her hair, smoothing it to silk. Loved being close to her, surrounded by the scent of flowers that rose from her hair and skin.

"You're such a good boy," she said.

He wriggled in pleasure. For this time, these precious few minutes, she was completely his. He wished it could last forever.

But always at the back of his mind, like a black, spreading cancer, was the knowledge that it wouldn't last. It was Friday night. Soon she wouldn't be his any longer.

"Don't go to work tonight, Mama. Please?" Eighty-eight strokes, eighty-nine, ninety. Almost done. Her hair was smooth as silk, shadow-dark against the white skin of her neck. His hand moved slower.

"I've got to work, honey. We've got rent to pay and food to buy," she said. "You're a big boy now, nearly seven years old. You're not afraid to stay by yourself for a few hours, are you?"

Yes. But he didn't say it; he was nearly seven years old, wasn't he? "No, Mama. I just wish you could stay with me. We could play a game or something. There's . . . there's a movie on, I think." Desperate, a child's voice gabbling the words.

"I can't." She climbed to her feet.

But I only got to ninety-six! "I'm not finished, Mama."

"I've got to go," she said, adjusting the straps of her halter top. "It's Friday night, baby. I make most of my money on the weekends."

But I only got to ninety-six! He didn't dare say anything, though. She'd remember what he'd said, and when she got home, smelling funny—not of flowers, but something else—she'd drag him out of bed and yell at him. Always the weekend. Friday and Saturday.

But I only got to ninety-six! Silently, he watched her walk out the door.

The living room faded to blackness, and the man found himself staring at the backs of his own eyelids. He opened his eyes. His hands were gripping the steering wheel with cramping force.

"You should have said it," he said through his teeth. "She always came home and did it to you anyway."

Peeling his fingers off the wheel, he flexed them slowly. Then he started the car and drove to the 7-Eleven that was just a few blocks away. He went to the pay phone outside and dialed the number of the Norfolk police.

"Detective Baedecker or Grange, please," he told the man who answered.

Another voice came on the line. "Grange here."

"There's a body you didn't find," David said.

"What's your name?"

"Never mind that. Take a look in the trees off Lytton Drive about a mile down from the overpass."

"Wait! Don't go yet!" the detective said, his voice urgent, too loud.

"Happy hunting." David hung up. He stood there for a moment, smiling, feeling the power bubble up inside him. Things must really be hopping at the station now. He couldn't wait to see the newspaper headlines tomorrow.

"Fame and fortune," he murmured as he dropped another quarter into the phone. "Fame and fortune."

This time he dialed *her* number. He wanted to hear her

voice again. There was this strange, growing urge to tell her all about his triumphs. He'd resisted it, resisted calling her. But after seeing her tonight, so near and so completely perfect, he couldn't hold back any longer. If she hadn't gotten home yet, he'd keep calling until she did. Her recorded voice was better than nothing.

But instead of her answering machine, he got a phone company recording telling him that her number had been changed. Breathing heavily, he leaned his forehead against the cool surface of the phone. He'd expected this—all those reporters hounding her. It was just that he'd needed to talk to her . . . Never mind. He'd take care of it. Straightening, he went back to his car and started the engine.

He took the Midtown tunnel into Portsmouth. The drive over the West Norfolk Bridge was always nicer at night; he could almost imagine what the scene must have been like a hundred years ago, before the chemical plants and docks and rusty metal barges had taken over.

Passing through Portsmouth without stopping, he took Kings Highway toward Chuckatuck and home. He liked living in the country. It was quiet, and a man could do what he pleased without people putting their noses into his business. He'd always lived in cities when he was a kid—his mother's profession required it—and there were always too many people around.

As he reached a stretch of road bordered by peanut fields and not much else, he saw a car parked on the shoulder of the road. The vehicle's emergency lights were flashing, and the hood was up. His headlights caught a woman standing in front of it.

He pulled onto the shoulder behind the disabled car, leaving his engine running and the lights on, and walked toward the woman. Gravel crunched under his feet. His heartbeat accelerated when he saw that she had dark hair.

"Do you need help, miss?" he asked.

She squinted at him, a wary look on her face. He realized that he was only a silhouette to her with the light at his back like this. Stopping, he shifted so she could see his face. That seemed to reassure her.

"I don't know what happened," she said, waving her hand at the engine in obvious disgust. "It was running fine, then all of a sudden it cut out. I haven't been able to get the stupid thing started again."

He moved closer. As he got his first good look at her, disappointment warred with the itch of anticipation that hung between his shoulder blades. She was considerably overweight—he'd never been much for large women. And her permed hair had been drawn back into a kinky ponytail that didn't appeal to him at all. Still, she had fallen into his lap, so to speak, so he couldn't waste her. Waste not, want not, as the proverb went.

"It couldn't be the battery," she said. "I just had a new one put in a couple of months ago."

"You didn't hear a noise before it quit?"

"No. Well, I had the stereo on, and it would have had to be a pretty loud noise for me to hear it."

"I don't know much about cars," he confessed, peering down into the convoluted innards of the engine. "Why don't I just drive you to a gas station and get you someone who knows what he's doing? You probably need a tow, anyway."

He saw her glance around, weighing going with him as opposed to sitting out here in the dark. Quietly, he waited for her to decide. *He* knew what she'd do. After all, it was ride with him or a very long walk. Besides, he was a clean-cut young man, polite manners, pleasant voice. The perfect Good Samaritan.

Finally she said, "I live about five miles down the road. If you could give me a ride home, I'd appreciate it."

"No problem at all." He closed the hood. "Why don't you turn your flashers off? You're just going to wear your battery down."

"All right." Reaching into the car, she turned off the emergency lights and retrieved her purse before following him back to his car.

He opened the passenger door for her and helped her with the seatbelt. Then he slid behind the wheel and put the car into gear. As he drove, he felt the power coursing through him. Sweet and sharp, and this time, fully in control. He glanced down at her stocking-covered legs.

This time he was going to improvise.

Chapter Thirteen

Kurt Baedecker and Jeff Grange stood on the shoulder of Lytton Drive and watched the Virgina Beach crew finish bagging the body. Found, Baedecker reflected, just where the caller said it would be. The night was full of flashing lights as Kenny Capeshaw, Homicide, came walking up to them.

"I can't tell you how much I appreciate you giving me a corpse late on Friday night," Kenny said.

Jeff chuckled. "Hey, anything for a friend."

Rubbing his cheek absently with one finger, Baedecker considered this new victim. Female, Caucasian, blond and blue, mid- to late twenties. By her clothes, she'd been a prostitute. Unlike Bambi Henks, however, this woman had been killed by one slash of the killer's knife—a single, tremendous stroke that had nearly severed her head. "How long do you think she's been here?" he asked the other two detectives.

Kenny shrugged. "Couple of weeks. He didn't do it here, not enough blood. A nice tidy job; he slit her throat, then brought her out here and tucked her in the bushes. If we hadn't been told where to look, I don't think she'd *ever* have been found."

Two weeks, Baedecker thought. That would put it right around the time of Charla Ross's murder. Curiouser and curiouser.

"That caller of yours is a real interesting guy," Kenny said. "I'd like to have a nice, long talk with him."

Baedecker gave a humorless bark of laughter. "Who wouldn't?"

"What I want to know," Kenny said, "is why he called you when he dumped her in Virginia Beach."

"Aha," Baedecker said. "Now that's the sixty-four-thousand-dollar question, isn't it? Either he isn't aware of the various jurisdictions around here, or he is—and wants to make sure we"—he indicated Jeff and himself—"know about this particular murder."

"Think it's the same boy who did Charla Ross and Bambi Henks?" Jeff asked.

Baedecker heaved a sigh. "I hate to think we've got two fellas who like knives and hate women."

"Yeah." Kenny pulled out a pack of cigarettes and lit one. The smoke curled above his head, reflecting the flashing red and blue lights eerily. "What say we go back and compare notes."

"I think we'd better," Baedecker said. "And notify the other city departments to keep their eyes and ears open. Just in case."

Garland was busy at The Tome all day Saturday. While Milo took care of customers, she sat on the floor in the back room looking through a new shipment of books. Pricing them, cataloging them, and putting them out on the shelves took most of the day. When the store closed at four o'clock, she was more than ready to go. Milo seemed to be in a bigger hurry than she was.

"Got a date tonight?" she asked, shrugging into her coat.

"Yeah. You should see this woman; she's just come here from Hawaii, a former Miss Wackahula or something. Really, really gorgeous. Really, really lonely." He twirled an imaginary mustache.

So are you, Garland thought, reaching up to pat his cheek. "Have a good time, Milo," she said.

As she drove home, she pondered the problem of Milo. Poor guy; he had women practically falling from trees onto him, and the one he truly wanted—Troll—didn't seem to be interested. So, Milo being Milo, he drowned himself in casual affairs instead of staying home alone.

"And who's to say he's wrong?" she said aloud. "At least he's not afraid to try."

Now *that* was a sobering thought. It put her mind on a loneliness/need/fear-of-getting-hurt-again loop that took her to the entrance to her neighborhood. As she made the turn onto her street, she saw Colin's Oldsmobile parked under the streetlight in front of her house. He was leaning against the rear fender, his shoulders hunched against the cold.

Temptation on the hoof. In the flesh, rather—and chilly flesh at that. Pulling into the driveway, she got out of her car and walked toward him. "You look cold," she said.

"I am." He blew into his cupped hands. "You're wondering why I didn't wait in the car."

"The thought did occur to me."

Instead of answering, he reached over and opened the rear door. The cat sailed out of the car, his tail held high in indignation. She swung round to stare at Colin, her own indignation surging to high tide.

"You didn't," she said.

He nodded. "A gift from my house to yours."

"Ah." Crossing her arms over her chest, she said, "This gift didn't want to come, or you wouldn't have been standing out here freezing your butt off."

"He didn't like the car," Colin admitted. "And he didn't like me for putting him in it."

"Colin, I can't take him."

"Why not? He likes *you.*"

"But . . ." She fumbled for an excuse, any excuse. "It wouldn't be fair; I'm gone most of the time."

"That's not what I hear. Anyway, *he* won't care as long as you stock plenty of canned tuna." Taking her by the arm, he ushered her toward the house. "Besides, he's a good watch . . . cat. Bit the mailman today."

"Dogs bite mailmen, not cats," Garland said.

"Tell *him* that."

"His name is Numbnuts, for God's sake."

Colin leaned into the car and pulled out a paper grocery sack. "I thought the least I could do was bring you a few cans of tuna."

The cat was sitting on the front porch waiting to be let in. Garland was now backed to her last line of defense. "You should have called first, Colin."

"And give you a chance to say no? Uh-uh."

"Ducks nest in my yard every spring."

Colin shook his head. "Not anymore."

"My neighbors have a big dog."

"So do mine. It took Numbnuts three days to teach the dog proper etiquette."

"What about my bird feeder?" she demanded as they went up the steps. "I love watching the birds."

"So does he."

Garland looked into the cat's slitted golden eyes, then into Colin's clear green ones. "I ought to throw you both out."

"Why don't you?" Colin asked softly.

Just as softly, she replied. "I don't know."

The cat rose and began to twine around her ankles, leaving a thick coating of hair on her jeans. He was hungry. With a sigh, Garland unlocked the door and pushed it open. The cat walked straight back to the kitchen.

While Garland put her purse and keys away, Colin set the bag on the kitchen counter and began unloading it. The cat sat at his feet, demanding that he hurry.

"Where's your can opener?" Colin asked.

"Second drawer to the right of the sink." Garland bustled into the kitchen, then stopped short at the sight of the pile of cans on the counter. "You didn't have to bring a lifetime supply, you know."

Colin opened cabinets until he found the dishes. "This is only two weeks' worth," he said, emptying the contents of the can into a bowl. "He eats two a day."

Making a mental note to wean the cat onto a regular cat diet, Garland said, "I'm not calling him Numbnuts. I won't own a cat called Numbnuts."

"Want to go get something to eat?" Colin asked.

"Well, actually, I ordered a pizza before leaving the store. It should be here in"—she glanced at her watch—"about five minutes. Why don't you stay and help me eat it?"

"If you let me buy."

She shook her head. "Let's call it part payment for that nasty remark I made the other day."

"Not necessary, Garland. I got pretty personal."

"Yes, you did." Looking straight into his eyes, she said, "With the ratio of women to men the way it is, I don't understand why you bother with a thirty-nine-year-old woman with as much baggage as I'm carrying. Hell, there are probably a couple of hundred young women out there with no wrinkles and no encumbrances who'd be thrilled to be with you."

He took a step closer, then another. Gently, he stroked her cheek with the back of his hand. "Is that what your ex-husband did? Found a younger woman?"

"Yeah." Her gaze wavered. "Twenty-three years old. She worshiped the ground he walked on."

"I don't want to be worshiped," Colin said.

"What do you want?"

"I want you. Thirty-nine years old, wrinkles, baggage and all."

"Why now? Why after all this time?"

"Admit it, Garland. You never looked at me before. I was just one of the Friday night crowd, all safe and secure and labeled nonthreatening." He took her hands and placed them flat against his chest. "Things have changed, though, haven't they?"

She drew in her breath sharply, surprised by the effect that contact had on her. He was solid, tight-packed with muscle, his heartbeat quick and strong beneath her palms. She stood frozen, her fingers splayed out across his chest. Even when he let go of her hands, she couldn't move them. Didn't want to move them. "I still haven't dealt with Charla's death," she whispered.

"You will. But it'll take time, and life isn't going to go

on hold while you do it."

"You mean *you're* not going to go on hold."

"I'm only human, Garland. This feels right, it feels good, and I've waited a damn long time already."

"I don't know if I can feel the right things. I don't know if I can feel at all." *Liar! You're afraid!*

"Why don't we try it and see?" Leaning forward, he kissed her cheek, her jaw, the corner of her mouth.

Tenderness surged through her, surprising companion to the tide of primal body heat that followed his caress. As welcome as the desire was, it was the tenderness that was truly precious. She'd thought it lost forever, burned out of her by another man's rejection. And here it was again; for Colin, with Colin.

"Does this feel wrong?" he murmured, nibbling on her lower lip. "Want me to stop?"

"No. Don't stop." She closed her eyes as he moved to nibble on her upper lip.

Instinctively, she shifted her head, seeking greater contact with his mouth. He refused it, however, running his parted lips over hers but not kissing her fully. She became more aggressive, wanting more, demanding more. Still he continued to tease her, kissing her neck, tracing the line of her open mouth with his tongue, but never giving her what she wanted.

"You're not playing fair," she gasped.

"Yes, I am." He ran his hands down her back, making her arch into his palms.

With a muttered sound of frustration, she moved against him fully, reveling in the discovery that he was as aroused as she was. He felt good—really good—his flesh sturdy and warm and comfortingly familiar. A rush of sweet, sharp desire made her tremble. She'd never expected this, didn't want to stop. It was such a surprise to feel this way now when her life seemed to be on a flight path to nowhere.

"Kiss me, damn it," she said.

He did, his mouth coming down on hers eagerly. But still gentle, still patient, still in control. Wanting to shatter that control, Garland wound her fingers in his hair and pulled him closer.

The doorbell rang, startling them both.

"Shit," Colin muttered. "I forgot about the pizza."

"I'll get it."

"No, let me." Sighing deeply, he let go of her and took a step backward. "You look like a kid who's been caught necking," he said.

Garland's face was as hot as her insides. "I *feel* like a kid who's been caught necking."

"We could shove the money under the door and tell him to leave the pizza on the porch."

Tempting, Garland thought. Oh, so tempting. But now that he wasn't touching her, the decision had become intellectual rather than visceral. And this was happening much too fast. Too fast, too strong. Regretfully, she shook her head.

His smile faded. Taking her by the elbows, he lifted her up onto her tiptoes and kissed her deeply. Even after he let her go to answer the door, she felt his touch on her skin like a memory of heat.

She was busy setting the table when Colin came back with the pizza. The cat was in attendance, loudly demanding a share.

"You'll get some, don't worry," Colin growled, gently moving the animal aside with his foot.

"What do you want to drink?" Garland asked.

"Do you have any beer?"

"Yes." She got two beers, popped them open, and brought them to the table.

Colin distributed slices of pizza—one to Garland, one to himself, one to the cat. "Why did you rush off last night?" he asked.

"That call was from a man who claimed to be Charla's lover. He said she planned to divorce Frank when she got back from Paris."

"Do you believe him?"

"Yes, I believe him." With a sigh, she leaned her elbows on the table. "He called to tell me about the affair because he thought Frank had something to do with her death."

Colin sat back, chewing his pizza thoughtfully. Swallowing, he said, "Frank was in California. There are a couple of hundred witnesses to that."

"I know. I've been through every logical argument I can think of, and I still can't shake the feeling that something strange is going on with Frank." She hesitated, trying to organize her thoughts; some hadn't been focused at all, but mere shadows flitting around her mind. Putting them into words, however, forced her to clarify them. And Colin, bless him, gave her the time she needed. Milo talked so much he never gave her a chance to think things through.

Finally she continued, "When I saw Frank throw that glass at Charla's face, I was stunned by the raw hate in every line of his body. I know it sounds crazy—"

"Not to an artist."

"What? Oh, you're right." She banged her fist down on the table. "I wish you'd been there! I mean, in retrospect the whole thing seems absurd. It might have been grief . . . well, not grief exactly, but frustration at not knowing whether her killer will ever be caught and punished. I *know* how that feels."

"But . . ." Colin prompted.

"But I can't shake it. It was anger, Colin. And not anger at himself—I know how that feels, too. Anger at Charla."

"Then he knows about the affair."

"I'm sure of it. The real kicker is: did he know *who* she was having an affair with?"

Colin cocked his head to one side. "Does it matter?"

"Every piece of the puzzle is important."

"Did you talk to Milo about this?" Colin asked.

Garland made a face. "Unfortunately. He has no problem believing Frank capable of murder; as Milo has said many times—usually in Frank's hearing—psychiatrists are crazier than their patients."

"Crazy enough to what . . . hire a hit man?" Colin slid a second piece of pizza onto his plate. "C'mon, Garland. You don't really buy that, do you?"

"No-o-o." Still, her mind worried at it, taking it apart, putting it back together. "But I can't help remembering what Detective Baedecker said about most murders being committed by someone who knows the victim and who has something to gain."

"Frank is already rich," Colin said through a mouthful.

"Some people don't like to share." She pushed her pizza around her plate with her finger. "And to quote Milo, 'Charla had a million bucks in insurance. Even to a Hollister, that's worth killing for.' "

"Too melodramatic."

"You're right." She lifted her shoulders. "What *I* think would pop Frank's cork is the divorce itself. You've been through it; think of what it would be like to have every private facet of your married life examined by the tabloids. Think what it would be like for *Frank*."

Colin dropped his half-eaten slice of pizza onto his plate. "Are you saying that you think Frank had your sister killed?"

"Well, no, not exactly. But if he does know who Charla's lover was, he's withholding that information from the police."

"And what if it has nothing to do with her murder?"

"What if it does?" she asked.

"Whoa. Take a breath, honey. Look, I'm the first guy to admit that divorce can severely test a person's scruples. But you're talking about a man letting his wife's murderer go free. That's real cold-blooded."

Cold-blooded. Now that certainly sounds like Frank. "Are you saying I'm wrong? That I misinterpreted what I saw?"

He shook his head slowly. "No. I believe you. I've seen rage in the attitudes of a person's body. I've seen hate. This hit you so strongly that I don't see how you could have been mistaken."

"Oh God, Colin! You don't know how good it is to hear that."

"But I know you. And I'm basing my judgment on that, not on the apparent facts of the case. You'll have trouble convincing the police."

"I've got to try. Something stinks here, and Frank's acting weird—even for him. I can't let it go until I find out why."

Colin studied her thoughtfully. After a moment he said, "What if the police can't find anything? Will you be able to let it go then?"

"I . . . don't know."

The phone shrilled. With a sigh, Garland went to answer it.

"Aunt Garland?"

Amber's voice sounded blurred, as though she'd been crying. Garland stiffened. "Is something the matter, sweetheart?" she asked.

"Can you come over?"

"Can I come over?" Garland repeated, raising her eyebrows interrogatively as she glanced at Colin. He crossed his arms over his chest, looking resigned. Returning her attention to Amber, she asked, "Is something wrong, sweetheart?"

"N-no. We just want to see you."

The child sounded too plaintive for that to be entirely true. "Is your father there, Amber?"

"No. He's still working. Are you going to come, Aunt Garland?"

"Let me talk to your nanny." Xenia came on the line, and Garland didn't even wait for her to say hello. "Xenia, this is Miss Ross. I'll be over shortly to visit my nieces."

The woman sounded flustered. "Well, I . . . have you asked Dr. Hollister?"

Screw Dr. Hollister. Aloud, however, Garland said, "No, I have not. Nor do I intend to."

"Very well, Miss Ross."

Garland hung up. There, she'd done it. Out-Hollistered the Hollisters. Putting her hands on her hips, she glared at Colin. "Go ahead and say it: I sounded just like Frank."

"You sounded just like Frank."

"I'll be damned if I'm going to let some hired nursemaid keep me away from Amber and Annalese."

"No, ma'am. Yes, ma'am. Whatever you say, ma'am." Colin ripped off a crisp salute, then climbed to his feet. "Take good care of her, cat," he said to Numbnuts.

"I thought . . . Aren't you coming with me?" Garland asked, surprised by his defection.

"Nope." A smile twitched the corners of his mouth upward. "Of all the things I had in mind for tonight, playing 'good old Uncle Colin' is at the bottom of my list."

"What's at the top?"

He reached out to cup her chin in his hand. "Making love to you."

"What's number two?"

"Neatly sidestepped," he said, tracing her bottom lip with his thumb. "Look, it's been a long day, a long week, and a hell of a long six months. Right now I'm feeling about as manageable as a bull during mating season, so unless you want to risk a tumble on that fancy white sofa in your sister's living room, don't try to change my mind about going."

It was tempting. *He* was tempting. And there was the vision of the Dragon Lady fainting away in horror at the sight of her two visitors cavorting on the sofa. But the issue went deeper than just sex; Colin wanted much more than that from her. He wanted everything. And she just wasn't ready yet. Yet. Looking deeply into his eyes, she said, "Mating season goes on longer than just one night, Colin. There's time."

"Yeah, there is. Good night, Garland." He kissed her once on the mouth, then turned away. Picking his jacket up from the back of a chair, he slipped it on and headed for the door. A moment later he was gone.

With a sigh, Garland began clearing off the table. Numbnuts wound his way around her ankles. *"Miaow!"* he complained.

"Pizza, pizza, pizza! Don't you think of anything besides your stomach?"

The cat shook his head so hard that his ears made a snapping sound.

"Don't tell me. Food and lady cats, and not necessarily

in that order. Sort of like someone else we know, huh?" Garland made a face. "What do you think, boy? Was I a fool for sending him away?"

"Miaow!"

"I'm afraid you're right," she said.

Chapter Fourteen

Garland opened The Tome at noon the next day. Sunday hours—one to four o'clock, dictated by the churchgoers. Business was brisk at first; many of their customers liked to browse among the stacks after services. But things soon slacked off, however. Garland found herself sitting in the steno chair beside the desk with nothing to do but think about calling Colin. An urge she resisted.

It was a relief when Milo breezed in a little after three, exuding fatuous self-satisfaction and a strong residue of Miss Wackahula's perfume.

"Hi, darlin'," he said, bending to kiss Garland's cheek.

She pushed him away, then tried to fan the scent from the air. "Holy cow, Milo, what *is* that stuff?"

"I dunno." He picked his collar up between his thumb and forefinger and pulled it over to his nose. "Jungle Gardenia, maybe?"

"Why are *you* wearing it?"

"I'm not exactly wearing it—Deanna gave me a kiss goodbye."

Garland laughed. "That must have been some kiss. I wonder how much heat has to be generated in order to transfer that much perfume from one person to another."

"Smart ass. How did things go last night?"

"Well enough," she said. "Once I got past Xenia the Dragon Lady."

clouds were piling up in a hurry, bringing premature darkness. The wind was beginning to gust, driving trash and leaves down the street before it.

"The weatherman said a warm front is moving in," Milo said. "We're going to be having thunderstorms off and on all night."

"We might as well close up, then. You unplug the computer and I'll get the lights."

Fifteen minutes later she was heading down I-264 toward home. It was beginning to rain, big, fat drops that sounded like pebbles hitting her windshield. She turned the stereo on, changing channels until she found someone talking about the weather.

". . . thunderstorm watch for Virginia Beach, Norfolk, and parts of Chesapeake," the announcer said. "And tomorrow, look for a temperature of sixty degrees. Yes, folks, typical Hampton Roads weather . . ."

She punched the Off button. The rain was coming harder now, forcing her to slow down. But it was only a mile or so before she reached the Military Highway exit and, from there, a few minutes to home. The first thing she saw was Numbnuts, his ears plastered tightly to his skull, sitting on the porch waiting to be let in.

There was enough lightning streaking the sky for her to see the tops of the tall loblolly pines whipping in the wind. A real humdinger of a storm, she thought as she ran for the door, splashing through the inch-deep water that covered the sidewalk. By the time she hit the porch, she was soaked from head to foot. The cat spat at her as she fumbled the key into the lock.

"Well, how do you think *I* feel?" she snarled back.

He was in the house the instant the door opened, leaving a line of muddy paw prints across the linoleum. Garland closed the door behind her and paused only long enough to shuck her shoes before following him, turning on lights as she went. His trail led down the hall to her bedroom, across the pale beige carpet and up onto her bed. And there he was, smack in the middle of her new bedspread, grooming himself in a veritable frenzy of feline outrage. He spared her a single burning glare before returning to his task.

Garland couldn't help laughing. "You think it's my fault. I ordered that storm just to get you wet, is that it?"

He ignored her. Still chuckling, she began undressing. "You stupid cat," she said. "You're lucky you're living with me, you know that? Someone else would have made a catskin rug out of you."

Thunder crashed almost directly overhead. The cat squalled and jumped off the bed. Garland gathered him into her arms, grimacing at the feel of cold, wet fur against her bare skin. There was another shuddering boom, and then the lights went out.

"Great, just great," Garland muttered. The cat squirmed in her arms. "You okay now, boy?" she asked.

He jumped down. Lightning illuminated the room long enough to see that he was ensconced on her bed again, tending to his *toilette*. Thunder followed hard on the lightning's heels, but this time the cat didn't even look up. Nerves of steel, Garland thought. At least after the first fright.

"I'd better call the power company," she said, moving through the room with the ease of long familiarity to find her robe and slippers. "I don't know why I'm talking to you, you stupid cat." *Yes, I do. It's being in a darkened house during a storm. Even a cat is better than no company at all.* "You couldn't care less whether or not we have electricity. It's tuna that worries you."

At the sound of the word "tuna," she heard a thump as he landed on the floor. Meowing eagerly, he ran toward the kitchen. "Great. He understands English, or at least those words pertaining to eating. Now, where did I leave the flashlight? Oh, yeah. The kitchen. Cat, you're in luck."

She tied the sash of her robe securely, then padded down the hall after him. The patio door curtains were open. The rain slashed against the glass, making the big sliding doors look like sheets of gray velvet. Then lightning flared outside, turning them into blazing platinum rectangles.

In that brief, brilliant flash of light, Garland saw someone crouched outside the doors. Thunder echoed her heart.

She found herself gripping the lapels of her robe with both hands, pulling the terrycloth fabric up around her throat. Unable to move, unable to breathe, she watched the spot where she'd seen that figure. It had looked shapeless and hulking, its head sunk between its shoulders. Creature of the night.

A bolt of lightning crackled overhead, then another and another, strobe-light fast and intense. Like frames in an animated movie, scenes flashed across her vision with each succeeding bolt: crouched figure, standing figure—hooded jacket/baseball cap/wide-shouldered male/something shiny in his hand—and then nothing. Nothing but the rain that came down so hard it seemed to bounce on the concrete patio.

She stared at the empty rectangle of glass, not quite believing he was gone. It had happened so fast that she hadn't even had time to scream. Her breath whooshed out, then in again. Almost sobbing with reaction, she ran to the phone and dialed 911.

"Miss Ross, can you describe this person?" the policeman asked.

Garland sighed. "Not much, Officer Firnay. I could only see him in the lightning flashes, you understand." She adjusted the wick of the oil lamp that sat on the table between them, wishing the electricity would come back on.

"Was he black, white, tall, short?"

"White. I remember his skin reflecting the light. Regular build, I guess. I couldn't be sure of his height; he might have been standing on the step, you see . . . and I'm afraid I wasn't looking at his feet."

"Can you remember what he was wearing?"

"Yes. One of those slick jackets that zip up the front. Um, navy blue or black, I think. And a red baseball cap. He'd pulled the hood of his jacket up over the hat, and I remember that red bill sticking out. It cast a shadow over his face." The memory of that dark, crouching figure made her heart race.

"Pants?" Firnay prompted.

"Ahhh, now that's a little fuzzy. They might have been blue jeans, only dark with water."

His pen moved across the paper, audible in the quiet room. The lamplight glinted off his uniform and badge. He was a large man in his late forties or early fifties, just beginning to run to fat. A comforting presence, Garland thought. She clasped her hands on the table in front of her, patiently waiting for him to finish.

"Let me take a look at the patio," he said after a moment. He got up and opened the sliding door, then stepped outside.

Garland followed him out onto the patio. There was only a fine mist of rain now, and a layer of fallen pine needles on the ground. It was at least ten degrees warmer than it had been before the storm.

Firnay used his flashlight to examine the patio and ground beyond. Garland didn't have much hope that he would find anything, not after that storm. It had rained hard enough to wash away any footprints the prowler might have left. She was still shaky with reaction; jamming her hands deep into the pocket of her jeans was the only way to keep them from trembling.

"Where exactly was he standing?" he asked.

Garland pointed. "There. At the right side of the door."

"The lock is on the left side." Firnay played the flashlight beam over the step, then up at the door.

"You're right," Garland said. "I was so scared I didn't

notice that. What do you think he was doing?"

The officer shook his head. "I can't speculate about that, Miss Ross." Suddenly he moved forward and picked up something that was wedged against the steps.

Garland peered over his shoulder. He was dangling a Bazooka Bubble Gum wrapper between his thumb and forefinger.

"Do you think he could have left it?" she asked.

"With that wind?" He shrugged. "It could have come from anywhere. Have you had any Peeping Tom incidents in the neighborhood?"

"No-o-o, not exactly," Garland said, combing her hair back with her fingers. "There's been some stuff with teenagers driving over people's lawns and switching mailboxes around, things like that. But surely kids wouldn't be larking around during a thunderstorm."

"I don't know. Kids do the damnedest things at the damnedest times, mostly to get a rise out of the old folks." His voice rang with the certainty of a man who had experienced teenagers. "But there's something else to consider, Miss Ross. You've been getting a lot of attention from the press lately. Your prowler might have been a reporter looking to catch you unawares."

"Maybe." The thought was reassuring; she hoped it was true. "If it was, I hope he gets pneumonia for scaring me out of my wits."

The officer chuckled. "I'll file a report on this, and feel free to call if anyone bothers you again." He played the flashlight beam over the door one more time, then went back into the house. Garland followed him.

"Look here, Miss Ross," he said, shining the flashlight over the aluminum track of the door. "Until you can get a proper lock, wedge a board between the inner door and the wall. It's not the perfect solution, but it will give you more security than what you've got now. It would take any reasonably competent burglar about two seconds to open that door."

Garland's skin crawled at the thought of someone

walking into her house so easily. "Thank you, Officer Firnay. I'll take care of it right away."

He called a cheery goodbye as he walked out the door, apparently unaware that he'd spooked Garland all over again. No matter how logical the explanation of the prowler's presence, there was still the memory of that sinister crouching figure. It brought back all those long-ago-but-still-remembered fears that had peopled her overly imaginative child-mind. The bogeyman—haunting the dark, peering into windows in the hope of scaring some poor helpless kid out of her wits.

The fine hairs at the nape of her neck lifted. Irritably, she scrubbed at them. Scared of the bogeyman at her age! As she stood watching the police cruiser disappear down the street, the electricity came back on. She went around the house, turning on every light she could.

She drank a cup of hot tea, more for the comfort of it than because she really wanted it, then went out into the garage and poked through the stack of scrap lumber there. By some miracle, there was a section of two-by-four that would fit the sliding door with only minor adjustment. She found her saw and set to work.

Numbnuts came into the garage to see what all the noise was about. *"Miaow!"* he said plaintively.

"Tell me about it," she agreed. "Once upon a time people in this neighborhood didn't bother locking their doors. Prowlers! Peeping Toms! Whoever that guy is, I hope *he* runs into the bogeyman."

Taking the board into the house, she slipped it into place. "There," she said, stepping back to look at her handiwork.

More security, the cop had said. The board sat wedged between the door and the wall, solid and real. It would take some doing to open that door now.

Somehow, though, she didn't *feel* more secure. Reaching out hurriedly, she drew the curtains to close the darkness away.

Chapter Fifteen

David parked his car in front of the apartments across from Garland Ross's house. These apartments were a godsend; without them, his presence might have been noticed. As it was, there were enough people coming and going that one more car didn't matter.

She was still home. He glanced at his watch. Quarter to nine. She'd be leaving soon; one of the things he liked best about her was that she was punctual. Now that her life was settling back into its normal routine, you could almost set your watch by her.

Except for Sunday. He'd come here in the afternoon expecting to have at least an hour to himself. But she'd shown up early. The storm, he supposed. He'd parked on the street beside her house, and had watched the lights go on one by one. Living room, hallway, bedroom—he knew she was changing her wet clothes. He'd left his car then, ignoring the rain. With the lights on and the patio-door curtains open, he'd had a clear view of the kitchen and dining area.

He knew she'd be blind to him with the light on. There had been another time when that had happened—at the bookstore. He'd been able to look at her to his heart's content. To see and not be seen. To know he was separated from her only by a few centimeters of glass.

The storm hadn't bothered him. He liked storms. They kept other people inside, kept them home. But not him. He'd been part of the storm, one with its power and violence. *Rider of the storm/Shed your heavy earth-bound form/Wind and rain and lightning bright/Will make you master of the night.* His breath coming swift and shallow in excitement, he'd waited for the woman to come into view.

But then the electricity had gone out. He'd dropped his keys, squatted to pick them up when the lightning had flashed overhead, leaving him as exposed as if he'd been standing in a spotlight. One moment, two. She'd seen him then. Her eyes had gone wide with shock and fear, but he couldn't savor it. He'd had to run, hoping she hadn't gotten a good look at his face.

He'd been cheated. She'd been right there—right there! He could have studied her to his heart's content. Betrayed, and by *his* storm! Three days passed before he'd dared to come back here. Three days of lying around the house watching TV and feeling as though the whole world was pressing on him. Suffocating. And the nights—dreams of her, dreams of the other. Intertwined, inextricable. He'd awakened from those dreams soaked with sweat, sobbing with rage and loss and frustration.

He looked around, startled by the sound of rapid footsteps. Someone was approaching the car—some guy jogging. David leaned over to open his glove compartment and pretended to look for something until the man passed.

Straightening, David settled back in his seat and returned his attention to the house. It sat prettily on the gently sloping lot, surrounded by pine trees. When he was a kid, he'd studied pictures of houses like these: red brick and white trim, black wooden shutters, neat flowerbeds bristling with daffodils that were nearly ready to bloom. And inside, people: Dad working hard to support the family, Mom taking care of the children. Clean clothes, hot food, bookbags, and lunch boxes with thermoses. And the weekends were family time.

He couldn't wait for the flowers to bloom; that would make the place perfect.

She came out then and began sweeping the porch and sidewalk. A homely task. His gaze followed every stroke of the broom. *Whisk, whisk.* It was too far away for him to actually hear it, but his imagination gave him what reality lacked. *Whisk, whisk.* He nearly whimpered when she finished and went back inside.

A few minutes later she came out again carrying her purse. She got into the van and drove away.

"Heigh ho, heigh ho, it's off to work we go," he sang.

He started the car and made a circuit around the block, then parked in front of the apartment again. No one was home here or next door, but there was someone in the house behind Garland Ross's. It would have to be the front door. The idea appealed to him; just walk right up and pretend he belonged there.

Whistling softly, he picked his toolbox up from the seat beside him and got out of the car. He looked down at the olive green jumpsuit he'd picked up at Sears Surplus. Handyman. Everyman. His camouflage, like the tiger's stripes in the tall grass, the leopard's spots in the dappled shade of the jungle.

He walked up to her front door, not slowly, but not hurrying either. Her locks were at least fifteen years old. Oh, she'd had the cylinders changed after her sister had died—he had seen the locksmith come out and do it—but the locks themselves were old, and they were regular door locks, not deadbolts. He was no burglar, but this was easy stuff. Taking a long, slim strip of metal out of his toolbox, he slid it into the crack between the door and the jamb. A moment later he had the door open.

He went inside. A blend of aromas hit him, stopping him in his tracks. Home smells, biscuits and fresh coffee. Scrambled eggs. His nostrils flared, savoring the inhaled air. Had she made the biscuits herself? he wondered. Betty Crocker/white apron/good-mother images—sweet and hurting.

His gaze flicked around the room, registering the contents. Furniture that had been lived on, but was clean and neat and obviously well taken care of. A group of framed snapshots hung on the wall behind the sofa.

Setting the toolbox down on the floor beside the door, he went to take a closer look at the photos. He passed quickly over the ones of two older people, focusing instead on the series of photographs of two girls, one blond, one dark, that took them from grade school to graduation and beyond. The child Garland had been serious and self-conscious in every picture, looking directly at the camera as though it were her enemy. Not like the other one. Smiling, smiling, big white teeth. Butterfly, tease—he knew the type. Whore. Gone now.

He traced the corner of one frame with his forefinger. There were no pictures from his childhood. They'd all been destroyed when . . . Whirling away from the sofa with a convulsive movement, he headed toward the kitchen. He didn't need pictures; the pictures in his head were clearer than photographs could ever be.

A huge orange tabby cat was sitting in the center of the kitchen floor. After a moment of open-mouthed surprise, the man held out his hand for inspection. "Hello, boy. You don't mind if I look around a little, do you?"

The cat stalked over and sniffed his fingers doubtfully, then sneezed. David bent and began scratching beneath the animal's chin. He liked cats. They were predators just like him.

"You're new here, aren't you?" he asked. "I don't remember seeing you before."

Those golden feline eyes never blinked, but the man's

scratching fingers elicited a buzz-saw purr from deep beneath that orange-striped hide.

"That's enough for you, big guy. I've got things to do," he said, straightening.

He saw a cup, plate, and small frying pan sitting in the drainer beside the sink, a washcloth hung neatly over the faucet; she'd tidied the kitchen before going to work. That pleased him. He hated dirty dishes . . . he hated dirt of any kind. In one corner of the kitchen were two bowls, one with water, one with dry cat food, which was obviously untouched.

Picking up the phone, he noticed she'd jotted her new, unlisted number beneath the old one. He grinned; where else do you write a new phone number down but under the old one? After all, why not? Who would expect someone to come into *your* house and look at *your* phone?

"Thank you," he murmured, without bothering to write it down. He'd always had a good head for numbers. Important ones, anyway.

He opened the refrigerator and looked inside, restraining the eager cat with his left hand. There was a package of sliced ham on the top shelf. He took two slices out—one for him, one for the cat.

Next, he went down the hall to her bedroom and spent a long time looking through her drawers. Sweaters, jogging suits, T-shirts. All neatly folded and in their proper place. Her lingerie was an interesting portrait of her: cotton nightgowns; plain white panties, slips, and bras; an array of pantyhose in various colors. He frowned. The hose was not in order at all, but jumbled together anyhow. Blue beside beige, gray next to black. He hesitated, his hands twitching as he tried not to fix them. Finally he began arranging the hose by color, off-white to flesh tone to navy to black. Lightest to darkest.

There. He stepped back to admire his handiwork.

Light to dark, that was the way it was supposed to be. He was surprised at her for not knowing that.

Shaking his head, he went into her bathroom and occupied himself sniffing her shampoo and conditioner, creams and goos. None of the scents sparked a memory cord, however, so he soon lost interest. She might as well have been a nun—no diaphragm, no condoms, no birth control pills. He didn't think she was the sort to play around without them. It pleased him.

She was his. Completely, with no intrusions.

"Perfect," he said. The hunger was there inside him, but quiescent now, belayed by his other need.

It was time to go; he'd spent far too much time here. As he walked toward the door, he noticed that one of the panes of the big picture window was broken. He understood why she hadn't done anything about it: she had no man to fix things for her. But really, broken things shouldn't be left lying around the house. As he opened the door, the cat slipped out between his legs. He grabbed for the animal, an instant too late. There was a streak of orange beneath the bushes in front of the house, a wild tossing of branches, and then nothing.

"Here, kitty," David called. "Heeere, kitty."

After a moment, he shrugged. Standing exposed like this was too dangerous, calling the stupid cat even more so. The woman would probably think she'd forgotten to let the animal in. People did that; human nature, just like writing her new number on her phone.

After glancing up and down the street to make sure no one was coming, he picked up his toolbox and slipped outside, locking the door behind him.

Security was *so* important these days.

Garland took off work at four o'clock, leaving Milo to handle The Tome alone until closing at six, and took the Midtown Tunnel to Portsmouth and then on to Churchland. She knew Churchland more as a pass-through than as a destination, so she took advantage of a red light to double-check the address Milo had given her. It was a long way to come when there were probably twenty private investigators on her own side of the river. But Milo had sworn—on various Bibles and ancestors' bones—that his lady friend the detective was very good at what she did.

"I only hope he means investigating, and not something else," Garland muttered under her breath. She wasn't sure it was a good idea doing business with one of Milo's huggy buddies, but her only other option was the Yellow Pages.

The light turned green. She cruised slowly now, watching for the doughnut shop that was supposed to be her landmark. Lo and behold, it was right where Milo said it would be, and behind it, the modest office of the lady detective. A small brass sign said MARCILLE INVESTIGATION SERVICES.

A bell jingled as she went in. The office was one starkly businesslike room; a desk, two chairs, telephone, answering machine, one wall of file cabinets and one of bookcases. The woman behind the desk looked up expectantly.

"Delores Marcille?" Garland asked.

The woman got up and held out her hand. "You're Garland Ross. Sit down, won't you?"

Garland took the chair the other woman indicated. The detective was somewhere in her thirties, tall and large-boned. She was more intelligent-looking than pretty, but then Milo had very catholic tastes. As succinctly as possible, Garland told her story. When she was finished, the detective sat quietly, seeming to digest the information.

"What exactly do you want from me, Miss Ross?" she asked at last.

"I want you to check my brother-in-law out," Garland said.

"Haven't the police done that already?"

Garland spread her hands. "They said they did. How thoroughly, I have no way of knowing. I get the impression they're pursuing another track entirely in this case."

The other woman pursed her lips, then nodded. "Okay, I'll take the job." Raising one finger, she added, "That is, I'll look into Dr. Hollister's personal situation—finances and things like that. I won't mess with the murder investigation itself."

"Fair enough," Garland said.

"Good. I'll start with the banks. If I'm lucky, I should have some information in, say, three or four days."

After writing out a check for retainer, Garland got to her feet. "Thanks. You've got both my numbers?"

"Yes. Thank *you*. Oh, Miss Ross!"

Garland paused in the act of opening the door to look back at the detective. "Yes?"

"If I do find anything out of the ordinary, I suggest you take it to the police."

"I hadn't thought to do otherwise," Garland said.

She let herself out. A few moments later, she was on her way. Fortunately, she was going opposite the flow of tunnel traffic—at least until she hit downtown Norfolk. From then on, it was bumper to bumper. If things were normal, she'd stop at Frank's house and visit until the worst of rush hour passed.

"Hell, I'm going to do it anyway," she said.

She slid into the left lane to make the turn onto Colley Avenue. A few minutes later she pulled up in front of her brother-in-law's house.

The Dragon Lady answered the door, her thin eyebrows going up in surprise. "Why, Miss Ross! We didn't expect you."

"I know. I was in the area, and just thought I'd drop in."

To Garland's surprise, Xenia's face thawed. Instead of looking sixty, she looked fifty, and human. She even smiled as she opened the door wider.

"Dr. Hollister is not at home now. Amber and Annalese are at their piano lesson right now, but I'm supposed to pick them up in a half hour. Do come in and wait, Miss Ross. I know they'll be delighted to see you."

Garland stepped inside a bit warily. *Xenia* was obviously delighted to see her, too, something that had never happened before. Every inch of the nanny's tall, thin frame fairly oozed welcome.

Xenia cleared her throat. "Miss Ross, do you think . . . well, could I possibly talk you into staying with the twins for a few hours tonight?" She patted her closely curled gray hair. "You see, with Dr. Hollister gone so much, I haven't had any time off. I asked that some sort of regular schedule be set, but he hasn't had time to consider it."

Garland studied the older woman from a new perspective. The Dragon Lady had suddenly become human, with wants and needs of her own. "Of course I'll stay with them, Xenia." She'd left Numbnuts with an ample supply of dry food, although she doubted he'd bother with it as long as there was hope of something better. Hell, here she was letting herself feel guilty because that spoiled, shiftless, no-good eating machine preferred tuna. Defiantly, she added, "Take as long as you want."

Xenia sighed. "Would it be all right if I left now?"

"Sure. I'll pick the girls up. Don't worry about Dr. Hollister; I'll call him and let him know what's going on." Taking her coat off, Garland tossed it onto the foyer table. Interesting that Xenia didn't react; last time she had snatched the garment up and hung it in the closet.

"Thank you, Miss Ross." Xenia made it out the door in record time. Garland watched her thoughtfully, thinking that Frank might be looking for another nanny soon. She'd seen this happen more than once before; Neither Frank nor Charla had ever understood that money couldn't buy twenty-four-hour-a-day loyalty.

She stood in the foyer a moment longer, the sight of the living room sofa pulling her thoughts to another track. The same track they'd been straying to with alarming frequency. One track: Colin. "We could take a tumble on that white sofa," he'd said Saturday, using light words to disguise what he'd really meant. Love, making love. The end of loneliness, the end of empty nights and a future filled only with work. Suddenly, the idea of making love with him on that expanse of smooth white fabric was very tempting.

A month ago, she'd been happy with her future. Sort of. She'd been happy without having a man around. Sort of. The bookstore and the twins had been enough for her to love. Sort of.

Her sister's death had rearranged her life like one of those jigsaw puzzles that can be put together six different ways to make six different pictures. The ones without Colin looked drab and uninviting. Stark, like this room. Safe, all the risky gradations buried in simple black and white. Safe, but sterile. Reassuring and unsatisfying.

And it was her decision. Take the safe way, and know how colorless her life was. Take the other, and with it the risk that it wouldn't last. Would the loneliness be worse for having tasted the brilliance? *Walk into the lion's den, put your head in its mouth.*

"Damn you, Colin, for making me see the possibilities," she said under her breath.

She tried calling Frank, but got only his answering machine. After leaving a message that the twins were going to be with her this evening, she put her coat back on and went out to the van.

By the time she reached the piano teacher's house, her guilt over Numbnuts had gotten a solid hold. And not just guilt; she was also afraid that he would do something to punish her for failing to deliver his can of tuna at the proper time.

"I should never have left him inside," she muttered as she rang the doorbell.

Mrs. Evvons, the piano teacher, answered the door. "Oh, hello, Garland. It's good to see you again."

"Hi, Mrs. Evvons. I gave Xenia the night off." Garland smiled; she'd always liked Mrs. Evvons. The piano teacher was a short, plump woman, perpetually out of breath. Her bouffant hairdo was thirty years out of date, but Garland couldn't imagine her wearing anything different.

"The twins have just finished," the older woman said. Raising her voice, she called, "Girls, your Aunt Garland is here."

She was answered by a squeal. A moment later Amber and Annalese charged into the room to envelop Garland in a whirlwind double hug.

"Where's Xenia?" Annalese asked.

Amber chimed in. "Did she tell you to come?"

"Can you eat with us? Can you play some games? Can you stay 'til bedtime?"

"Whoa," Garland said, smiling at Mrs. Evvons over their heads. "I've got a better idea. How would you like to come out to my house for a while?

"Sure! Can we see the cat?" Annalese demanded.

Garland laughed, amused by the twins' priorities. "I'll even let you feed him."

"How about us? Can we have pizza?"

"You've got pizza on the brain," Garland said. "How 'bout grilled cheese sandwiches and chips—"

"Yay!"

"And broccoli."

Two voices, one groan.

After calling a goodbye to Mrs. Evvons, Garland herded the girls out to the van. They talked constantly. She enjoyed every minute of it, the solid drone of voices blotting out her thoughts like white noise.

Once on the daily-familiar stretch of I-264 that ran between downtown and home, Garland found a comfortable slot in the traffic and let her mind slip into autopilot. A sudden cessation in talk behind her, however, jerked her back to awareness.

"Is everything all right back there?" she asked.

The silence remained for a long, awkward moment before Amber spoke. "Aunt Garland, will you take us out to see Mom sometime?"

The words seemed to hang in the air, taking on more solidity every passing second. Garland reached up and tilted the rearview mirror so that she could see the twins' faces. "Sure. The cemetery is closed now, but I'll be glad to take you over there Saturday. I'll talk to your father about it." After a moment's hesitation, she asked, "Has he talked to you about your mom?"

They nodded slowly, as though unsure. Garland let her breath out in a soft hiss of frustration. He'd probably told them the stages of grief in easy-to-understand steps. Knowing the man, it had been a clinical overview, completely ignoring the fact that confused, grieving children need love. Extra love. But remembering what Colin had said about stretching them between the two adults they needed most, she kept her mouth shut.

The girls seemed satisfied with the little she'd offered them, however, and moved on to other things.

"Where does Numbnuts sleep?" Amber asked.

Startled, Garland counted to ten before trusting herself to speak. "Where did you hear that name?" she asked as casually as she could.

"That was real smart," Annalese hissed, giving her

sister a shove. "You weren't supposed to—"

"Well, it's his *name,* stupid." Amber said.

"You're the stupid one. You messed up."

"So what?"

"Big mouth!"

"Toad face!"

"Puke-head!"

Puke-head? Garland was tempted to let things go on just to hear what came next. But this fight was a smokescreen, pure and simple—calculated to keep her off the subject of Numbnuts. So she shouted, "Time!" When things were quiet again, she said, "I believe I asked a question."

"What question?" Amber countered.

After another count to ten, Garland asked, "Where did you hear that name?"

"You mean Numbnuts? We heard you talking to Colin about it." Amber elbowed Annalese, who giggled. "And don't worry about us not knowing what nuts are—Richie Berrand at school told us."

Completely at a loss as to how to answer *that* little item, Garland merely said, "The cat sleeps on my bed," and then dropped the subject. At least they hadn't asked anything about reproduction. Then again, maybe Richie had already told them everything they needed to know.

The twins lapsed into little-girl chatter for the rest of the trip home. Garland returned the rearview mirror to its normal position. The girls were so like their mother. Garland couldn't remember how many times Charla had used an argument to deflect her big sister's questions. Kids learned by example—and they learned fast. Sudden tears misted Garland's vision, and she blinked them away hurriedly.

It was a relief to leave the highway for the almost-deserted street that led to the neighborhood. The house and yard was brightly lit, thanks to the floodlights that faithfully came on at dusk every day. Garland pulled into the driveway, inordinately glad to get home again. Home—warm and welcoming.

The twins had their seat belts off and the door open before she'd turned the ignition off. Amber cupped her hands around her mouth. "Here—"

"Don't you dare!" Garland shouted out the open door.

"—Kitty!" Glaring at Garland over her shoulder, Amber said, "Gee, Aunt Garland, chill *out.*"

Garland couldn't help laughing. "Okay, I'll chill out. I know you're civilized enough not to scream 'Numbnuts' through the neighborhood—not even to push my buttons. But you might as well save your breath, 'cause I left him—"

The cat came running around the corner of the house, tail held high, expressing his hunger with a plaintive wail. There must be some Siamese in his ancestry somewhere, Garland thought as he launched himself into her arms, ignoring the twins completely.

"Hey!" Amber said, looking hurt.

"Don't worry, honey," Garland said. *"I'm* food, you're play, and right now he wants to eat." Frowning, she looked down at his scarred orange head. "I thought I left you inside."

His reply was an even more plaintive demand for food.

"Strange, I could've sworn I left you in the house," she said again. Then she shrugged; her life was so topsy-turvy nowadays she couldn't be sure of *anything.* "Well, come on, and I'll feed you."

Annalese held out her arms. "Give him to me."

The cat, apparently mollified by Garland's promise of a meal, allowed himself to be taken from her and carried up onto the porch. Greedy *and* lazy, Garland thought.

She paused a moment to admire the daffodils, which

were very near blooming. The buds had swollen, changing from pea green to yellow. Tomorrow or maybe the next day there would be a riot of yellow flowers out here. Daffodils were her favorite; they came at the time she was most hungry for color.

"Come on, Aunt Garland," Amber said. "We're all starving."

"Okay, okay." Unlocking the door, Garland pushed it open and let the girls—and cat—stampede in ahead of her.

"The tuna is on the bottom shelf of the pantry," she called after them. "Just give him one can."

Dropping her purse and jacket on the sofa, she went into her bedroom to change into a sweater and jeans. She waited until the electric-can-opener and spoon-scraping-metal sounds ended, then called, "He's going to be busy for a while. Why don't you change your clothes in the meantime? I bought you some new T-shirts the other day—they're in the dresser in the spare room."

That precipitated another rush, this time down the hall. Smiling, Garland ran a brush through her hair before going out to the kitchen. Her answering machine was blinking. She took a notepad out of the drawer and hit the Play button. The first message was from Detective Baedecker, a curt sentence telling her that there were no new developments in her sister's case. Garland stuck her tongue out at the machine, getting a great deal of satisfaction from the childish gesture. After that were a couple of hang-ups, then Colin's voice came over the speaker. "I'm not going to be able to make the Friday night get-together," he said. "But how about dinner Saturday night? Or Sunday, Monday, Tuesday, Wednesday, et cetera. Make that and/or Sunday, Monday, Tuesday, Wednesday, et cetera. 555-3441."

The tape rewound itself, leaving her in silence. She glanced at the calendar that hung above the phone, but she didn't need to look at it to know that every weekend and evening was empty. As empty as her life had been. And as long as she refused to let anyone inside her carefully constructed little shell, it would stay empty. What the hell, Colin was *already* in; all that remained was for her to do something about it.

She dialed his number, her heart beating wildly as the phone rang once, twice, three times. Then it clicked, and his answering machine came on.

"This seems to be my night to talk to people's machines," she muttered. After the beep, she said, "Colin, this is Garland. Uh . . . Saturday night will be fine. I'll . . ." And then she went blank, completely, utterly without speech. Realizing that there would be several seconds of silence on his tape, she hung up hurriedly.

"Well, it's done," she said. "Done, done, done."

She felt nervous, yes, but also relieved and a bit elated. The step had been taken, the words had been spoken, the commitment made. Even if she broke the date, Colin would know she'd taken that step. As Milo would say, "Batten down the hatches, we's on a roll!"

The girls came back in, wearing the oversized Union Jack T-shirts Garland had bought for them at Waterside.

"These are cool," Annalese said. "Thanks, Aunt Garland."

"You're welcome." Garland gathered them both in for a quick hug, then turned to the refrigerator. "Let's eat, I'm starved."

Chapter Sixteen

Friday morning, Garland woke to the sound of the phone ringing. With her eyes still closed, she sat up and groped for it. Numbnuts complained loudly as her movement disturbed him.

"Oh, shut up, lazy," Garland said as she picked the receiver up. "Hello?"

There was no answer. But someone was there on the other end; Garland could hear breathing. *Damned if I'm going to say hello again!*

Then, "Hello." A man's voice. "I'm looking for . . . Jane."

"I'm sorry, you have the wrong number."

"I like your voice," he said.

Surprise held her motionless. "What?"

"Your voice. It's dark and sweet. Perfect. Will you talk to me?"

Reason came flooding back. She banged the receiver back into the cradle. "Damn weirdo," she muttered.

She swung her legs over the side of the bed and got up, stretching to get the kinks out. Then she took a look at the clock.

"Holy cow, it's almost eight! Why didn't you wake me up earlier?" she asked the cat as she ran for the shower.

After making the water as hot as she could stand it, she set the shower head to "massage" and let the water pummel her into wakefulness. Tonight was the Friday night gab session. She didn't feel like going. Maybe it was stress, maybe just the fact that Colin wasn't going to be there. Frank had agreed to let the twins stay with her for the night; maybe they'd just take in a movie.

Frank, Frank, Frank. All these years he'd seemed to be a cardboard cutout of a man, a gray backdrop for Charla's vivacity and brilliant plumage. But now, with his wife gone, he was beginning to dominate all their lives. Control, that was what he had, control over Garland's visits with the twins, even controlling to an extent the local press; lately, the articles about Charla had been low-key and respectful, evidence of the clout the Hollisters wielded in this city.

Garland turned around, letting the hot water needles pelt her front. "I wonder, Frank old boy, if Charla was as free as she made out." She had a sudden vision of Charla the vivid butterfly firmly tethered to an earthbound Frank. Implacable hands holding the chain, allowing the illusion of freedom while maintaining iron control.

Sighing, she turned the water off and stepped out of the shower. Makeup and hair took her all of fifteen minutes. After considering her clothing options, she took a sweater and a beige suede skirt out of the closet. Opening her hosiery drawer, she reached for the first flesh-colored pair she saw. Then she stopped, her hand hovering over the drawer.

"Funny, I don't remember doing that," she muttered, staring at the neat ranks of hosiery. Color coordinated. Oh, she did put them in order like that from time to time, but she just didn't remember doing it anytime recently.

Then she shrugged. This wasn't the first time she'd done something like this. Under stress, she had a tendency to organize things, her hands moving while her brain was engaged elsewhere. And yesterday she'd run the coffeemaker without water.

"Hell, I'm getting absentminded. First sign of old age, they say," she said, closing the drawer with a bang. "And so is talking to yourself."

Numbnuts sat in front of the closed bedroom door, watching her impatiently. When she didn't respond immediately, he scratched to go out, leaving four parallel grooves in the door.

"There's always the SPCA," she said.

He scratched again. Four more grooves. This time she moved to obey. Smiling at the impertinent angle of his tail, she followed him down the hall to the sliding glass door. It was raining outside, a steady drizzle that looked like it was going to last all day. The cat looked up at her accusingly.

"Don't look at me," she said. "I had nothing to do with it." Putting her hands on her hips, she added, "It's God's way of punishing you for your sins: greed, sloth, and disregard for the possessions of others."

He shook his head in obvious disbelief. When she opened the door, he eased through, then sat on the top step contemplating the rain. Finally he stepped out into the grass, slinking along as though to slide between the drops.

"Good luck, Fatso," Garland called before closing the door.

Humming under her breath, she went into the kitchen to get herself a cup of coffee. The timer on the brewer had been set for six-thirty, so the coffee was well cooked. Hey, she told herself, it couldn't be any worse than Milo's. Just put an extra spoonful of sugar in it and let the caffeine do its thing.

A notation on the calendar caught her eye. "Oh, damn," she said. "I forgot about that hair appointment." Four o'clock. That would take more than an hour out of her day, and she'd planned to spend the whole afternoon getting some much-needed cataloging done. Oh well, she might as well look good for Colin; until now, the poor guy had suffered Garland at her worst.

She carried the coffee over to the table and sat down. While she drank, she idly watched the rain drip from the trees. It was a grim, gray day.

"Whoops," she muttered, glancing at her watch. "Gotta go." There wasn't time to make something to eat.

When she went to the back door to let Numbnuts in, he was nowhere in sight. Garland was surprised; she'd expected to find him plastered to the glass, begging to be let in. She tried a whistle, with no luck.

"Look, I'm late," she said. "Your fat orange butt is just going to have to stay out in the rain."

Just as she turned away, she caught sight of him crouched beneath a bush in the back flowerbed. He was *very* absorbed in what he was doing. Then he shifted, and Garland glimpsed something red between his paws.

She opened the door and went outside, her rubber-soled shoes slipping a bit on the wet concrete steps. Not wanting to spook the cat, she walked slowly and casually toward him. He never looked up, even when she was standing right over him. Hell, he was so engrossed in what he was doing that she could have dropped a bomb beside him and he wouldn't have noticed.

"What have you got?" she asked, although she knew. The empty hole a few feet away and the small pile of scarlet feathers between his paws was evidence enough. He'd dug up the cardinal.

Startled, he glanced up. Alarm went through his

yellow cat eyes, then defiance. He growled low in his throat.

Garland knew better than to reach for the bird. She wasn't even sure why she wanted to take it from him. But she did. "I've got tuna for you," she said.

The magic word. He abandoned his prize like a shot and headed for the house. Gingerly, Garland picked the pitiful thing up. There wasn't much left but skin and feathers. No wonder he'd dropped it so quickly. There was no point in trying to bury it again; he'd only dig it up. She smoothed the still-bright plumage, then carried the corpse to the trash can and wrapped it in a piece of old newspaper before laying it gently to rest atop the can's contents.

She went back inside, washed her hands, and fed the cat two cans of tuna instead of one as compensation.

On his last few visits to Garland's home, David had noticed that the neighbor behind her left every day at three. So he timed his next visit for three-fifteen. It was Friday. On Fridays, she got home around five, later if she went to pick the little girls up. That would give him almost an hour and a half. Plenty of time.

He made a careful circuit of the block before parking in front of the apartments again. Taking his toolbox and a brown-paper-wrapped package out of his trunk, he carried them up to the house.

Quickly, he replaced the broken windowpane, then cleaned everything up neatly and carried the discards out to the trash. Catching a glimpse of something red in a neatly folded piece of newspaper, he investigated and found the carcass of a bird. Red . . . now, what was that red one called? He couldn't remember. Anyway, it was pretty, so he took it with him and tucked it away in his toolbox.

Then he used his slender piece of metal to jimmie the lock again. He stopped to wipe his shoes on the throw rug by the door. Didn't want to track dirt into her nice clean house. He looked up as the cat sauntered out of the kitchen to meet him.

"Hello, big fella," he said. "Got a big weekend coming up?"

A shiver went up his spine. It was Friday night, and he didn't have a thing planned. It was getting so all he could think about was Garland Ross. He'd call her. Maybe he'd actually talk to her.

"What do you think?" he asked the cat. "Is it too soon?"

Tail held straight up, the cat turned and stalked away. His round sphincter seemed to stare at the man like an insolent eye.

"Maybe it *is* too soon," he said. "After all, I wouldn't want to frighten her."

The phone rang. A moment later he heard the answering machine click on and give its recorded message. The sound of that sweet, dark voice drew him into the kitchen.

When the machine beeped, another woman's voice came on. "Miss Ross, this is Delores Marcille. I tried reaching you at The Tome, but Milo said you'd gone for a haircut. I've got some information about your brother-in-law's research into the homeless you might find interesting. Nothing earth-shaking, mind you, but interesting. Give me a call when you get in. I'll be here at the office until seven. 555-0828."

Click. David picked up the phone and dialed the number the caller had given.

"Marcille Investigation, Delores Marcille speaking."

Smiling, he hung up and began to search through

the drawers for the Yellow Pages. Ah, there it was! He flipped through it until he found a listing for Marcille Investigation Services, 9099 Western Branch Boulevard.

Now wasn't this his lucky day? The investigator's office was practically right on his way home. If he left now, he could beat the worst of the tunnel traffic. Whistling under his breath, he wiped the tape.

He trotted back to Garland's bedroom and opened the drawer in which she kept her hosiery. It was still in order, every color in its proper place. The fact that she hadn't changed it pleased him; he felt as though she'd accepted his little gift. Now, which ones should he take?

He closed his eyes and waved his hand over the open drawer. "Eenie, meenie, miney, moe, catch a la-a-ady by the toe. If she hollers, let her go . . . No, no, that's not right. If she hollers, *make* her go. Eenie, meenie, miney, moe!"

When he opened his eyes, he saw that he was pointing to a pair of sheer black pantyhose. Ahhh, good! Right at the end of a row—wouldn't get things out of order at all. He tucked the hose into his pocket, then closed the drawer and headed for the front door. This time he was careful not to let the cat get out when he left.

Traffic in the tunnel was already getting heavy, and it took him nearly an hour to get to Portsmouth. Finally, though, he backed into a parking place in front of the investigator's office. He had no plan beyond walking in, but he was sure things were going to work out perfectly. The power was running high now, a great, singing tide in his veins. Nothing ever went wrong when he felt like this.

The woman looked up as he came in. Her hair was a sort of muddy beige color, neither blond nor brown. She was big, almost as tall as he was. He glanced at the breadth of her shoulders and decided that stealth, not strength, was the way to go with this one. A hunter had to adapt.

"May I help you?" she asked.

"I hope so. My name is . . . David Smith. And my wife is . . . my . . ." He didn't have to fake the tremor in his voice; excitement was running so high in him that it was all he could do to speak at all. "I think my wife is seeing another man."

She pointed him to a chair. He perched on the edge of it, clasping his hands in front of him.

"What makes you think your wife is having an affair, Mr. Smith?" she asked.

"She has meetings at night. She never had meetings at night before. And phone calls. When I answer, he hangs up."

"I see. And what do you want me to do?"

"I just want to know if she is or isn't," he said. "How much do . . . do you charge for this sort of thing?"

His heartbeat pounded in his ears so loudly that he missed her reply. Then she said something about a standard contract and swiveled her chair so that she faced the file cabinets behind her. He was all instinct now. Jungle predator, killer. Before she could turn around again, he leaped out of his chair and looped the pantyhose around her neck.

She heaved and bucked like a wild horse under his hands. He tightened the pantyhose, pulling it with a force that turned his knuckles white. God, she was strong! But he was stronger. He kept the pressure up until jagged flashes seared across his vision. Her struggles grew weaker and weaker, then stopped. She was a dead weight in his hands. Dead weight. Dead. Dead, dead, dead. His breath whistled between his teeth.

She had soiled herself in her dying, and the smell brought him to his senses. He opened his hands and let her drop, then stepped over her to lock the door. It wouldn't do for someone to come in now.

He began searching the office, beginning with the desk. This *was* his lucky night, because right on top of her briefcase was a manila folder labeled ROSS. He folded it up and stuffed it into his pocket, then went through the file cabinets. Finding nothing under ROSS or HOLLISTER, he decided he'd gotten the only copy.

He peered through the miniblinds covering the single window. It was dark now, and although the doughnut shop was just across the narrow parking lot, only a blind, windowless wall faced this way. In fact, the shop acted as the perfect shield from the busy street beyond.

Unlocking the door, he slipped outside and opened the trunk of his car to get the box of plastic bags he always kept there. Lawn and leaf bags—the thirty-nine-gallon size. *This* one, however, might take two. Leaving the trunk open, he went back into the office.

He was right; it took two bags to cover the body. With a great deal of effort, he picked her up, carried her out to the trunk, and dumped her in. Closed the lid. Safe. He went back into the office and found the tiny bathroom tucked into one corner of the storage area at the rear. Just a toilet and sink. There was a bucket and cleaning supplies in the cabinet beneath the sink. A pair of rubber gloves hung like shriveled udders over the drain pipe. He stripped his own gloves off and put the rubber ones on.

He poured half the bottle of cleaner and dumped it into the bucket, then ran water into it. A sharp, clean scent stung his nostrils, wiping away the death stink.

Pine power, full strength for big jobs.

When he was finished washing the carpet where the woman had lain, he flushed the dirty water and put the bucket back neatly. He kept the rag, though, using it to polish the handles of the file cabinets, the desktop, doorknobs, anything he thought he might have touched. He polished his way right out of the office and used the rag to lock and close the door.

"Now, where do I put you?" he murmured, rapping the trunk lid as he passed. "It has to be a place where you won't be found."

The aroma of fresh-baked bread wafted to him on the breeze. Mmmmm, cinnamon rolls, fresh from the oven. He could almost taste them. He'd like to have some right now. Hey, why not? He had a couple of hours to kill.

He drove the short distance to the doughnut shop. It was a great place, with shiny counters and those little round stools that spun around. There were a couple of other men there, sitting at widely spaced intervals along the counter as though to make sure no one thought they were together.

The waitress was just going through the door to the back, so he sat down and twirled his stool until she returned. An old woman with wiry gray hair that was drawn into a coil at the back of her neck. He'd never found gray hair interesting.

"What can I get you, young man?" she asked.

"Are those cinnamon buns I smell?"

She smiled. "Just out of the oven. Would you like one?"

"Two," he said. "And a glass of milk. Oh, is there somewhere I can get a newspaper?"

"There's a dispenser right outside the door."

He fished two quarters out of his pocket and went outside to get a newspaper. When he came back in, his milk and cinnamon buns were waiting for him.

The buns were delicious—rich and buttery, oozing with creamy frosting. He took his time eating.

Once he'd licked every last drop of frosting off his fingers, he opened the newspaper, looking for something about the woman he'd plucked from the shoulder of Kings Highway. He was proud of her; she'd been his first real innovation. There was nothing, however.

He drummed his fingertips on the counter, considering that. They had to have found the car; it had been sitting on the shoulder of the road in plain sight. Interesting. He'd just have to see how things developed.

Sudden inspiration hit. Glancing at his watch, he saw it was nearly seven. He paid his bill and hurried out to his car. Lytton Drive was clear across Tidewater, and it took him more than an hour to get there. But once there, he knew he'd made the right decision. The street was deserted, the nearby trees a solid mass of darkness against the faintly moonlit sky.

The police had finished here; all that was left of the crime scene were some scraps of plastic ribbon and a few scattered cigarette butts. With the investigation complete, this was probably the last place the police would look for another victim.

David took one last look up and down the street, then opened his trunk and grabbed the body. She was stiff now, hard to handle. He'd curled her into a fetal position to fit her into the trunk, and now her arms and legs remained bent even when he hauled her up and out and dumped her on the grass beside the car.

Taking a blanket out of his car, he rolled her into it. Then, a flashlight in one hand and a corner of the blanket in the other, he dragged her far into the trees. He found a fallen tree and shoved her beneath it, wedging her so tightly that he couldn't get the blanket out. Shrugging, he tucked the fabric in around her and then piled brush over everything.

"Good boy," he murmured, wiping shreds of bark off his palms. "No one will ever find her here."

It was a good start to the weekend.

Chapter Seventeen

"I think I'm going to pop," Garland said, sliding down as far as her seat would allow.

Colin laughed. "What do you expect after eating three plates—let's call a spade a spade and say platters—of seafood?"

"It's human nature to overeat at a buffet. I just wanted to get your money's worth."

"Well, you certainly did *that.*" He slid along the booth's leather seat until their thighs were almost touching.

Garland waited for her usual alarm bell of reluctance to go off, but it wasn't there. Relief washed through her; tonight was important to her; she wanted everything to be right, to *feel* right. She'd gone out today and bought a whole new outfit—a sapphire blue dress, matching shoes, hose, purse, underwear, the works. Judging by the look on his face and the way he'd been hovering close all evening, she'd done all right.

This restaurant faced the ocean, and one whole wall of the building was glass to take advantage of it. The Atlantic was in a gentle mood tonight, sending ranks of placid, white-tipped waves toward the sand. Garland's blood seemed to pick up that languid rhythm, and when Colin put his arm around her, she moved into the warmth of his side.

"Look at that sky," she said.

"If it were summer, we could take a walk on the beach," he murmured.

She felt reckless, giddy with the currents of anticipation that were coursing through her. "Why don't we do it anyway?"

His eyebrows went up. "Now?"

"Where's your sense of adventure?"

"Garland, it's forty degrees out there!"

"Just for a minute?"

"You're out of your mind." But he gestured for their waiter. "Check, please."

They walked outside and ran across the sand toward the ocean. Garland didn't care that the breeze coming in off the water was brutally cold; she felt like a kid again, and she was determined to enjoy it while it lasted. Turning her back to Colin, she kicked her shoes off and peeled her pantyhose off. Then she skirted the water, flirting with it, letting the edges of the dying waves chase her along the sand.

Colin caught up with her, barefoot, his pant legs rolled up over the big knots of his calf muscles. He took her hand. They walked along the line of demarcation between wet sand and dry. Her feeling of giddiness had passed, but contentment remained, a feeling of peacefulness she hadn't felt in years. When Colin stopped and turned her to face him, she found herself eager for his kiss. Would loving him be worthwhile later, when the heat passed? She didn't know. All she had now was this, and it would have to be enough.

His mouth was firm and warm and sweet. She pressed closer, wanting more. He pulled her in tighter, his hands going up under her jacket to rove restlessly over her back. She sighed deep in her throat, wishing he'd do more. He cupped her buttocks in his hands and lifted her against him. He was hard and oh, so hot.

"This is insane," he muttered against her mouth.

"The whole world is insane," she said. "At least this is the madness *I* choose."

"My feet are numb. Let's go home." In between each word, he kissed her, tiny, biting kisses she felt right to her toes. "Your house or mine?"

"Mine. I've got to feed the cat."

"That damned cat," he said. "Even after I manage to get rid of him, he's still running my life."

He released her, then took her by the hand and started running back toward the parking lot. Garland scooped her shoes and pantyhose up on the way. By the time they reached the car, she was shivering. Colin got a blanket out of the trunk and handed it to her.

"Get in before you freeze," he said, swinging the car door open for her.

Her teeth were chattering in earnest now. Under the cover of the blanket, she put her hose and shoes back on, then tucked the material around her legs. Colin slid behind the wheel and started the car, but the heater blew cold air for what seemed like a very long time.

"Has your stray burst of adventure worn off?" he asked, making the turn to get back on the freeway.

"Frozen off, more likely," she said. "God, did I really do that?"

He laughed. "It was the oysters."

"*You* had oysters."

"So I did."

"If we'd been twenty years younger, the cold wouldn't have mattered," she said.

"Actually, it wasn't the cold that bothered me. It was the fact that we were in full view of everyone in that restaurant."

Garland drew in her breath with a hiss. "Holy cow! I never thought of that at all!" She ran through the scene in her mind, trying to remember exactly what they'd done and how much might have been seen.

"Don't worry," Colin said as though reading her thoughts, "all they saw was a couple of fools running around barefoot in the cold."

The heater was beginning to put out hot air. With a sigh, Garland put her feet under the vent. Her flesh had just begun to thaw when Colin pulled to a stop in front of her house.

"Would you like a cup of coffee?" she asked, thinking that she ought to be nervous. But she wasn't; the decision had been made, and she was surprisingly comfortable with it.

"Yes."

He turned the ignition off and came around to open her door. As they walked up the porch steps, Garland noticed a prettily wrapped package sitting beside the door. The card read *To Garland, from Uncle Milo.*

"Uncle Milo!" Garland said, giving the box an experimental shake. "What's he up to?"

"Maybe it's a gift," Colin offered.

"From Milo? Now I'm really scared." Garland let him hold the box while she fished her keys out of her purse and opened the door.

Numbnuts came running. Garland picked him up with one hand then awkwardly unbuttoned her jacket with the other. While Colin hung their coats up, she went into the kitchen to feed the cat and get the coffee maker started.

"Why do you feed him so late?" Colin asked from behind her.

"Because if I don't, he's hungry again at six A.M."

Colin gave a snort. "You don't let him wake you up!"

"Colin, he sits on my face. It's pretty hard to sleep through that."

She took the box from him and untied the ribbon. Tearing the paper off impatiently, she opened the lid.

There were a bunch of small packets inside. Confused, she picked one up. "Condoms!" she cried. "I'm going to kill him!"

Colin burst out laughing. She stared at him, not getting the joke.

"It . . . it's fluorescent," he gasped, pointing at the small square package she was holding by one corner. "Glow-in-the-dark rubbers!"

Garland wanted to be outraged. If this had happened with anyone but Colin, she might have managed it. And Milo, damn him, knew that very well. And it *was* funny, in a twisted, Milo-ish way. "Look, Colin!" she said, pulling another condom from the box. "This one's blue."

He dipped into the box, took out a handful. "Here's an Excita Extra, Ultra Ribbed. A King Tut. Hey, here's an extra large—"

"Couldn't be one of *his,*" Garland said.

"Couldn't," Colin agreed, grinning.

"I've got to think of something really awful to do to him in revenge." She tapped her chin thoughtfully with her forefinger. "I'll have to go through some of my books on herbal lore to see if there's anything that induces temporary impotence."

"I hope you don't find it, and not only for Milo's sake. Why don't we just give Numbnuts to him?"

"That's *too* cruel," she said.

Colin reached into the box again. "Ah, here's a note. He says, "Things have changed since you've been on the market, darlin'. Personally, I recommend the Excita. And tell Colin the extra large *is* one of mine."

"I'm going to kill him," she said again.

"Maybe I'll help you." Chuckling, he tossed the condoms back into the box. "Coffee's done. Where do you keep your cups?"

"The door above the drainboard."

A few moments later he came over, two mugs of steaming coffee in his hands. "Why did you pick your house?" he asked. "And don't tell me it was the cat."

"I guess because this is my turf. There's nothing worse than being kicked out of someone else's world."

He set the mugs down on the table. "Haven't I made it clear enough that I *want* you in my world?"

"For how long?"

"For as long as you want to stay."

And there it was. The future, put right in her hands and left for her to decide. "I'd rather stay here," she said. Then, seeing the hurt and disappointment on his face, she took a step closer and added, "With you."

He pulled her in then, fitting her to him slowly. He kissed the curve of her cheek and the corners of her mouth. He did teasing, promising things with his hands that made her try to urge him to greater contact. His mouth came down on hers with sudden fierceness, and she met him eagerly, straining against him. Wanting more, wanting everything.

He sighed into her open mouth, then pulled away to look down at her. His eyes were clear spring green, the pupils dilated with passion. "This is it, Garland," he murmured. "The real thing, head over heels and fathoms deep."

"Does it scare you?" she asked. It did *her,* the intensity of it.

"The only thing that frightens me is that you'll slip away from me."

She didn't answer him. There *was* no answer, at least not a verbal one. But there was a better way to reassure him. Winding her fingers into his hair, she pulled his mouth down to hers. He kissed her back, pulling her up on her tiptoes.

They were both shaking when they broke for air. Smiling a bit crookedly, Colin took her by the hand

and led her to the bedroom.

"It's hot in here," she said, opening the window an inch. A cold breeze, welcome against her too-hot skin, belled the curtains out.

Colin slid his arms around her waist, pulling her back against him. She arched her back, sighing, as his hands caressed her breasts and hips and belly, dipping down to grasp the hem of her dress and pull it up over her head. Her bra, slip, and panties followed, leaving her naked.

"You're beautiful," he said, turning her around to face him.

She ought to be embarrassed. But the look on his face showed that he really *did* admire her, and that made her believe he was telling the truth. For the first time in her life, she felt beautiful. Smiling, she ran her hands over his chest, then down his torso to the line of his erection.

Drawing his breath in with a hiss, he bent to kiss her again. Working together, they managed to get his clothes off without breaking the kiss. And then they were both naked, trembling with the need to touch each other.

He picked her up and laid her on the bed. She held out her arms, welcoming him, and he came to her eagerly. Hot skin against hot skin. Mouths clinging, hands stroking, exploring, bringing even greater heat—Garland lost track of time and place, everything but what he was making her feel. There was no holding back; every caress, every gasp of pleasure was given with no thought of restraint. There were no more doubts, no shyness or playing of games. Just two people coming together in love and in passion.

She cried out when he entered her at last, and then it really *was* perfect. They moved in complete unison, seeking the same goal, seeking it together. Garland felt her climax coming and tried to hold back. But he buried his face against the side of her neck and encouraged her with words and with his body, forcing her over the edge. Faintly through the roaring in her ears, she heard him call out as he followed her.

Garland slowly came back to reality. A sound at the window caught her attention, but when she raised her head to look, she saw only the curtain stirring in the breeze. She relaxed again, reaching up to run her hands down the strong line of Colin's back.

He propped his weight on one elbow and studied her. A small smile curved the corners of his mouth upward. Then he began to move again, leisurely, taking her back up the slope to passion.

Her awareness of the world faded, her boundaries narrowing until they contained only him.

The wind shifted the curtain again, giving David a clear view of the bedroom once more. And framed in the window, the bed. The *bed.* Where she and the man lay. Naked, touching each other, doing things . . .

He whimpered. Clapping his hands over his mouth to stifle the noise, he tried to look away. But he couldn't. He was trapped by curiosity and disgust and a taut, quivering tension. Those twining, sweating bodies . . . the man's mouth on her breasts, sucking . . . her hand on his penis, stroking it . . . And then the man moved between her legs. David began to shake violently, seeing how their bodies moved together, straining, thrusting. Gasps and moans. Clutching hands. Whispers. Release. Hers, theirs, his. *His!*

He ran away then, stumbling through the grass toward his car. But he tripped over a fallen branch and sprawled heavily. He didn't try to get up. Tears began to run down his face. *Not her! Oh God, not her!* There was wetness in the front of his pants. Not pee. Ugly, ugly, ugly—as disgusting as what was going on in the bedroom.

He pressed the heels of his hands against his eyes, trying to push the tears back inside. He pressed so hard that he saw jagged flashes of light on the inside of his eyelids. Why did people do *that?* Why did they like it? Once, when he was eight years old, he'd walked into his mother's room late one night. There had been a man in bed with her. David had stood transfixed in horror at the sight of the man's flexing buttocks, his big, red, glistening *thing* ramming into his mother's body. She squealed.

Run, David. Run, run as fast as you can. To the kitchen. Get a knife, stick it in. Right in one of those flabby, bouncing cheeks.

The man had jumped up with a howl. His mother had jumped up, too, but not to thank him for saving her. Her face had been twisted with rage, her hands curved into claws. Chased into his cubbyhole of a room, cornered, he had gotten the worst beating ever. "But I was only trying to help you!" he'd cried. Mother screaming, her naked breasts bouncing as her arm lifted and fell, lifted and fell.

She'd been a drunk. A whore. She'd liked being a whore, would have done it even if she hadn't gotten paid for it.

"Garland, I trusted you! You were supposed to be different!" he moaned under his breath. Different. Chaste. He'd thought she was. But she wasn't. Like any other woman, she'd fallen for the first hard dick that came around. Women always went for the fucking. Fucking, fucking.

His memory played back both scenes. Mother/Garland, Garland/mother—legs spread, eagerly accepting the invasion of their bodies. Skin sheened with sweat, the red, wet flesh of secret places, licking tongues and thrusting penises. *And they liked it.*

His stomach heaved. Scrambling onto his hands and knees, he vomited into the grass.

Afterward, he stayed in that position for a long time. He ought to feel purged. But although his memories were held at bay—sort of—they hovered close, threatening to come sweeping back.

He glanced back at the window. *They didn't even bother to turn out the light.* He climbed slowly to his feet and went back to the window, trembling with mingled repulsion and anticipation at what he might see there.

But the bed was empty. The room was empty, only the scattered clothes showing what had happened there. Then he heard the sound of running water. The shower. So, they were trying to get clean again. He knew that wasn't the way. No amount of soap and water could scrub *that* from anyone's skin.

"Slut," he muttered, pressing his forehead against the cold glass of the window. "Slut, slut, slut."

Chapter Eighteen

David was dreaming. He knew he was dreaming, tried to get out of it. But he couldn't. He never could.

He runs, his legs churning in slow-motion terror. Skinny kid-legs, full of knobs and bruises. *Run, run as fast as you can/You can't catch me, I'm the Gingerbread Man!* His treasure box held in front of him, the lid off, the cat's-eye marbles bouncing like pinballs inside.

Run, run as fast as you can/You can't . . . Fingers winding in his collar, dragging him to a halt.

Her mouth opening and closing, unsyncronized with her words like a badly dubbed movie. Her voice slurred and angry, flavored with bourbon. "What are you hiding in there, you little bastard? You got some money?"

"Nothing, Mommy, nothing!" Clutching the box with desperate ten-year-old strength. Not enough. She shoves him away. Sprawled on his back, he sees her bloated face peering into his box. Tears squirt from his eyes. "That's mine!" he shrieks.

"Shit, nothing but trash!" She turns toward the fireplace. Bright orange and yellow flames dance there, the apartment's only heat.

Terror/outrage/fury pull him off the floor. He grabs one end of the box and struggles to take it away from her. "You can't have it! It's all I've got!"

Cursing, she wrenches at the box. Cardboard tears and the marbles spill out, bouncing on the floor. He goes scrambling to retrieve them, skinning his knees on the dirty linoleum.

"You can't, you can't!" he sobs.

She's laughing now. Kicks at him as he scuttles buglike across the floor, sends him sprawling. Then, as he watches in horror, she tosses Teddy and the mutilated box into the fireplace.

"Nooooo!" Plunging his bare hands into the flames, he pulls Teddy out. Pain makes him let go. She kicks the burning piece of fur, sending it against the tattered curtains.

Smoke fills the room with incredible swiftness, punctuated by the crackle and heat of flames. Fire blocks the door, follows him as he races to the bedroom. The ancient window is swollen shut, so he snatches up a chair and hurls it through the glass.

A dark shape stumbles blindly through the smoke toward him, hands outstretched, groping.

"David, honey, where are you?" Sweet, dark voice, not shouting now. He crouches on the floor beneath the window where the air is freshest. *Mommy.* So nice now, needing him. But she'd change.

She is coughing now. Coming closer. "David, I can't see. Come help Mommy. Please, David."

It's hot, so hot, and he's choking. All he has to do is stand up, reach out touch the open window, and he'll be safe. But her voice holds him there with the smoke and fire. Trapped. He'll never get away, never, never. No matter how fast he runs, she always catches him.

Suddenly she's standing right over him. Tiny flames lick at the trailing sleeve of her kimono. Smoke wreathes her; he watches her head turn from side to side as she tries to find him. A gust of air from the window sends her hair whipping around her face amid a comet trail of sparks. She sees him: her face swoops close, ugly and twisted. The nice voice—a lie, as he'd known it was—becomes a scream as she grabs his shirt. "You little fucker! What do you think you're doing? Help me—"

His hand closes over a long shard of glass from the window. He can feel the edge sink through his skin, into his flesh, feel the blood well out around it. Without willing it, he's on his feet, lashing out blindly at the hovering shape. There's a scream, whether hers or his, he doesn't know. Something wet spurts into his face.

He can't hear her voice any longer. *Free at last!* Letting the piece of glass drop, he turns back to the window. He clambers through the opening, the fire licking at his heels.

A man's voice cuts through the roaring in his ears, strong hands pull him to his feet. "Jeez, kid, are you okay?"

"Mommy," he whispers, coughing.

"Your mother's in there?" The man's hands tighten on his shoulders, but he hardly feels them.

Mommy. He smiles, turns to look at the house so the man won't see it. The fire is beautiful. Great, hungry flames eating up everything inside.

Sirens split the night. Men run past, shouting. Hoses like pale serpents snake past him. He'd like to tell them they're too late, but he's afraid that if he tries to talk he'll start laughing. Someone puts something over his nose and mouth, telling him to breathe deep. Someone else puts something on his cut hand that stings. He hears/sees/understands, but doesn't respond to any of their questions.

"He's in shock," someone says.

It isn't shock, he knows. He could talk if he wanted to. But his freedom is so new, so fine, that all he wants to do is wrap it around himself like a nice, warm coat.

"His mother's still in there, some guy said." Another

voice, another pair of hands. "No chance of anyone getting out of there; that place is going up like newspaper." And then, belatedly, "Poor kid."

David feels the roughness of a blanket being wrapped around his shoulders. He curls his hands against his chest; they feel dead, like lumps of wood.

"What's the matter, son?" Someone gently takes him by the wrists and pulls his hands away from his body. "Christ!" Horror in the voice, and sympathy. "When is the ambulance due? Tell them to hurry!"

Another man says, "Look at all the blood on him. It can't all be his."

"Maybe his mother got cut getting him out that window."

Yes! David thinks. Later, he'll tell them that. But right now he's too busy watching the fire. Blood-red flames are shooting out all the windows of the old house. A pillar of black smoke coils upward into the night sky.

And then comes that voice, sweet and rich and hated, rising high with the smoke, growing louder and larger until it encompasses all the world. "David, you little shit! I'm going to get you for this. David . . . David . . . David . . ."

Shut up! His mind screams. *Shut up, shut up, shut up!*

But she doesn't. He curls down inside himself, running, hiding, running again. But there is nowhere he can go that she can't follow.

It is then that he realizes he's going to have to keep finding ways to shut her up. Over and over, until she goes away forever.

He woke to screaming, his voice hoarse with it. Sweat covered him, running in hot rivulets down his face and chest. He forced air into his lungs and out again. In.

Out. In. His heartbeat began to slow.

Trembling, he reached up to wipe the sweat from his face and caught sight of his hand. Ridged with fire scars front and back, the palm bisected by a long, puckered scar. Holding it up in front of his face, he turned it from side to side. His legacy. Other kids inherited houses and cars and photo albums. He got these.

The phone shrilled, echo of sirens. He answered it hastily and heard a familiar voice.

"Hello, David."

"Hello."

"You sound strange. Did I wake you?"

David scrubbed the back of his hand across his eyes. "I had the dream again. You said it wouldn't come back. You said if I did what you wanted, you'd make it go away."

"But you *haven't* been doing what I wanted, have you, David? I told you how dangerous it was for you to keep on with this, didn't I?"

"Yes." Sullenly.

"I think it would be best if you came down to see me this afternoon."

David cocked his head to one side, considering that. "Why?"

"Because I'm your friend and I want to help you."

"Okay." He glanced at the clock. "I can come at three."

"Fine. I'll see you then."

David hung up, then lay facedown across the bed, groping beneath it until he found his treasure box. Although he knew *she* couldn't reach out of a dream and take it, he needed to reassure himself.

The box was intact. Smooth, brightly colored cardboard, crisp tissue paper rustling inside. He opened it. Carefully, he took out his treasures.

Hanks of hair, reminders of the women who had gone before. He arranged the daintily beribboned ponytails on the bed. Light to dark. There were two spaces there, colors he hadn't yet collected. One was forever out of his reach. But the other, well, he'd have it soon. He'd allowed himself to get distracted, but that was over.

He was a man now. Beyond *her* reach. She was only a pale shadow haunting his dreams, easily exorcised. He knew how to do that—he'd done it many times already. Power coursed through him, and with it, dark need that was even hotter than the fire in his nightmare. He was stronger than he'd ever been before, his power fueled by the black vortex of hate within him.

"And all thanks to Garland," he muttered, stroking each swatch of hair with his forefinger before putting it away.

Garland rose on one elbow to look at the clock. It was nearly eight, time to get up. The room was cold; she'd forgotten to close the window.

Colin was still asleep. He lay on his back, his arms flung wide. A bed hogger. At least he didn't snore. Evidently used to sleeping in a cold room, he had pushed the covers down to his hips. The body that looked squat in clothing looked powerfully masculine without. No one would ever call him lean, but his bulk was muscle, not fat.

She put her hand on his chest, feeling his heartbeat and the slow, steady rise and fall of his breathing. He didn't waken. With a smile, she moved closer to the nightstand and dialed Milo's number. It took him a long time to answer.

"Hello?" he mumbled at last.

"Milo, this is Garland."

"Mmmm? Whaddyawant?"

"I'm going to be a little late this morning. Can you cover for me?" She'd lost count of the times he'd done this very thing to her; payback was sweet.

"Oh, you are?" He sounded wide awake now. "Why is that?"

"I've got things to do."

"Is Colin there?"

Yes, Colin was there, and awake; his hand was making slow, interesting patterns on her back and hip. "That's none of your beeswax," she said into the phone.

"Did you get my package?" Milo asked.

"Yes, I did. Someone needs to talk to you about your choice of gifts, Milo. A gentleman sends flowers or candy."

Milo snickered. "I know. How late are you going to be?"

"Oh, an hour, I suppose." She looked over her shoulder at Colin, who held up two fingers. "Make that two hours," she amended.

"Take the day, stupid," Milo said. "How many Sundays have you worked for me?"

"Hundreds."

"Bullshit. But this one's on me. Have a good time, my children."

"Thanks, Milo. See you tomorrow."

"Hey, before you hang up. I forgot to ask you earlier—did Delores ever tag up with you?"

Garland frowned. "Delores? No, she never called."

"She called *here,*" Milo said. "Said she was going to try you at home."

"When did she call?"

"Friday afternoon just after you left."

"Friday?" Swinging her legs over the side of the bed, she sat up and fumbled in the drawer of the nightstand for pen and paper. "Do you have her number handy?"

"Just a sec . . ." Garland heard rustling noises. After a moment he came back on. "703-2444. Home number 703-8961."

"Thanks, Milo. Bye." Garland tried both numbers but got no answer at either. Strange, she thought, that the investigator didn't have an answering machine at her office phone.

"Problems?" Colin asked.

"I don't know." Garland shook her head slowly. "I wish I knew what she was going to tell me."

"Does that mean we have to get up?"

She turned to look at him. "Not yet."

"Then come here." He held the blankets open, inviting her into his warmth.

"Milo's going to work the store alone," she said, sliding under the covers. "We've got the whole day to ourselves. Are you going to tell me you've got other plans?"

"Not on your life." He pressed her close, skin to skin. "You're cold," he murmured, pulling the covers up around them.

Soon she was *too* hot, however, and pushed the blankets away again. A short time after that, awareness of her surroundings faded, and all she knew was Colin.

It was almost noon by the time they decided to enter the real world again. Colin was the first to finish getting dressed.

"I'm going to put a pot of coffee on," he said. "Then we'll go out for brunch somewhere."

"There's plenty of food here."

"Why bother with dirty dishes when you've got another option? Afterward, how about going to the Chrysler Museum?"

"What better way to spend a Sunday afternoon?"

"I could think of something," he said with a leer Milo would have envied.

Garland snorted. "Are you going to make me dress to match you, or can I wear pants?"

"Wear pants. We'll swing by my house so I can change to match *you.*"

She took her time getting dressed, enjoying the sounds of him puttering around in the kitchen. The smell of fresh-brewed coffee finally lured her out of the bedroom. Numbnuts coiled his body around her ankles, as sinuous as a snake despite his bulk. He complained vigorously.

"Don't believe a word of it," Colin said. "He's been fed, been out, and is back in again thinking to con you out of a second can of tuna."

"Bad cat," Garland crooned, picking the animal up.

He sat on her lap while she drank her coffee, his yellow eyes half-slitted in contentment. Garland saw how intently Colin was looking at her. His big, square hands moved restlessly on the table top, and she knew he wanted to draw. It was nice to be loved, she mused. With sudden intuition, she realized that her ex-husband had never loved her. He had enjoyed *being* loved. By her, and by the various women he'd had all during their marriage.

Garland put the cat down and went around the table to kiss Colin.

"Mmmm. What was that for?" he asked when she raised her head again.

"Just because," she said. "Now either take me out, or let me fix something here. I'm starved."

"I'll take you to the biggest brunch in town."

While he was getting their coats, Garland made her usual round of the kitchen to make sure everything was turned off. He opened the door for her, stepping back to let her go out first.

She stopped, teetering on the threshold to keep from stepping on the giant bouquet of daffodils that lay on the porch. With a sick feeling in the pit of her stomach, she looked out over her flower beds. Every bloom had been stripped.

"Oh, no!" she whispered.

She knelt and reached to gather the flowers up. As she did, the blooms fell away, leaving her holding bare stems. The butter-yellow trumpets lay scattered on the tile like tiny severed heads.

"What the hell is that?" Colin demanded.

"My . . . my daffodils."

Still clutching the stems, she turned to look at him. He grasped her by the elbows and pulled her up and into his arms. The stems were crushed between them, and the scent of ruined greenery rose, sharp and ugly. Her shock turned to anger, and she flung the stems away. "I can't believe anyone would do this!"

"It's a damned nasty prank," Colin said.

"They didn't even leave me enough stem so I could put them in water."

Colin stirred the murdered blooms with his foot. "Whoever did that wasn't interested in letting you enjoy them, honey."

She bent and began to pick the blooms up. Her hands trembled with reaction. She'd had a few problems in the past with teenagers driving across her lawn, kids putting a couple of BB holes in her windows, things like that. But as Colin had said, this had a nasty feel to it. And it had been aimed directly at her; no one else on the street had been bothered.

"Garland."

Head down, she kept working.

"Garland." Colin knelt behind her. "Stop."

She took a deep, shuddering breath and leaned against him. "Why, Colin? Why would someone do this?"

"I don't know." He got to his feet and retrieved the

newspaper from the driveway. Stripping the rubber band from around it, he shook it open and dropped it into her lap. "Put the flowers in there."

She scooped the blooms up and wrapped them in the paper, then crumpled it violently between her hands. Hot tears ran down her cheeks.

"Take it easy, Garland." Colin knelt beside her and put his arm around her shoulders. "Don't let it get to you."

She turned her head to look at him. There was regret in his clear green eyes. Their idyll was over; she knew it, and so did he. The real world had come to intrude, and it wasn't a very pretty one.

"I'm sorry, Colin," she said. "I warned you about the baggage."

"And I told you I didn't care." He got to his feet, lifting her with him. "Are you still in the mood to eat?"

"Yes." She lifted her chin defiantly; she was damned if she was going to let some nut ruin her day. "Just let me go in for a minute to repair my makeup."

Colin was bent over the kitchen table when she came out of the bedroom. His pencil was moving swiftly over a piece of paper. Garland went to peer over his shoulder.

Her breath went out in a harsh gasp. It was a powerful drawing, done with broad, bold strokes of the pencil. He'd caught her at the moment she'd knelt to pick the daffodils up from the porch. The shorn heads were scattered around her, and she was looking up with such a shattered expression on her face that she turned her back on the picture, unable to bear it.

"Why does it bother you so much?" Colin asked.

"Do you always strip people like that? Put their souls on paper?"

"I draw what I see," he said.

She turned back around. Gently extracting the picture from him, she forced herself to study it. The initial impact faded a bit, and she was able to look at it with some objectivity. "You're very good," she said. "It's a waste not to do more with your talent."

"Maybe." He swiveled around in his chair to face her. "Should I begin my exhibition with this one?"

"No. May I have it?" Alarm spread across his face, and she held up her hands to reassure him. "I'm not going to destroy it, Colin. I may not ever frame it and put it up on the wall, but I'd like to have it."

"Only if you take me with it."

She smiled a bit shakily. "I thought I already had. Weren't we going to pick up your toothbrush and clothes?"

"Full household rights?"

"Trial run." She folded her arms over her chest. "One thing we've got to get straight right away: when the girls are with me, you either sleep on the sofa or at your place."

"Same thing with my Kathy. Old-fashioned morals."

"Exactly."

He grinned. "The twins are what, eight years old? They'll be hitting puberty before you know it. You don't want to give them ideas."

"Exactly," she said again.

"There's a way we can fix that problem."

Too fast, too strong. And too, too dangerous. "Please, Colin. Don't. I've come a long way in just a couple of weeks, but this is all I can handle right now. Look, I haven't even met your daughter."

"Scared?"

"Terrified."

"She'll love you." He smiled. "Actually, the hard part is over with. That first step was the worst; everything else can be worked out."

"If you believe that, you're more of a romantic than Milo."

"I thought he was a cynic."

"Cynics don't fall in love." She put her hands on her hips. "You know how I'd draw *you?* Three little Colin monkeys with signs hung around their necks: see no faults, hear no arguments, speak no doubts."

"Ouch!"

She sighed. "Let's go eat, Colin. At least that's something I can deal with this morning."

Chapter Nineteen

The front door was open. David walked back to the inner office and knocked softly.

"Is that you, David?"

"Yes."

"Come in."

He opened the door and went in. The portrait behind the desk dominated the room. Such warm colors, such a pretty woman. Gone now. A slut like all the rest of them. A slut like her sister.

"Thank you for coming, David. Please, sit down. Can I get you something to drink?"

"No, I don't want anything," he said, settling into one of the chairs that faced the desk.

The older man clasped his hands on the polished wood in front of him. "Why don't you tell me what's bothering you?"

"I told you. The dream came back." When there was no reply, he raised his voice. "You said you'd make it go away, Frank."

"It *did* go away."

"But it's back. Worse than ever." David rubbed his hands along the leather arms of the chair, feeling the cool hardness of the rivets under his fingertips.

"Did you take the medication I gave you?"

He nodded.

"Then perhaps I should increase the dosage," Frank said. "Let me—"

"No. No more medicine. I want to be free of her." David jabbed his thumb toward the portrait. "Just like you wanted to be free of your wife."

"Now, David, we agreed not to talk about that. You were to put those . . . things behind you."

"I do."

He watched the doctor's face turn the same shade of gray as his hair. Was it anger, he wondered, or fear? Interesting.

"Why did you kill that teacher, David?"

"Because she was there. Given to me, like a gift. What's the problem? *You're* the one who said I should branch out, that choosing the same kind of woman over and over again would get me caught. You should be proud; I even improvised."

The doctor's face grew even paler. "There was only supposed to be the one."

"The one *you* wanted. What about what *I* wanted?"

"You promised to stop. But you broke that promise, didn't you?" Frank's voice was pitched higher than normal. "Perhaps that is why the dream has recurred. Perhaps she's come back to punish you for what you've been doing."

She. His stomach clenched with dread. He spoke, the words coming out of his mouth without his willing them. "I'm a *good* boy."

The doctor didn't answer, just sat there looking at him with a half-smile on his face. David jumped to his feet and leaned over the desk.

"I'M A *GOOD* BOY!" he shouted.

And then he saw the fear on the other man's face. A glow of satisfaction replaced his anger.

"Of course you're a good boy," Frank soothed. "I never said otherwise, did I?"

David sat back down. Fear, fear, fear—in the man's eyes, in his white-knuckled hands.

"Now, David, I want you to remember that I'm your friend. And as your friend, I only want what's best for you."

"Then get rid of the dream."

"I can't as long as you're still doing . . . things. If you really want me to help you, you should commit yourself to Donlevy Psychiatric Center. With the proper medication and therapy, we should be able to deal with your nightmare."

Frank continued to talk, making arrangements as though the younger man had agreed to his suggestion.

But David tuned out the smooth emotionless voice, the smooth emotionless face. The doctor had seemed so friendly the first time David had come here last November. He'd been broke—nowhere to go, nowhere to stay—and the man at the Downtown Mission had referred him to the nice psychiatrist who paid five dollars an hour to talk to the homeless.

David found himself enjoying talking to such an attentive listener. Not many people had ever listened to him. So he kept going back. Reassured by the doctor that everything he said was completely confidential, he began to talk about some of the things he'd done back in Indiana. Frank had been fascinated. Eager to help, eager to give advice. Eager to be friends. He had let David stay for free in a house he owned, given him money for a car, clothes, gasoline.

But now, looking into Frank's cold, calculating eyes, David realized now that it hadn't been friendship that had motivated the doctor. *He thinks he can control me. Do this, David, do that, David. Think this, David, think that, David. Push the buttons and watch me go.*

Well, two could push buttons. Cutting the doctor off in mid-word, he said, "Your sister-in-law hired a private investigator to check you out," he said.

"What?" Frank looked completely stunned, as though

someone had punched him in the belly.

Amusement curled David's insides. He repeated, "Your sister-in-law hired an investigator to look into your doings, Frank."

"H-how do you know?"

"Don't worry, I took care of the problem for you. It was a *lady* investigator."

"David." The doctor's voice shook. "How do you know what Garland is doing?"

He smiled. "I heard it on her answering machine."

"What were you doing in her house?"

He smiled again.

Frank stood up and put his palms flat on the desk. "You can't. The police will have a link between two of the victims. Don't you understand how dangerous that is?"

"I don't have any connection with them."

"But I do! If both my wife and her sister are killed, the police are going to come straight to me."

"But Garland is perfect," David said. "The best one yet."

Muscles jumped spasmodically in the doctor's face. After a moment they smoothed out, leaving his face as coolly expressionless as usual. "I'm going to give you some money, David. I want you to leave Norfolk. It isn't safe for you any longer."

"I like it here," David said. *He'd like to keep me from Garland. He'd like to stop me.*

"David, you've got to listen to me. The only reason you weren't caught long ago is the fact that you chose prostitutes. No one cares what happens to a prostitute. But you've started taking others, women with connections and families."

"So what? You were the one who said I shouldn't stay with the same kind of woman all the time."

"I said—"

"You said exactly that, *Doctor* Hollister. My memory is very good. I never liked blondes. I still don't. But I've learned to accept them. You should be proud to know you did such a good job 'removing my fixation on small, dark women.' "

Frank sank heavily into the chair.

David continued, "I'm grateful to you for introducing me to Garland. I've been looking for her for a very long time. She's the one who will free me, you know."

"From your dream?" Frank whispered.

"Yes. I should have known none of the others would do." His gaze strayed to Charla Ross's portrait, then returned to the older man's face. "Only Garland."

The slack look of shock on the doctor's face showed that he realized the extent of his miscalculation. Good, David thought. Frank knew the truth now. Secure in his superior education, his supposed understanding of human nature, he had thought to use David Cudahy. A tool was all he wanted. Something to be used, then discarded when it served its purpose.

But this wasn't the world Frank assumed it to be. This was the hunter's realm. The jungle.

David smiled. Garland would be the culmination of his whole life. His final step. His catharsis. Nothing else mattered. Frank was incapable of seeing that.

Still smiling, David got up and pushed his chair back. This would be his last visit.

"Where are you going?" Frank asked.

Without bothering to answer, he turned on his heel and headed for the door.

"David, wait!"

He kept walking.

"David, we've got to talk! Dav—"

He closed the door behind him, shutting off the voice.

* * *

"Whew, what a day!" Garland said.

Milo locked the door and turned the sign to CLOSED. "It's been the busiest Monday *I* remember. Did everyone in Norfolk decide to clean out all the books in their attics yesterday?"

"Whatever. We got some really neat stuff." Hands on hips, she surveyed the boxes that were stacked around the desk. "I guess we'll just put them in the Tomb until we can get to them."

"Hand me a couple."

It took them almost a half hour to move the boxes back to the storeroom. Afterward, Milo sat on the desk and waited while Garland tried calling Delores Marcille. There was still no answer.

"I've tried several times today," she said. "Doesn't she have an answering machine?"

"Sure she does. You mean it isn't on?"

"No, and I get no answer at her home phone either."

"That's odd," Milo said. "She usually leaves them both on whenever she's out of town or something."

"Did she say what she wanted when she called Friday?"

He shook his head. "Delores goes by the book; she would no more discuss your business with me than she would with Frank."

"I wonder what she found," Garland said.

"She'll get back to you, don't worry." Milo slid off the desk and reached for their coats. "Let's go. We've both got things to do."

Having something to do after work was still new to her. As she drove toward home, she found herself looking forward to going there. But still, hovering at the edges of her contentment like a dark shadow was the question of what would happen between her and Colin once the glow wore off. As it surely would—that was a cold, hard fact of life.

With a hiss of exasperation, she turned the stereo up loud, hoping to drive her self-doubts out of her head. What a fool she was! Anyone else would grab for happiness with both hands and be content with it while it lasted. But she couldn't. She had to worry at the edges of it, looking for flaws, frightened by the holes made by her own insecurities.

As she pulled into her driveway, she saw that Colin wasn't back yet. She hurried up the walk, trying not to look at the butchered daffodils.

"Hello, cat," she murmured as Numbnuts came to greet her. "Did you miss me?"

"Miaow," he replied.

He probably missed his tuna, not me, she thought. Carrying him like a baby, she headed for the kitchen. "You've got no dignity at all, do you know that?"

Evidently he didn't care, for he stayed in the same position, feet in the air, his tail draped across her arm. He didn't move until she got near the cabinet in which she kept his tuna. Then he jumped down and began to twine around her ankles.

"Okay, okay, take it easy," she said.

While she was opening the can, she heard a key in the lock. It was strange having someone else come into her house this way after years of living alone. She couldn't quite decide if it was good-strange or disturbing-strange. Maybe she'd get used to it in time.

"Hi," he said, coming around the corner. He was carrying a grocery bag. His hair was ruffled from the wind.

"Hi."

She expected him to kiss her, but walked past her to set the bag on the table. He pulled something out of it and turned toward her. It was a copy of the *Galaxie News,* one of the worst of the tabloids. Her stomach knotted.

Feeling like a lamb being led to the slaughter, she held out her hand for it. Quickly, she scanned the front page. Among the headlines about Elvis sightings and the leak in Dolly Parton's breasts was one that read, GALAXIE EXCLUSIVE: MURDERED MODEL POSED FOR NUDE PICTURES.

She closed her eyes. "They didn't. They *couldn't.*"

"I'm sorry, but they did. Your sister's agent gave them the photos—nearly half the article is about *him.*"

Her hands shook as she flipped through the paper. And there they were: pictures of Charla. Charla standing, Charla reclining, Charla posing playfully on her hands and knees. Narrow black-ink rectangles titillated as well as concealed.

Garland threw the paper as far from her as she could. The pages fluttered to the floor, the pictures of Charla coming to rest uppermost. Garland hugged herself to hide her trembling from Colin. This was the last straw, the final outrage!

When she could trust herself to speak again, she went to the phone and dialed Ted Ballard's number. Heaven must have been looking down on her, for he answered on the first ring.

"Mr. Ballard, this is Garland Ross," she said.

His voice was hearty. "Well, hey, Garland. How are you doing?"

"I saw the article in *Galaxie News.*"

"Ah, yes. Charla made those photos when she was young and hungry to break into the business. Marvelous, aren't they?"

"No!"

"Believe me, Charla would have wanted it this way. She *loved* publicity."

Garland took a deep breath, hating his oily heartiness, his use of Charla's tragedy to line his own pockets. "I'm going to sue you blind," she shouted. "I'm going to—"

"Now, now, let's not get nasty about this. Everything I did was absolutely legal." There was amusement in his gravelly voice. "I've got signed releases for every one of those pictures, sweetheart."

"You're a jerk, Mr. Ballard. A total—"

The line went dead. Garland stood with the phone in her hand, too furious to speak. Finally Colin took the phone from her and hung it up.

Putting his hands on her shoulders, he turned her around to face him. "Sorry, honey."

"He didn't give a damn about her! She was nothing but dollars and cents to him. A body to put on the block and sell to line his pockets! She couldn't have been more than eighteen when she'd made those photos. From beginning to end, she'd been taken advantage of."

She continued talking—raving, really, but she couldn't seem to stop herself. Colin merely held her, letting her wind down. When she could think rationally again, she said, "I don't know why you put up with this."

"Well, one thing's for sure: life with you isn't dull."

He bent and began picking up the scattered newspaper. "At least this explains the daffodils."

"What?"

"The daffodils. Scandal brings the kooks running like cockroaches."

"You're right." A steady throb of pain settled into her head, and she pressed her fingertips against her temples, trying to will it away. "Lousy world, lousy people. But I guess it's better than no explanation at all."

He got to his feet and took her chin in his hand to study her eyes. "You look awful. Why don't you go lie down? I'll call you when dinner's ready."

She obeyed, sinking into the welcome softness of her pillow with a sigh. The cat jumped onto the bed and settled against the back of her legs. The last thing she heard before sleep claimed her was his buzz saw of a purr.

Chapter Twenty

Garland woke to the unmistakable smell of meatloaf cooking. Propping herself up on one elbow, she peered at the clock. It was nearly eight-thirty. She'd been asleep nearly two hours. The cat was no longer in the room; at some point Colin must have let him out.

She got out of bed, brushed her hair and teeth, then went out into the kitchen. Colin was stirring something on the stove. The table was set, and the delicious aroma of biscuits was starting to seep out of the oven.

"I hope this is a sign of what the future holds," she said.

He switched the burner off and turned around to face her. "Feeling better?"

"A lot. I don't know what happened to me. I just kind of passed out."

"It was emotional overload, honey. I'm surprised it didn't happen earlier."

He opened his arms, and she walked into them. It felt good to be held. "I was dead to the world. I didn't even hear you let the cat out."

The timer went off. "That's the biscuits," he said, letting go of her. "Canned ones, I'm afraid."

"What other kind are there?" she asked, smiling.

He laughed. "My mother used to bake the fluffiest, tastiest homemade biscuits in town."

"My mom was a secretary. Her boss worked long

hours, so she did, too. I did most of the cooking. Canned biscuits were all I could manage."

"Then you'll feel right at home tonight."

She went into the kitchen to help him, and a few minutes later they sat down to eat. Just when she'd taken her first bite, however, the doorbell rang.

"I'll get it," she said, pushing her chair back.

Colin came with her, reaching around her to open the door. Garland touched him on the arm reassuringly when she saw one of her neighbors standing on the porch. She didn't know Dave Younston well, but they'd had pleasant dealings over the years.

"Hi, Dave. Come on in," she said. She introduced the two men casually.

"We've got a new mailman," Dave said.

"Not again!" She turned to Colin. "Dave's address is almost the same as mine, except he lives at 237 Maravid *Court*. Whenever a new mailman is assigned to this neighborhood, our mail is screwed up until he gets acclimated."

Dave held out a manila envelope. "This is yours. Anything else I get, I'll dump in your mailbox." Nodding to Colin, he added, "I smell your dinner. I'll let you get back to it. Nice meeting you, Colin."

"You, too." Colin closed the door and leaned his back against it. "This is my *friend,* Colin Kingsley?"

"What was I supposed to say?" she countered. "This is my squeeze, my lover, my prospective cohabitee?"

He laughed. "Cohabitee? Shit, Garland, that sounds like a disease. Come on, let's eat while the food is hot."

Garland let him steer her back to the table. "I wonder what this is," she said, turning the envelope over. The return address said Marcille Investigation Services. Her name and address was written in such a scrawl that it was a miracle the thing had made it even to Dave's house.

She opened it, then pushed her plate aside. It was a

computer printout, long columns of numbers with pluses and minuses in front of them.

"What the hell?" she muttered. A large blue Post-It note was stuck on the front, written in the same terrible hand as the envelope. "Colin, listen to this."

" 'Dear Miss Ross,' " she read. " 'Sorry this is so disorganized, but I wanted to get this to you in case we don't get together before I go out of town next week. Getting this info was a bear; the Hollisters—singly and collectively—have their fingers in a lot of pies. Tracing Frank's was like unwinding a tangle of yarn. As you will see in the highlighted areas, he's taken nearly sixty thousand dollars from different places and funneled it into his practice in the past three months.

" 'This could mean his practice isn't doing well, or it could mean something else entirely. Without looking at his books, I won't be able to find out what he's used it for. Let me know what you want me to do next. Delores Marcille.' "

Garland put the letter aside and thumbed through the printout. Or rather, printouts; it looked like Frank had dealings with at least four different banks. "She's right. He's taken a little here and a little there and skinned it through one account or another. But all of it ended up in the same place. His practice."

"May I?" Colin held out his hand for the printouts. After a couple of minutes he looked up again. "You can't say he's hurting for money. There's a lot of fat here. Hell, his savings account is more than I made in the past five years."

"Right. Then why didn't he take the sixty thousand out of it instead of taking a bit from here and a bit from there?"

"Maybe he's consolidating."

"Maybe. But he's spent almost twenty thousand of it in the past few weeks." She ran her fingertip along one column. "Look, here, here and here. Nice, big chunks—

five thousand, seven thousand, and three thousand just the other day."

Colin spread his hands. "Research?"

"The only research I know about is something about incidence of mental illness among the homeless. He pays them five bucks an hour to talk to him. I don't think there are enough homeless in Tidewater to go through twenty thousand in a couple of weeks. Come on, Colin, what's wrong with you?"

"I'm just playing devil's advocate." Spearing another square of meatloaf, he added, "Seeing where this is going."

She fended off the proffered food. "I have to know what he did with that money."

"What are you doing to do? Send the investigator to burglarize his office?"

"I wouldn't ask anyone else to break the law." Pushing her chair back, she went into the kitchen and began rummaging around inside the junk drawer. Finally she straightened, a well-stocked key ring dangling from her thumb and forefinger. "Ta-daah. Charla gave me copies of all her keys long ago. And she made sure she had a key to *everything.*"

Colin shook his head. "I don't believe you'd actually consider this. Give it to Detective Baedecker. Let him deal with it, that's his job."

"He already thinks I'm a little strange. If I go to him with just this, he'll laugh me out of his office." She walked back to her chair and grasped the back of it. Her hands were trembling enough to make the wood creak. "Someone killed my little sister, Colin. If Frank's hiding something, I've got to find out what and why. Maybe it'll have no bearing on her murder. Maybe he's just a lousy businessman and doesn't want anyone else to know. But I have to be sure. I can't look at him day after day . . . Okay, I'll say it before you do: I can't let my nieces live in that house with him unless I know."

With a sigh, he got to his feet. "I guess this means I don't get dessert."

"I don't want you to go. If I get caught, I don't want to have you on my conscience. Besides, I may need somebody to bail me out of jail."

"Milo can bail us both out."

"No."

"Yes."

"No!"

He smiled. "I'm bigger than you are."

"Colin . . ." She broke off, seeing the stubborn set of his jaw. A new aspect of Colin. It wasn't a nasty kind of stubbornness, but just as unreasonable. She could talk herself blue in the face, but she wasn't going to change his mind.

"You call around and see if you can find out where Frank is," he said. "I'll put the food away. And yes"—he spoke to the cat—"you will get some meatloaf."

Garland called Frank's office. Getting no answer there, she tried the house next. Xenia answered. "Yes, Miss Ross, he's at home. But he's resting just now. May I have him call you?"

"I'll call back later. Are the twins available?"

"No, I'm sorry, they're at a friend's house."

"Well, give them a kiss for me. Thank you, Xenia."

She hung up and went to get her coat. Colin checked to make sure the oven was off, then followed her.

It was a quiet ride downtown. Although Colin made several attempts at conversation, Garland was too nervous to help him out much. She was as tightly-strung as a guy wire by the time they pulled up in front of Frank's office. The big trees hung over the building, seeming to gather the darkness even more thickly beneath their branches. The only light in the building was the brass coachlight beside the door.

"Spooky," Colin said in a stage whisper. "Did you notice there's a full moon tonight?"

"Don't make fun," Garland said. "Breaking and entering is serious business."

"Who's making fun?" He parked the car and turned the engine off. "What if your key doesn't work?"

"Then I'll have to think of something else." She undid her seat belt. "Now look—we go right up to the door and act like we're supposed to be here. That way, if someone happens to see us, they'll think everything's okay."

"You sound like you've done this before."

"Are you always like this in stressful situations?" she asked.

"Pretty much."

"I might as well have brought Milo." She got out of the car and walked up to the building, conscious of Colin behind her. The key worked.

"Let me go first," Colin said, all business now. Taking a flashlight out of his pocket, he led the way inside.

The beam moved around the waiting room, picking out a chair here, a magazine cover there, reflecting off the glass window that separated this room from the secretary's office.

"Which way?" Colin asked.

"He'll keep his books in his private office," she said, pushing him toward the back hallway.

Reaching Frank's office at last, they turned the light on and surveyed the territory. There was a lot of it to cover: three four-drawer file cabinets, Frank's desk, and the storage cabinet on the far wall. The big portrait of Charla dominated the room. No matter where Garland was when she looked at the portrait, Charla's eyes seemed to be focused on her.

"I'll take the armoire thing over here, you take the file cabinets," Colin said. Garland saw him run his fingers lightly over the polished wood of the cabinet. "Is this an antique?"

"No, just a very expensive reproduction." Turning to

the file cabinets, she opened the top drawer and flipped quickly through its contents. All patient files. Closing that one, she went to the one below. Ditto. And ditto for the other two.

She moved on to another file cabinet. *God, what's happening to me? Breaking into Frank's office, looking through his records. Is it the murder, or him, or me?* She could still feel the portrait staring at her. Not in disapproval; if Charla could actually see her staid older sister burglarizing Frank's office, she'd think it hilarious.

"Nothing in here," Colin muttered. "I'm going to try the desk." After a moment he said, "The drawers are locked."

Garland turned to look at him. He raked his hands through his hair in obvious frustration.

"Look, Garland. Going through his stuff is one thing, prying locks open is another. I don't feel right about it."

She sighed. "Okay, I don't, either. But—"

"A commendable attitude." It was Frank's voice, sounding even more clipped than usual.

Garland whirled around to see her brother-in-law standing in the doorway. "Frank!"

"I'm glad to see you have *some* scruples," he said. "It's obvious you didn't expect me. How fortunate that I decided to come down here and get some work done." He came farther into the room. Although he was wearing slacks and a sweater, he made them look as stiff and formal as his suits. Hands on hips, he looked at Colin, then Garland, and then past her to the open drawer of the file cabinet. "Would either of you like to explain this?"

Garland lifted her chin, deciding to take the bull by the horns. "We were trying to find out what you did with that sixty thousand dollars, Frank."

"What sixty thousand dollars?"

"You've been funneling money from your personal to your business account," she said.

"Yes, I have."

Garland blinked; calm admission wasn't what she expected. Before she could say anything, however, Frank went to the file cabinet and gently closed the drawer. He turned around again, and she saw how gaunt his face was, the skin tightly-stretched over the bones. But there was no emotion showing; he might be anything from terrified to furious. God, she wished she knew what went on in that cold, methodical mind of his!

Frank sat down behind the desk and clasped his hands in front of him. "I won't belabor the fact that the money was mine, and what I did with it is entirely my business. What is important here is your welfare, Garland."

"My welfare?" She gaped at him in astonishment. That was absolutely the last thing she expected to hear.

"Grief can do terrible things to people," he said.

"What do you mean?"

"Why don't you sit down?" He indicated the chairs in front of the desk.

Garland crossed her arms over her chest. "I'd rather stand."

"Very well." His coolly dignified gaze didn't waver. "It's perfectly natural to want to blame someone for Charla's death. With her murderer not found, there's no one to point to and say, 'He's the one to blame.' But you've gone a bit overboard with this, don't you think?"

Surprise turned to anger, a swift, hot rush through her body. "Now just a minute—"

"Please let me finish." Somehow, Frank managed to talk right over her without raising either the pitch or volume of his voice. "I strongly suggest you get help. Of course I can't treat you myself, but I can recommend several excellent doctors with expertise in this subject."

Garland was too angry to speak. Her field of view narrowed to his eyes. The light from the lamp was reflected in them, making his pupils look like tiny leaping flames. It was the only warmth she'd ever seen in him, and even it was borrowed. Her welfare! Who was he kidding?

Her voice returned with a rush. It was too shrill, but she was past trying to control it. "There's not one goddamn thing wrong with me. It's the situation that isn't normal!"

"Of course the situation isn't normal," Frank soothed. "There's nothing wrong with getting help in dealing with it."

"I *am* dealing with it!" she shouted. "And I'm going to continue dealing with it until Charla's murderer is caught!"

"Is this"—Frank indicated their presence in his office—"a rational way of dealing with it?"

"You're hiding something, Frank."

"Nonsense." He looked past her, toward Colin. "I take it you're . . . involved with my sister-in-law, Mr., ah . . ."

"Kingsley."

"Mr. Kingsley, do you care for her well-being?"

Colin nodded. "Very much."

"Then help her. Get her to someone competent to deal with—"

"Frank." Garland put her hands flat on the desk and leaned forward. "If you have something to say, say it to me."

He tilted his head back to look at her. "Would you listen to me if I did?"

"Probably not."

"Come now, Garland. Can you say that breaking in here was a totally rational act?"

Easy, Garland. Easy, he's doing it to you again. "It seemed to be."

"I wonder if the police would think so."

"Why don't you call them and ask?" She forced herself to smile, hoping it didn't look as unnatural as it felt.

Frank's hands remained clasped on the desktop. "I wouldn't do that to you. You've got enough problems."

"What are you hiding?" she asked again.

"I have nothing to hide."

"Don't give me that crap," she hissed. "You didn't funnel sixty thousand dollars into your practice to pay the light bill."

"What I do with my money is my business," he said.

"And Charla is *my* business."

"No, Garland. Charla is the police department's business, and God's, but certainly not yours."

She drew in her breath harshly. "Neither the police nor God is doing a whole hell of a lot to find her killer."

"Perhaps you think I've hidden him in my file cabinets," he said.

"You knew she was going to divorce you."

"Ah, that again. I'm afraid my answer will be the same as it was before. Charla and I had no plans to separate. That is truth, that is reality. I'm sorry if you cannot accept that. The police have." Frank got up and went to the minibar. "Let me get you something to drink. Some soda, perhaps?"

"I saw you throw your drink at her portrait," she said.

"And that is what you base your judgment on?" He shook his head sadly.

The sympathy in his voice was not reflected in his eyes. An excellent performance, Garland thought. He'd hit just the right note, found just the right words. No matter what she said, she'd look bad. "Damn it to hell, Frank! I know what I saw!"

"Do you?" he asked, smiling faintly.

That smile was *it*. She wanted to throw things, to leap across the desk and shake Frank until he rattled like a castanet. Then she caught sight of Colin's face. He was watching her, not Frank, and his eyes contained love and concern . . . and doubt.

With a muttered exclamation, she flung herself away from the desk and went to stand in front of the window. Her hands were shaking, so she clasped them together in an effort to control them. *Ohhhhh, Frank is slick! Five minutes, and he's already working Colin over.*

She'd played right into his hands. Straight man to the oh, so kind and solicitous doctor. Even Colin, who *wanted* to believe her, was having doubts.

There was silence in the room, and she could feel both men's gazes on her. Finally Colin said, "Let's go, Garland."

"Just a moment," Frank said. "I assume you used a key to get in?"

Garland nodded.

"I'll take it, if you don't mind."

She did mind, but there was nothing she could do. But she was *damned* if she was going to hand it to him. Instead, she dropped it on the desk as she walked past it toward the door.

Garland glanced at Frank over her shoulder. He was standing in front of the bar, his face looking as pale and hard as marble. Then he reached up and smoothed his hair.

Colin hustled her out to the car. She managed to hold everything inside until he was strapped in beside her. Then the tears started, tears of mingled rage and frustration.

"He sounds so damned reasonable!" she said. "Do it Frank's way, think the way Frank wants you to. If you disagree with Frank, you need help."

Colin pulled a couple of tissues out of the box he kept on the dashboard. "Take it easy, Garland. Remember, he could have had us in jail tonight."

She stared down at her lap, folding the tissue into smaller and smaller squares. "That was it, my only shot. Whatever is in his office won't be there an hour from now."

"Maybe there wasn't anything in his office."

"Sure there was. Why else do you think he refrained from calling the police?"

He put the car into gear and pulled out of the parking lot.

Garland stared blindly out the window. It wasn't until they were on the highway heading for home that she said, "He did it to you, didn't he?"

"Did what?" he asked.

"I saw it in your face. You actually started to believe what he was saying."

"Garland, I . . ." With an irritated movement, he raked his hand through his hair. "Look. I love you. I'm with you, no matter what happens. But we could be wrong about Frank. He didn't act guilty, didn't act mad, didn't react in any way I expected. Now I don't know what to think."

She let her breath out in a long sigh. She had no proof, nothing. Frank held all the cards; if he could make Colin doubt her, he'd have Baedecker convinced she was a candidate for the funny farm. She'd have to depend on Delores Marcille to dig something up. *If you spend that other forty thousand, Frank, better make sure you've got a receipt.*

Colin seemed content to let the silence continue. After a few moments he started whistling something under his breath. Nerves, she thought. He'd been great so far. Certainly he'd had more faith than *she* would under the circumstances.

But faith, like love, can be stretched too far.

Chapter Twenty-one

David parked his car across the street from Garland's house. He'd come here the night before, ready to walk into her house and take her. But the man had been there. Again. He was still there, his car parked right in the driveway for all the world to see.

"Slut," David whispered through his teeth.

The man wasn't going to stop him. She'd been marked. The hunter's prey. No one ever escaped him.

He smiled, but his lips felt stiff and strange. The air was cold on his bared teeth. Thursdays she worked in the bookstore until 8 P.M. Alone.

Run, run as fast as you can . . . He closed the door on that refrain fast. It held too much of his past. Too much of her. *But you're going to be rid of her soon. Both with one stroke—the quick and the dead. Exorcised.*

Garland came out of the house and walked toward her van. He stiffened, every sense springing to alertness. His prey. Would there be time to run across the street . . . No, the man came out of the house to join her.

They stood beside Garland's van, their heads close together in conversation. The man put his arm around her waist, a possessive gesture. David felt his lips writhe back in a snarl. The pair looked as though they were wrapped in their own little world. A private world of the flesh, where there was room for only two. No one else could share. No trespassing. Keep out!

The man leaned down and kissed her, then opened the door of the van for her. David watched her drive away. When he turned to look at the house again, the man's car was gone, too.

Whistling under his breath, David slid out from behind the wheel and trotted across the street. Getting in was as easy as ever, a quick flip of his thin piece of metal and the door was open. The house smelled of breakfast. This time it wasn't a welcoming sort of smell, because he knew it wasn't meant for him.

He walked back to the bedroom. The bed was neatly made, but the room smelled of *them*. He knew what they'd been doing. With a jerk of his wrist, he opened the nightstand drawer. There were several condoms inside. Safe sex. His lip curled contemptuously. *Nothing* was going to be safe for her.

Then he noticed the picture lying on top of the chest of drawers. His hands trembled as he picked it up. It was a drawing of Garland holding the flowers he'd left for her. She was kneeling, and the expression on her face made the hairs rise up on the back of his neck. Mingled shock, bewilderment, horror—he'd seen that look on many women's faces before, but it had never been so . . . pleasurable. He had to have this for himself.

Rolling the drawing so as not to crease it, he slipped it into his left pocket. "I'll just leave something in return," he murmured. From his right pocket, he took the mummified cardinal he'd removed from her trash days ago. Smiling, he dropped it onto the chest.

"A message from me to you," he said, adding, "Although you probably won't get it until it's too late."

There were a lot of things she wouldn't get until it was too late.

He left the house, carefully locking the door behind him. Strange, he thought, there had been no sign of the cat. Maybe it was for the best; he kind of liked the cat.

As he slid behind the wheel of his car, a moving van

came around the corner and pulled up at the curb behind him. For a moment his heart pounded in fear; no one was supposed to be home at these apartments this time of day. Had someone seen him? He hoped not; he'd have to silence whoever it was, and that would be distracting. His purpose was pure, the course of his hunt a straight, uncluttered road stretching ahead of him. He wouldn't want distractions. He watched in the rearview mirror as the driver of the van got out and went up to knock on the door of the apartment. After a few moments, a man opened the door. His red hair was wet, and he was wearing only a towel wrapped around his hips. He swung the door wide to let the driver in.

David smiled. The guy in the apartment couldn't have seen him leave Garland's house. Good. After waiting a few minutes, he got out of his car and walked up to the apartment. He knocked on the open door and called, "Hello?"

The redhead reappeared. This time he was wearing a pair of jeans and a sweatshirt. "What can I do for you? If you're selling—"

"I'm not selling anything," David said. "I'm looking for an apartment and happened to see the moving van here. Is this place going to be available soon?"

"Sorry. A friend of mine is going to be moving in here in a couple of weeks to finish out my lease."

A couple of weeks, David thought. Plenty of time. He looked over the other man's shoulder at the interior. The apartment looked clean and in good repair; even if the landlord knew about the subleasing arrangement, he might not bother much with a well-kept-up place.

"Here's the landlord's card." The redhead pulled a business card from his back pocket and handed it to David. "These places stay pretty full, but he can tell you if anything else is going to be open soon."

"Thanks." David took the card without looking at it. "Are these places kept up pretty well? I mean, does the landlord go in and clean them up between tenants?"

The other man shrugged. "They're all right, I guess. Look, I'm pretty busy right now."

"Sure. Thanks for the card." David turned and headed back to his car. The apartment was perfect—safe and private, with a nice, big picture window that looked straight at Garland's house.

Things were falling into place. The power flowed within him, making everything happen the way he wanted. He could do no wrong, make no mistakes.

Smiling, he started the car. It was going to be a busy day today. *Things to do, places to go, people to see. People to talk to.* There were things he had to reveal about himself—no, not himself, but his works—so that Garland might begin to understand the hunt.

He could hear Frank's voice, a dim echo in his mind. "Be careful, David. Think things through. Know your enemies' strengths and weaknesses. Be in control."

"Yes," he said. It was good advice. A hunter is adaptable. A hunter uses everything around him. Even the technology that was set up to aid the police, if used properly, could be his ally.

Whistling, he put the car in gear and drove away.

A burning sensation spread through Baedecker's gut. Grimacing, he fumbled in the top drawer of his desk for his antacid tablets. Damned if this case wasn't going to give him an ulcer.

He'd just come from the first meeting of the task force set up to handle this case. *And guess who has the ball-crunching job of leading it. Let Baedecker handle it; he knows everybody.* Shit. Ten years ago he'd have jumped at the chance. But this case smelled bad from beginning to end.

He reached for the stack of reports that had accumulated. Everything was there: interviews with Bambi

Henks's friends, data on all the victims, their similarities, their differences. Age/occupation/habits, how they died, when and where found, everything down to what they'd had in their stomachs at the time they were killed. Facts upon facts upon facts.

They told him nothing. He'd looked at the data so many times he knew it by heart. And he didn't know any more now than he had the first time around. Stumped, dead-ended. He'd feel worse if every other man in the Task Force wasn't in the same boat. There were some similarities with a couple of files in National Criminal Information Center computer, but not enough to call it a match. And there was still data coming in, any of which might skew everything in a different direction.

His phone rang. Pushing the papers aside, he picked it up. "Baedecker."

"Hello, Detective." A man's voice, tenor and unremarkable.

Baedecker punched the button on the Caller ID box beside the phone, then jotted the number down. "What can I do for you, Mr.—?"

"I know where that missing Suffolk schoolteacher is."

"You do? Where is she?"

"Where I put her."

A rush of adrenaline went through Baedecker. He stood up and began making violent gestures at his partner, who was across the room getting a cup of coffee. Jeff looked up, dropped his half-full cup on the floor, and ran to snatch the paper Baedecker held out to him. A moment later he was at his own desk dialing the phone company.

"Is she dead?" Baedecker asked.

"Of course. But not like the others. I strangled *her*."

"Why?"

"Why not?"

There was silence, and for a heart-stopping instant Baedecker thought he'd lost him. "Talk to me," he urged, poising his pen over his paper. *Please, please, please!*

"There's a spot on Kings Highway just outside Chuckatuck where the kudzu has overgrown the trees. Behind it is a shallow gully. Look there."

Jeff held up a piece of paper. "Pay phone in Smithfield. Hold him!"

Baedecker nodded. "Why did you—"

The phone went dead. He shook the receiver as though to revive it, then tossed it back into the cradle. "Damn!"

"Lose him?" Jeff asked.

"Yeah." With a sigh, he ripped the top sheet off the pad. "Call Suffolk. We've got Winona Olyar. It's our boy, all right. He said he strangled her."

Jeff put his hand on the phone but didn't pick it up. There was a sick look on his face that echoed the cramp in Baedecker's gut. They'd been working together long enough that Kurt knew what he was thinking: cross off everything they thought they knew about the man and start over. He couldn't be slotted in any category except "killer." He could be anyone.

He was smart, he was adaptable, and that made him doubly dangerous. And unless some miracle happened, they weren't going to catch him.

Garland got home just after dark. Business had been good all day, although she'd cringed at the prospect that every stranger might be a reporter come to ask her about Charla's nude pictures. No one had, however; all she and Milo had done was sell a lot of books.

She slammed the door of the van and strode up the walk, muttering "That goddamned Ted Ballard" under her breath. "What a world! Money, money, money, and not a single thought for people's feelings . . ."

The moment she opened the door, Numbnuts rushed the opening. He was moving so fast that he was a glimpse of orange fur as he made the turn into the bedroom.

She dumped her coat and purse on the sofa and went into the kitchen to get a can of tuna out for him. He was nowhere in sight, but she knew from experience that he'd come running the minute she started the electric can opener.

The phone rang just as she inserted the can beneath the cutter. With a muttered curse, she picked it up. "Hello?"

"It's me," Milo said. "You missed some fun a few minutes ago."

"Just a second, Milo," she said. "Let me get this can open before his lordship comes in here and shreds my legs." Cradling the phone between her ear and shoulder, she opened the can and dumped its contents into the cat's bowl.

"Okay," she said. "What fun? And where are you, by the way?"

"I'm still at the store. While I was locking up, a man drove up and stopped me. You should have seen it—the whole trunk of his car was full of books."

She felt a stirring of excitement. "Yeah? Anything good?"

"Lots of good. The guy had just inherited his uncle's estate. Uncle was a reader, he was not. He had a pretty good idea of what they were worth, but I did okay. Gave him a check on the spot."

"I can't wait to see them."

"We've got a lot of logging-in to do with this lot and the stuff we bought last week. What say we both work Thursday night? If we close the store for a few hours, we can get everything priced and out on the shelves for the weekend."

"Sounds good to me," she said.

"Hey, did you hear from Delores?"

Glancing at the steady light on her answering machine,

she said, "No, not a word. I've called her office several times, but there's no answer. I guess she's still out of town."

"I'll see if I can track her down for you."

"Thanks, Milo. Be careful driving home; the freeway is a mess. Oh, and there's a radar trap just before the Military Highway exit."

"I'm always careful, darlin'. Bye."

"Bye, Milo." There had been no mention of Miss Wackahula for the last few days. Evidently the relationship had soured like . . . like overripe coconuts. The thought of coconuts brought to mind Milo's description of his woman-of-the-moment's breasts. It should have been funny, but Garland found it rather sad. Poor Milo. His relationships barely lasted long enough to win that title; love, fast and furious, while he pined for Troll, who wouldn't have him.

She stretched, leaning from side to side to get the kinks out of her spine. Then she glanced down at the cat's bowl. Where was the old glutton anyway? He never missed a meal.

"Numbnuts? Where are you, fella?" she called.

Then she remembered he'd headed for the bedroom the moment he'd come inside. *Now what are you up to, you old rakehell?* It couldn't be anything good if it took precedence over food. She hurried toward the back of the house.

The first thing she saw when she walked into the bedroom was scarlet feathers scattered over her bedspread. Numbnuts sat in the center of the bed, looking up at her with an innocent expression on his striped cat face.

Garland jammed her fists onto her hips and surveyed the mess. Somehow this demon in cat form had sneaked the bird out of the trash can before the sanitation truck came. That was bad enough. But dragging the poor, mutilated thing in here and smearing it all over her good bedspread . . .

"What are you, Houdini?" she demanded. "Get off the bed."

He stood—or rather, sat—his ground. She grasped the edge of the spread with both hands and began to pull. The cat came with the cover. Garland reeled him in, dropping the spread to catch his dead weight as he slipped over the edge of the bed.

"You're a horrible animal," she said. A red feather clung to the long fur on his belly, and she plucked it off. He grabbed her hand and brought it to his mouth so he could chew the feather. "What's the matter with you? And don't give me that cat stuff about wanting to show off your hunting skill; I happen to know this particular corpse's history. Besides, you're too fat to catch anything."

He didn't even have the grace to look embarrassed. Laughing, Garland tossed him back onto the bed. Gathering up the bedspread, she took it out into the garage and stuffed it, feathers and all, into the washing machine.

As the water level rose, bright red feathers began to float up to the surface. Garland picked them off and tossed them into the trash can, then dumped a double scoop of detergent into the washer. Feathers were one thing, but she was *not* going to pick bird parts off by hand, at least not until they'd gone through the wash cycle.

The phone rang, barely heard through the noise of the machine. Garland banged the lid down and ran to answer it.

"Hello?" she said breathlessly.

"Hi. What are you doing?"

It was a sort-of-familiar male voice, but she couldn't quite place it. "Who is this?"

"Don't you know?"

"No, I don't."

"You will."

She heaved a sigh. "Look, who is this?"

"Why don't you try guessing? If you think hard enough, I'm sure you'll remember me."

"Oh, brother," Garland muttered under her breath. Raising her voice so the caller could hear her, she said, "I think you've got the wrong number. Either tell me who you are or hang up and go bother someone else."

"You're not very nice."

"You're right. I'm not." With that, she hung up.

She started scrubbing potatoes for dinner, taking out her irritation on the vegetables while waiting for the phone to ring again. But it didn't, and she decided he'd just dialed her number by chance. Hear a female voice and take advantage.

"What a creep," she muttered.

She heard Colin's key in the lock, and a moment later the sound of the door opening and closing. The rustle of paper and the smell of Chinese food wafted in from the living room. Abandoning the potatoes, she went to meet him.

"What've you got?" she asked.

He set the bag on the coffee table and peeled his coat off. "Eggrolls, fried rice, Kung-Pao chicken, and a dozen fortune cookies. I love those things." His gaze moved to a spot behind Garland. "I did *not* call your name."

Garland didn't have to look behind her to know who was there. "Speak of the devil. Colin, you wouldn't believe what he did today."

"I'd believe anything anybody said about that cat." Colin pulled her close, his hands making smooth, possessive strokes along the curve of her back. "You ought to close the front curtain at night, Garland. I could see right into the house."

"I forgot." She glanced at the picture window and saw that he'd already closed them. "The cat distracted me. And besides, I'm not in the habit of doing anything that would shock the neighbors."

"Times have changed, honey," he said.

During that short exchange, he managed to work her sweater up and over her head. He flung it over his shoulder carelessly. Her bra followed. As his hands explored her, she arched her back to welcome him. Again, his touch sent shock waves of desire through her, warming her to her toes. She felt cherished and safe, and the rest of the world very far away just now.

"What about the food?" she asked. "It's going to get cold."

"That's what microwaves are for." Lifting her, he turned and laid her on the sofa. He finished undressing her, his big, square hands gentle and sure, yet trembling in a way that aroused her unbearably. Her own hands fumbled with haste at his buttons and zipper.

When they were both naked at last, he flipped her up and over so that she was lying on top of him. She wanted to touch every part of him, do everything all at once, but settled for a kiss that left them shaking and breathless.

"Is it always going to be like this?" she whispered.

"God, I hope so," he said, pulling her down for another kiss.

Chapter Twenty-two

Garland tallied up the day's receipts while Milo went down to the deli to get something to eat. He came back in a few minutes later, a giant-sized cup of iced tea in one hand, a newspaper in the other.

"Take a look at that," he said, tossing the paper down on the desk.

SERIAL KILLER STALKS AREA! the headline screamed. Below, in smaller letters, was *Charla Ross only the beginning. Suffolk teacher found near Chuckatuck said to be killer's fourth victim.* Garland scanned the article below. She couldn't find out who had "said" anything official about a serial killer; all Baedecker had had to say in his interview was "no comment."

But the journalist's argument was convincing, especially when he compared the details of all four cases. Garland sat there, stunned, trying to take it all in. A serial killer—murder without reason, a victim chosen at random for reasons no sane person could understand. All the things she'd been thinking about Frank suddenly added up to zero.

"I was wrong about Frank," she said.

Milo spread his hands. "It wasn't as if you had no reason—"

"I accused him of holding back information about Charla's death." She leaned her elbows on the desk, feeling as if all the life were draining out of her. "That isn't the worst. Colin and I broke into his office and he caught us."

"Shit, Garland! Are you out of your mind?"

"Apparently so." *I was so sure about Frank. How could I have been so wrong? So completely, utterly wrong?*

"Baedecker had to have known. That's why he didn't want to listen to anything about Frank."

"I guess so. All I'm sure of right now is that I owe Frank an apology. And the sooner the better." She reached for the phone and tried calling Frank's office. There was no answer, so she tried the house next.

To her surprise, Frank answered.

"Frank, this is Garland. I'd like to talk to you. May I come over?"

There was a moment of silence, and she drummed her fingers on the table. Finally he said, "Xenia and the girls are at a movie."

"I'd rather talk to you privately."

"All right, Garland."

"Give me fifteen minutes." She hung up and reached for her jacket. "Lock up for me, will you, Milo?"

"Want me to come with you?"

She shook her head. "I got myself into this, now I've got to get myself out of it. But thanks."

The ten-minute drive to Frank's house seemed like an hour. Garland's stomach felt as if nails were shooting through it. Wrong or not, she didn't like Frank any more than she had before. But not liking a man was one thing and thinking him capable of abetting his wife's murder another. She owed him. And if he spit in her eye, she'd take it.

When she reached the house, its two picture windows stared at her like accusing eyes. Swallowing her nervousness, she went up and rang the bell. Frank swung the door open and stood there, framed in the rectangle of light.

Garland clutched her purse in both hands to keep

them from trembling. "Hello, Frank."

"Hello, Garland." He stepped back to let her in.

Without taking her jacket off, she sat down on the edge of the white sofa and waited for him to join her. He took the chair opposite. His maroon sweater was a solid block of color against the pale fabric of the chair.

"What may I do for you?" he asked.

Garland set her purse down on the sofa beside her and clasped her hands in her lap. "I came to apologize."

"Ah. You saw the newspaper then."

She nodded. "You were right the other night in your office. Charla's death really hurt me, and I guess I lashed out at the only person I could. I was unfair to you, and I'm sorry."

He didn't reply. Garland studied his face, trying to assess his mood, but he was closed to her. As he always had been. And, she realized now, always would be.

"I never held any grudges against you," he said. "It was *you* who held the grudge."

No forgiveness there, she thought.

"And you still don't like me very much," he continued.

"Is it necessary that we like each other"—she paused to take a deep breath—"as long as the twins are happy?"

"Ah. You sound like a wife who is staying in a bad marriage 'for the children.' "

"So?" She spread her hands. "Like it or not, I'm the closest thing to a mother they have right now, Frank. They need me. They need both of us."

"If it weren't for the girls, would you have come here to apologize?" he asked.

"Yes. The apology was owed, and I always pay my debts."

His mouth stretched in a smile that didn't reach his

eyes. "Then I accept it." Raising one finger in an admonishing gesture, he added, "If you promise to stay out of my business."

"I promise."

"And no more breaking into my office?"

"Cross my heart and hope to die."

He smoothed his hair in that gesture she was coming to know very well. There were a lot of things going on behind those cold granite eyes of his, but his face showed none of them.

"I wish you'd consider going away for a while," he said. "You've been under a great deal of stress lately. A month or two amid different scenery would do you good."

"It's a great suggestion, Frank, but I've got a business to run. A month or two is out of the question." She cocked her head to one side. "But I might be able to swing a week. I could take the girls down to Florida with me."

"That . . . would not be possible."

"Why not?"

"I don't want them missing any more school than they already have."

She met his gaze levelly. "Spill it, Frank. Is it because you don't want them going with *me?*"

"Not at all. I gave you my reason for not allowing it."

Allowing. Garland clasped her hands in her lap again and stared down at them. Subtly and succinctly, Frank had just summed up his position. He had control. She might see the twins, but he'd say where and when and how long. And as much as she might not like it, she was going to have to abide by it.

Frank's voice brought her head up. "You have a new relationship going now," he said. "Why don't you and Mr., ah . . ."

"Kingsley. Colin Kingsley."

"Why don't you and Mr. Kingsley take off somewhere?"

"He has a business to run, too."

"So I can't convince you to go?" Frank asked.

"I'm afraid not." She watched with interest as his hands went up to stroke the sides of his hair again. Something was really bothering him. "Did you see the pictures of Charla—"

"Yes." His mouth congealed into a thin line. Propping his elbows on the armrests of his chair, he steepled his hands in front of his face.

Garland studied him thoughtfully. He'd curled in on himself, withdrawing visibly and completely. It would be awful for anyone to have to see pictures of his naked wife splashed across the tabloids, but it must have been hell for someone as private as Frank. As much as she sympathized with him, however, there were others more important.

"About those pictures, Frank," she began. "I think—"

"I don't want to discuss them."

"We have to decide what to tell the girls."

His fingers intertwined, squeezing so hard that his knuckles turned white. "We don't have to tell them anything. I'm sure they don't read the tabloids."

Garland stared at him in surprise. He couldn't be that naive surely! "Don't you think the kids at school are going to show them?"

"I . . . never thought of that." He pushed himself up from his chair slowly, then turned his back to her. "Do what you think is best."

He just can't deal with it, she thought. *How sad. He's trained to help people with their problems, and he can't even face his own.* "Okay, Frank. I'll talk to them about it."

He didn't reply, nor did he turn around. His right

hand, however, went up to smooth the back of his hair. Garland watched those long, clever physician's fingers of his, thinking that they looked strangely bloodless against the iron gray hair.

There was nothing more to do here, nothing more to talk about. Garland rose from her chair. "Well, it's getting late. I'd better be going; Colin will be wondering what happened to me. Thanks for letting me have my say, Frank."

"How could I not after everything you've done for Amber and Annalese?" he said, turning around to look at her. "We'll just call the little incident in my office a . . . momentary lapse in our relationship, shall we?"

"Sounds good to me." She held out her hand.

He shook hands with her, his palm feeling dry and cool against hers.

"I'll walk you to your car," he said.

"Oh, don't bother."

"It's no bother." Opening the front door, he stood waiting for her.

It really was ridiculous, but Garland didn't want to strain their newly forged truce by arguing. Frank was silent as they walked down the sidewalk toward the van.

"Will you say hi to the girls for me?" she asked. "And tell them I'll be calling tomorrow?"

"Of course."

"Good night, Frank." As Garland put her hand on the door handle, she noticed something strange about the seat. "What on earth . . ." She swung the door open and gasped.

Someone had slashed the upholstery on the driver's seat. And not just a little; the fabric was in ribbons. Pale foam showed through the rents like flesh through clothing. Rage, outrage, as well as a shivering sense of violation went through her. "God damn them to hell!" she cried.

"What's the matter?" Frank asked, coming around to her side of the car. "You look . . . Good God!

His voice lowered to a croak on those last two words, and Garland saw his face go chalk-white. He was holding on to her side-view mirror, and his hand looked like wires strung on bones.

"Take it easy," she soothed, afraid he was going to faint.

"Get in the house."

She stared at him. "What?"

"Get in the house!"

"Frank, it's not—"

He grabbed her upper arm in a painful grip and all but dragged her around the car and down the sidewalk. It was the urgency of his voice more than the pull of his hand that made her run to keep up with his longer strides. The moment they were inside, Frank slammed the door closed and leaned his back against it.

"Are you out of your mind?" she demanded, rubbing the spot where he'd held her.

Then she got a good look at his face. His eyes were closed, his cheeks sunken, his lips stretched tightly over his teeth. Alarm shot through her; was he going to have a stroke right here?

"Frank, are you all right?"

His eyes opened. It took him a moment to focus on her. Then he took a deep breath, and it was like a shutter coming down over his face. Once again he was Frank Hollister, the imperturbable doctor.

"Now it's *my* turn to apologize," he said. "I spooked like a skittish horse."

"I've never seen you so upset, Frank."

"I thought . . . whoever it was might still be around. Sorry if I frightened you."

Garland stared at him speculatively. Although she'd been upset by the sight of her shredded upholstery, it had been more outrage than anything else. Frank had out-and-out panicked. In fact, his overreaction bothered her more than the act of vandalism itself.

"Is something wrong?" she asked.

"No, of course not. I'm just not accustomed to things like that happening right in front of my house."

There was no sign of emotion in that smooth, controlled voice. But she knew better now. "I think I'll report this to the police," she said.

"Yes, I think you'd better." He ran his hands along the sides of his hair.

Interesting, Garland thought. "Is it all right if I use the phone in Charla's . . . in the office?"

"Of course."

Just before leaving the foyer, she glanced over her shoulder at him. His face was as smooth and pale as marble, and as hard. *Strike stone hard enough, and it'll shatter.*

Going back into Charla's office felt strange. Strange, because everything was the same, and yet completely changed. The array of pictures was still on the wall, Charla's calendar, memo pad, and stationery in their accustomed places on the desk. But the woman who owned them was gone.

Pushing the bleak thoughts aside, Garland called the Norfolk police. She got a gruff-nice sergeant who sympathized with her about the slashed seat, but could offer her nothing more than to send a patrol car out to take her report.

"It's these kids, miss," he said. "They roam the streets without supervision. Last Saturday night we had twelve smashed windshields in one neighborhood, about thirty lawns 'turfed' and God knows how many other pranks. Hey, one night someone stole a concrete bench from in front of the elementary school. Thing weighed several hundred pounds."

"In my day it was switching people's mailboxes around," Garland said.

"Mine, too. Dates *us,* doesn't it?" He chuckled. "I wish I could do more."

"That's all right, Sergeant. At least I can still drive my car, which is more than I could do if they'd smashed the windshield. Thanks anyway."

"Thank *you.* And next time lock your car door no matter how nice the neighborhood. Goodbye, Miss Ross."

"Goodbye." Garland hung up, muttering under her breath, "With all the Mercedeses and BMWs there are around here, you'd think my van would be the last car anyone would bother."

She sat for a moment, idly flipping the pages of Charla's appointment book. Frank worried her. He must be wound up as tight as a jack-in-the-box for something like the slashed seat to send him off the way it had. What was it? Damn it, she'd come over here thinking she'd misinterpreted all the little nuances of his behavior that had bothered her before. But she couldn't have been wrong about what had happened tonight, she *couldn't.*

"Why not, stupid?" she said aloud. "You've been wrong about a hell of a lot of other things."

Suddenly it seemed as though Charla was staring at her from the ranked pictures on the wall. It was hard to imagine Charla dead, even now. There was so *much* of Charla left in this house, in her children, in Garland's memories. Even Frank's pain seemed to revolve around a woman who would never come back.

Garland sighed. So many things left unfinished, so many questions left unanswered. Her gaze skipped from one picture to the next. Charla Ross, preserved forever. Glossy images of that beautiful face—large ones, small ones, smiling, serious—they all seemed to be looking at her. Eyes, eyes, eyes, all seeming to want something. Seeking . . . what? A message? If there was one, she didn't get it.

"Product of an overactive imagination," she muttered, raking her hand through her hair in exasperation. "Back to Earth, Garland, or you really will be as nutty as Baedecker thinks you are."

But unable to face those silent stares any longer, she left the room.

Chapter Twenty-three

Garland sat at the front desk and subtracted the last few entries in her checkbook while Milo tended to the last, lingering customer. She checked her watch. Six-thirty, but it felt like midnight. It had been the busiest Thursday she remembered, the steady stream of browsers and buyers keeping them both occupied here in the store. It was a good thing they'd decided to close to get their stock inventoried, or they'd never get it done.

"Thanks, Mrs. Buchner," Milo said, escorting the tall, angular elderly woman to the door.

"It was nice of you to keep the store open just for me," she said. "I didn't realize I'd taken so long to make up my mind."

"It was only a few minutes," he said.

"More like thirty." She smiled. "But that's why I keep coming here." Still smiling, she patted his cheek before stepping outside.

He locked the door and turned to Garland. "I wouldn't put myself out for very many people, but Nora Buchner is definitely on my list."

"A real lady, in the classic sense of the word," Garland agreed.

Milo picked up his coffee cup and headed toward the back of the store. His voice floated out from between the stacks. "Hey, why don't I run out and get us some dinner?"

"Italian?"

"Chinese."

"Aw, come on, Milo. I just had that the other night."

"Okay, how 'bout one of those steak subs from Ernie's? Nice and juicy, smothered in onions—"

"You've got me!"

He came back up to the front and lifted his jacket from the hook. "I'll just be gone a couple of minutes."

"Don't worry about me. I'm going to the Tomb to get a head start."

Someone rattled the handle of the door. Garland turned to see Colin peering in, his breath fogging the cold glass. She unlocked the door and let him in.

"Hi. What are you doing here?" she asked.

He waved to Milo, then leaned down to kiss her lightly on the mouth. His nose was cold. "And I thought you'd be happy to see me."

"I'm thrilled. But confused."

"I stopped by the upholstery shop to see how they're coming along with your seat, and lo and behold, they're done. I thought I'd see if you wanted a ride down there." He glanced at his watch. "We've just got time if you want to go."

"Yeah, I want to go. I've spent more than enough time without a car." She turned to look at Milo. "I'll run over there with Colin and pick up the food on the way back. Remember, I'm almost finished sorting that stack of fiction that came in last week, so don't mess with that one."

"Okey-dokey." Milo ripped off a salute, then tossed her jacket to her.

"And don't forget . . ."

Colin grasped her by the wrist and pulled her outside. His van, its white paint softened to cream by the light that came from the store window, sat at the curb. "We're only going to be gone a few minutes," he said.

"Even Milo couldn't burn the store down in that short a time."

"He bombed the hard drive a couple of weeks ago."

"How did he do that?" Colin demanded.

"Hell if *I* know. He certainly doesn't."

Colin opened the door for her, then went around to his side of the van and got in. "I'm afraid this repair job is going to cost you a bundle," he said. "He said there wasn't much he could salvage."

"That's what insurance is for," she said.

"This really bothers me, Garland. Things are getting weird. First the daffodils, then somebody breaking into your car and slashing it up like that . . ." He raked his hand through his hair. "I don't like it. I don't like it at all."

She swiveled to look at him. "I don't like it either, but what can I do? I reported it dutifully, and the police did everything *they* could, which was nothing. We'll just have to tough it out until all the publicity dies down."

"It's weird."

"Sure it's weird. There's no dearth of weirdness in this world. You wouldn't believe what passes for pranks these days."

"If slashing seats is a prank . . . what's next—mow your neighbor down with an Uzi? Now that would be a real chuckle." He put the van in drive and pulled out into traffic.

There wasn't anything she could say to make him feel better about it, so she remained silent. Colin had been upset since she'd shown him the ruined seat; her own feeling of violation seemed to be magnified in him. So instead of going to him for comfort, she'd played down her own feelings about it.

She hadn't told him about Frank's reaction to the incident either. After what had happened the night they'd broken into Frank's office, she didn't think Colin had much faith in her judgment when it came to her brother-in-law. Hell, *she* didn't trust her judgment as far as that went. Maybe Frank was scared of something, or maybe he was just a man who wasn't handling his wife's violent death very well.

Suddenly she stiffened, remembering that her checkbook was still sitting on the desk. Retrieving her purse from the floor of the van, she began looking through it to see what else she had. It was slim pickings: twenty-three dollars in cash and her Mastercard. "I left my damned checkbook back at the store, Colin. Does that place take credit cards by any chance?"

"No, but don't worry about it. I've got enough to cover it."

"Thanks, but . . ." The statement died unspoken. If he paid, she knew he'd never let her pay him back. What was she going to say that he'd understand? That she was wary of mixing finances so early in their relationship? That letting him pay was giving him even more influence in her life? "Let's just swing back by the store. It'll only take a minute."

"Whatever you say."

David hunkered down in the tiny closet that was tucked away in one corner of the storeroom. A few minutes before The Tome had closed, he'd come in behind a group of young men and women. Their chatter had masked his silence. Garland had been sitting at the desk. She had looked up when they came in, but her face registered only the awareness of several people before she glanced away.

"That's okay," he muttered. "You'll know me soon enough."

He'd slipped into the storeroom when no one was

looking, then settled into this closet to wait. It was dark and private in this lair, all sounds muffled by the heavy wood door. He liked it. He always welcomed quiet. But Garland's conversation with her partner about dinner, pitched to carry from one end of the store to the other, was easily heard. And even more welcome than silence. She would be alone soon. He was riding the power tonight; he could do no wrong. He would strike fast, capture his prey, and take her to a private place where they could be alone. Just the two of them.

He'd even prepared the way by unbolting the back door. She wouldn't scream, even when he walked her outside to his car. They never did, not with the point of a knife jammed against their ribs; deferred death was much better than immediate death. Hope was part of the human condition. A man named Nietzsche had said it best of all: "Hope in reality is the worst of all evils, because it prolongs the torments of man."

He felt his upper lip curl. Frank had read that to him during one of their visits, had even lent him the book. David had read the book but hadn't understood any of it. Nothing except that single, wonderful quote. A nugget of gold in a sea of muck.

Hearing the front door open and close, he snapped to alertness. She would be coming soon. Any moment now. At last she would be his, and she would set him free. He stood up, opened the fuse box on the wall to his left. This was an old place, and had those glass screw-in fuses. His gloves made him fumble a bit, but he managed to unscrew all the fuses.

His heartbeat accelerated as the lights went out. His blood was like thunder in his ears, like lightning coursing through his veins. His breath shot out of his nostrils, hot and deep. In and out, in and out. In. And. Out. Be calm, he cautioned himself. A hunter must be in control at all times. Excitement shivered along his nerves.

He unlatched the door to his closet and swung it ajar an inch. It was as dark out there as inside. Good. She'd be coming in blind. So small, so fragile. Perfect.

The outer storeroom door opened. His hearing was sharpened by anticipation; every noise, from the skitter of a nearby insect to the sound of the light switch being flicked seemed loud to him. A shoe scraped on wood. She *thought* she was coming to check the fuse box, but he knew better. She was coming to him.

Small sounds, coming closer. He could feel the air move across his oversensitive skin like sandpaper. She was right outside the door now; he could hear breathing. Soft. His knife was in his hand, but he didn't remember reaching into his pocket for it.

The door swung open with an audible creak. He went with it, using the noise to mask his movement. Grabbed clothing, twisting to bring the wearer against him.

"What the hell . . . ?" *A man's voice!*

Not Garland, but a man!

Panic. Sick, raw fear. *The power had failed him!* There was no power, no hunter's reflexes, just David. He recoiled frantically, wanting only to get away.

"Hey!" the man shouted. "What the fuck are you doing here?"

David backpedaled, heard someone whimpering. Dimly, he realized he was the one making the noise. His knife dropped to the floor with a clatter. He followed it, scrambling on hands and knees to retrieve it. Just as he felt the other man's hands close on his shirt, he found it. With a hoarse scream of terror, he surged to his feet and lashed out with the weapon. Felt the edge slice something, felt the hot spurt of blood on his face. He lashed out again, and again connected.

With a liquid gurgle, his opponent went down. David stood in the dark room, surrounded by the coppery smell of blood. Filled with it. He closed his eyes, dark upon dark, and breathed it in. For it was strength. It was power.

"Milo?" Another man's voice, bringing David out of his trance. "Milo, where are you? Milo?"

The intermittent gleam of a flashlight pierced the darkness of the store. He rushed out of the storeroom, his feet sliding a bit on the wet floor, and ran toward the back door, which he'd unlocked earlier.

Her voice, crying, "Colin, look! There by the back door!"

The beam of light speared him, nearly blinding him. Flinging one arm up to shield his eyes, he tore the door open and hurtled out into the dark alley.

Just before he turned the corner, he heard Garland begin to scream.

Chapter Twenty-four

Garland came up behind Colin in time to catch a glimpse of a man running toward the back door. A single moment of sight, a brief but unforgettable picture as he moved into and out of the flashlight beam. There was blood on his face, his hands, a banner of it across his shirt. A knife in his hand, silver gleaming through a coating of crimson.

"Milo!" she shrieked, grabbing the flashlight from Colin's hands. "Milo, answer me!"

Pointing the light toward the floor, she saw a line of bloody footprints leading from the storeroom. She followed them, her steps becoming swifter the closer she got. Colin was behind her, his breath harsh in her ear.

There was a bloody handprint on the door frame, startlingly red in the beam of light. More red upon the floor, a glistening scarlet pool surrounding a sprawled form.

"Milo!"

She ran to him, her shoes sliding horribly in the wetness. A wet, red wound crossed his neck, oozing blood to add to what was already on the floor. Falling to her knees beside him, she felt for a pulse.

"He's alive!" she cried. "Colin, call 911!"

Then she pressed her fingers against the wound, trying to stop the bleeding. Trying to hold his life in. She heard Colin talking to someone on the phone, giving them the address, telling them to hurry.

When he hung up, she said, "The fuse box. In the closet, on the left wall. There's another flashlight in the center drawer of the desk."

A second beam of light snapped into being. It moved over Milo briefly, then picked out the closet door. Colin went past her, moving fast, and a moment later the overhead light came on.

It was worse in the light. Garland saw that she and Milo were the center of a small lake of blood, more than she would have believed could come from a single human body.

"The ambulance is on its way," Colin said. "Want me to take over?"

She shook her head. "By some miracle I've got the right spot. I'm afraid to let go for a second."

"Is there a blanket around here?" he asked.

"Ahhh, in the closet . . ." She ducked her head against her upper arm to wipe sweat away from her eyes. "Second shelf on the right, I think."

Colin squeezed her shoulder briefly, giving her what quick comfort he could, then moved away. A moment later he returned and put the blanket over Milo.

"Hold on, Milo," she said. "An ambulance is coming. Just hold on. Hold on."

Somehow, he did. One minute, two. Garland kept pressure on the wound, knowing each lost drop might make the difference between life and death. He'd lost so much blood already. Much too much. Her arms trembled from the strain, but she controlled them. His life depended on her. If her hands slipped, she might not find the right place again.

She could hear sirens in the distance. Closing her eyes, she prayed they'd get here soon.

"A couple of minutes more," Colin whispered in her ear. Then, louder, "Do you hear those sirens, Milo? Help is almost here. Hang on a little longer, buddy."

Milo's eyelids fluttered for a moment. Garland drew in her breath with a little sob. "Breathe!" she rasped through clenched teeth. "Breathe!"

The sirens were right outside. Colin jumped to his feet and ran out of the room. A moment later the place was full of people. White uniforms, blue uniforms, a clamor of voices. Garland was beyond differentiating who was who; all her attention was focused on Milo's chest, as though she could keep it rising and falling by sheer strength of will.

Someone's hands slid down her forearms to her fingers. "When I say go," a voice said in her ear, "lift your hands."

She nodded.

"Go!"

She jerked her hands back. Someone snatched her away from Milo and thrust her at Colin. Milo was surrounded by white-clad bodies wielding clamps and tubes and IV bags. A stretcher was brought in, slid under him and raised. They began wheeling him out.

Colin gave her a push. "Go with them. I'll stay and talk to the police."

She ran after them. "Let me go with you!"

One of the men turned to look at her, then nodded. "Ride up front with the driver."

She ran around the side of the ambulance as they lifted Milo in. They were really hustling; the driver hit his seat the same time she hit hers, and threw the vehicle into gear immediately.

The ambulance screamed down Brambleton Avenue, scattering cars before it. Garland hung on to the door handle, wishing they'd go faster. Wishing they could fly. Thank God they were within a few minutes of Sentara Norfolk General, which had the best trauma unit in the area. If Milo had hung on this long, maybe he'd make it. *Just a little longer, Milo.*

The ambulance pulled up at the hospital's emergency entrance. Garland had her door open before the vehicle had completely stopped, but still she didn't move fast enough. People swarmed out of the building and surrounded the stretcher. A moment later, the efficient crowd had whisked Milo away.

Garland pushed through the double glass doors and ran after the fast-moving stretcher, but a white-clad woman caught her by the arm and held her back. Garland tried to twist free, registering only that the woman was tall and lean and had gray hair.

"Let go!"

The woman hung on. "You can't go with him now. They're taking him down to surgery."

"But . . . all right. I'll wait." Garland pushed her hair back from her forehead with the back of her hand. When she started to sit down, however, the other woman tightened her grip.

"Why don't you let me help you get cleaned up?" she asked.

Garland looked down at herself. Her hands were completely crusted with dried blood, as were her arms up to the elbows. The blood was like glue; she had to force her fingers apart. Her jeans were heavy and stiff where she'd knelt beside Milo. Moving slowly, as though in a dream, she lifted her hands up in front of her face and turned them over, then over again. This was Milo's life upon her skin.

A rustle of paper nearby made her look up. Everyone in the waiting room was staring at her. Reaction set in. Those curious faces began to bob like balloons.

"Are you all right?" the uniformed woman asked. "Miss?"

"I . . . I have to wash." Garland started to put her hands over her face, then thought better of it.

Putting her arm around Garland's shoulders, the

woman said, "Come with me."

The bathroom was a tiny cubbyhole, just a toilet, a sink, and a shelf for cups. With an effort, Garland kept herself from swaying. "I'll be all right now, thank you."

"Are you sure you don't need help?" the woman asked.

"I'm sure."

As soon as the door closed, Garland fell to her knees in front of the toilet. There was nothing in her stomach to come up, but she spent what felt like an eternity straining with dry heaves.

Finally the nausea stopped. With a sigh, she climbed slowly to her feet and began washing her face and arms in the sink. She rubbed the soap along her arms, building a good lather. Red lather. Streaks of red swirling in the sink, red bubbles on the soap and in the soap dish. She scrubbed until her skin was sore, until the water ran clear instead of red. But somehow, she could still feel the blood.

"Are you all right in there?" the woman called through the door.

"Better." Garland pulled a handful of paper towels from the dispenser and wiped her arms before opening the door. It was only now that she had enough presence of mind to read the woman's name tag: K. SPRINGFELD. Holding the damp paper in a grip that made her hands ache, she asked, "How is he?"

"Still in surgery. Afterward the doctor will come and talk to you."

"Okay." Garland felt tears coming and pressed the damp towel to her face to stop them.

"Look, I know you're not feeling up to this, but there's a policeman waiting to talk to you."

"Oh, damn," Garland said into the towel. *Relive it while it's raw.* She took a deep breath, then tossed the crumpled towels into the trash can under the sink. "Okay, I'm ready."

Instead of taking her back to the waiting room, the woman led her down an interior hallway. As they walked, she asked, "Does the patient have family here in town I should call?"

"No," Garland said. "His mother lives in Phoenix. Lois Freeman. But I'd rather call her myself; it's better coming from someone she knows."

"Is there anyone else?"

"Some very good friends," Garland said. "I'll call them when I find out . . . if he's going to make it or not."

"Your friend is in the best of hands. Dr. Carlson is one of the ablest surgeons in the business. Here we are," she said, indicating a closed door. "I'm going to leave you now, but if you need anything, just ask for me." She put her hand briefly on Garland's shoulder. "Look, for what it's worth, I hear you did all the right things for your friend. You gave him a shot at it; a lot of people would have stood there and watched him bleed to death."

"Thanks," Garland said, watching the woman walk away. A stranger's kindness, a stranger's sympathy felt even more precious because it was unexpected.

Straightening her shoulders, she opened the door and walked into a room that seemed like a cozy upholstered hand waiting to gather her in. A uniformed policeman stood at the window looking down into the parking lot below. Colin was there, too, sprawled in a modernistic chair that looked too small to hold him comfortably.

Colin jumped up and put his arm around her waist. "Are you all right?"

"I'm fine."

"You always say you're fine, even when you're not," he whispered, then raised his voice so that the other man could hear. "Garland, this is Officer Rickerson. He wants to ask you a few questions."

"Okay." Garland sat down and folded her hands in her lap. The policeman didn't look a day over twenty; the wholesomeness of his round, snub-nosed countenance was only enhanced by glasses. One of Milo's sayings popped into her head: You know that middle age has struck when doctors and cops start to look young. She sighed. "What do you want first, Officer?"

"I want you to tell me exactly what happened from the time you entered The Tome to the time you found Mr. Freeman," he said, flipping open a notebook.

Garland gave it to him as best as she could remember. It all sounded so dry and useless: *I walked here, I stood there, I heard that*. She was afraid that she might have missed something significant, perhaps not noticed it at all.

"Can you describe this man you saw running from the store?" Rickerson prompted.

She closed her eyes to bring the memory into sharper focus. "He was maybe . . . six feet tall, maybe six-one. Lean—he had his sleeves rolled up to his elbows, and I remember the tendons standing out on the arm with the knife."

"Which hand?"

"The right," she said. Then her eyes popped open in surprise. "He was wearing gloves. I remember that now. Funny, how that just shot into my mind."

"You're right, you know. He was wearing gloves." There was satisfaction in his voice. "Please continue."

"Ah, his hair was short. Brownish. There was blood on his face like . . ." She spread her hand out over her own face, indicating a mask over nose, mouth, and left cheek. "I didn't see his eyes. But I think he was fairly young. He moved . . . easily. Aggressively, if you know what I mean."

He nodded, then pulled a piece of paper out of his notebook. "See if this corresponds with what you remember."

She took the paper from him. It was one of Colin's drawings—a copy of a drawing actually. Milo's attacker was there just as she remembered him, his torso thrust forward as he ran. A bandit's mask of blood on his face, a diagonal slash of it across his shirt. Pen-and-ink streaks of it on his hands and forearms, stark against the white paper. Colin, too, had caught the gloves. But not the features; only the patterned blood was delineated. Still, it was raw and powerful. Murder in black and white.

Garland drew in a long, shuddering breath. "Yes, that's him. For what good it does."

"Would you recognize him if you saw him again?" Rickerson asked.

"I don't know. In a way, I feel I'd know him anywhere, but in different clothes in a different situation, I just don't know." She handed the drawing back to him, then absently wiped her hands on her jeans. Realizing after a moment what she was doing, she clasped her hands in her lap again.

He put the drawing away carefully and got to his feet. "Well, you've both been very helpful. I wish all witnesses were so observant. We'll be in touch. If you think of anything else, give me a call."

The door closed behind him, leaving them alone in the quiet room. Garland wished she could climb into his lap like a child and pretend this had never happened. Looking into his eyes, she realized he wanted to make the world right for her—for them—and was as helpless to hold it together as she was.

"What have they told you about Milo?" he asked.

"Nothing but that he's still in surgery. I guess no news is good news at this stage."

"Yeah." He raked his hand through his hair.

There was a moment of awkward silence. Garland didn't know what to say next, and obviously neither did he. Finally she rose to her feet. "I've got to call Milo's mother. And Troll, Robbie, and George will want to know."

"And then what?"

"And then we wait. And pray."

Some of the bleakness left his eyes. "Once you told me you'd forgotten how."

"The words are gone, but the important stuff seems to be still here," she said, tapping the center of her chest. "Funny how you find it again in times like this."

Chapter Twenty-five

Garland paced the confines of the room once again. It was sixteen paces wide, twenty long. She'd been walking the same path for most of the night and had come to learn every inch of the beige carpet intimately. The wall clock read a quarter to five. Dawn would be coming soon. She could only hope Milo would be able to see it.

"I wish you'd sit down," Colin said.

She turned to look at him. He was slumped in his chair, looking as comfortable as a cat on a warm pillow.

"How can you sit like that?" she demanded. "I'm ready to climb the walls!"

"There isn't room for both of us to pace the floor."

"What's taking so long? He's been in surgery for *hours!*"

She whirled as the door opened. A man peered into the room. "Miss Ross?"

"That's me."

He was middle-aged, short, and plump, with skin the color of bittersweet chocolate. He was wearing surgical greens and his eyes looked very tired behind his glasses. "I'm Dr. Carlson. I thought you'd like to know that Mr. Freeman's surgery was a success. He's in recovery now."

"Will he be all right?" was all she could get out.

"Barring complications, I think he's going to be fine."

"Thank God!" She fell into the nearest chair, numb with relief. "Oh, and thank *you,* too, Dr. Carlson."

"I think God deserves this one." The surgeon smiled.

"Mr. Freeman has a long road before regaining his health completely, but he's a fighter. I think he'll do fine."

"Can we see him?" she asked.

"He's in intensive care. Only the family—"

"Right now, we're all he has," she said.

"Well"—Dr. Carlson glanced at his watch—"just for a moment. He's still heavily sedated. Come with me."

He led them through a pair of doors and down another hallway to the intensive care unit. Milo lay on the bed, surrounded by a staggering array of tubes and wires and electronic equipment. A thick square of gauze covered the wound on his neck. There was another bandage on his chest. Although he was pale, he looked a hundred percent better than he had when he'd come in.

Carefully, Garland reached through the maze of tubes to lay her hand on his. His eyelids fluttered. "Milo," she said, leaning as close to his ear as the equipment allowed. "We've sent for your mother. She should be here in a couple of hours."

His mouth formed a word. Garland understood it, although it was obvious from the look on their faces that Colin and the doctor did not. "Troll" was what he'd tried to say.

"She'll be here soon," Garland said. Glancing up, she saw Dr. Carlson gesture toward the door. She nodded, then returned her attention to the man in the bed. "Get some sleep now, and maybe you'll be able to chase some nurses afterward."

His hand moved slightly under hers. She pressed it lightly, then stepped away from the bed. She even managed to keep the tears inside until she was out of the room.

"I-I'm sorry," she said, wiping the moisture from her face with the back of her hand. "He just looks so pitiful lying there like that."

Colin put his arm around her. "Why did he have a bandage on his chest, Dr. Carlson?"

"He'd been stabbed in the chest," the surgeon said. "It punctured his lung and missed his heart by a fraction of an inch."

Garland gasped. "I never even saw it. There was so much blood . . ."

"The neck wound was the most critical at the time, Miss Ross." He glanced down at Garland's blood-stained jeans. "I think we can consider Mr. Freeman a very lucky man."

A nearby speaker came to life. *"Dr. Carlson, you're wanted in ER, Dr. Carlson . . ."*

"Goodbye, and good luck," the surgeon said. Before Garland could say anything, he loped away down the hall.

She leaned into the comfort of Colin's solid bulk. "Stabbed in the chest, too. That . . . bastard tried hard to kill him."

"Yeah." Colin held her close for a moment, then pushed her out to arms' length. "You look like hell. I'm taking you home."

"But I've got to pick Milo's mother up at the airport at six-forty."

"I'll meet her. One look at you will send her running off in screaming fits. I won't be so naive as to suggest you get some sleep—"

"Wise choice."

He continued as though she hadn't spoken. "But you can at least grab a shower and change your clothes. I can drop you off at the house on the way to the airport and pick you up on the way back to the hospital."

"Okay, okay." She raised her hands, indicating defeat. The thought of a shower was just too hard to resist.

The ride back to the house was a quiet one. Although Garland would have thought she was still too keyed up to sleep, the motion of the van put her into a doze almost immediately. She didn't wake up until Colin pulled into the driveway.

"Damn, I hoped you'd stay asleep," he said. Reaching behind her seat, he extracted her purse and dropped it into her lap. "You forgot this last night."

"Thanks, Colin." She opened the door and slid out. "You'd better get going, or you'll be late. You won't have any problem recognizing Lois; she looks just like Milo, only older."

He waved, combining reassurance and farewell in one gesture. Garland turned toward the house in time to see Numbnuts shoot out from beneath one of the azaleas.

"I'm sorry, fella," she said, holding out her arms to pick him up. "Things got a little crazy last night. I figured you could fend for yourself for a few hours. But it's time for tuna now, isn't it?"

He dug the claws of one paw into the fabric of her jacket and murmured in agreement.

"I'm forgiven, then?" she asked, juggling purse and cat and keys in front of the door.

She managed to get inside at last. The living room was streaked with bars of golden morning sunlight, dust motes drifting lazily through the beams. Home, sweet home. Sanity after a night of terror. She breathed a sigh of relief and set the cat down on the floor.

As she turned to close the door, something in the window caught her eye. Or rather, *nothing* caught her eye, and something ought to. Memory ran through her mind like a newsreel: the shot sound of impact, the cracked windowpane, then the discovery of the dead cardinal on the porch. There could be no mistake. She had heard it, seen it, felt it, buried the bird with her own hands. It had happened, and nothing on this earth could convince her otherwise.

But there was no cracked pane now.

And the cat hadn't gone into the kitchen. He was sitting at her feet, his ears pressed tightly to his head. Realization seared through her like lightning. The phone calls, the flowers, the windowpane. *The pantyhose in her drawer.*

Standing in a pool of blazing sunlight, Garland suddenly felt very cold. The hallway was dark, as it always was this time of day, but it wasn't a friendly sort of dark. She strained to see, strained to hear, but there was nothing. Even the normal creaks and pops characteristic of an aging building were absent, as though the house were holding its breath. Waiting.

This was no bogeyman-fancy of the dark. This was real.

Without taking her gaze off the hallway, she bent and picked the cat up. He growled deep in his throat. But not at her; he, too, was looking at the hall. Tucking him beneath one arm, she reached behind her for the doorknob.

The door swung open, and she stepped backward onto the porch. Closing the door silently, she walked backward down the steps and along the sidewalk. Only when she reached the driveway did she dare turn around and run next door.

And as she ran, she felt her spine crawling with anticipation of a blow, anticipation of being dragged back, dragged down.

Praying that Mrs. Beeman was home, she rang the bell again and again. "Come on," she muttered. "Come on."

She shifted the cat's weight to her other arm and looked back at her own house. Was that a shadow moving behind the living room window? Oh God, please let it be her imagination, please! Because if it wasn't . . . *he* could see her.

Mrs. Beeman opened the door so suddenly it startled her. The old woman was wearing a faded blue robe, and her head bristled with pink foam curlers. "Why, Garland! And the nice cat, too?" Then she peered more closely through the glass of the storm door. "Why, whatever is wrong, dear? You look like you've seen a ghost."

Her gaze went to Garland's clothes, and her eyes widened.

"Please let me use your phone," Garland panted. "I think . . . I think there may be a burglar in my house."

"Good Heavens! Get in here, child." The old woman fumbled with the latch of the storm door.

It was all Garland could do not to wrench the thing off its hinges. *Let me in! Close the door and lock it—can't you tell he's watching?*

Finally she was inside, the door locked and bolted. Safe? Perhaps. Perhaps not.

"The phone is in here," the old woman said, tugging at her arm. "The kitchen, Garland. Are you going to call 911?"

Garland shook her head. Handing the cat to the old woman—by some miracle, he allowed it—she slipped her purse off her shoulder and retrieved Detective Baedecker's card from her wallet.

He picked up on the first ring. "Baedecker." Never had a human voice sounded so welcome, Garland thought.

"Detective Baedecker, this is Garland Ross."

"I heard about the attack on your partner—"

"He's been in my house. I think he may be there now."

"What?" He spoke to someone else briefly. "Where are you?"

"At my next-door neighbor's."

"A squad car's on its way. And I'll be there in ten minutes. Stick tight, and whatever you do, don't go back in there."

"You don't have to worry about that," she said.

Chapter Twenty-six

A short time later Garland found herself sitting in a chair in front of Detective Baedecker's desk. His partner, a huge, handsome black man by the name of Jeff Grange sat nearby, taking notes. A chest-high partition separated this section from the rest of the busy office, but the drone of many conversations seeped over the panels.

She glanced at Colin, who sat beside her. He was still a little pale. He'd driven up to see three police cars parked in front and a swarm of policemen going through her house. Not a pleasant surprise. He'd come hurtling out of his car almost before it had fully stopped, his face looking like that of a man who'd received a mortal blow, and hadn't calmed down until he'd seen she was safe. He hadn't left her side since, however; it was at his suggestion that a squad car had been dispatched to drive Milo's mother to the hospital.

He isn't the only one reeling from shock, she thought. She felt as though she'd fallen into the Twilight Zone. Things like this didn't happen in real life. But it had. If she hadn't noticed the window, if she'd walked back into the house . . . Hastily, she clamped down on that thought. Too much of that, and she was going to lose control completely.

"So," Baedecker began, "tell me when this all started, Miss Ross."

Garland tried to collect her straying thoughts. "I

started getting some crank calls; no talk, just breathing."

"Didn't you tell anyone?" the detective asked.

"No. Not that they didn't bother me, but I've gotten calls like that before—lots of women do. Some of these weirdos go through the phone book checking for listings of women's names. Anyone will do, as long as they're female. And some of the calls came to Charla's house, so I didn't assume they were for me."

A uniformed policeman leaned over the partition and tossed a manila folder and a brown envelope onto the desk in front of Baedecker. He opened the folder and scanned its contents, then passed it to Grange.

Baedecker leaned his elbows on the desk. "Well, he was in your house. We can't tell if it was this morning or another time, but he was definitely there."

"It was this morning," Garland said. "He was waiting for me. I wasn't imagining it."

"No," Baedecker agreed. "I don't think you were. Now, let's get back to the calls. When did they begin?"

"It was just about the time Charla disappeared, maybe a few days before . . ." She faltered to a stop, realizing exactly what she was saying. "You mean . . . he might have been following me even then?"

Baedecker spread his hands. "Let's get a little more information before we start speculating. You've told us about the window. What else can you remember that might be out of the ordinary?"

"Okay." She closed her eyes to better remember. "God, *everything's* been so nuts lately it's hard to pick anything out. One night I saw someone standing outside my patio doors. I-I called the police, so there'll be a report somewhere—"

"The flowers," Colin said.

Baedecker sat forward. "*What* flowers?"

"Someone cut down all my daffodils," Garland said. "Besides that, he also snipped the blooms from the stems and arranged them so they'd fall off when I picked the flowers up. It really upset me. But the worst was the pantyhose he put in order—"

"How?" Baedecker asked, glancing at his partner.

"By color. Light to dark, everything rolled up neatly. I didn't think anything much about it at the time; there was just too much going on with Charla's death and all. But when I saw that the window had been fixed, everything sort of clicked into place."

Jeff Grange got up from the chair and went to pick up the phone on the other desk. He dialed a number, his finger stabbing the buttons imperatively. "Stonebridge? This is Jeff Grange. Plug in your computer and give me anything you might have with flowers and slashed car seats. And arranging things by color, especially pantyhose. Yeah, pantyhose. Okay, call me back."

He tossed the receiver back into the cradle and sat down again. "NCIC computer system," he explained. "National Criminal Information Center. We've been keeping tabs on our boy to see if we can match him to killings in other cities, maybe even get lucky and ID him."

"The same guy has been doing them all?" Garland asked. "Charla, too?"

"We think so."

"Oh," she whispered. "Oh." All the pieces were falling into place now. She cleared her throat and spoke louder. "Milo and I'd had a conversation about getting some food, and he was the one who was supposed to go. It was only at the last minute that Colin showed up . . ." She took a deep, shuddering breath. "That means he didn't break in at all. He was in the store all along. Waiting. For me, not Milo. That's why he went to my house afterward. To finish the job."

Noticing that Colin was gripping the chair arm so hard his knuckles were white, she put her hand over his, silently urging control.

"Let's all have a cup of coffee," Baedecker said, evidently realizing that a distraction was needed. He got up from his chair and hovered like a waiter ready to take orders. "How do you like it? By the way, there's no cream."

"Black will be fine," Colin said.

Garland's teeth were chattering. "H-hot and sweet."

A few moments later she was clutching a Styrofoam cup between her hands, hoping the heat of the coffee might penetrate her fear-chilled palms. She took a sip. Oddly, the thought that came to mind was that Baedecker's coffee was worse than Milo's worst. Something for the record books. She'd have to tell Milo about it someday.

She forced herself to relax. Sips of coffee helped, more because of the heat than the taste. Baedecker must have been gauging her closely, for the moment she stopped shaking, he got back to business.

"Ready?" he asked.

She nodded.

"Good. Let's see what's in here," he said, picking up the brown envelope that had so far been ignored. He ripped it open and reached inside, pulling out a small cassette tape. "This is the one from your answering machine, Miss Ross."

He dropped it into his machine and hit Play. A man's voice came out of the speaker. "Hi, Garland. I'm coming for you." *Click.* And again, "Hi, Garland. I'm coming for you." The same message played over and over for the entire fifteen minutes of the tape. Confirmation, harsh and ugly, of her fears.

She listened, stunned by the thought that this man—this faceless, unknown person—wanted to kill her. When the tape ended, she shook her head in mingled fear and disbelief. "I know that voice. He's the one who called me. But he didn't say anything that showed he knew me. He . . . just seemed weird."

"What did he say?" Baedecker asked.

"Just that he liked my voice."

Baedecker slid two fingers into the envelope and gingerly extracted a piece of paper. He laid it on the desk in front of Garland. It was the drawing Colin had made of her the morning she'd found the shorn daffodils. The portrait's face was untouched, but the rest of the drawing had been stabbed so many times there was hardly anything left but shreds of paper.

Such hate. Such anger. *That's what he wants to do to me,* Garland thought. Her imagination supplied the picture of that bloodstained man from last night, shoulders hunched, slashing at the picture over and over. Wishing it were she. The rip of paper unsatisfying, a pale substitute for flesh and bone and blood. She reached out blindly to Colin, and he took her hand in a grip that hurt.

"Why?" she asked. "I've never done anything to him. I don't even know him!"

"We may never understand his motives, Miss Ross," Baedecker said. "We just have to stop him."

The phone rang. Jeff Grange answered it, then tucked the receiver between his ear and shoulder and began to scribble in his notebook. After a few moments he hung up and returned to his seat. Garland leaned forward, hoping that the new information might be able to put some sense into this insane situation.

He flipped the notebook back to the first page. "There was a fella in Tell City, Indiana, who killed nine women in a thirteen-month period. Victim number nine, one Betty Jean Cowli, had her flowers cut down and the blooms lopped from the stems. Phone calls, too."

"He's done this *before?"* Garland gasped.

"If it's the same man, yes. The Tell City Stalker, the newspapers called him." Grange turned a page. "All nine victims were petite and dark-haired."

Like me, Garland thought. Then she sat forward. "You mean he's after me because I'm small and have dark hair?"

"That's it," Colin said, getting to his feet. "I'm taking

you out of town until they catch this guy."

He reached down and took Garland by the arm, but she shook him off without taking her gaze from Baedecker. "They were all small, dark women, Detective. *I'm* small and dark. But my sister wasn't. Why did he kill her?"

He exchanged a glance with Jeff Grange, who spread his hands and shrugged. Baedecker sighed. "I don't know. Hell, it might not be the same man at all, but there are enough similarities for us to pursue. I won't even guess at the whys and wherefores until I get a lot more information. But if I were you, I'd take Mr. Kingsley's advice."

I wish I could, she thought. *Run and run and run and never look back.* "Come on, Baedecker. What are the odds you'll find him? The Indiana police never did."

"He left Indiana," Grange said. "He might leave Tidewater, too. This is a frequent pattern for this type of killer."

"That's great, but how long do I wait? My life is here. I could close the bookstore for a week or so, but any longer than that, and I'm out of business." She lifted her chin. "Besides, if he wants me so badly, why wouldn't he follow me, or just wait until I got back? What's the attention span of this kind of personality—a month, two months, a year?"

The detectives glanced at each other, and she knew she'd hit it right.

She went on before anyone could start arguing. "This guy killed my sister. I want him caught. I want him put away for a thousand years."

"That's not your job," Colin said.

She swiveled to face him. "Yes, it is."

"You can't be serious."

"I am, more than you'll ever know."

He shook his head, at a loss for words. She turned back to the two detectives.

"Well, what do you say?" she asked.

Baedecker's face showed no emotion, but there was a glitter of excitement in his eyes. "Are you offering to help lure him in?"

"I'm insisting on it."

"No!" Colin's fist crashed down on the desk, making them all jump. "I won't allow it!"

Garland stood up. "This is my decision to make, Colin. Either support me, or walk out now."

He stared back at her, his eyes narrowed to green slits of anger. Then he whipped around and left. She resisted the impulse to run after him. He'd probably come back if she did, and it was better this way. *I told you it wouldn't work, Colin. Not now. I'm no good for anybody now.* It was easy enough to say, much harder to endure. Grief shafted through her, and sharp regret for the loss of something precious.

She turned back to the two detectives. Baedecker's face was like stone, but the sympathy on Jeff Grange's twisted her guts into knots. She couldn't bear sympathy right now. So, wanting to put her thoughts on a level she could handle, she asked, "What do you want me to do?"

"You're sure about this?" Baedecker asked.

"I'm sure."

He wagged his forefinger from side to side. "You'll have to talk to him if he calls, draw him into conversation. It's going to be grim, Miss Ross. Grim and scary. There will be a police officer with you at all times, but—"

"Accidents happen," she finished for him. "I'll take the risk."

"It's a big risk to take just for revenge," Grange said. "You can make your peace with your sister's death another way."

Ahh, so Grange was the philosopher of this detective team, Garland thought. It was a shame that philosophers never seemed to care whether or not they trod on someone else's holy ground.

She crossed her legs and clasped her hands over her knee. “And what if this nut moves to another city and kills a dozen more women, Detective Grange?” she asked. “How will I make my peace with that?”

“It isn’t your responsibility.”

“I want him stopped,” she said.

Baedecker slapped his palms down on the desk. “Okay, Miss Ross. You’re in. I’ve got some things to work out, but I’ll get it put together by tomorrow. Meanwhile, I’ll make sure someone stays with you twenty-four hours a day.”

“What about The Tome?” she asked.

“You said before you could close it for a week or so. Better do it. There’s no way we can adequately protect you there.” He ran his thumbnail over his chin. “One good thing about this guy having killed before: Tell City probably has a psychological profile on him we can use. We’ll have our own boys do more work on him, however, since he seems to be changing his methods.”

“How so?” she asked.

“Well, picking blond victims, for one.” Baedecker’s gaze was hard and straight. “Some of the other things you don’t want to know.”

“You’re probably right,” she said. Her voice sounded a bit hollow, even to her. “But tell me anyway.”

Chapter Twenty-seven

Baedecker drove her home in an unmarked police car. Following behind them in Garland's minivan was a policewoman by the name of Juana Otto. Officer Otto was an almost terrifyingly efficient person. With her straight, dark, shoulder-length hair, she also looked a bit like Garland, at least when she was sitting down.

"Are you setting him up with two targets?" Garland asked.

Baedecker smiled, a brief upturning of thin lips. "It never hurts to hedge your bets. Grabbing Officer Otto in the dark would be a mistake for anyone."

He made the turn onto her street. Garland gave a start of surprise when she saw Colin's Oldsmobile parked in front of her house. He was leaning against the car's fender, arms folded over his chest—just like the day he'd brought Numbnuts to her. That day had been a beginning for them. Would this be another?

"Are you surprised to see him?" Baedecker asked. "I'm not. He's no quitter."

"No," Garland said, without taking her gaze from Colin. "I guess he isn't." A variety of emotions churned through her: frustration, dread, resignation—and joy.

Baedecker parked in the driveway, and the van pulled in beside him. "I'll check things out." He held out his hand. "Keys, please."

Garland dropped her key ring into his palm, then slid out of the car. With Officer Otto hovering a few paces behind her, she went to meet Colin. He unfolded his arms as she came near.

"Hi," she said.

"Hi."

"Did you go by the hospital to see Milo?"

He nodded. "He's doing great, the doctor said. And there's plenty of company; besides his mother, George, Troll, and Robbie are dancing attendance."

"How is Lois taking it?"

"As well as can be expected."

Garland clasped her hands in front of her to keep them from shaking. "I didn't expect to see you again. Not after the ultimatum I gave you."

He smiled. "Maybe I'll make you pay for that later. Right now, I'm going to stick to you like glue."

"Why?" she asked.

"Didn't you ever hear about couples staying together through bad times along with the good?" Gently, he laid his hands on her shoulders. "What the hell kind of men are you used to, Garland?"

"Not your kind," she whispered.

"Let's go inside," the policewoman said, evidently uncomfortable with standing out there in the open.

Colin slipped his arm around Garland's waist and urged her toward the house.

"What did you do with my cat?" she asked.

"George is going to keep him for us. I don't think this is the best place for him right now." His arm tightened. "You should have seen it: George spoke to him in that wonderful voice of his, and the cat just turned to jelly."

Baedecker appeared in the doorway. "The house is clear."

Going inside was scary, even with company. Her house, her sanctuary, had been violated. How many times had *he* been in here without her knowledge? How many of her things had he touched, how deeply had he probed into her privacy?

"There's a message on your answering machine," Baedecker said. "I think you ought to hear it."

"From . . . from him?"

The detective nodded. She knew he'd played it already, and had a reason for telling her to listen to it. It was a test to see if she had the guts to go through with this.

She disengaged herself from Colin's encircling arm. Feeling like a lamb going to the slaughter, she walked into the kitchen. The red light on the answering machine seemed to stare at her balefully. She took a deep breath and pushed the Play button. A voice came out of the speaker.

His voice. A stranger's voice, but more familiar now than her own. "Hi, Garland," he said. His tone was strange, triumph and anger and anticipation all rolled together. "The police aren't going to be able to help you. You've been marked by the hunter, and he never fails. Remember your sister? She was only an exercise, you know. I don't really like blondes. But I'll always be grateful to her for leading me to you. You're special, and I have something special saved just for you."

Click.

She stared at the wall, trying to take it all in. He'd killed Charla for an exercise. An *exercise!* A new fear came into Garland, a fear beyond that of dying. He wouldn't take her quickly. He'd make her suffer. She couldn't even imagine what a mind like that would consider "special."

It was only when Colin reached around her to take her finger off the Play button that she realized the message had ended. She closed her eyes, praying for strength, then turned to face the others. Colin's eyes reflected the horror she felt; Baedecker and Otto's, calculation.

"It's going to get worse," Baedecker said. "Are you up to this?"

Garland almost said no. Every instinct she possessed screamed at her to get out now. But then she remembered how the killer had passed over Charla's death as though it hadn't mattered at all, and pushed her instincts aside. "I want him caught," she said. "Paint a bull's-eye on me and set me out in the street if you have to, but catch him."

Baedecker nodded, and for the first time Garland saw something like approval in his eyes. "We'll have Caller ID hooked up here by this evening," he said. "We'll trace him if he calls again."

"What are the odds he'll call from home?"

"Not good. He's been pretty careful up 'til now. But even if he calls from a public phone, we can trace it. It's only a matter of getting a car there fast enough. The longer you can keep him talking, the better chance we'll have of grabbing him."

Realizing that her hands were clenched into fists, Garland forced herself to relax. "I'll be Chatty Cathy. The Garland Ross Answer Line."

"That's what we need," Baedecker said. She turned away, but he tapped her on the shoulder, bringing her around again. "About your brother-in-law . . ."

"I got a little crazy about Frank," she said. "Sorry I gave you a hard time."

He shrugged. "You've got good antennae. Something felt wrong. Your logic was fine: you had a marriage on the rocks, a million-dollar insurance policy, and your sister married to a man you disliked. Everything was there."

"Yeah," she said, trying not to sound as bitter as she felt. Everything was there, but it was wrong."

Colin put his arm around her shoulders. "That's not important now. What *is* important, however, is us getting a couple of hours' sleep so we can think straight. Right, Detective?"

"Right."

"But I want to see Milo—"

"Later," Colin said. "Troll is there now, and Lois. He

won't need either of us for a while. We can go to the hospital later."

Garland nodded. He made too much sense, and even if he didn't, she was just too damned tired to argue. "You'll wake me up if *he* calls?" she asked Baedecker.

Baedecker smiled. A genuine smile this time, one that warmed his eyes. "You can count on it."

Numb with everything that had happened, she let Colin urge her down the hall to the bedroom. It wasn't until he'd shut the door, however, that exhaustion hit her fully. Her purse, by some miracle still hanging on her shoulder after all this, suddenly felt like it was full of concrete. She slipped the strap off her shoulder and let the bag drop to the floor.

The bed spread out before her, as welcoming as though it had held arms out to her. Clean sheets, a soft pillow . . . heaven. She kicked off her shoes and peeled her jeans down. Where Milo's blood had dried, the denim was as stiff as cardboard. She tossed them in the trash; even if she could get them clean, she wouldn't want to wear them again.

Colin stripped his jacket off and tossed it on the foot of the bed. Garland's mouth dropped open when she saw that he was wearing a shoulder holster, the smooth brown butt of a gun showing beneath his arm.

"What the hell is that?" she demanded.

"What does it look like?" He reached behind him, pulled another, smaller gun out from under his belt, and held it out to her. "This one's for you. It's a .38 special. It's got stopping power and is light enough for you to handle. If you don't know how to use it, I'll take you out to the shooting range today and show you."

Garland looked at it lying across his palm, smooth and deadly. "My dad was a hunter. He taught me how to handle a gun. But why—"

"Insurance, honey. Baedecker will do the best he can, but there's no way he can guarantee your safety. This increases your safety a little bit, which makes me mighty happy."

"Christ Almighty, Colin, what do you think this is, the Wild West?"

"I'd back a gun against a knife any day."

"You've got a point."

"You bet I do," he said. "Take the gun, Garland."

She obeyed, hefting it to refamiliarize herself with the weight of a gun. She didn't like it much. After her father had died, she'd sold his guns to one of his hunting buddies. But just now the weapon seemed like cold, hard, blue-steel security.

"I wouldn't tell Baedecker about it," Colin said. "He'd probably take it away from you."

With a sigh, Garland dropped the gun into her purse. It might help. And right now she had the feeling she was going to need all the help she could get.

David squatted on his heels in the empty apartment across the street from Garland's house. The sun was going down. Its dying rays slanted between the ranked trees, sending attenuated shadows stretching across the street. He shifted position to one side of the window. There were two cops in the house, as well as an unmarked car patrolling the street at frequent intervals. No way could he get her there.

He reached into his duffel bag and pulled out a paper lunch sack, the top carefully folded, not rolled. In it was an apple, a peanut butter and grape jelly sandwich wrapped in wax paper, and two cookies. The kind of lunch he'd wanted all during school and never got.

The sandwich first. All the good kids ate their sandwiches first, just the way their mothers had told them. Pulling his big hunting knife out of the duffel bag, he carefully cut the sandwich into fourths. Diamonds, not squares. He didn't like squares. Then he hunkered down and began to eat.

All the while, he watched the house. The cops in the unmarked car made a few more passes around the block, then parked in the street where they'd have a view of the rear of the house.

He finished the meal, washing it down with lukewarm apple juice. Still he waited, the patient hunter. An hour passed, then another. He checked his watch, wondering if they were going to settle in for the night.

At eight-fifteen, they came out. The slut, her lover, and the two cops. David smiled when he got a good look at the policewoman. They thought to tempt him, did they? Well, they could forget it; no one could possibly be as good as Garland.

He gathered up his trash and thrust it into his duffel bag, then let himself out of the apartment. Casually, as though he belonged there. The policewoman spotted him. He raised one hand in greeting; it was the neighborly thing to do. Garland didn't even look up.

He drove away, not worried that he might lose them. There was one entrance to this neighborhood, one street to access it. All he had to do was wait at the 7-Eleven just before the overpass. No matter what their destination, they had to go past him.

A few minutes later the gray minivan went by. Garland sat in the passenger seat, looking wan and tired. David waited until the van entered the overpass ramp to Military Highway, then followed—at a safe distance, of course.

He stayed with them until they pulled into the hospital parking lot. So, they were going to visit that other man, the partner. David felt a little uneasy at the thought of how close that had been, the surprise and fear he'd felt when he'd realized he'd grabbed a man instead of Garland. Then another thought came to him, and he smiled.

Last night had seemed like a mistake, but he could see now that it wasn't. This hospital visit had pulled her out of the house as nothing else could have. At the house, surrounded by her protectors, he wouldn't be able to get to her. And the longer he waited, the more closely woven the net of protection would get. But now, here, he didn't have to go through anyone else. All he had to do was get *her* to come to him.

"No problem," he said. He was focused, sure of himself, sure of the power. "Noooooo problem."

Chapter Twenty-eight

David stopped at a pay phone and called Frank's office. The answering machine picked up, but he hung up without leaving a message. Next, he dialed Frank's home. A woman answered.

"Is Dr. Hollister at home?" David asked.

"Yes, but he's unavailable just now," the woman said. "May I have him return your call?"

"No, thank you. I'll call back."

Good. Everything is falling into place. But he had to move fast. Strike hard, for another chance might not come. He got back in the car and headed toward Frank's house. He'd never been inside the doctor's big, imposing house. Personally, he preferred Garland's. It was homier.

Anticipation made his palms slick with sweat. It was Friday night. TGIF. "Everything is working right/On Thank-God-It's-Friday night," he muttered under his breath.

The house was lit up like Christmas; every downstairs light seemed to be on. The sign of a nervous man. David parked a block or so down the street, then donned the leather sheath-belt that held his hunting knife.

After buttoning his jacket over the weapon, he went up to the door and rang the bell. He peered at his reflection in the polished brass knocker, turning his face this way and that, amused by the distortion caused by the curved surface. Especially the one where his teeth looked like big, white squares in a pointed pinhead. He grinned widely, opening and closing his mouth. Chop, chop. He hoped the woman would answer the door; that would make things a lot easier.

The door opened as far as the chain allowed, and a lean, middle-aged woman peered out at him. "Yes?" she asked, her mouth nested in wrinkles of suspicion.

"I'm sorry to bother you so late," David said. "But my car broke down and I wonder if I might use your phone."

She looked him up and down. David smiled his best clean-cut-good-boy smile, counting on it and his neat appearance to make up her mind for her.

"All right," she said at last. "Come on in."

"Oh, thank you!" Just in case, he put his palm flat on the door as she nearly closed it to remove the chain. But then it swung open again, inviting him inside.

She turned away, beckoning him to follow. "The phone is just over—"

He clamped his hand over her mouth hard, pulling her up against him, then pulled his knife out and drew it across her throat in one smooth gesture. A fan of blood sprayed out across the foyer. The woman sagged. He let her go, and she slid to the floor in a quivering heap.

To avoid walking through the rapidly spreading pool of blood, he detoured through the living room. An ugly room—black and white and hard. He was glad to leave red footprints on the thick white carpeting.

Now for Frank. Since the stairs were close, he checked the bedrooms first. All he found were the two little girls, sound asleep. He left them alone. *They* were precious. Closing the door to their room, he padded downstairs again. Silently, the hunter stalking his prey.

He found Frank in an office/den sort of room, all rich wood paneling and leather furniture. The doctor was seated at a big rolltop desk, his back to the door.

Holding the knife close to his side where it wouldn't be *too* obvious, David said, "Hi, Frank."

The doctor whirled, his mouth an O of surprise. His

gaze moved down to David's blood-spattered shoes, and fear replaced the astonishment in his eyes. "Why, David! W-What brings you here?"

"You know why I'm here," he said, coming farther into the room.

The older man shook his head. "If you'd wanted to meet with me, it would have been better at the office. Why don't you sit down over there and tell me what's bothering you tonight?"

David felt a stab of admiration; even now Frank was trying to exert control over him. To put him in the position of patient, and Frank as mentor. "It's a little late for talk, don't you think?" he asked.

"It's never too late to work things out." Without looking away from him, the doctor opened a nearby drawer. "Just let me get my notebook—"

David sprang forward to slam the drawer closed with his foot. Holding the edge of the blade against Frank's throat, he said, "Don't move. Don't make me kill you." Then he eased the drawer open. Inside was a gun, which he took out and put in his pocket.

Then he turned and looked at Frank. "That wasn't very nice, Frank. I thought you were my friend."

"I am," the doctor said, his voice barely audible.

"Then you won't mind helping me, will you?"

Frank shook his head. His eyes were wide, his skin as pale and dry as chalk. The big vein in his temple throbbed spasmodically. *Fear, fear, fear,* David thought. *A man looking at death. Yes, but not yet. Turnabout was fair play; the user becomes the used.*

"Of course you don't mind helping out a friend." David smiled. "Now, let me tell you what I want you to do."

When Garland and her companions got to the hospital, they found that Milo had been moved from intensive care into a private room. He was still hooked up to a great many tubes and wires, but nothing like before.

Troll was still here, curled up asleep in the chair beside the bed. She'd been combing her hair with her fingers again; reddish spikes stood up all over her head.

Lois Freeman stood at the foot of the bed looking down at her son. The light picked out the white strands among the blond, making her hair look frosted with ice.

"Lois," Garland whispered.

The older woman turned, then came forward to take Garland's hands in hers. "Hello, dear." She nodded a greeting to Colin, then looked inquiringly at Baedecker and Otto.

"These are police officers," Garland explained, introducing them.

"Ah. Two officers were waiting most of the afternoon to ask my son some questions, but he wasn't awake long enough to do them any good."

"How is he?" Baedecker asked.

"Mending," Lois said. "Mending. I do believe he's going to be just fine."

"I'm so glad." Garland squeezed the other woman's hand. "Did he notice that Troll is here?"

"Troll . . ." After a moment of obvious bewilderment, Lois smiled. "Oh, you mean Linda. Yes, I think he did. Poor girl—she's exhausted, but I can't convince her to go home. Colin, see if you can do anything with her."

Colin went to Troll and shook her gently. Her eyes opened, and a moment later she sat up with the fuzzily embarrassed look of someone caught sleeping on duty.

Rubbing her eyes with her fists like a child, she asked, "Garland, are you all right?"

"Right enough," Garland lied, conscious of the gun-heavy weight of the purse on her shoulder. "Go home, Troll. Get some more sleep before you fall down."

"I think I will. I think I'd better; I was so worried last night that I didn't sleep at all." With a huge yawn, Troll levered herself out of the chair and got her purse and coat. "Bye, Lois," she said, pausing to kiss the older woman on the cheek.

"Such a nice girl," Lois murmured, watching Troll leave. "Too intelligent for her own good, perhaps."

Nothing gets past Lois, Garland thought as she urged the older woman to take the seat Troll had vacated. *So that's where Milo gets his crystal-ball-reading abilities.*

The phone rang as she got Lois settled. Garland reached for it, but Baedecker stepped forward, shaking his head, and she lowered her hand.

The detective lifted the receiver. "Hello? Yes, this is Mr. Freeman's room. Oh, right . . . Dr. Hollister. I thought I recognized your voice. Sure, you can speak to Garland."

He handed her the phone and moved away. Garland put it to her ear. "Hello, Frank. Are you at home?"

"Yes. I . . . I'm at home."

The tension in his voice sang along her nerves like fingernails on a blackboard. "Frank, is everything okay there? The girls aren't sick, are they?"

"No, they aren't sick," he said. "Garland, I—"

A new voice came on the line. "Hi, Garland." *His* voice. The killer.

She felt her insides shrivel like a spider on a hot grill. *He's in the house. With Frank. With the girls.* She glanced at Baedecker, but he'd already turned away, satisfied that she was talking to her brother-in-law. Even as she raised her hand to get the detective's attention, the man spoke again.

"I know you've got cops there. If I hear sirens, those little girls are dead."

She lowered her hand. Her throat tightened with fear for the twins, for herself. *Stay in control. Keep* him *in control.* "So," she asked, forcing her voice to remain calm, "how are the girls, Frank?"

"Very good," the killer said. "No one would ever know you're afraid. You *are* afraid, aren't you?"

"Yes."

"Frank is afraid, too. I bet you've never seen him afraid before, have you?"

"No."

"He's going to get even more afraid."

Her mind tilted and turned, seeking a foundation in a world that had become chaos. Poor Frank. He must be terrified, for himself and for his daughters. And all because he knew a woman named Garland Ross.

"Look," she said. "This isn't necessary. Why don't we meet somewhere and try to work this thing out? Just the two of us."

There was a sharp exhalation of breath on the other end, almost a sigh. "Have I ever told you how much I like your voice?"

"Once you did," she said. "But I didn't understand then."

He laughed softly. "Do you understand now?"

"I think I do. How are the girls . . . Frank?"

"They're fine," the killer said. "They're fast asleep in their beds with visions of sugarplums dancing in their heads."

Garland fought her rising panic. The voice was so calm, so, so *ordinary.* A shudder rippled up her spine. This was a monster. A monster in the body of a man, looking, walking and talking like a man, but inside, something else entirely.

"Will you do what I tell you?" he asked.

"You know I'll do anything for the girls."

"Yes," he said, laughter in his voice. "I know."

Her brain felt like an overcrowded mass of cogs and gears, grinding, grinding, searching for a way to reach him. She would take any risk to get him out of the house. God, she'd bare her throat for him, stretch it out like a chicken for the cookpot, and hope Baedecker was as good as he ought to be.

"Why don't we meet somewhere—" she began.

"Here."

Anywhere but there! "The girls don't need to be involved in this. I told you I'd be willing—"

"Garland, you're arguing." There was a steely timbre to

his voice, knife-sharp and terrifying. "You don't want me to hang up, do you? If I hang up, I'll just have to go upstairs."

"No, don't do that." Fear, sick and cloying, clamped her throat.

"Besides, we *have* to meet here. Those girls can't stay here alone without a babysitter, you know. Wouldn't be right. And Frank's kind of tied up right now."

Oh God, Garland thought. Xenia. Was it the nanny's day off? She couldn't remember, couldn't think. The killer was breathing into the phone, waiting for her to figure it out. Waiting for her to ask. Damn him, he was playing with her!

She had to ask, knowing as she did that he wasn't going to answer. "Is Xenia there?"

"What will it be, Garland? Are you going to come, or should I go upstairs and wake those little girls up?"

"I may be a while," she said. "You know I'm tied up here at the hospital."

"That's okay. I know it may take some time for you to ditch the cops. But I've been watching you long enough to know you're smart enough to find a way out of there. Just come as soon as you can. *I've* got all night."

Garland closed her eyes when she heard the triumph in his voice. Triumph, and a creepy sort of possessiveness.

"And remember," he said, a note of menace darkening his tone. "If I even think you've sold me out, those little girls are going to pay for it. Got it?"

"Got it," she whispered.

"See you later."

The line went dead. She replaced the receiver gently, hoping her expression looked normal. It didn't feel normal; her face felt stiff and cold. But no one seemed to notice. Colin and Baedecker were deep in conversation by the door, and Officer Otto was leaning against the far wall, reading.

Her protectors. All she had to do was open her mouth and tell them what had happened, and everything would be taken out of her hands. But that "everything" happened to be her family's lives, and maybe Xenia's, too. If she made a mistake now, they would pay for it.

She didn't want that kind of responsibility. She wanted to give it to Baedecker. He would take it, too, handling this "case" as he had many others. She had a sickening vision of a dozen police cars surrounding Frank's house, complete with flashing lights and bullhorns, and the people inside dying while the doors were still being broken down. The police would get their man in the end, dead or alive.

But Garland didn't give a damn about getting the man. She wanted her family, and she wanted them alive. The police, FBI, Army, Navy, and Marines put together couldn't get into that house before the killer slit the hostages' throats. Only Yours Truly. She knew what Baedecker would say. "We can't let him have another hostage, Miss Ross. Catching the killer isn't your job; you let us handle it." So she'd sit here, safe among her protectors, and listen to the sirens that would spell the deaths of Frank and the girls.

She simply couldn't do it. The killer knew that. He'd been following her, watching her, learning her strengths and weaknesses, and he'd set her up. She'd been hooked, played like a fish on the end of a line.

"Garland, dear," Lois said, her voice overloud in Garland's ears, "would you like to play some gin rummy to pass the time?"

"Huh?" Garland stared at the older woman blankly, literally not comprehending the words.

"Are you all right?" Lois asked.

"Oh . . . yeah, I'm fine." Garland brushed her hair back from her face with her hands, gaining time, putting her thoughts back in some sort of order. "Sorry, I was just thinking. What did you say?"

"I asked you if you'd like to play gin rummy. You see, playing cards settles my nerves. But other people don't—"

"I'll be glad to play," Garland said. Anything to keep from having to talk to Baedecker, and most especially, to Colin.

She sighed. God, she wanted to stay here, protected by walls and guns and shrewd-eyed detectives! Baedecker's voice rose, and she realized the men were talking baseball. Baseball—the image of fun, of normalcy, of a world that had been safe and orderly. Controlled. But she had entered the killer's world now, where he made the rules and called the tunes. And she'd dance to them. Oh yes, she'd dance.

"Come sit down on the bed, dear," Lois said. "Don't worry, you won't wake Milo." She pulled a deck of cards out of her purse and began shuffling expertly. "I carry these everywhere I go. You never know when you might need a deck."

Like an automaton, Garland sat down on the edge of the bed and picked up the cards as they were dealt to her. Everything had an air of unreality; even the cards remained a blur of red and black. How strange that she might be spending her last few hours on earth playing gin rummy. How prosaic.

"Your play," Lois said.

Garland drew the top card, put it into her hand at random, then discarded just as randomly. She glanced at Colin, wishing she could confide in him, hold him, wishing she could say goodbye. Wishing . . . a lot of things.

The killer was smart. He'd cut right through the bullshit to the heart. To *her* heart, knowing she'd walk right through the net of protectors to him. This was between him and her; had she kept it that way, he wouldn't be in Frank's house now. If she'd known . . . If she'd known, she wouldn't have believed it, for then she hadn't known he was a monster. No lives, not Frank's, not the girls', mattered to him in the least.

Only mine.

Getting out of here was going to be tricky; Baedecker wasn't going to just let her leave. Somehow, she had to find a way. The killer had given her time, but how much? He could kill them out of anger, out of boredom, or simply for fun.

A monster's game, a monster's rules: hide from your friends, run to your killer. The thought pounded in her skull as though trying to beat its way out. Imperative, frightening.

"Gin," Lois said, laying her hand down. "You lose."

Yeah.

Chapter Twenty-nine

"Garland, I don't think your mind is really on the cards," Lois said.

Garland looked up, realizing that she'd just lost another game. No wonder; she'd played the entire game without having a clue as to what was in her hand. "You're right, Lois. I'm sorry. I guess I'm too preoccupied for this."

All she could think about was the killer, and the lives he was holding. Had he gotten tired of waiting? Was he walking upstairs right now, going down the hall to the twins' room? That fluffy pink and white confection of a bed spattered . . .

Unable to finish the thought, Garland got up and ran her hands through her hair. She checked her watch unobtrusively. A half hour had passed since that phone call. During that time, Colin had left the room twice, Baedecker once, and Juana Otto once. But never together. And now everyone looked as though they were settling in for the duration, Juana engrossed in her book, Colin nodding off in his chair, Baedecker sitting on the foot of the bed, his feet propped on his briefcase.

Garland swallowed convulsively, her frustration pressing up against her diaphragm. She had to get *out* of here! Her mind churned frantically, grasping one plan after another, but discarding each as either unworkable or absurd. She found herself staring at the door, one short breath from bolting.

Maybe she was making things too difficult. Maybe

they *would* just let her walk out of here. "I'm starved," she said. "I think I'll just run downstairs to the cafeteria—"

Baedecker's feet hit the floor, and Juana Otto closed her book. The policewoman rose to her feet, crushing Garland's hopes. Damn. Now she was going to have to eat a meal she didn't want, keep a conversation she couldn't keep track of, while the minutes ticked by. Minutes of her family's lives.

Then Colin groaned and stretched. "Why don't I go down and get something for all of us? If I don't get my blood moving, Milo's going to be sharing that nice, soft bed."

Baedecker nodded; Juana Otto returned to her book. After trailing his fingers down Garland's cheek in farewell, Colin left the room. Garland repressed a grimace as Baedecker's too-sharp gaze focused on her face. *Don't let him see!*

"Are you feeling okay?" he asked.

She shrugged. Shoulders up, shoulders down, a marionette's gesture, conveying an indifference she didn't feel. "I guess so. Considering."

"It's all going to work out," he said. "Just try to relax."

Those twin-bore eyes looked away. Garland went to the window and looked down at the rooftop below, where pipes and vents oozed pale wraith-smoke into the night air. She put her hands flat on the glass, feeling the cold against her palms. If wanting were enough, she'd be invisible now. But it wasn't enough; it never was.

"Damn," she muttered under her breath. "Damn, damn, damn."

Milo shifted restlessly, and she turned to look at him. His eyes opened, moved without focus for a moment, then slowly became more lucid. She hurried to the side of the bed, leaning over to put herself into his field of view.

"Hi, buddy." Careful of his IV, she took his hand. "I'm glad to see you're feeling better."

He couldn't talk because of the tube in his mouth, but the look in his eyes spoke volumes.

"So, you aren't feeling better," she said. "At least you're feeling."

Baedecker, notebook in hand, came to stand beside her. "I'd like to ask you some questions, Mr. Freeman. I know you can't talk, but if you blink once for yes and twice for no, we ought to be able to communicate well enough."

Milo blinked once.

"This man who attacked you—did you see him at all?" the detective asked.

Two blinks.

Baedecker nodded. "Did he come in the storeroom behind you?"

Two blinks.

"Was he waiting there?"

One blink.

As the questioning continued, Garland glanced around the room in time to see Officer Otto go into the bathroom. Lois and Baedecker were concentrating on Milo, and Colin was still gone. This was her chance; she'd better take it.

Casually, she stepped back from the bed, putting herself out of Baedecker's line of sight. Scooping her purse up from the floor, she slipped out of the room and took the stairs down to the ground floor. No one even seemed to notice her. But then, the sight of white-faced, worried people was all too common in a hospital. Even death was a frequent visitor here.

But not mine! Her jacket was still upstairs, and she began to shiver when she hit the cool night air. Hopefully the jacket would buy her some time; Baedecker would probably search the hospital for her, mad as hell because she'd been careless. By the time he figured out she was gone, it would be too late.

As she ran across the parking lot, she could almost hear George's mellifluous voice, quoting from one of his favorites: "Life hurries on, a frantic refugee,/And Death, with great forced marches, follows fast." There was more, but she couldn't remember the rest.

"Shit," she muttered, zigzagging through a line of parked cars to the van. A few minutes later, she was headed for Frank's.

As she drove, her right hand kept straying to her purse. She never thought she'd find a gun comforting, but it was. The great equalizer. Would it make her equal enough? She hoped so. God, she hoped so.

It was possible he'd already killed Frank and the girls. Strangely, however, she didn't think so. Not yet. Not until he'd gotten his hands on his sacrificial lamb.

But then she knew all bets were off. Maybe he was planning to kill Frank and the girls in front of her, just for fun. Just to liven things up a bit. Maybe that was the "special something" he'd planned for her.

"Well, it's not going to happen if I can help it," she muttered under her breath.

She wasn't out of the game yet. He might hold all the aces, but she had one trump card, and that was the fact that he didn't know exactly *when* she was coming. And he didn't know she had a gun.

She parked a short way down the street, out of sight behind some trees, then walked the short distance to the house. The windows were dark and blind, but the porch light was on, casting knife-edged shadows on the walk and shrubbery. It was the sort of thing any homeowner would do for an invited guest. But here, the gesture was frighteningly alien, a monster aping human behavior.

And why had he turned off all the lights inside? To frighten her more? It might be possible to be more scared than she was right now, but she hoped she wouldn't have to find out. She scanned the dark rectangles of the windows, looking for movement, but the house seemed as quiet as a . . . Hastily, she pushed that thought aside. It was a stupid cliché anyway.

"Where are you?" she muttered under her breath. "Front or back . . . where, where, where?"

She decided to go in the back; it was closer to the stairs. Taking the gun from her purse, she dropped it into her pocket. Then she slipped around to the back of the house and used her key to open the gate.

A few moments later she was in the kitchen. The black and white squares of the floor seemed full of movement in the dim light that came from the windows. Wedges of thick shadow were pooled in the lee of the center island and in the corners. The doorway leading to the hallway was a pitch-black oblong. Somewhere out there, the killer was waiting.

And so were Amber and Annalese. Garland took the gun out of her pocket as she walked toward the door. The weapon felt cold and slick in her hand, reptilian.

She slid out into the hallway and pressed herself against the wall. It was quiet, so quiet, as though the world were on hold. Her eyes were adjusting to the dark, and she was able to pick out the shapes of the hall table a few feet away, the lesser darkness framed by the arch that led to the living room.

Garland was suddenly glad of the darkness. Maybe the killer had made his first mistake. She knew this house almost as well as she knew her own. *He* didn't. It was a small advantage, as advantages went, but she'd take anything she could get.

She moved toward the archway, holding the gun ready. Point and shoot, her father had always told her. Trust your instincts. Well, her instincts said to leave this house, to run as far and fast as she could. But that was impossible. Damn it to hell, he'd killed Charla; he wasn't going to get her children, too.

She stood just inside the archway for a moment, holding her breath as she listened for movement. Nothing. Her eyes were beginning to adjust to the dark now. She could see into the living room. There were the familiar shapes of the sofa, chairs and tables, the white ones seeming to absorb what light came in through the windows, the dark pieces almost blending into the shadows. A line of dark footprints marked the pale rug.

I hope that's mud, she thought. But it hadn't rained in a while. Fear knotted her insides.

Then she noticed a mound lying on the floor of the foyer. She stared at it for several interminable moments, but it didn't stir. Finally she moved closer. Her shoes slid in something wet, a sickening replay of the night before. She knew what she would find as she bent to touch that still form.

Her groping hand encountered a cold, limp arm, the softness of a woman's breast, moved upward and touched something wet and open and horrible. She recoiled, pressing the back of her hand against her mouth to stifle a cry.

For a moment she stood, fighting panic. Poor Xenia. Killed for . . . nothing. She'd gotten in his way, and had been discarded. Like Charla. Slowly, Garland forced herself into relative calmness. If she panicked, she wasn't going to be able to do Frank or the girls any good.

As soon as her breathing settled down, she moved to the stairway. It was totally dark, without even the faint illumination from the street outside. There were two landings above her, one on the second floor, another on the third, where the twins' room was.

Walking blindly up those stairs was the hardest thing she'd ever done. The darkness and her own terror seemed to congeal the very air, like gelatin thickening around her. But she made it to the first landing unchallenged, and the second. A moment later she reached the girls' bedroom and slipped inside. *He might be in here,* she thought. *He might have picked this as the perfect spot to wait.*

There was no sound in the room. Garland felt as though someone were twanging her nerves like guitar strings. She had to see. She had to *know.* Even if he were standing in the corner beside her, she had to know.

She opened the curtain on the nearest window, letting the lamplight from outside into the room. The colors of the bedspread sprang into being. Pink and white—no red. The twins began to stir, wakened by the light. *Thank God. Oh, thank God! I thought . . . I was so afraid!* Her shoulders sagged with relief.

"Amber, Annalese, it's Aunt Garland," she whispered. "Wake up now. Shhhh. Quietly."

They sat up and blinked at her sleepily. Garland put her finger on her lips, cautioning silence. By some miracle they sensed her urgency and obeyed.

"There's someone in the house," she whispered. "We've got to get out of here, and we've got to do it fast and quiet." She held out her hand. "Amber, come take my hand. Annalese, take Amber's. Hold tight, now. Whatever you do, don't get in front of me. And if I say run, you run."

Without a word, they slid out of bed and came to her. She could tell they were afraid by the way they crowded close, as though just her presence was their guarantee of safety. *Trust is a wonderful thing,* Garland thought. *I hope it isn't misplaced.*

She pressed herself against the wall beside the door, felt the girls do the same. Slowly, she opened the door a crack and peered out into the hallway. It looked and sounded empty.

"Okay," she whispered. "Let's go."

They moved out single file. The girls bare feet were silent on the carpeted stairs, their breathing controlled. Garland was proud of them. Brave girls. She wouldn't let them down.

"Hi, Garland." *His* voice.

He was right beside her! She brought the gun up and fired at the spot from which his voice had come. Light and sound filled the stairway for an instant. Both girls shrieked, a shrill counterpoint to the thunder echoes of gunfire. Then the darkness swooped back in. Something hard struck Garland's wrist, sending the gun flying out of her hand. She heard it land somewhere close. But the killer was closer.

"Run!" she cried, pulling the twins with her down the hallway. There was a spare bedroom just a short way away—if she could just . . . running footsteps sounded behind her, too close. Then she heard him blunder against a wall and curse. It gave her enough time to reach the bedroom and lock the three of them inside.

A fist pounded the door, then a shoulder. The wood shuddered from the force of the blows. Garland ran to the window and opened it. The flower bed was just below. Two floors—a long drop, but it was the best—the only—chance she could give them.

"Come on, girls," she panted. "One at a time. Remember gymnastics class; drop and roll. Okay?"

Annalese was nearest. Garland helped her sit on the windowsill. "Don't wait for me. As soon as you're down, run next door and tell them to call the police. Ready, sweetheart?"

"Ready."

Grasping the child's wrists, Garland swung her over and out. There was enough moonlight to see her small, frightened face. "It'll be all right," she said, then dropped her.

There was a soft thump of landing, a tumbled sprawl of limbs that made Garland's heart nearly stop beating. Then Annalese stood up and moved out of the way.

The door shuddered again, and Garland heard wood crack. "Amber!" she hissed, in a hurry now.

Amber hopped up onto the windowsill. Quickly, Garland swung her out and dropped her to the ground below. She, too, made it unscathed. Then, hand in hand, the girls disappeared into the darkness.

With a shriek of splintering wood, the door burst open. Garland swung her leg over the sill, preferring a blind drop to the killer, but he caught hold of her shirt and dragged her back into the room.

No! Not like this! With a cry of denial, she kicked backward, bringing her heel down onto his foot as hard as she could. He grunted with pain and jerked her almost off her feet before losing his hold on her shirt.

She reeled, coming up hard against the bed so hard the breath was knocked out of her. She sank to her knees, dragging the bedspread down with her. Her attacker recovered first. As she knelt, gasping, he closed the window and locked it, then went to stand between her and the door. A menacing shadow, gray against the greater darkness of the hallway.

"That wasn't very nice," he said. "But then, I've found out that *you* aren't very nice. We need to talk about that."

He moved toward her. Garland saw the gleam of something shiny in his hand. *This is it,* she thought, clutching the fabric to her chest as though it might shield her from him. From it.

"No!" she shrieked. Surging to her feet, she flung the bedspread at him. Without waiting to see whether or not she'd hit the mark, she ran for the door.

Chapter Thirty

Garland made it to the bottom of the stairs before she heard his footsteps behind her. He was coming down two at a time. Too fast. She'd never get to the door.

He was only a few yards behind her now. She bolted down the hallway, ducked into the family room, and started to slam the door closed. Before she could latch it, however, he reached the other side. Her toes sliding on the carpet, she threw her weight against the door. But he forced it wider.

It wasn't going to work. She flung herself away from the door, and he all but fell into the room. Enough light came in through the curtains for her to see that he had pale skin and dark hair cut very short. She ran to the bookcase and began hurling books, knickknacks—anything she could find—in his direction.

He kept coming, one forearm raised to deflect the missiles. She dropped to her hands and knees and crawled behind the sofa, where there was a wedge of greater darkness. He was standing in front of the bookcases now, his face turning from side to side as he scanned the room.

"You might as well come out, Garland," he said, his voice loud in the otherwise silent room. You'll never get away. All I have to do is turn the light on, you know."

But he didn't. Garland knew he was enjoying this sick cat-and-mouse game. He'd make her run, make her hope, and then he'd kill her. She *would* run. She *would* hope. It was either that, or walk up to that knife and stretch out her throat. Time. She needed time. How long would it take Amber and Annalese to rouse the neighbors? How long to make the phone call, how long to get someone out here?

"I've been watching you for a long time," he said. "At first I thought you were nice. But you're a slut. Just like the rest of them."

Garland cocked her head, confused. *Who* were all sluts? Women in general, or a particular kind of woman?

"I had to kill them, you know." His voice was strange now, sing-song. "I thought I'd killed enough of them, but then the dream came back. I knew the only way to be free was to kill you, too."

That she understood. She tightened her crouch, wishing she could disappear entirely. The killer's breath was coming audibly now. Then, far in the distance, came the treble wail of sirens. They had to be coming here, they just had to! But they seemed so far away. Maybe he'd be frightened and run . . . No. He'd come back. Someday, somehow, he'd come after her again. It had to end here, tonight, one way or another.

He moved toward her. "I know where you are," he said. "Ready or not, here I come."

She backed farther into the shadow until her back hit the unyielding surface of the sofa. He came around the far end of the sofa, holding the knife out in front of him. Light reflected off his teeth. Garland couldn't tell if he was smiling or grimacing.

She moved away from him, still keeping her back against the sofa. Her hand came into contact with something hard and smooth. A glass—no, a heavy mug. A bizarre thought popped into her mind: *How many times have I told the girls to take their dirty dishes into the kitchen?* Thank God they hadn't listened to her. Jumping to her feet, she flung the mug at the killer with all her strength.

It bounced off his shoulder, pushing him off balance. He stumbled and fell, bringing the table lamp down with him. She was up in the same instant, darting past him into the hall. Using her hand on the wall as a guide, she headed for the kitchen and outside.

When she reached the back door, however, she found that the deadbolt had been locked. Damn him! *Damn him!* Her keys were in her purse, her purse . . . somewhere else. She hesitated for a moment, torn between hiding and trying for the living room.

But then she heard him coming and knew there was no longer any choice. She dove behind the center island just as he came into the room. He was wearing tennis shoes; they squeaked on the tile floor. She duck-walked along the line of cabinets to the opposite end.

He was standing still now. Listening. She breathed through her nose shallowly, not daring to make the slightest sound.

The sirens were perceptibly closer. How long, she wondered, until they got here? *Probably too long.* She shrank back against the cabinet as he began to move again.

"Come out, come out, wherever you are," he called.

Garland pressed her fist against her teeth until it hurt. She wanted to bolt like a frightened animal, but that would be suicide. That's what he wanted. He'd drag her down from behind and slaughter her like poor Xenia.

He came farther into the room. Judging his progress by sound, she slid around the corner of the island, then around the next corner to the side facing the door. He was stalking her, moving her from spot to spot. Soon there wouldn't be anywhere left to go. *Squeak,* went his shoes. *Squeak.* He was moving toward the garage now.

Garland gathered herself, crouching like a cat about to spring. *Please let him go in, please!*

She heard the door open and close. Her breath coming in harsh rasps, she leaped to her feet and ran toward the hallway. The overhead light flared to life, blinding her momentarily.

Squeak, squeak, squeak! He hadn't gone into the garage! *Squeak, squeak, squeaksqueaksqueaksqueak* . . . His hand fell heavily on her shoulder, clamping there, his fingers digging cruelly into her flesh.

"Surprise!" he said. His voice was high and excited, like a kid's. But there was nothing ludicrous about it, or him.

She thought he'd kill her then, but he only wound his hand into her hair and used that hold to make her look at him. Shock jolted through her as she recognized him as the man she'd seen in Frank's waiting room.

"But . . . but I know you!" she stammered. "You're one of Frank's patients!"

His lashless eyes glittered. Excitement/anticipation/blood lust—the eyes of a killer. "Not a patient," he said. "Haven't you figured it out, Garland?"

"What?"

He dragged her out into the hall and down to Frank's office. There, sitting behind his desk, was her brother-in-law. His forearms were bound to the chair arms with duct tape. Blood had flowed down from his cut throat, soaking a wide crimson stain into the carpet. His face was blue-gray, his eyes wide with horror, his mouth open as though he'd tried to scream.

"Dear God, Frank!" she moaned.

She tried to look away, but the killer jerked her hair, forcing her to face the horrible sight. "God had nothing to do with *him*. He lied to me. He said he was trying to help me, but all he wanted was for me to kill his wife. I didn't want to. I told him I didn't like blondes. But he kept saying 'You're going to get caught if you keep killing the same kind of woman all the time. You must adapt, David.' And then he'd point to that big picture of his wife that hangs over his desk and say, 'Think about killing her, David. The only difference between her and the other women you've killed is the blond hair. Ignore that, and you won't have a bit of trouble.' "

"I—"

"And don't tell me you didn't suspect Frank had something to do with it, or you wouldn't have hired that private investigator. She's gone, too, by the way. I put her where no one would ever think to look: in the same spot they found another one of my women."

Not Delores, too! Oh, Frank! Frank had been so damned sure he knew all the answers. Push the right buttons, make people jump. But Frank had pushed the wrong button with this . . . whatever this man was. Now Frank was dead. Just like Charla, just like all the other women he had put in the killer's hands.

Who's going to take care of the girls? She'd never know. She closed her eyes. The killer yanked her hair, pulling her hair up.

"You're not paying attention," he said.

Garland was ready to do whatever she had to in order to live long enough for those sirens to get here. He didn't seem to hear them at all; maybe he didn't care whether he escaped or not as long as he took her with him. *Keep him talking. As long as he's talking, he's not doing . . . anything else.* "I'm listening," she said. "Tell me why you picked me out."

"You look like *her.* They all have to look like her, or it isn't any good. Sluts, every one of them. Just like her."

"Who are you talking about?"

"Her. She . . . was small and dark, just like you. Your voice even sounds the same. You're . . . going to free me from her."

With an effort, Garland kept from screaming. "Who?"

"Her, her, her!"

The knife hovered above Garland's face. She saw that his hand was striated with puckered burn scars, ugly, monstrous, nearly as frightening as the weapon. He put the edge of the knife against her throat almost gently.

She went up on tiptoes, trying to put some distance between herself and the blade.

The sirens were closer now, their shrieking voices seeming to split the night. But not close enough. Not nearly close enough.

"But I've never done anything to you. I don't even know you," she gabbled in an attempt to gain a few moments more of life. "Why are you doing this?"

"I told you before: you're going to set me free," he said, his breath hot in her ear. "Do you know that your sister begged for her life? She got on her knees and begged me not to kill her. Will you beg for *your* life, Garland?"

Reckless outrage surged through her. This . . . beast had tormented Charla before killing her with no more compunction than he'd have stepping on an insect. And now he was going to do the same to *her.* Watch her crawl, listen to her plead, then kill her anyway. Beg? Damn it to hell, she wasn't about to give him the satisfaction!

"No, I'm not going to beg!" she snapped. "I'm not afraid of you!"

The hand holding the knife trembled. Garland didn't know whether that was a prelude to thrusting it in or some other reaction, but she kept talking anyway. As long as she could, she was going to have her say. "You've got your nerve watching me, sneaking around my house and messing with my things! You little shit!"

To her astonishment, he let go of her hair. Hope shafted through her, sharp and sweet. If she could get away from him, she might be able to reach the stairs. Somewhere on that second landing was a gun.

"I've been a good boy," he said. "I was only trying to help."

A good boy? What an odd thing to say to anyone but . . . *His mother! He's talking to his mother!* Realization burst on Garland with a jolt. Something she'd said had set off some echoing chord of memory, perhaps of reflex. There was only one chance for her. Such a slim chance. "Of course you've been a good boy," she said. "But now it's time to stop."

The knife trembled, drew a fraction of an inch away.

He said his name before. What was it . . . Oh, yeah. David. "David, things have gone too far. I know Frank told you to do things, but you shouldn't listen—"

"No, *you* listen!" he cried. "I thought you were different. You seemed so perfect. I saw how you cared for those little girls, how you did things for them. You didn't seem to care about men. I almost . . . loved you. Then you let *him* fuck you. I watched it. I watched everything you did." His voice broke like a teenager's. "And then I knew you were no good. A lie, a cheap lie, like all the rest. And I knew you weren't right for me."

Black terror churned her guts. She'd chosen wrong; he wasn't looking for his mother. He'd been killing her. But in his tirade, he'd forgotten to hold the knife against her throat. It hovered in front of her, though, close enough to do the job. But maybe, just maybe, far enough.

She jabbed her elbow into his solar plexus with all her strength. As his breath whooshed out, she slapped the knife aside and ran for the stairs. He was after her in a heartbeat, even got his hand on her shirt as she scrambled up the first flight. But she kicked backward, hit something soft that made him grunt and go to his knees.

She made the first landing, bounced off the far wall, then hurtled up the next section of stairs. He was coming again, fast and angry, the rasping of his breath loud in the enclosed space. She darted to the right as he lunged for her, gaining herself another second of time. The gun was lying on the step just below the landing.

His hand closed on her ankle, dragging her down to her hands and knees. Scrabbling forward desperately, she just managed to grasp the gun. Turning onto her side, she fired up at his looming form. "Point and shoot," her father had said, and that was what she did. A crimson flower blossomed on his shirt, but he only moved closer, the knife glittering hungrily.

She fired again, and still he didn't go down. Steadying the pistol with both hands, she fired twice more. His arm, the one holding the knife, went up like a ballet dancer's. The blade flew from his hand, a silver blur spinning away. Two more splotches spread rapidly across the front of his shirt, and a fine crimson spray hit the wall behind him.

He seemed to hover there forever. Then he began to tilt at the waist like a marionette with a broken string. At last he fell. His body thumped and slithered down the stairs to the landing, leaving a trail of smeared blood in its wake.

Garland curled up where she was. The stairwell was filled with the smell of death. But not hers. Not tonight. "Thank you, God," she muttered.

A whimper drifted up from below. Not a man's cry, but a child's. Holding the gun ready, she walked down the stairs. The killer was lying with his head on the landing, his feet propped on the stairway. He wasn't going to get up; Garland could see halfway through his chest. Although he was still breathing, his lungs were sucking more liquid than air.

I did that, she thought. Right now it didn't hurt. Maybe it never would.

She sat down on the step above him. His hands were turned palm upward, and she could see more burn scars. He began to cry, frightened sobs like those of a child scared of the dark. Garland didn't want to hear it, didn't want to watch him die. But she couldn't seem to move. Something strange had happened during their time together; terror and hate had tied them together, a bond only death could break. So she sat and waited, glad that the death was his and not hers.

"I'm sorry, I'm sorry, I didn't mean to be bad," he moaned. "Please, Mommy don't hurt me anymore."

Garland tried to imagine what had been done to him to make him into a monster, but failed. He was beyond her understanding. All she knew was that he didn't look menacing any longer. He didn't look like a monster. The muted light that came from downstairs blurred his features until they looked child-soft. As he lay dying at her feet, she could only think how young he looked. So terribly young to have done the things he'd done. All those women, all those lives, sacrificed to his personal demon.

His shattered lung bubbled and wheezed. He whimpered again, a high, agonized sound that twisted in her guts like a knife.

"It's dark," he muttered. A man's voice, but a child's pain, a child's need. "And cold. I can't see you, Mommy. I'm scared. I tried so hard . . . to be a good boy." He was winding down, his voice growing weaker with each word.

Then he looked straight at Garland. His eyes were wide, blurred with tears. "Mommy. Please . . . tell me I'm a good boy. Please, Mommy . . . don't let me go alone."

Garland's teeth chattered. Death was near; she could feel it in the stairway like a chill breeze. And *he* was looking at her.

She levered herself off the stair and bent over him. His eyes tracked her, avid, beseeching, needing her—the eyes of a dying child. Bending, she put her hand on his forehead. "You're a good boy, David."

It was a benediction. Not for the Stalker. For the child.

His breath went out in a long sigh. The liquid gurgle of his breathing stopped. She moved her hand downward, closing his eyes.

The sirens were right outside now, the night full of flashing blue lights. Garland recognized Baedecker's voice outside and, a moment later, Colin's.

She dropped the gun to the floor beside the killer, then went to open the door.

Chapter Thirty-one

"So it's over," Milo said after Garland finished telling her story. He pushed himself up higher in his hospital bed.

"Yes, it's over," Garland said. Eight days had passed since her meeting with the killer. They'd been busy ones, so she hadn't had time to visit the hospital as much as she would have liked. Milo had prospered without her—thanks, no doubt, to Troll's loyal presence. "They've tied him in to several murders in Indiana, too. All small, dark women who resembled his mother."

"Hell, makes you feel old, doesn't it?" He waggled his eyebrows. "Being mistaken for some psychotic killer's *mother?*"

Garland folded her arms over her chest. If he was strong enough to make age jokes, he was strong enough for what she was about to tell him. "Milo, he killed Delores."

"Delores?" He stared at her blankly, then leaned back against the pillow and put his arm across his eyes. "Oh God. Why?"

"Because she was working for me."

"But I don't understand. She was investigating Frank, not Charla's murder!"

Garland was glad he couldn't see her, for she was going to lie to him about something very important. "Frank had nothing to do with it. The guy was a complete nut. Who can say what his reasons were?"

"I really liked Delores."

"I know." Garland clasped her hands on the bed rail and stared down at them. She hadn't told anyone but Colin about Frank's involvement with the killer. Nor did she intend to. It wasn't to preserve Frank's reputation. But the twins had suffered enough losing both parents to violent deaths, and didn't need to know what Frank had done.

Strangely, she held no hatred for the killer. Yes, she was glad he was dead. But that was because *she* wanted to live. She couldn't judge David; there were no standards she knew to apply, no way to understand what had driven him. But Frank was another story. She'd never never forget what he'd done to her sister, never forgive him for making her protect him for the twins' sakes. She could only hope there was a special place in hell for Frank Hollister.

When she looked down at Milo again, she saw that his arm had dropped to his side. His eyes were closed. Thinking he'd fallen asleep, she turned to leave.

"Don't go," he said. When she returned to her place beside the bed, he reached out and took her hand. "How are the girls taking it? Losing their father and all."

"They're going through counseling, and will continue to for a long time. But I'm their guardian, so part of their world is still intact. We'll handle it." She disengaged herself gently and propped another pillow behind him. "But tell me about you. When are you getting out of here?

"Three or four days," he said. "Maybe sooner."

"To Troll?"

"Troll?"

"She's been pretty constant at your bedside, you know."

"Didn't she tell you?" Milo smiled a bit crookedly. "The day this happened"—he touched his throat—"she and Robbie were married. She didn't tell me until they were sure I was going to live, I guess."

It was Garland's turn to stare. *"Robbie?"*

"Robbie," Milo said. "Now they can argue about Milton for the rest of their lives. By the way, they're moving to Boston at the end of the month."

"Milo, I'm sorry."

He shrugged. "I'll live."

She wanted to stroke his hair as she'd done to the twins so many times lately, but she didn't think he'd welcome it right now. Troll had stayed by Milo's bedside because he'd needed her—just as any friend would have done. She didn't have to love him. And now she was moving on, as they all had to do.

"Hi, guys." Colin, his hands full of soft drink cans, pushed the door open with his shoulder. "I've got the soda. The nurse took the chips away from me, though. You ought to marry that one, Milo; she's just sharp enough to keep you in line."

Milo perked up a bit. "You mean the little redheaded one?"

"Uh-huh." Colin popped the tab on one can and handed it to the other man. "Look, I hate to drink and run, but it's almost five, and we promised to take the girls out to Pizza Hut tonight."

"Go, my children," Milo said, making shooing motions with his hands. He winked. "I think I'm about to have a relapse anyway. I'm bound to need a lot of special attention."

Garland went to kiss him on the forehead. "Good luck."

Colin tucked her hand into the crook of his arm and led her out to the elevator. While they were waiting, he said, "I invited Kathy to go with us. I hope you don't mind. She's been asking to meet you, and I thought this would be a good time."

"Okay."

He didn't seem to register her answer. "I know you've been nervous about meeting my daughter, but I know you'll like each other—"

"Colin, I said okay."
"You did?"
"I did."
He took her chin in his hand and tilted her face upward. "Things have changed, haven't they? You're not scared of anything anymore."
"I'm afraid of a lot of things. But I'm not frightened of the future any longer, if that's what you mean. And I'd love to meet your daughter."
"What about us?" he asked, looking as though his heart hung in the balance. "Have you stopped being afraid of that, too?"
"Well . . . marriage is a pretty big step." Then smiling, she put her hand on his cheek. She'd tormented the poor man enough. It was time to fess up. "But doesn't it fall under the category of 'future'?"
"God, I hope so!"
He kissed her right there in the busy hospital corridor. The elevator came and went, but neither of them cared in the least.